W9-AGW-428

DISCARDED

VANISHED

SEASON OF PASSION
THE PROMISE
NOW AND FOREVER
PASSION'S PROMISE

Danielle Steel

Vanished

Delacorte Press

LARGE PRINT EDITION

Published by
Delacorte Press
Bantam Doubleday Dell Publishing Group, Inc.
1540 Broadway
New York, New York 10036

Library of Congress Cataloging in Publication Data

Steel, Danielle.
Vanished / Danielle Steel.
p.   cm.
ISBN 0-385-30603-2 (hardcover).
ISBN 0-385-31043-9 (lg. print)
I. Title.
PS3569.T33828V36   1993
813′.54—dc20   92-37118   CIP

Manufactured in the United States of America

Published simultaneously in Canada

August 1993

10 9 8 7 6 5 4 3 2 1

BVG

**This Large Print Book carries the
Seal of Approval of N.A.V.H.**

To Nick

For the pain of having a mother who follows you everywhere, and the agony of so many years of not being able to do what you want, when you want to. For the person you are, and the person you will become. The fine man, the good friend, and maybe even the great writer!

With all my love, Mom,

And to John,

The best Daddy, the best friend, the greatest love, the sweetest man, the most extraordinary blessing in my life . . . how lucky we all are to have you!
With all my love and heart, always,

Olive.

1

Charles Delauney limped only slightly as he walked slowly up the steps of Saint Patrick's Cathedral, as a bitter wind reached its icy fingers deep into his collar. It was two weeks before Christmas, and he had forgotten how cold it was in New York in December. It was years since he'd been back to New York . . . years since he'd seen his father. His father was eighty-seven now, his mother had been gone for years. She died when he was thirteen, and all he could remember of her was that she had been very beautiful, and very gentle. His father was senile and ill, bedridden and infirm. The attorneys had insisted that Charles come home, at least for a few months, to try and get

the family affairs in order. He had no sib-
lings and the entire burden of the Delauney
affairs rested on his shoulders. Landholdings
throughout the state, an enormous estate near
Newburgh, New York, coal, oil, steel, and
some very important real estate in downtown
Manhattan. A fortune that had been amassed
not by Charles, or even by his father, but by
both of his grandfathers. And none of it interested Charles for a single moment.

His face was young, but weather-lined, and
showed the wear of pain and battle. He had
just spent almost two years in Spain, fighting
for a cause that was not his own, but about
which he cared deeply. It was one of the few
things he did care about . . . something he
truly burned for. He had joined the Lincoln
Brigade to fight the Fascists almost two years
before, in February of 1937, and he'd been in
Spain ever since, fighting the battle. In August
he had been wounded again, near Gandesa
during the battle of Ebro, in a ferocious con-
frontation. It was not the first time he had
been wounded. At fifteen, in the last year of
the Great War, he had run away and joined the
army and been wounded in the leg at Saint-
Mihiel. His father had been furious about it
then. But there was nothing he could do now.
He knew nothing of the world, or his son, or

the fight in Spain. He no longer even recognized Charles, and perhaps, Charles had decided as he watched him sleeping in his enormous bed, perhaps it was better. They would have argued and fought. He would have hated what his son had become, his ideas about freedom and liberty, his hatred of "fascists." His father had always disapproved of his living abroad. Born late in his father's life, it made no sense to the elder Delauney that Charles wanted to live over there, raising hell in Europe. Charles had gone back to Europe at eighteen, in 1921, and had lived there for seventeen years since then, working occasionally for friends, or selling an occasional short story in his youth, but in recent years primarily living from his very substantial trust fund. The size of his income had always irritated him. "No normal man needs that much money to live on," he'd once confided to a close friend, and for years he'd given most of his income to charitable causes, although he still derived great pleasure from making a small sum from one of his short stories.

He had studied at Oxford, and then at the Sorbonne, and finally, for a brief while, he had gone to Florence. He had been more than a little wild in those days. Drinking as much fine Bordeaux as he could consume, an occasional

absinthe, and carousing with a fascinating ar-
ray of women. At twenty-one, he had thought
himself a man of the world, after three very
uncontrolled years in Europe. He had met
people others only read about, did things few
men dreamed, and met women others only
longed for. And then . . . there had been
Marielle . . . but that was another story. A
story he tried not to let himself think of anymore. The memory of her was still too painful.

She wandered into his dreams at night
sometimes, especially when he was in danger,
or afraid, asleep in a trench somewhere, with
bullets whistling past his head . . . and then
the memory of her crept in . . . her face
. . . those unforgettable eyes . . . her lips
. . . and the bottomless sorrow she wore like
a wound the last time he saw her. He hadn't
seen her since, and that was almost seven
years before. Seven years without seeing her,
touching her . . . holding her . . . or even
knowing where she was, and telling himself it
no longer mattered. Once, when he was
wounded and convinced he would die, he had
allowed himself to wallow in the memories,
and the medics had found him unconscious in
a pool of blood, but when he awoke, he could
have sworn he saw her standing just behind
them.

She had been only eighteen when they met
in Paris. She had a face so beautiful and alive it
looked as though it had been freshly painted.
He had been twenty-three, and he had seen
her as he sat in a cafe with a friend. He had
been taken with her instantly as he watched
her. And as she glanced at him, she had a face
full of mischief. She had run away then, back
to her hotel, but he had seen her again, at an
ambassador's dinner. They had been introduced formally, and everything had been very
circumspect except Marielle still had those
laughing eyes that had bowled him over. But
her parents were far less taken with him. Her
father was a serious man, much older than his
wife, and he knew of Charles's reputation. Her
father was a contemporary of his own father's,
and Charles thought they knew each other
slightly. Her mother was half French, and always seemed to Charles to be incredibly
proper and extremely dreary. They kept Marielle on a ridiculously short leash, and insisted
that she dance attendance on them every moment. They had no idea what a flirt she was, or
how funny she could be too. But there was a
serious side to her as well, and Charles found
he could talk to her by the hour. She had been
vastly amused to discover him at the embassy,
and remembered seeing him at the cafe, al-

though she didn't admit it to him, until much later when he teased her. He was fascinated by her, and she by him. To her, he was a very intriguing young man, unlike any she had ever known. She seemed to want to know everything about him, where he came from, why he was there, how he came to speak such good French. And she was impressed from the first by his ambitions and abilities as a writer. She painted a little, she'd explained to him rather shyly at first. And later when they knew each other better, she had shown him some astoundingly good drawings. But that first night, it was neither literature nor art which appealed to either of them, it was something in their souls which drew them irrevocably together. Her parents noticed it too, and after her mother had seen them chatting with each other for a while, she attempted to pull Marielle away and introduce her to some other young people who had been invited. But Charles had followed her everywhere, a ghost who could no longer stand to be without her.

They met at the Deux Magots the following afternoon, and afterward went for a long walk along the Seine, like two mischievous children. She told him everything about herself, her life, her dreams, of wanting to be an artist one day, and then marrying someone she loved and having nine or ten children. He was less amused by that but fascinated by her. There was something ephemeral and delicate and wonderful about the girl, and yet underneath it something powerful and resilient and alive. She was like lace delicately placed over exquisitely carved white marble. Even her skin had the translucence of the statues he'd seen in Florence when he first arrived from the States, and her eyes shone like deep blue sapphires as she listened to how he felt about his own dreams about writing. He hoped, one day, to publish a collection of his short stories. She seemed to understand everything, and to care so much about all the things that mattered so deeply to him.

Her parents had taken her to Deauville, and he had followed her there, and then on to Rome . . . Pompeii . . . Capri . . . London and finally back to Paris. Everywhere she went, he had friends, and he would conveniently appear, and as often as possible go for long walks with her, or escort her to balls, and spend extremely boring evenings with her parents. But she was like a drug to him now, and wherever he was, wherever he went, he knew he had to have her. Absinthe had never been as fascinating as this girl. And by August . . .

in Rome . . . as she looked at him, her eyes were filled with the same unbridled passion.

Her parents were nervous about him, but they knew the family after all, and he was well mannered, intelligent, and it was difficult to ignore the fact that he was the sole heir to an enormous fortune. The fortune meant nothing to Marielle, her parents were comfortable, and it was something she never thought about. She thought only about Charles, the strength of his hands, his shoulders, his arms, the wild look in his eyes after they kissed, the chiseled beauty of his features, like an ancient Greek coin, the gentleness of his hands when he touched her body.

He had no intention of ever returning to the States, he'd explained early on, he and his father hadn't gotten along since he'd gone off to the war at fifteen, and returning to New York afterward had been a nightmare. He felt as though the place was too small for him, too boring, too restrictive. Too much was expected of him, and they were all things he had no intention of doing. Social obligations, family responsibilities, learning about investments and holdings and trusts, and the things his father bought and sold which one day he would inherit. There was more to life than that, Charles had explained to Marielle as he ran

long, gentle fingers through her silky cinnamon-colored hair, which hung long past her
shoulders. She was a tall girl, but she was
dwarfed next to him, and with him she felt
delicate and frail and yet wonderfully protected.

He had lived in Paris for five years when
they met, and it was obvious that he adored it.
His life was there, his friends, his writing, his
soul, his inspiration. But in September, she
was due to sail home on the *Paris*. To the gentle life they had in store for her, to the men
she would meet, and the girls who were her
friends, and the small but elegant brownstone
on East Sixty-second. In no way did it compare with the Delauney home, only ten blocks
north, but it was respectable certainly . . .
respectable . . . and very boring. In no way
did it compare with his garret on the rue du
Bac, rented to him by an impoverished noble-
woman who owned the entire *hôtel particulier*
below it. Charles had taken Marielle there one
day, and they had all but made love. But at the
last moment, he had come to his senses, and
left the room hastily for a few moments to
compose himself. And when he returned with
a serious air, he sat down next to her on the
bed, as she tried to straighten her dress and
regain her composure.

"I'm sorry . . ." His dark hair and fiery green eyes made him look even more dramatic, but there was an anguished air about him too, which always touched her. She had never known anyone even remotely like him, or done the things she suddenly wanted to do with him. She knew she was losing her head over him, but she couldn't help it.

"Marielle . . ." He spoke very gently as the soft reddish brown hair concealed half her face. "I can't do this anymore . . . you're driving me mad." But he was doing the same to her, and she loved it. Neither of them had ever felt anything like this before.

She smiled at him, seeming very old and wise, as he leaned over and kissed her. He felt almost drunk when he was near her. The only thing he knew for sure was that he didn't want to lose her. Not now, not ever. He didn't want to go back to New York for her, now or later, to plead for her hand, or negotiate with her father. He didn't want to wait another hour. He wanted her now. In this room, in this house. In Paris. He wanted her with him always. "Marielle?" He looked at her very soberly and her eyes grew dark.

"Yes?" She spoke very softly. She was so young, yet she was so in love with him, and he knew her well enough to sense how strong her spirit.

"Will you marry me?"

He heard her gasp, and then she laughed. "Are you serious?"

"I am . . . God knows . . . will you?" He was terrified. What if she said no? His whole life seemed to depend on what she would say in the next minute. What if she wouldn't marry him? What if she wanted to go home with her parents after all? What if it was only a game to her? But he knew from the look in her eyes that his worries were foolish.

"When?" She was giggling she was so excited.

"Now." And he meant it.

"You're not serious."

"I am." He stood up and began to pace the room, like a very handsome young lion, running a hand through his hair as he made plans and watched her. "I am very serious, Marielle." He stopped dead and looked at her, everything about him taut and electric. "You still haven't answered my question." He rushed to her side, and held her tightly in his arms until she laughed he was being so absurd.

"You're crazy."

"Yes, I am. And so are you. Will you?" He held her tighter and she pretended to scream.

He held her tighter still, and she laughed un-
controllably and then he kissed her, teasing
her until he forced an answer from her lips
between the kisses.

"Yes . . . yes . . . yes . . . I will." She
was breathless, and they were both smiling.
"When will you ask my father?" She sat back
with a blissful expression, and Charles's face
clouded over.

"He'll never agree. And if he does, he'll in-
sist we go back to the States and start a serious
life there where he can watch us." He looked
like a caged lion again as he spoke and once
more began to pace the room. "I'll tell you
right now, I won't do that."

"Won't ask my father, or go back to New
York?" She looked suddenly worried, as she
stretched her long, graceful legs in front of
her, and he tried desperately not to notice.

"New York, for sure . . . and . . ." He
stopped and looked at her again, his black hair
looking wild, his eyes boring into hers. "What
if we elope?"

"Here?" She looked stunned, and he nodded. He was serious, she knew him well
enough to know that. "My God, they'll kill
me."

"I won't let them." He sat down next to her,
as they both thought it over. "You sail in two

weeks, if we're going to do it, we'd better do it quickly." She nodded quietly, thinking it over, weighing it in her mind, but she already knew there was no choice, no question, no decision. She would have gone to the end of the world with him. And when he kissed her again, she was certain.

"Do you think they'll forgive us eventually?" She was concerned about them as well. Like him, she was an only child, and her father was so much older. And they expected so much of her, particularly her mother. Marielle had been presented to Society in New York the winter before, and now they had done the Grand Tour, their expectation was that in a short while, she would find a suitable husband. And in some ways, Charles was certainly that, in terms of his family at least, but there was no denying that his life-style was, at the present time, a little eccentric. But in time, her father would say, he would settle down. But when she tried to broach the subject to him that night, he suggested that she wait until he did that.

"Wait and see how you like him when he comes back to New York, my dear. And in the meantime, there are lots of handsome young men waiting for you there. There's no need to fall head over heels over this one." A young

Vanderbilt had pursued her for a time that spring, and there was a handsome young Astor her mother had her eye on. But they were of no interest to Marielle now, and never had been. And she had no intention of waiting for Charles to move back to New York. She was quite certain he never would, not the way he felt about New York, or even the United States, and more specifically his father. He was happy where he was, he had flourished in the past five years. Paris suited him to perfection.

They eloped three days before her parents were to set sail, leaving a note for her parents at the Hotel Crillon. She felt more than a little guilty about the grief they would feel, but on the other hand, she knew her parents well enough to know that they'd be pleased she was marrying a Delauney. She wasn't entirely right on that score, given the reputation Charles had for running wild, but it certainly soothed them a little. Her note had urged them to go ahead and set sail, and she and Charles would come to New York to visit them over Christmas, but they were not as cavalier as that, and they waited patiently, and very angrily, for the young lovers' return, with every hope of annulling the marriage and squelching the entire affair before it became a proper scandal. Of course the ambassador knew what she'd done, because they'd sought his help, and he had made discreet inquiries. But all he knew was that they had gotten married in Nice, and he had reason to believe they had driven across the border into Italy shortly after.

They had an exquisite honeymoon in Umbria, Tuscany, Rome, Venice, Florence, Lake Como, they had ventured into Switzerland, and two months later, as October drew to a close, they made their way leisurely back to Paris. Her parents were still at the Crillon and when the honeymooners returned, there was a note waiting for them at Charles's lodgings.

Marielle couldn't believe they were still there, but she was amazed to discover that they had indeed waited. And two months had done nothing to warm their hearts on the subject of their only daughter's elopement. When Marielle and Charles appeared at the hotel hand in hand, looking happy and peaceful, they demanded that Charles leave at once, and announced that they were setting the annulment en route in the morning.

"I wouldn't do that if I were you," Marielle said quietly, causing Charles to smile at the firm stand she took on his behalf. For a shy, quiet girl, she had a remarkable way of taking extremely definitive positions. And he was pleased that this was one of those times. Pleased, and a moment later, very startled.

"Don't you tell me what to do!" her father roared at her, and at the same time her mother ranted about how ungrateful she was, how dangerous her life would be with Charles, how they had only wanted her happiness, and now it was all ruined. It made a Greek chorus to the ears, and Marielle stood in the eye of the storm, watching them all calmly. At eighteen, she had suddenly become a woman, and one Charles knew he was going to adore for an entire lifetime.

"I can't get an annulment, Papa." Marielle spoke quietly again. "I'm having a baby."

This time Charles stared, and then suddenly he was amused. It was most likely not true, but it was the perfect way to make them give up the idea of an annulment. But as soon as she said the words, all hell broke loose, her mother cried louder still, and her father sat down and began to gasp, insisting he was having chest pains. Her mother said Marielle was killing him, and when the old man was ushered from the room, with his good wife's help, Charles suggested that they go back to the rue du Bac, and discuss the matter with his in-laws later. He and Marielle left shortly afterward, and as they walked a few blocks in the warm air, Charles looked vastly amused as he pulled her close to him and kissed her.

"That was brilliant. I should have thought of it myself."

"It wasn't brilliant." She looked amused too. "It's true." She looked very pleased with herself, the little girl she had been only moments before was now going to be a mother. He looked stunned.

"Are you serious?"

She nodded her head and looked up at him.

"When did that happen?" He looked startled more than worried.

"I'm not sure . . . Rome? . . . maybe Venice . . . I wasn't entirely sure until last week."

"Well, you sneaky little thing . . ." But as he held her close to him, he looked pleased. "And when is the Delauney heir due?"

"June, I think. Something like that."

He had never given much thought to being a father. It should have frightened him, given the life he'd led of such great freedom, but the truth was he was thrilled. He hailed a cab for her, and they rode home toward the rue du Bac, kissing in the backseat like two children, instead of two prospective parents.

Her own parents were just as distraught the next day, but after two weeks of arguments, they finally relented. Marielle's mother had taken her to an American doctor on the Champs-Elysées, and there was no doubt about it, she was pregnant. The idea of an annulment was out of the question. And their daughter was certainly happy enough. And like it or not, they knew they had to live with the reality of Charles Delauney. He promised them, before they finally left, to get a better apartment, a maid, a nurse for the child, a car. He was going to become a "respectable man," her father extracted from him. But respectable or not, the obvious fact was that the two were deliriously happy.

Marielle's parents left shortly after that on the *France,* and after all the excitement and fuss and strain and exhaustion of dealing with them, she and Charles agreed that they were not going to New York for Christmas, or maybe ever. They were happy in their garret on the Left Bank, with their life together, his friends, even his writing had never been better. In Paris, in 1926, for one brief shining moment, life had been perfect.

As Charles pulled open the enormously heavy cathedral doors, even his bones felt chilled, and the leg throbbed more than usual. It had been just as bitter a winter in Europe. It had been so long since he'd been in New York, so long since he'd been in a church, as he walked inside and looked up at the enormous vaulted ceiling. In some ways, he was sorry he had come. It was depressing to see his father so ill, and so unaware of his surroundings and those around him. For an instant, he had seemed to recognize Charles, and then the moment passed, the eyes were blank and then closed as his father dozed heavily on his pillows. It made Charles feel lonely whenever he watched him. It was as though the older Delauney was already gone. He might as well have been. And for Charles, there was no one left now. They were all gone . . . even the friends he had fought with in Spain. There were almost too many to pray for.

He watched a priest in black robes cross his path, and Charles walked slowly to the back of the church, to a tiny altar. Two nuns prayed there, and the younger of the two smiled at him as he knelt stiffly beside them. His black hair was flecked with gray, but his eyes still had the same electricity they'd had when he was fifteen, and he still exuded energy and strength and power. Even the young nun could feel it. But there was sorrow in his eyes too as he bowed his head, and thought of all of them, the people who had meant so much to him, those he had loved, those he had fought with. But he had not come here to pray for them. He had come here because it was the anniversary of the worst day of his life . . . nine years before . . . two weeks before Christmas. A day he would never forget . . . the day he had almost killed her. He had been insane, out of his mind with rage and pain . . . a pain so terrible he truly couldn't bear it. He wanted to tear her limb from limb to make it stop, to turn back the clock, to make it not happen . . . and yet he had loved her so much . . . loved them both . . . he couldn't bear thinking of it now, as he bowed his head, unable to pray for him or her, or himself, or anyone, unable to think . . . the pain of it still so great, barely dim, the only difference was that now he seldom allowed himself to think about it. But when he touched the place in his heart where they still lived, the pain of it still took his breath away, and he almost couldn't bear it. A tear ran slowly down his cheek as he stared unseeingly straight ahead and the young nun watched him. He knelt that way for a long time, seeing nothing, thinking of them, and what had been in a life that was no more, in a place he seldom allowed himself to remember. But today, he had wanted to come here just to feel a little closer to them. And it always made it worse that the date fell just before Christmas.

In Spain he would have found a church somewhere, a little chapel, a shack, and he would have had the same thoughts, the same excruciating pain too, but in the simplicity of his life there, there would have been comfort. Here, there was nothing, except strangers in a vast cathedral and cold gray stone, not unlike the cold gray stone of the mansion he now shared with his dying father. And as he stood up slowly, he knew he would not stay long in the States. He wanted to get back to Spain before much longer. He was needed there. He wasn't needed in New York, except by lawyers and bankers, and he cared nothing for that. He never had. If anything, he cared less now than he had years before. He had never become the "respectable man" his father-in-law had dreamed of. He smiled at the thought, as he remembered his in-laws, they were dead now too. Everyone was. At thirty-five, Charles Delauney felt as though he had already lived ten lifetimes.

He stood for a long time, looking at the statue of the Madonna and child . . . remembering them . . . and then he walked slowly back the way he had come, feeling worse than he had before, instead of better. He wanted to feel close to André again, wanted to feel him close to him, the delicious warmth of his flesh, the softness of his cheek, the tiny hand that had always held his so tightly.

Charles was blinded by tears as he walked slowly back toward the main door of the cathedral. The leg seemed to pain him more, and the wind was whistling through the church, as something happened to him which hadn't happened in a long time. But it used to happen frequently. Sometimes even on the battlefield, he imagined he saw her.

He saw her in the distance now, swathed in furs, walking past him, like a ghost, going toward something he couldn't see, unable to see him. He stood for a long moment, watching her, aching for her again, as he hadn't in so long, a memory come to life, as he stared, and then he realized it was no ghost, it was a woman who looked just like her. She was tall and thin and serious, and very beautiful. She was wearing a somber black dress covered by a sable coat that almost swept the floor and seemed to frame her face with softness. A hat tried to conceal all but one eye, but even with so little of her visible, it was as though he sensed her, the way she moved, the way she looked, the way she quietly took off one black glove, and then sank to her knees at another small altar. She was as graceful as she had ever been, as long and lean, except now she seemed so much thinner. She covered her face with graceful hands, and for a long time she seemed to be praying. He knew why. They had both come here for the same reason. It was Marielle, he realized as he stared at her, unable to believe it.

It seemed an eternity before she turned and looked at him, but when she did, it was obvious that she hadn't seen him. She lit four candles, and slipped some money into the collection box, and then she stood and stared at the altar again, and there were tears on her cheeks too. And then, head bowed, she pulled the fur coat more tightly around her. She began to walk slowly between the pews, as though her whole body ached, and her soul with it. She was only inches from him, when he gently reached out a hand and stopped her. She looked startled when he did, and she glanced up at him with a look of astonishment, as though she had been wakened from a distant dream. But as she looked into his eyes, she gasped and stared at him. Her hand flew to her mouth, her eyes brimmed with the tears she had shed at the altar.

"Oh my God . . ." It couldn't be. But it

was. She hadn't seen him in almost seven years. It was impossible to believe it.

He touched her hand without making a sound, and as he did, without hesitating she melted into him, without a thought, without a word, and he put his arms around her. It seemed right that they had both come here, that they should be together today, and they clung to each other in the church like two drowning people. It was a long time before she pulled away, and looked up at him. He looked older than he had before, more battle worn, more weary in many ways. There were small scars on his face, a bad one she couldn't see on his arm, the leg of course, and gray in his hair, and yet as she looked at him, she felt eighteen, and her heart pounded as it had when she was a girl in Paris. She had known for years that there was a part of her that would never release Charles Delauney. She had known that for a long time, and she had come to live with it. It was something she had to accept, like pain, like the leg he had to drag at times, or that irked him so much when the weather was cold or damp. It was a pain like the others she had learned to carry. "I don't know what to say," she smiled sadly at him, wiping her own tears away, "after all this time, 'how are you?' seems so stupid." It did, but what else was there to say? She had heard echoes of him from time to time, but nothing in many years now. She had known for some time that his father was ill. Her own parents had died, within months of each other, before she'd come home from Europe. But Charles knew that.

"You look incredible." He could only stare at her. At thirty, she was even more beautiful than she'd been at eighteen when they were married. It was as though her promise had been fulfilled, and yet her eyes were still so sad. It hurt him just to see them. "Are you all right?" He meant it in a thousand ways, and as she always had before, she understood him. Eventually, they had become like one dance, one song, one movement. He would have half a thought and she could finish it without saying a word. They just knew each other so well. It was as though they were the identical halves of a single person. But no more, they were two halves now . . . or were they whole? He wondered as he watched her. She was expensively dressed, and the sable coat was incredible. The hat had been done for her by Lily Daché, and made quite an effect the way she wore it. She was certainly more sophisticated than she had been as a young girl. Like this, she might have frightened him then, he smiled to himself, or perhaps not appealed to him in the same way. But she didn't frighten him now, she tore at his heart, as she had for years. Why had she been so damn stubborn the last time he saw her?

"You look so serious, Marielle." His eyes seemed to bore into hers, wanting the answers to a thousand questions.

She tried to smile, and turned away before she looked at him again. "It's a difficult day . . . for both of us . . ." If it were otherwise, they wouldn't have been there. It still seemed remarkable to her that they were standing here together, after all these years, in Saint Patrick's Cathedral. "Have you come home for good?" She was curious about him. He looked bigger and stronger than he had before, more powerful, and as though he would tolerate even less nonsense. And difficult as it was to believe, his nerves seemed even closer to the surface.

He shook his head, wishing they could slip into a pew and talk all day. "I don't think I could stand it here. I've been back for three weeks, and I'm already itching to go back to Spain."

"Spain?" She raised an eyebrow. His life seemed so integrally interwoven with Paris

and their memories there, it was hard to imagine him somewhere else now.

"The war there. I've been there for two
years."

She nodded then. It made perfect sense. "I
wondered once if you were there." It was his
kind of battle. "Somehow I had a feeling you
would go." She'd been right, and he had no
reason not to. Nothing to lose. Nothing to
gain. Nothing to stay home for.

"And you?" He looked pointedly at her. It
was odd asking each other for news here, and
yet they each wanted to know what the other
had been doing.

It was a long moment before she spoke, and
then she answered him very softly. "I'm married."

He nodded, trying not to look as though she
had caused him pain, although in truth she
had run a dagger into a wound that had long
festered. "Anyone I know?" It was unlikely, as
he had lived abroad for the last seventeen
years, but she looked as though she were married to at least an Astor.

"I don't know." But she knew that her husband had been a friend of his father's. Her
husband was twenty-five years her senior.
"Malcolm Patterson." There was no joy in her
eyes as she said his name, no pride, and sud-

denly the hat concealed her expression from him completely. He sensed something he didn't like, and she looked anything but happy. So this was what she'd done with the past seven years. He didn't look impressed. He looked annoyed. Very much so.

"I know the name," Charles said coolly, and then waited to look her in the eye again. "And are you happy?" Was it worth refusing to come back to him? It was obvious to him that it wasn't.

She wasn't sure what to say to him. There were things about her marriage that she cherished. Malcolm had promised to take care of her, at a time in her life when she needed that desperately and he had done that. He had never let her down. He was always kind. But she hadn't realized at first how cool he would be, how aloof, and how busy. And yet, in some ways, he was the perfect husband. Polite, intelligent, chivalrous, charming. But he was not Charles . . . he was not the flame and passion of her youth . . . he wasn't the face she dreamt of when she hovered between life and death . . . or the name she called . . . and they both knew he never would be. "I'm at peace, Charles. That means a great deal." There had been no peace with Charles . . . there was only joy, and excitement, and love, and passion . . . and eventually despair. As great as the joy had been, so had the sorrow.

"I saw you . . . in Spain . . . when I was shot . . ." he said almost dreamily.

. . . And I saw you every night for years . . . she wanted to tell him, but knew she couldn't. Instead, she only smiled. "We all have ghosts, Charles." Some were just more painful than others.

"Is that it then? Are we ghosts? Nothing more?"

"Maybe." It had taken her two years in a sanatorium to understand that it was over, to live with the pain, to be able to go on after what had happened. She couldn't jeopardize that now, not even for him, especially not for him. She couldn't allow herself to step back, no matter how much she thought she still loved him. She touched his hand and then his cheek, and he bent to kiss her, but she turned her head just a fraction. He kissed her cheek, just near her lips, and she closed her eyes for a long moment as he held her.

"I love you . . . I will always love you . . ." His eyes were blazing with the passion she knew so well, as he said it. It was not the passion born of desire, but of believing and wanting and caring so much it almost kills you. Charles cared about everything that way, and she knew that one day it would kill him. She had barely survived his flame, and now she knew that she could no longer risk it. He had his scars, and she had her own, no less fierce because they hadn't been won in battle.

"I love you too," she whispered, knowing that she shouldn't say those words to him. But it was a whisper from the past, a salute to all that had been and had died with André.

"Will you see me before I leave for Spain again?" It was so like him to pressure her, to make her feel responsible for him once he went into battle. She smiled at him, but she shook her head this time.

"I can't, Charles. I'm married."

"Does he know about me?" Slowly, with a look of agony, she shook her head in answer.

"No, he doesn't. He thinks I went a little wild one summer on the Grand Tour, and got a little out of hand, as I think my father described it to his friends. That's what my father said years ago, something about a 'little romance.' And that's all Malcolm knows. He has never allowed me to discuss it. Malcolm has no idea we were ever married." It was so like her father to tell people that. He had never told people of her life with Charles and their staying in Europe had made it easier for him. All he cared about were appearances, and reputation. He had lied to protect her, and told everyone she had stayed in Europe to study. He had to save face at all costs, and he had wanted to save Marielle from her "terrible mistake" when she married Charles Delauney. And now, Marielle's husband still believed the lie, because she let him.

Charles couldn't believe she had never told her husband the truth. They had told each other everything. They had shared all their secrets. But at eighteen, what was there to hide? At thirty, it was different.

"He knows none of it, Charles. Why tell him?" Why tell him she had spent twenty-six months in a sanatorium, wanting to die . . . that she had tried to slash her wrists . . . take pills . . . drown herself in the bathtub . . . why tell him any of that? Charles knew, he had paid the bills . . . and she had recovered.

"Will you tell him you saw me today?" He was curious about her, and them. What kind of marriage could they have if she told him nothing? Did she love him, or he her? She had said "I love you" so easily after all these years, and Charles believed her. And now she shook her head in answer to his question.

"How can I tell him I saw you, when he doesn't know you exist in my life anyway?"

Her eyes were very calm, and her face very lovely. She seemed at peace, and that was something.

"Do you love him?" He didn't believe she did, and he wanted to hear it.

"Of course. I'm his wife." But the truth was she respected him, she admired him, she owed him. She had never loved him as she loved Charles, and she never would. What's more, she didn't want to. A love like that caused too much pain, and she no longer had the courage. She glanced at her watch and then back at Charles. "I have to go."

"Why? What will happen if you don't go home, if you come home with me instead?" He looked as though he meant it.

"You haven't changed. You're still the man who convinced me to elope with him in Paris." She smiled at the memory, and so did he.

"You were easier to convince in those days."

"Everything was easier then, we were young."

"You still are." But in her heart, she knew she wasn't.

She pulled her coat more tightly around her, and slipped on her other glove, and he began to walk her slowly toward the main door of the cathedral.

"I want to see you again before I go."

She sighed, and stopped to look up at him. "Charles, how can we do that?"

"If you don't, I'll come to your house and ring your doorbell."

"You probably would." She laughed in spite of the sorrow of the day that had brought them together.

"You'll have a hell of a time explaining that." Just thinking about it almost brought on one of her migraines. "You know where I am. I'm at my father's. Call. Or I will."

After seven years, here he was threatening her, and looking so damn handsome while he did it.

"And if I don't call?"

"I'll find you."

"I don't want to be found." She looked serious, and so did he when he answered.

"I'm not sure I believe that. And after all these years, we can't just . . . I can't just let go, Marielle . . . I can't . . . I'm sorry." He looked so forlorn, and in an odd way, almost broken.

"I know." She slipped a hand into his arm, and they walked through the door, just as Malcolm's chauffeur darted through a side door. He had spent an interesting hour watching them. It was a side to Marielle he hadn't seen before, but in some ways it didn't surprise

him. Malcolm had his own life too, and she
was a beautiful young woman. Beautiful, and
frightened, he knew. She was intimidated by
everyone, especially her husband. And he
wondered who would pay more for the intelligence of what he'd just seen, in time . . .
Mrs. Patterson herself? Or her husband?

Charles and Marielle were walking slowly
down the steps arm in arm, and he held her
close to him as they reached the bottom. "I
won't press it if you don't want me to, but I'd
like to see you before I go." But he really
looked as though he meant it.

"Why?" She looked straight at him, and he
gave her the only answer he could have.

"I still love you."

Tears filled her eyes as she looked away
from him. She didn't want to love him anymore, or be loved by him, didn't want the
memories, the pain, the anguish. She looked
up at him again. "I can't call you."

"You can do anything you want. And whatever you do, I'll still . . . is it just as hard for
you . . ." He glanced back at the church,
thinking of the day that had brought them
here, and then he looked down at her, his eyes
filled with tears, as hers overflowed in answer,
and she nodded.

"Yes, it's just as hard. It doesn't go away."

And it never would. She understood that now. She had to live with it, like constant pain. She looked up at him again. "I'm so sorry . . ." She had wanted to say those words to him for years, and now she had, but nothing was different.

He shook his head, pulled her tight against his chest, and then let her go. And with a last look at her, he walked away, up Fifth Avenue, without saying good-bye to her. But the truth was, he couldn't. She watched him for a long time, and then she slipped into Malcolm's car. As the chauffeur drove her home, she was thinking about Charles . . . a life long lost, never to be found again . . . and André.

2

Patrick, the driver, took Marielle home, driving north up Fifth Avenue, but she didn't see Charles there. And finally, they drove east on Sixty-fourth Street, to the house where she had lived for six years with Malcolm. The house was between Madison and Fifth, just around the corner from the park, and it was a beautiful home, but it had never been hers. It was Malcolm's. She had felt ill at ease there from the first. It was an awesome establishment, with a huge staff, and it had once belonged to Malcolm's parents. He had maintained it almost as a memorial to them, with priceless collections everywhere, added to only by the rare objects he collected on his travels, or sometimes by curators of museums. Sometimes Marielle felt like a precious object there, something to be displayed, but never played with. A doll to be admired on a shelf and never handled. His servants treated her politely, for the most part, but they had always made it clear that they worked not for her, but for her husband. Many of them had been there for years, and after six years, she still felt she scarcely knew them. Malcolm always urged her to keep her distance. She had, and so had they. There was no warmth in their exchanges with her. And from the first, Malcolm had let her make no changes. It was still his home, everything was done his way, and if her orders differed from his at all, they were politely ignored, and the matter never mentioned. He hired the staff himself, and most of them were Irish or English or German. Malcolm had an enormous fondness for all things German. He had gone to Heidelberg University in his youth, and he spoke the language to perfection.

Marielle wondered sometimes if the reason the staff resented her, albeit secretly, was because she had worked for Malcolm. It had been impossible for her to get a job when she came back from Europe in 1932. The Depression was in full swing, even men with college

degrees were unemployed, and she had absolutely no training. She had never worked for
anyone before, and her parents had left her
nothing. Her father lost everything in the
crash of '29, which basically had killed him.
He'd been too old to survive the strain, to start
over again. In the end, his heart had given out,
but before it, his spirit. And there was nothing
left but a few hundred dollars when his wife
died six months later. Marielle had still been
in Europe then, and Charles had arranged for
their house to be sold in order to pay their
debts. She'd been too ill to take care of it herself, and when she went back to New York
eventually, she was left with nothing and had
no home to go to. She stayed in a hotel on the
East Side, and started looking for a job the
week she'd arrived. She had two thousand dollars she'd borrowed from Charles. It was all
she'd let him give her. She was totally alone.
And in many ways, Malcolm had saved her.
She was grateful to him for that still, and she
always would be.

She had appeared in his office on a wintry
February day, and the face that smiled at her
across the desk was like a ray of sunshine. She
had gone to him because she knew he was one

of her father's friends, and she hoped that somehow he might know of a job, or someone who needed a companion who spoke French. It was all she knew other than her graceful drawings, but she hadn't drawn now in years. She had no secretarial skills at all, but after speaking to her for an hour, he hired her, and until she found a place of her own, he even paid for her hotel bill. She had tried to repay him afterward, but he wouldn't hear of it. He knew what dire straits she was in, and he was happy to help her.

She learned quickly and she worked well, as an assistant to his senior secretary, an English-woman who clearly did not approve of Marielle, but was always civil. And it came as no surprise to anyone when Malcolm started inviting her, first to quiet lunches, and then to romantic dinners. Eventually, he started taking her to important social events with him, always discreetly suggesting that she buy a new dress for the occasion, at a store where they knew him. It troubled her at first. She didn't want to take advantage of him, didn't want to put herself in an awkward position. Yet, he was always so kind to her, so intelligent, so amusing, so understanding. He never pressed her about what her previous life had been, why she had lived in Europe for six

years, or why she had finally returned. They
kept their conversations strictly to the present.
She was surprised that she was always comfortable with him. He was so polite, and so
kind, and so easy to be with. All her earlier
resistance to him disappeared, and she was
particularly surprised that he never made im-
proper advances. He just seemed to like her
company, being seen with a beautiful young
woman in the expensive clothes he paid for.
She was painfully shy then, and sometimes she
still felt a little shaky. But he never seemed to
notice it, and when she was with him, she always felt more confident, and surprisingly
stronger than she had in a long time. She
wasn't her old self anymore, but at least she
was a new one she could live with.

With Malcolm, no one asked her anything.
People wanted to know who she was, of
course, but beyond her name, they never
wanted to know where she'd been or why she
wore such a serious expression. They were impressed with her because of whom she was
with, and how she looked, and sometimes she
even found it amusing. She felt so safe with
him, he protected her from everything, and
that was precisely what he offered her, when
he asked her to marry him at Thanksgiving.
He offered to protect and take care of her for

as long as he lived, which wouldn't be as long
as she lived, because he was so much older.
He made no pretense of loving her, and yet
in some ways, she felt that he did, because
he was always so considerate and kind, so
thoughtful, and so decent. In fact, she wanted
nothing more from him. She couldn't have
taken the risk, or been able to stand the pain,
if anything went wrong, or something happened. Even the memories of Charles were
still exquisitely painful, and the rest was something she still couldn't talk about, even to Malcolm. She had tried to be honest with him, to
tell him that there were things in her past that
had caused her great pain, but he didn't want
to hear it.

"We each have a past, my dear." He had
smiled gently at her, as they dined at the
Plaza. "But at twenty-four, I suspect that yours
is still a little more wholesome." He was so
tolerant of her, so accepting. She could come
to him with her past and her pain and her
wounds and find solace there, and protection.
It was that that she wanted from him, not his
house, or his jewels or his money. He had
been married twice before, and she knew from
those who talked too much, that his generosity
had been legend. But all she wanted from him
was a port in the storm, a place to hide for the

rest of her life, and that was what he promised.
He sensed easily how frightened she was, although even he did not suspect how battered.
And all he required of her was that she be
willing to bear his children. Neither of his previous wives had, and at forty-nine, it was
something he wanted very much, an heir for
the Patterson empire. His money had been
made in steel, and several generations earlier
it had been far less genteel, but by the time
Malcolm was born, the name was highly respected. And in his lifetime, Malcolm had
made it even more so.

She'd been stunned by his proposal at first,
and for a brief moment, she even thought he
was joking. They had certainly been out together many times, and he had been unspeak-
ably generous with her, but until then, he had
never even kissed her.

"I . . . I don't know what to say . . . are
you serious?" He smiled coolly at her, and
took her hand in his, amused by her astonishment. She still looked like a child to him, and
he gently raised her hand to his lips and kissed
her fingers.

"Of course I'm serious, Marielle." His eyes
met hers, and in some ways he seemed more
like a father. But that was part of what she
liked about him, and more than that, it was

what she so desperately needed. She had been back in the States by then for less than a year, and she had no one in the world, except Malcolm. "I want you to be my wife. I will take very good care of you, my dear. I promise you that. And if we're lucky enough to have children, I will be grateful to you for the remainder of my lifetime." It was an odd offer, as she listened to him, and in some ways it almost sounded more like a business arrangement than a marriage. He wanted children from her, and she wanted and needed his protection. He hadn't told her he loved her, or looked at her adoringly, she wasn't head over heels in love with him. It was totally different from what she had had with Charles, but that was precisely what she wanted. Only the idea of having children frightened her now. She wasn't sure she wanted to take that risk again, but she didn't dare explain that to him.

"And if there are no children?" Her eyes searched his with a worried expression, as he wondered if there was something he didn't know. He had thought he knew everything about her.

"Then we will be friends." He looked peaceful as he said it, and that reassured her, but she still couldn't understand why he wanted her, with so many other women who

would have died to have him. And in fact, he
scarcely knew her.

"But why me? There are . . . so many
other . . . more suitable . . ." She blushed
as she said the words. She had no money, no
social status anymore. Her parents had been
respectable certainly, but not in his league,
and they had left her without a penny. But all
of that was part of what appealed to him. She
was a girl with no ties, no family, no obligations. She was "his" in a way, or she would be
if she married him, and he liked that. Malcolm
Patterson was a man who was obsessed by pos-
sessions, his houses, his cars, his paintings, his
Fabergé collection, his "things." Marielle was
something more for him to possess . . . a
very important possession if she could give
him children. Besides which, she was a very
quiet, undemanding girl, and he liked that.
She would be a dignified, attractive wife and
perhaps, with luck, one day, a very good
mother.

"Perhaps I should say I love you," he said
very gently, but they both knew he didn't.
"But I'm not sure that's important to either of
us." He knew her well, better than she had
realized. "Perhaps that doesn't matter at all.
Perhaps it will be better like this, and we will
come to love each other in time, won't we?"

She nodded, still awed by what he was saying. And then he looked down at her expectantly, as though she knew what she was expected to say, and he was waiting for her to say it. "Do you have an answer for me?"

She hesitated, but only for an instant. "I . . ." She looked at him worriedly. . . . "Are you sure? . . ." She was afraid for him, more than for herself. What if she was a disappointment to him? What if . . . what if she fell apart again? The past year hadn't been easy. The Lindbergh child had been kidnapped two weeks after her return, and the horror of it had mesmerized her at first, and in May when the world heard that he was dead, she felt a pain in her heart for them that she knew she would always remember. For days she had stayed in bed, claiming to have the flu. But in truth, she had been unable to function. Finally, in a wave of terror, she had called her doctor in Switzerland, and he had been able to reassure her. But what if that happened again? What if Malcolm knew. . . . "I'm not sure it's fair to you." Marielle lowered her eyes, and tears clustered on her lashes. Suddenly he wanted to pull her into his arms and make love to her. It was the first time she had actually inspired him with any kind of passion, and for an instant he wondered if he really might come to love her.

"Darling . . . please . . . marry me. . . . I'll do everything for you . . ." It was the only language he knew, but she looked up at him with a sad smile, and shook her head.

"You don't have to do that. All you have to do is be kind to me, and you always have been. Too kind. I don't deserve it."

"That's nonsense. You deserve more than I can give you. You deserve a handsome young husband who is so mad about you he's half insane, and takes you dancing every night. Not an old man you'll have to push around in a wheelchair when you're forty." She laughed at the picture he painted, it was difficult to imagine Malcolm ever being anything but vital and youthful. He was a powerful, vibrant man who, despite his mane of prematurely white hair, looked ten years younger than he was. The white hair only made him look more important. "So, now that I've told you what the future holds, will you accept my offer?" Her eyes met his, and almost imperceptibly, she nodded. She felt her breath catch as she looked at him, and he pulled her into his arms and crushed her against him. She felt tears fill her eyes as she looked at him. She wanted to be as good to him as he was to her, she wanted to promise him everything, and she swore to herself she would never disappoint him.

The wedding was tiny and discreet. They were married on New Year's Day by a judge who was a close friend of his, at Malcolm's home, with fewer than a dozen of his friends present. She knew no one to invite anyway, except the women she had met when she was working in his office. But they resented her now anyway. Her Cinderella story did not fill them with happiness for her. She had walked off with what they had always wanted, but they had wanted him for very different reasons than she did. They wanted his money, and all Marielle wanted was his protection.

She wore a beige satin suit that he bought for her from Mainbocher, with a matching hat that had been made by Sally Victor. And she had never looked lovelier than she did that day, with her dark auburn hair in an elegant chignon, and her deep blue eyes filled with emotion. She had cried when the judge declared them man and wife, and she stood very close to him all day, as though she was afraid that if she didn't, some evil spirit might come between them.

They honeymooned in the Caribbean, on a private island near Antigua. It belonged to a friend, and there was a fabulous house, a

yacht, and an army of discreet, extremely well
trained British servants. It had been perfect in
every way, and she found that her affection for
him was rapidly growing deeper. His thoughtful, gentle ways touched her more often than
she was able to tell him. And he approached
their physical life together with wisdom, kindness, and enormous caution. He was anxious
for a child, but not so much so that he was
ever rough or hasty with her, and he spent
most of their honeymoon learning the ways
that brought her pleasure. He was an experienced man, and she enjoyed the time she
spent in bed with him, but there was no hiding
from the fact that there was something missing
between them. But they enjoyed each other's
company, and when they returned to New
York three weeks later, they were good
friends, and she walked into his house with a
confident air, and a bounce in her step that
hadn't been there in years. But once home
again, the reality of their life together had hit
her. They lived in *his* house, saw *his* friends,
day and night, she was surrounded by *his* servants and Marielle had to do everything *he*
wanted. For the most part, the servants considered her a fortune hunter, and treated her like
an intruder. Knowing she had previously
worked for him, jealousy stoked the fires of

their hatred. Her orders were ignored, her requests were secretly ridiculed, her belongings either disappeared or were "accidentally" destroyed, and when she finally tried to mention it to Malcolm, he treated her complaints with amusement, which upset her even more. He told her to give "his people" time to get used to her, and in time they would come to love her as much as he did.

Once back in New York, he was busy at the office again. He kept to himself much of the time, and led his own life, and Marielle became very lonely. He still enjoyed being seen with her, and he was always kind to her, but it was clear that she was not going to share his entire life, or even his bedroom. He explained that he stayed up very late at night, reading documents, or making overseas calls, and it was important to him to have privacy while he did that, and he didn't want to disturb her. She had suggested that they shift their rooms around, and that he have an office next to their bedroom, where he could work at night, but he was adamant that he didn't want to change anything. And in the end, he didn't. Not one single thing changed in Malcolm's life after he married Marielle, except that they went out together a little more often. But more than once, in spite of his kindness, she felt as though she was still one of his employees.

She got an allowance now, which was discreetly shifted into an account on the first of every month, and he encouraged her to shop anywhere and buy anything she wanted. But the servants were still his, the house still looked exactly as it had before, the people they saw were all his friends, and he still traveled without her when he went on business. In fact, Marielle had traveled more with him before, when she was only an undersecretary to him. She would have been angry at the new secretary who did travel with him, except that Marielle liked her. Brigitte was a pretty German girl from Berlin. Her behavior and reputation were impeccable, and she treated Marielle with enormous deference. She had pale blond hair, and bright red fingernails. She carried herself well, and was highly efficient. More than that, she was always kind to Marielle, to the point of being friendly. As they had been of Marielle, the older secretaries were jealous of her, and Marielle felt sorry for her more than once when she noticed the raised eyebrows of Brigitte's colleagues. Brigitte was always very respectful to her, and very helpful whenever Marielle called the office. And she was particularly nice to Marielle when she got

pregnant, sending small but thoughtful gifts
for the baby. She even knitted him a blanket,
and several sweaters, which also deeply
touched Malcolm. The rest of the time, he
seemed to scarcely notice her existence. But
he had other things on his mind, important
business deals, and his wife, and eventually,
the son he had wanted so badly.

Marielle had expected to get pregnant easily. She had before, and she was surprised
when it hadn't happened after the first few
months of their marriage. And after six
months, Malcolm insisted that she go to a spe-
cialist in Boston. He had taken her there himself, and he had left her at the hospital for the
afternoon, while a team of specialists checked
her over. In the end, they found nothing
wrong with her, and they encouraged her and
Malcolm to continue trying. They felt that it
was just a matter of time, and they made some
suggestions which embarrassed her, but Malcolm was more than willing to try them. But
six months later, their suggestions still hadn't
worked, and both of them were deeply worried. It was then that she spent a quiet afternoon with her own doctor. He had no new
explanations to offer her, and he very gently
said that some women just weren't made to
have babies. He had seen it happen before,

healthy young women who had nothing wrong
with them, but simply never conceived. It was
no one's fault, but "Sometimes," he said quietly, "God just doesn't want it to happen." She
was beginning to get hysterical every month
when she saw that she was not pregnant again,
and the strain of it had started her migraines.

"It has happened before," she said softly,
almost afraid to look at him. It was something
she still hadn't told Malcolm, particularly now
since she'd been unable to have his baby.

"You've been pregnant?" The doctor looked
intrigued. He had wondered once when he examined her, but he hadn't been certain and
hadn't asked her. And she had never said anything to him. They had asked her in Boston
several times, but she had denied it. But she
felt more confidence in this man to keep her
secrets to himself. She had found him herself,
and he was one of the few people in her life
who did not owe any special allegiance to Malcolm.

"Yes," she nodded.

"Did you have an abortion?" That really
worried him. In his experience, women who
had the kind of abortions that were available
in dark alleys and back streets, were seldom
able to have other children. They went to

butchers and were lucky if they lived, let alone were still able to have babies.

"No, I didn't."

"I see . . ." He looked suddenly more sympathetic. "You lost it."

"No," she started to say, and then winced as though he had caused her physical pain. "I mean, yes . . . I had him . . . and he died . . . later. . . ."

"I'm so sorry." She told him about it then, and she cried endlessly, but she felt relieved two hours later when she left his office. And in some ways it was like a weight being lifted from her shoulders. He reassured her by saying that he felt certain she would get pregnant again eventually. There was absolutely no reason for her not to.

And he was right. Two months later, with amazement and delight she discovered that she was pregnant. She had just begun to think that it was never going to happen at all, and she had even begun morosely wondering if she should offer Malcolm a divorce, if that was what he wanted, since she had been unable to bear his children. But suddenly, the light had shined, and Malcolm was beside himself with gratitude and excitement. He showered jewelry and gifts on her, came home at lunch to check on her, treated her like the rarest jewel, and seemed to spend every hour making plans for their baby. It was obvious that he wanted a son from her, and yet he was even prepared to be pleased with a daughter. "We'll just have to have more, if it's a girl," he said happily, and Marielle laughed. By then, she could no longer see her feet and hadn't slept decently in weeks. The prospect of more was a little daunting. On the other hand, she had blossomed in pregnancy, and the pain of the last several years seemed dimmer now with the excitement of life inside her. She sat for hours feeling the baby move, and waiting for the hour when she could hold it. It would fill a void that had been aching for years, and she knew that nothing would fill that void again except another baby. She had to tell herself again and again that it would not be André this time, it would be another child . . . he would never return, and still, no matter who this child was, she knew she would welcome him or her with her whole heart, and so would Malcolm.

He ordered everyone in the house to take care of her, to cater to her every whim, to feed her practically every hour on the hour, and make sure she didn't fall or trip or get tired, but his staff was far less enthusiastic about her pregnancy than he was. They seemed to see it as an opportunity to be even more disagreeable to her, particularly the housekeeper who had been there for twenty years, through both previous wives, and continued to view Marielle as a very temporary intruder. The prospect of the baby made her a greater threat, so instead of being pleased, the most malevolent of them were actually angry. The housekeeper, the maids, the driver, Patrick, an Irishman Marielle had disliked since they'd first met, and even the cook and her staff of underlings were all annoyed at having to cater to Marielle's few whims, or even making special tea for her when she had one of her migraine headaches. They seemed to consider her headaches a sign of weakness in her, and they were often rude about her indisposition. Even the baby nurse Malcolm hired for her seemed to view Marielle as something of a lesser being. She was an Englishwoman Malcolm had hired on one of his trips abroad, and she had a face like a stone wall and a heart to match it. It was difficult to imagine her giving any kind of warmth or tenderness to a newborn baby. And when she arrived a month before the baby was due, Marielle was horrified when she saw her.

"She looks like a prison warden, Malcolm. How can we let her take care of our child?" The real issue for Marielle was, why did they need her? She had taken care of André herself, but then the memory of that was too painful to endure, and there was no way now that she could discuss that with Malcolm. "I can take care of the baby myself." But he only laughed at her and told her she was being silly. He wanted her to let everyone spoil her.

"You'll be exhausted when the baby comes. You'll need to rest. Miss Griffin will be perfect. She has excellent references, is hospital trained. She's just what you need, and you don't even know it. You'll see, babies aren't as easy as you think." She knew for a fact they were easier than he thought, but she couldn't tell him. At eighteen, she had taken care of her own baby, with no assistance from the likes of Miss Griffin.

Miss Griffin announced early on that Marielle's migraines were bad for the child, and probably a sign of some very dangerous weakness in the mother. It was as though she wanted to shame Marielle out of them, but they were too severe for anything except a dark room and bed rest. A thousand things brought them on. Tension, worry, an argument with Malcolm, a cruel remark from a maid, a head cold, a virus, a late night, too much rich food, even a glass of wine. They were torture for Marielle, and she was always apologizing for them, as though they were a serious character disorder, just as Miss Griffin had suggested.

Only Haverford, the English butler, was ever kind to her. He had never shown any undue interest in her, but he was unfailingly polite and always pleasant. Unlike Miss Griffin, who was intent on allying herself with Malcolm, who had hired her in the first place. And like everyone else in the house, she rapidly began treating Marielle like an intruder. She treated Marielle like the unpleasant but necessary vehicle they had to put up with in order to get the baby. Eventually, it began to make Marielle feel frightened. She wanted to be with people who loved her now, and she longed for her happy days with Charles before their baby. Sometimes she just lay on her bed and cried, and on more than one occasion, Malcolm was shocked when he found her.

"You're just sensitive right now. Try not to take it all so much to heart," he tried to tell her. But after talking to Miss Griffin, he did think she was being a little foolish. She seemed to cry all the time. She even got upset when she came to the office and saw Brigitte. Marielle felt so fat and ugly in comparison to her that for three days she refused to go anywhere with Malcolm. But he was always patient with her, and tried to be understanding. But it was obvious even to him that Marielle was desperately overwrought at the end of her pregnancy. It was as though she was terrified, and barely able to cope, but he did all he could to help her. Miss Griffin explained that some women are so afraid of delivery that they go crazy in anticipation of the pain. It seemed to support her general theory that Marielle was weak, and worse yet, a coward.

She wanted to have the baby at home, she had insisted on it early on, but Malcolm was equally insistent that the baby be born at Doctors' Hospital, with every possible modern development near at hand in case there was a problem. Marielle felt it would be more peaceful to have the baby at home, and she was worried about kidnapping, as she confessed to Malcolm. Bruno Richard Hauptmann had been arrested in September for kidnapping the Lindbergh child and she became obsessed with the Lindbergh kidnapping again, but Malcolm decided she was just unduly nervous because she was six and a half months pregnant. It was a difficult time for her, in ways no one else knew. Only her doctor realized what she was going through, and whenever she saw him, he tried to soothe her and reassure her that this time everything would be different.

They were at home the night the baby came, she was reading in her room, and Malcolm was working on some papers in his bedroom when the first pains came. She waited for a while, and then she went to tell him, and he rushed to her side the moment he saw her. Patrick drove them to the hospital and Malcolm stayed with her as long as the doctor would let him, and then they wheeled her away to have their baby. She was groggy from the medication they'd given her by then, and she was telling Malcolm something about how different it had been in Paris. The doctor smiled at him, and the two men exchanged looks of understanding, she was in a dream world.

"It should go easily for her," the doctor said softly as the nurses took her away. "I'll come back to you very quickly." He smiled and Malcolm settled into a chair to wait in the huge private suite of rooms they'd reserved for her. It was midnight by then, and Theodore Whitman Patterson was born at four twenty-three that morning.

Marielle saw him first through a kind of haze, and the doctor held him out to her swaddled in a blanket. He had a round pink face and a shock of blondish hair, and he looked at her with surprise as though he'd been expect-

ing someone else, and then he gave a long
loud wail, and everyone in the delivery room
smiled while tears coursed down Marielle's
cheeks. She had thought he was gone . . .
she remembered him so well . . . the same
round cheeks, those surprised eyes . . . but
his hair had been black, like Charles's . . .
shiny black hair like a raven . . . this wasn't
him and yet it looked so like him. She nuzzled
her cheek next to his, feeling a primeval ache
in her soul, and at the same time a rush of joy
and tenderness and completion. They took
him away to clean him up and introduce him
to his father, while Marielle dozed, and the
doctors did some minor repair work.

It was morning when they brought her back
to her room again, and Malcolm was dozing
peacefully there, waiting for her return, and
there was champagne cooling in a silver
bucket near her bedside. He woke as soon as
the gurney entered the room, and she was
more awake than she had been the last time
she saw him. Awake, and sore, and happier
than she'd been in years . . . and proud . . .
she had finally fulfilled Malcolm's dreams, and
their agreement.

"Did you see him?" she asked as Malcolm
bent and kissed her cheek, her eyes tired but
content as he watched her.

"I did." There were tears in Malcolm's eyes now too. This was all he had ever wanted. "He's so beautiful, and he looks just like you."

"No, he doesn't." She shook her head, wanting to say the forbidden words . . . he looks like André. . . . "He's so sweet . . . where is he?" She looked at the nurse, suddenly terrified . . . what if he was gone? . . . if something happened to him . . . if someone took him. . . .

"He'll be back in a little while. He's sleeping in the nursery."

"I want him here, in my room." Marielle looked nervously at Malcolm and he took her hand in his own.

"He'll be all right."

"I know . . . but I want to see him. . . ." She was never going to take her eyes from him, never going to let him go, never going to let it happen again . . . never . . . she began to feel frantic as she looked around the room for him, and for an instant she was afraid she was getting a headache. But the moment passed and Malcolm poured her a glass of champagne, which she only pretended to sip at. After all she'd been through and the medication they'd given her, even the Cristal he'd brought wasn't too appealing.

They brought the baby back to her after

that, and she held him close to her while he
slept, and when he woke, she unbuttoned her
nightgown and nursed him. It all came back so
easily, as though nothing had happened since,
no grief, no loss, no tragedy . . . nothing
. . . the eternity of motherhood was hers, and
she was lost in love at the hands of this tiny
baby.

Malcolm watched in fascination as she
nursed, and he held the baby afterward,
watching his son in adoring silence. And later
that morning, Malcolm went home, and slept
peacefully in his own bedroom, knowing that
his life was full, complete, and almost perfect.
And despite any doubts he may have had in
the past two years, he was glad now that he
had married Marielle. The child had made it
all worth it.

The heavy oak door swung open somberly, as
Marielle stepped into the house on silent feet.
She was still serious, from having seen Charles
after so many years. It had been a shock, but it
had also touched her.

"Good afternoon, Madam." The butler took
her coat from her, as one of the maids stood by
to help her. And Marielle sighed as she saw
them. It had been a difficult afternoon, a diffi-

cult day. She could still feel the chill of the church in her bones as she took off her gloves and laid them beside her black suede handbag.

"Good afternoon, Haverford." She spoke to the old butler. "Is Mr. Patterson at home?"

"I don't believe so."

She nodded, and walked up the stairs, torn as to whether she should go to her own room, or the third floor. Often, when she wanted to visit him, she decided not to. At first, much to her own surprise, she had had mixed reactions to Malcolm's child. She had a passion and a love for him she had never expected . . . more even than the first time . . . more than she'd been capable of at eighteen . . . more than she had known she could ever love another human being. And yet at the same time, outwardly she held back from him, and often the love she felt for him was a well-kept secret. It was too dangerous to allow herself to fall that much in love with him. She knew that, this time, if something happened, it would kill her. So she forced herself to stay away from him, or even appear to be a little indifferent. But there were times when she couldn't feign the pose, times when she had to be with him, times when she crept upstairs at night on bare feet, and just looked at him while he was sleeping. He was more beautiful than any child she had ever seen, warmer, rounder, sweeter, lovelier, more perfect . . . he was the reward for all her pain, the gift from God for all she'd lost. He was everything she lived for.

Of course Malcolm adored him as well, particularly his bright mind and easy ways. He had none of her tension or fears or anxieties about Teddy's safety. He was just an easy, happy child who brought joy to all who knew him.

He had made Malcolm greedy for more for a time, and for the first year after Teddy's birth, Malcolm had hoped to get Marielle pregnant. But once again, their efforts had been in vain, and now with Teddy, Malcolm was less anxious to pursue it. His efforts were abandoned before success was gained, and now he and Marielle kept to their own rooms discreetly. She didn't seem to mind and both of them were content with the lives they led. At thirty, Marielle had a child she adored, a husband who treated her well, it was more than most women had these days, and Malcolm had the heir he had longed for. It was enough for both of them.

And Marielle seemed calmer now in some ways, except on the subject of Teddy's safety. There she was leonine in her defenses. The

Lindbergh kidnapper had been put to death more than two years before, but she still acted as though there was a potential kidnapper on every corner.

Malcolm was grateful to her, she took excellent care of his child, she was a fine mother, a good wife, and she had given him the perfect, beautiful, bright, blond baby of his dreams. It was all he had ever wanted.

As Marielle walked slowly up the stairs, she debated whether or not to go on, she wasn't really in the mood to endure the nurse, and she didn't want to disturb Teddy with Miss Griffin. But suddenly, she heard him. There was a chortle of laughter far away down an upstairs hall, and as she heard it, she smiled. She had already seen him that morning, and sometimes she tried to ration herself. She had to, or he would become an all-consuming passion. It was a game she constantly played with herself, never allowing herself quite enough, never being with him as often as she wanted, because she knew that if she did, she would go mad if anything ever happened. But in truth, the child was already woven into the very fiber of her soul in such a way that she couldn't have torn herself from him. But if she rationed her time with him, she could allow herself to think that she had kept some distance and freedom. Unfortunately, as a result, he spent the rest of the time in the constant care of the indomitable Miss Griffin. Malcolm had insisted she stay with them, and after four years Marielle still disliked her. And Miss Griffin still treated her like a somewhat deficient being. Her migraines, her nerves, her fear of kidnappers, her barely concealed, and obviously unhealthy, passion for the child, alternating with periods of restraint, Miss Griffin felt it was all symptomatic of a truly unworthy person, a view she was not embarrassed to share with any and all who would listen whenever she visited the kitchen. It was Malcolm whom the governess adored, Malcolm she respected, and secretly dreamed of. He was her senior by a mere four years, and had fate been kinder to her, it was Miss Griffin who would have stood in Marielle's shoes, not that pathetic, nervous weakling, as she sometimes called her. She still talked about the Lindbergh child, about how traumatic it had been, and where she'd been when she heard the news. Of course it had been an unpleasant business, but it had happened six years before, and after all, the Lindberghs had had two sons since then.

Marielle stood for a long moment in the hall, listening to the child, smiling to herself, and then, as though pulled by unseen forces, she walked slowly up the marble stairs to the third floor, her elegant suede shoes resounding down the long hallway as she walked toward him. The door of the nursery was closed, and as she reached it, she could hear him giggle. She should have knocked, she knew, Miss Griffin would be shocked by it, but she preferred the element of surprise, and slowly she pressed down the brass handle of the door and it swung slowly open. As it did, a small child turned, with golden curls and huge blue eyes, and his face exploded into smiles when he saw her.

"Mommy!" He flew across the room and into her arms, as her own face melted into a smile and she held him. She picked him up and held him close to her as he nuzzled her neck and breathed deep of her perfume. "You smell so good." He always noticed things like that, the way she smelled and looked, and she loved it when he thought she looked really pretty. The rest of the women around him were so plain, except Brigitte, Daddy's secretary, who sometimes came to visit him and brought him German storybooks and German candies. She said everything was better in Germany, but Miss Griffin said that wasn't true. Miss Griffin said everything was really better in England.

"How are you today, my handsome prince?"
She kissed his cheek and set him down again,
as the governess looked at her with disapproval.

"We're very well thank you, Mrs. Patterson.
We were about to have tea before you interrupted." Marielle never thought that he
should drink any of it, but Miss Griffin felt it
was a sacred ritual, and Malcolm had long
since given their afternoon tea parties his official stamp of approval. As usual, Marielle was
overruled, she thought milk and cookies would
have been healthier, and in truth Teddy preferred them.

"Good afternoon, Nanny." Marielle smiled
uncertainly at her, she was never quite sure of
how she would be received, and it made her
feel awkward to be around her. But explaining
that to Malcolm had been impossible over the
years, and sometimes it seemed as though
Miss Griffin would stay forever. And at four, it
was too soon to say that Teddy didn't need her.

The nurserymaid served tea to the three of
them. She was an unpleasant Irish girl Marielle had never liked, but the housekeeper had
hired her, and Miss Griffin adored her. She
and the driver were also fast friends, and her
name was Edith. She had dyed red hair and
familiar ways, but she did Teddy's and Miss

Griffin's laundry to perfection. And she always kept an interested eye on Marielle's wardrobe.

"And what did you do today?" Marielle asked Teddy conspiratorially over their tea. He looked very serious as he answered.

"I played with Alexander Wilson. He has a train," he said with enormous importance, and went on to explain to her how it worked, how there were little bridges set up and villages and stations, and how he wished he'd gotten one for his birthday. His birthday had been two weeks before. December was a strange month for her, so much to rejoice over, so much to mourn.

"Maybe Santa Claus will bring you a train." In fact, she knew that Malcolm had already bought one, and there had been men working in the basement for weeks, to set up a special train room, with mountains and hills and lakes and exactly the kind of villages he had just described seeing at the Wilsons'.

"I hope so." He looked pensive, and then he smiled up at her again, moving imperceptibly closer. He loved being close to her, smelling her perfume, feeling the silk of her hair, and letting her kiss him the way she had when she first saw him. She was the most exciting person he knew, and he loved her more than anything . . . even trains . . . "Did you do

something nice today?" He always asked, as
though he really cared, just as he asked Malcolm and Brigitte how things were at the office. It made Malcolm smile. And he always
said Brigitte was very beautiful, almost as
beautiful as his mommy, which pleased the
girl from Berlin. She thought him an adorable
child, and Marielle had allowed her to take
him to the zoo on several occasions, and once
she had taken him to the Empire State Building, which he said was the most exciting thing
he'd ever done. When he came home that day
he'd been so emphatic, he even told Brigitte
he loved her.

"I went to church today," Marielle said quietly, as Miss Griffin watched her. Teddy
looked surprised, usually he went with her,
but today he hadn't.

"Is today Sunday?"

"No," she smiled, wondering if she would
ever tell him. Perhaps when he was a man, she
suspected even now that one day he would be
the kind of person you could talk to. "But I
went anyway."

"Was it nice?" She nodded. It had been
"nice" . . . and sad . . . and she had seen
Charles, after all these years. She hadn't had
the courage to tell him about Teddy. It seemed
unfair. He was fighting wars in Spain, risking

his life, perhaps hoping to die, as she had. But now she had this wonderful child, this ray of hope and sunshine to fill her days and life. On this particular day of the year, she couldn't bring herself to tell Charles that she'd had another baby. All she had told him was about Malcolm. And she knew she wouldn't call him again. She couldn't . . . it wasn't right . . . he was part of another lifetime.

"I went to Saint Patrick's Cathedral. You know, the big, big church. We went there last year, at Easter."

He nodded, like a small, wise man. "I remember. Can we go again?" He liked watching the ice skaters across the street, at Rockefeller Center.

She stayed with him for a long time, talking to him, holding him, and reading him a story, until Miss Griffin said it was time for his bath, and Teddy turned imploringly to look at his mother.

"Can't you stay? Please . . ." She wanted to, more than anything, but she knew that disrupting Miss Griffin's routine was a breach of conduct the nurse would not easily forgive her.

"I can give him his bath," she said hesitantly, knowing full well what was going to be the reaction. Miss Griffin hated interference.

"There's no need, thank you, Mrs. Patterson." She stood up crisply. "Kiss your mother good night, please, Theodore, and tell her you'll see her in the morning." It was a hint of sorts. And Marielle understood it.

"But I don't want to see her in the morning. I want to see her now . . ." And I want to see you now too, she wanted to tell him . . . I want to give you your bath, and make dinner for you, and put you in my bed and hold you till you fall asleep, and kiss your little eyes and cheeks and nose while you're sleeping. But they wouldn't let her do things like that. She had to visit the nursery, and have tea with him, and say good night to him hours before bedtime.

"We'll go to the park tomorrow, sweetheart. Maybe to the boat pond."

"There's a birthday party at the Oldenfields' tomorrow afternoon, Mrs. Patterson." Marielle was clearly interfering with their more important social engagements.

"Then I'll take him in the morning." She looked at Miss Griffin defiantly, but to no avail, the older woman always won, and she had Malcolm's support and knew it. Marielle always felt so powerless here, so out of control, as though she didn't exist and had never existed. "We'll go tomorrow morning." She looked at Teddy reassuringly but there were tears running down his little round cheeks anyway. Tomorrow was too far away, for both of them, and he knew it.

"Can't you stay?" She shook her head sadly in answer, and held him close to her for a moment. And then she stood up, trying to look lighthearted, as he was led away, crying, to his bathroom. As she left, Marielle closed the door softly behind her. She always felt so cruel leaving him, he was being brought up by strangers, not even friends, and Marielle herself didn't dare defy them. She had been brought into this house to have this child, and once she had, she no longer seemed to serve any purpose whatsoever. It was hard to live with that, hard to feel useless and unwelcome. And yet her life with Malcolm was something she was grateful for, and she had the child . . . but that was all she had, and why he was so infinitely, desperately precious to her.

She went to her own dressing room then, thinking of him, and changed into a long, pink satin dressing gown, and looked at herself long and hard in the mirror. In some ways, the years had been kind to her. Her figure had stayed the same, despite two children, but her face seemed older now, more sharply etched, more defined and wiser. The eyes were what gave her away, they said she had lived several lifetimes. And as she sat there, she found herself thinking of Charles again, only a few blocks away, and for an insane moment, she wanted to call him, but she knew she couldn't. There was nothing left to say to him except recriminations and apologies and regrets. There were no answers to their questions and now they both knew there never would be.

Malcolm came home shortly after that, and told her he had a business dinner scheduled for that evening. It had come up unexpectedly, and he apologized, as he kissed the top of her head and disappeared hastily to his own bedroom. She ordered a tray in her room that night, and tried to read the same page of the same book over and over, but she found she couldn't make sense of it, no matter how hard she tried. Her mind was elsewhere.

All through the evening, memories of Charles kept intruding on her . . . Charles in Paris when he was so brave, so wild, so young . . . in Venice . . . in Rome on their honeymoon . . . of Charles laughing . . . teasing her . . . swimming in a lake . . . running through a field . . . and then the last time . . . in Switzerland . . . and now, today. . . . She laid her head down, and cried finally, unable to bear the memories a moment longer. And finally, late that night, as the house lay still, she tiptoed silently upstairs and looked at the sleeping child. She knelt on the floor next to his bed and kissed the velvet of his forehead, and then tiptoed back downstairs to the room where she slept alone. She was aching to call Charles, but she owed Malcolm too much. He had done too much for her. She could not call Charles, no matter what . . . no matter what she still felt, or what he had said . . . she knew her days with Charles Delauney were over forever.

3

The next morning, Marielle made one of her rare appearances in the dining room for breakfast. Usually, she had her breakfast in her room on a tray, but this morning she had woken early. She found Malcolm downstairs, finishing his coffee and eggs, and reading the morning paper. In Italy, Mussolini had just demanded that France hand over Corsica and Tunisia.

"Good morning, my dear." He was always courteous, always kind, always seemed pleased to see her, like a charming houseguest he hadn't expected to encounter quite so early. "Did you sleep well?"

"Not very," she said honestly, which was

rare. Usually it was easier to just say what was expected . . . fine . . . thank you . . . excellent . . . marvelous . . . but her night had been filled with nightmares.

"One of your headaches again?" He put down the paper to look her over, but she seemed well. In fact, she looked better than she had in a while, he decided.

"No, just a long night. I probably drank too much coffee after dinner."

"You should drink wine, or champagne." He smiled. "That'll put you to sleep."

She smiled in answer. "Are you home tonight?"

"I think so. We'll spend a quiet evening by the fire." Everything was always such a frenzy right before Christmas, the week before they had been out five evenings in a row, at least this week was quiet. "What are you doing today?"

"I thought I'd take Teddy to the park this morning." She led such a small life, he felt. She seldom went out, never had lunch with friends. He had introduced her to everyone, yet even after all these years, she kept to herself. She was a very quiet young woman. And when he pressed her about it from time to time, she always said she didn't have time, but the truth was she didn't have the courage. And only she knew what terrible sins she thought she was hiding.

"I want to take him to *Snow White* too. Do you think he's too young?" Marielle asked him. It had just opened earlier that year, and it was an enormous hit.

Malcolm shook his head as he set down his paper. "Not at all. I think he'll love it. That reminds me. I want to check on the progress of the train room. They're working down there like elves." It was only twelve days until Christmas.

"Will it be ready in time?" She knew it would, with Malcolm in charge of the project. He tolerated no broken deadlines.

"I certainly hope so. By the way, I'm going to Washington next week. Would you like to come?"

"To see your friends again?" He had impor-tant friends in the War Department, and he loved going to Washington to see them. He nodded. "About some important business I'm doing. And then I have an appointment with the German ambassador, about a project in Berlin."

"You sound as though you'll be very busy."

"I will, but you're more than welcome to come with me." But she knew perfectly well that he would have no time for her there, and despite his invitation, she would only be a burden. And she had so much to do before Christmas.

"I'd really love to stay here and get organized. Would you be upset if I didn't come?"

"Of course not, my dear. It's up to you. I'll be back very quickly."

"Maybe after the New Year," she suggested, wondering if she was failing him, or if he'd be angry at her not going. She was always afraid of doing the wrong thing, or hurting someone, or letting him down, or not being wherever, or not doing something she should be. But where should she be? With Malcolm in Washington, or here with Teddy? Those decisions had become difficult for her over the last nine years, because if you made the wrong choice, it could cost you all you had. She had learned that lesson and paid for it dearly. "Is that all right?" she asked nervously.

"It's fine." He was quick to reassure her. He kissed her good-bye then, and a little while later, she went upstairs to dress. And later that morning, as promised, she went out with Teddy. Miss Griffin had attempted to accompany her, but for once Marielle had been firm and told her that she and Teddy wanted to be alone for the morning. He was thrilled with what she said, and Miss Griffin was so outraged that, as Marielle and Teddy made their way downstairs, they heard the nursery door bang smartly behind them. Teddy only laughed, and Marielle smiled as she put his coat on, and Brigitte stopped to chat with them for a minute, on her way upstairs to see Malcolm.

"Are you going somewhere exciting this morning, Theodore?" She said it with her very slight German accent, and her eyes exchanged a warm smile with Marielle. Marielle had always felt that the two of them might have been friends, had circumstances been different. But Malcolm would never have tolerated Marielle befriending his employees.

"We're going to the park," Teddy said proudly, glancing at Marielle with the full measure of his affection. And then, noticing the blue dress his father's secretary had on, he executed a little bow that brought a smile to Brigitte's lips. "I like your dress, Briggy. You look *very* pretty."

The young German woman laughed, and blushed faintly. "Perhaps you will tell me that again in another twenty years, young man, yes?" Teddy looked a little baffled by the suggestion, as both women smiled. "Never mind, thank you very much. I think you look *very* handsome too. Is that a new coat?" It was the navy blue English coat with matching cap which Miss Griffin had ordered for him, and which he hated.

"No." He shook his head matter-of-factly. "It's my old one." And then he looked up at his mother. She had her fur coat on, and they were both ready.

"All set?" She smiled down at him and he nodded, and then stood on tiptoe to plant a kiss on Brigitte's cheek, noticing the faint musk of her perfume.

"Have a good time, Theodore." She waved, as he left, hand in hand with his mother, and he turned back once for a last wave at Brigitte.

It was freezing outside, as it had been the day before, and she decided to have Patrick drive them up Fifth Avenue, to bring them closer to the boat pond. Teddy chatted all along, and as they walked into Central Park from Fifth, Marielle was telling him about Paris when she lived there. Malcolm loved telling him about his trips to Berlin, and she knew that Miss Griffin was always rhapsodizing to him about England.

"One day we'll go on a trip to Europe, on a big ship, like the *Normandie*," and then she told him all about that, as he listened to her wide-eyed.

"Will Daddy come too?" The idea of a trip on a ship really thrilled him.

"Of course. We'll all go." She loved going on trips with him. She hated leaving him behind, which was one of the reasons why she didn't like traveling with Malcolm and was relieved that he seldom asked her.

Teddy looked thoughtful as they walked along hand in hand, the wind bitter cold on their faces. His nose was red and her eyes watered but they were well bundled up in coats and hats and scarves and mittens. "Maybe Daddy will be too busy," he said with regret, and Marielle tried to reassure him.

"No, I'm sure he'll come if we take a trip like that." She tried to sound lighthearted as she said it. But he was right, Malcolm was always busy, especially lately.

"Maybe we could meet him in Berlin, if he's too busy to come with us," Teddy said with a matter-of-fact air. He was so bright. He noticed everything. Even that Malcolm did a lot of business with the Germans. It was why Brigitte was so useful to him, and probably why she had lasted for six years in his office. She was incredibly efficient, as well as nice, and his dealings with Germany seemed to have tripled over the years of their marriage.

"Maybe we could go to London too," Teddy

added out of kindness to Miss Griffin. "And we could see Big Ben, and the Tower of London . . . and Buckingham Palace . . . and the King!" He seemed very impressed by everything Miss Griffin had told him and Marielle smiled as they walked along and finally reached the boat pond. But there was a thin layer of ice on it today, and she felt a shiver run through her. Marielle pulled the child close to her, as though something evil waited for them there, and pulled him away from it very quickly.

"There's no one here today. Let's go see the Carousel." But she was very pale in the chill wind as she said it.

"I wanted to see the boats." He looked so disappointed.

"There are none." She was looking frightened, but he was too young to know it. "Come on . . . let's go."

"Can we walk on the ice?" he asked, fascinated by the thin crust that lay across most of the boat pond, but she pulled him away even harder. "Never, ever do that, Teddy, do you hear me?" He nodded, startled by the vehemence of her reaction. It was then that she looked across the ice, and thought she saw him. It seemed impossible this time, as though her mind were playing tricks on her again.

Maybe she was finally going mad. Maybe coming here today, to the pond, with its thin veil of ice on it, had been too much for her. She closed her eyes for a moment, as though to clear her vision, and then opened them again, very quickly.

"We're going home." Her voice was a croak of terror as her eyes darted between Teddy and the man she thought she saw across the lake, as though she were still not sure of what she was seeing.

"Now?" Teddy looked as though he might cry. "We just got here. I don't want to go home. Can't we go to the Carousel?"

"I'm sorry . . . we'll go for a drive . . . the zoo . . . tea . . . maybe the skaters . . ." anything to get away from here. As she stood there, her whole body began shaking. But as she tried to lead the child away, the man she had seen ran as fast as he could around the lake, coming toward them. And as he reached her, his black hair was disheveled, his eyes looked wild, and she saw with dismay that she knew she hadn't been mistaken. As Teddy saw the look on his mother's face, he was suddenly frightened. His mother had always instilled in him a vague terror about strangers, and this one looked particularly dreadful. He was tall and disheveled and he seemed to swoop down on them breathlessly, and without warning, he grabbed both of Marielle's shoulders in his hands, looked her in the eye, and then stared down at Teddy. But at least she knew now she wasn't mad. She hadn't dreamed him. It was Charles, and then she remembered how close the boat pond was to the Delauney mansion. He had had a long drunken, sleepless night himself, and had come out for some air to sober up before a meeting with his father's lawyers.

"What are you doing here?" He looked at her, and then at the boy. "And who is that?" There was something of André in his face, and yet he was so different. There was something almost angelic about this child's face, it was a face you wanted to kiss, with eyes that made you want to laugh the moment you saw him.

"This is Teddy," she said quietly, her voice still shaking.

"Teddy who?" He stared at her accusingly, and she suspected instantly that he was not entirely sober. "This is Teddy Patterson." She straightened her chin and looked Charles in the eye. He couldn't do this to her, couldn't make her feel guilty again, couldn't ruin her life . . . or could he? . . . "My son." Teddy held tightly to her hand wondering who the man was. He thought he looked pretty scary.

"You didn't tell me that yesterday. You only told me about Malcolm." His eyes bore into hers so hard it was almost painful to meet his gaze, but nonetheless she met it. She was braver than Malcolm thought. But Charles had always known that.

"It didn't seem the time or place to tell you."

"Why not?" He was accusing her again. He was angry at her. "Why didn't you tell me?" She knew his anger too well. It was the same anger which, nine years before, had almost killed her.

"It seemed unfair to tell you about him yesterday."

"And now?" His eyes were furious and his face was right next to hers, as Teddy watched in terror. In a minute, he was going to scream, if he could, if only to protect her. "Is it unfair?" Charles asked again, this time louder, seeming very drunk now. But she was calm, and in total control. She had Teddy with her, and she was not going to let Charles hurt them. No matter what had happened in the past, he no longer scared her. She could not let him.

"I don't think we should discuss this now." She pulled Teddy closer to her, and gently touched his face so he wouldn't be afraid. But it only seemed to make Charles more angry. He was still such a striking-looking man, and she still felt weak in the knees when she looked at him, but he seemed so out of control now.

"Why do you have a child?" He shouted at her as she tried not to flinch, so she wouldn't frighten Teddy. "What do I have?"

"I don't know . . . your battles in Spain . . . your beliefs . . . your friends . . . your writing . . . if you have nothing else, perhaps that's a choice you made." She was desperate not to discuss it in front of Teddy, but she was afraid just to walk away and make Charles even more angry. She held tightly to the child's hand, trying to give him courage with her pressure.

"That's a choice *you* made, seven years ago when you left me," Charles shot at her. "You made that choice for me. We could have had more children."

"We have to go now." She began to cry as she said the words and Teddy stared at them, wondering what it all meant as she spoke to Charles again, this time more softly. "What kind of life could we have had? You hated me, and you were right then, I hated myself too . . . maybe I always will . . . but Charles, I couldn't have stood it. I couldn't have looked you in the eye, knowing how you felt about me." She had told him all that seven years ago, before she left Europe.

"I told you I wanted you back," he said stubbornly.

"It was too late then." She took a breath and wiped her eyes, forgetting Teddy for an instant. "I think you'd always have blamed me, just as I blamed myself."

She had still loved him in some ways, but she could never have stayed with him, not after what happened.

Charles looked down at Teddy then, as though he still could not believe he even existed. He was a beautiful child, in some ways, even more beautiful than André. And then Charles looked at Marielle again, wanting desperately to hurt her. "You don't deserve this," he raised his voice to her, and for an insane moment, he wanted to slap her. Why had she married again? Why did she have this child? Why in God's name had she left him? But they both knew why, and perhaps it could never have been any different. "You don't deserve him," he said with the cruelty she still remembered. It was the other side of their great love, the side that had battered her before she left him.

"Perhaps not."

"You shouldn't have left me."

"I had no choice. If I'd stayed, it would have killed me." And he knew that was true too. They had both gone more than a little crazy. She with attempted suicides, he with his wild attack on her the night it happened. But they had both been so mortally wounded by what had happened.

"Perhaps we would all have been better off dead. . . ." There were tears in his eyes now too, as Teddy drew even closer to his mother.

"That's a terrible thing to say."

"For you, maybe . . . you have a life now . . . a husband . . . a child. And why should you? Why should you, dammit, when I still wake up every day thinking of him . . . and of you . . . wishing I had died with him. Do you ever think of him? Do you ever remember . . . or is it all forgotten?" But as he said the words, fury suddenly raged in her eyes. Fury born of years of pain and anguish, about which Charles knew nothing.

"How dare you? There isn't a day that I don't remember, that I don't think about him . . . that I don't see his face if I close my eyes . . . or even yours. . . ." Just as she had seen them the night before as she lay sleepless, remembering, fighting herself not to call him. "But nothing is going to bring him back, no matter how badly we destroy our lives now, or each other. He's gone . . . he's at peace . . . perhaps it's time for us to be at peace too."

"I will never be at peace without you." He raged at her, looking young again, and this time she smiled at him, and shook her head. In some ways, despite the fact that he was older, he seemed even more childish. He hadn't gone on, hadn't grown, hadn't healed, he had just stayed there, doing the same crazy things he had done as a boy, playing the expatriate, fighting other people's wars, and in some ways, hiding from being a grown-up.

"That's a stupid thing to say. You don't even know who I am now. Or maybe even who I was then. Maybe it would have all died a normal death anyway, if things had been different." She looked down at Teddy then, and smiled at him, and pulled him close beside her. "Teddy, this is an old friend. His name is Charles, and sometimes he acts a little crazy, but he's a nice man. Would you like to say hello?" Teddy shook his head firmly and hid in the folds of her fur coat. They had spoken much too freely, but at four, a lot of it had missed him. The tone hadn't, the anger, the passion, but the history was too complicated for him to follow.

"I'm sorry if I frightened him." He looked

briefly remorseful, but still like a madman. He hadn't shaved since the day before, and everything about him looked wild and woolly.

"You should be. And for what? Can you really hold this against me?" He looked at her and then at the boy long and hard, and when he looked back at her, the look in his eyes hadn't mellowed. Instead he frightened her more, and he seemed even drunker. For the first time in a long time, she knew real terror. It reminded her of the bad times when Charles had become a stranger.

"He should be mine. By all rights . . . he should be." He was staring hard at Teddy, hidden in her coat, and Marielle looked at Charles firmly.

"But he isn't yours, Charles."

"What right did you have to move on . . . to do this . . . to have a child without me?" As he said the words, his fury seemed to be growing.

"You agreed to the divorce, I had every right." She refused to be bullied.

"You said that if I didn't, it would kill you."

"It nearly did." And they both knew she meant it.

"I'd rather you were dead than have this child without me." His eyes were like daggers into her heart as he said it, and she shrunk back from him, frightened and disgusted, wondering how she had ever loved him, reminded of how irrational he could be, and why she had left him.

"Charles, stop it." He reached out and grabbed her arm then, and Teddy let out a small shriek and jumped behind her. "You're frightening the child. It's not fair. *Stop it!*"

"I don't give a damn. He's mine . . . by all rights, he should be."

"Stop!" She spat the word at him, no longer afraid of him or anyone as she wrenched her arm free. She was not going to watch her life fall around her. "He's not yours, and neither am I . . . and André wasn't ours either. No one belongs to anyone else in this world. We all belong to God, and we're here on loan to each other . . . and when the loan is up, it's over . . . and it's terrible . . . and it hurts like hell . . . and sometimes it comes much too soon . . . but we didn't own him . . . you didn't own me, or I you . . . and I don't own Teddy."

"You love him, don't you?"

"Of course I do."

"And he loves you?"

"Yes."

"Why do you have that, and I have nothing?"

"Maybe because I'm lucky. Or maybe because Malcolm felt sorry for me . . . or maybe just because that's the way it is, or I'm willing to pay a price you aren't."

"And what price is that? What price did you pay to marry him?" She had married a man she didn't love and who didn't love her and she knew it. It was not as easy as one might have thought. But it was also something Charles would never even have considered doing for a moment. "What exactly did you give up when you married him?"

Hope . . . love . . . tenderness . . . the kind of love and passion they had once shared . . . the kind of love that she knew existed. "Everybody gives up something when they get married." Out of loyalty to Malcolm, she would never have told Charles the truth. "Perhaps I gave up the past."

"I'm deeply impressed by your sacrifice," he said scornfully, glaring at her through the booze.

"I'm deeply impressed by your behavior. You're as bad as ever." He had upset Teddy and her, and they had resolved nothing. There was nothing to resolve anymore. It was over. "There's no reason to do this to me, or yourself. What do you think you're going to accomplish?" But he was staring at Teddy again, and the way he looked at him made her nervous. He was like that when he drank. It had happened in the old days too, he would drink too much and stay drunk all night and the next morning, and finally go more than a little crazy. He had destroyed an entire hotel room once, and a bar, and a restaurant, and nearly killed two men . . . and her, but only once. Only once . . . but she knew what he was capable of. It was hard to forget it.

"I apologize." He looked at her unhappily, but he didn't sound as though he meant it. He looked down at Teddy then, who was peeking around his mother. "I apologize to you too, young man. I have been extremely rude to you and your mother. It's a bad habit I have, but I've known her for a long time, almost since we were children." They had almost been children then. Eighteen and twenty-three . . . My God, they'd been babies. And then he looked at Teddy more seriously. "One day, I would like to get to know you." Teddy didn't look as though he reciprocated the feeling, but he nodded politely. "I had a little boy once too . . . his name was André. . . ." Charles's eyes filled with tears as he looked at Marielle again. "I'm sorry . . . maybe it's just because yesterday was so difficult . . . and seeing you . . . dammit . . ." He looked away and sniffed to try to clear his head. "Why is it always just there? Why does it hurt so damn much? Is it like that for you too?" He looked at her questioningly, but he was calmer again, and she nodded.

She had told him that at church the day before too, but he'd forgotten. And he'd started drinking the moment he left her.

"We should go back now," she said again. "It's getting late." Teddy had to have lunch, and go to the birthday party he was attending with Miss Griffin. In the end, it hadn't been much of a morning. In fact, it had been horrendous. And she was sorry. Her time with Teddy was so precious. "I'm sorry we ran into you like this." It had been easier the day before, before he knew about her son. Now he was filled with anger and resentment. All during the night, he had drowned himself in alcohol and self-pity. But now he had set his feelings ablaze with the incendiary fumes of jealousy and fury.

"I'm leaving next week. I decided yesterday. Will you see me?"

She shook her head, holding Teddy's hand firmly in her own.

"Why not?"

"You know why. You're angry at me anyway, if we see each other it will just make things worse. Why torture ourselves with what we can't have now?"

"Who's to say what we can't have? You're not happy, it's written all over you. You're nervous, taut, wound up like a tight screw, your insides all tied in a knot. We can have anything we damn well want, if we've got the guts to take it." He seemed threatening somehow, when he said it.

"That's a nice attitude, Charles."

"I can do whatever I damn well please."

"How fortunate for you."

"I want you."

"Don't say that." Her eyes blazed at him. "And even if you do, so what? We 'take it,' as you put it, and you leave and go back to Spain. Where would that leave me?" She was trying to reason with him, but it wasn't easy in the state he was in.

"Maybe it'll leave you happier than you are today. Or maybe you'd like to come with me." The simplicity of it almost made her laugh. After six years she was supposed to just walk out on Malcolm, and their child, and go back to Europe with Charles as though nothing had ever happened. He really was more than a little crazy. "You could even bring the boy."

"Your hospitality overwhelms me. And Malcolm? What happens to him after all this?"

"You win . . . you lose . . . he loses . . ."

"That's a rotten thing to suggest, Charles, and you know it. You also know me well enough to know I wouldn't do it."

"Perhaps," he said, grabbing her wrist in his powerful hand, "perhaps . . . you could be forced. . . ."

"Charles, this is not Spain, and you are not fighting for my freedom. This is ridiculous," but she was trying to cover the fact that the look in his eyes had scared her.

"How ridiculous would it be if I took something you wanted—or loved—very much . . . and then perhaps you could be . . . induced, shall we say . . . to join me?"

"What exactly are you saying?" Even the thought of what he was suggesting terrified her.

"I think you understand me."

"You wouldn't do a thing like that." He was suggesting that he kidnap Teddy in order to make her go with him, but he was mad, and even he wouldn't do that. Or would he? His eyes said he would. But history said he couldn't. Or could he?

"It all depends on how desperate I am, doesn't it? . . . doesn't it? . . ." He suddenly let go of her wrist and laughed, and she looked at him with terror. It would be a relief when she knew that he was gone again. She was suddenly sorry that she had run into him at the church the day before. Perhaps he still mourned for André too, but it had obviously twisted him into someone she no longer knew and didn't want to.

"If you ever did anything like that, I want you to know that you would never get away with it, and instead of making me follow you . . . I would kill you . . . and so would my husband."

"You terrify me." He laughed drunkenly again.

"You make me sick. We had something beautiful that I've cherished in my heart for twelve years . . . along with the memory of someone sweet and pure . . . and you use it in this vile way to poison yourself and everyone around you. That isn't what he was about, and it isn't what you were about then."

"Perhaps I've changed." He smiled evilly at her, but the tragedy for both of them was that he really hadn't. He still loved her, still longed for their child, wished she'd return, and that they could recapture a past long gone and never to be forgotten.

"Good-bye." She looked at him sadly for a long moment, and smiled gently down at Teddy, as they walked away. "We're going home now." There was nothing more to say to Charles and he was staring at them as they walked away, but this time he didn't ask her to call him. He was angry at her, angrier than he had ever been. She felt colder than ever as they walked back to the car, and Teddy said not a word until they reached it.

"I don't like him," he said quietly, as the chauffeur closed the doors of the Pierce-Arrow. Patrick had followed them into the park, according to Malcolm's orders to him, to ensure their safety, and he had seen Charles again, but he had heard none of the conversation. He recognized him from the church, and he was ever more intrigued by what Marielle was up to. It was odd that she had taken the boy with her, but maybe she wanted the boy to meet him.

"He's not a bad man," Marielle said sadly as they drove toward home. "He's very unhappy. We used to be very good friends."

Teddy nodded, trying to understand it. And then he looked at her again, and asked a question she hadn't expected. "Who's André?" Her breath caught as he asked and she took a moment before she answered.

"André was his little boy. He died . . . a long time ago . . . and Charles has been very sad ever since then. That's what makes him act so crazy." Teddy nodded then, as though now everything was clear to him. And then he looked up at his mother.

"Did you know André too?" She fought back tears as she nodded and held his hand tightly. She had wanted to tell him one day, but not like this, and not hiding behind the subterfuge she had to use now. But he was too young, and it was too soon. And she still had to try and answer his questions.

"I knew him too," she said sadly, wiping a tear from her cheek.

"Was he nice?" That was always important to Teddy, and Marielle felt a sob lodge in her throat, begging to spring forward, but she wouldn't let it.

"He was very sweet . . . and very young when he died." There were tears rolling slowly down her cheeks, and she wasn't sure what to say to Teddy. There was really nothing more to say to him. She just held him close to her, more grateful than ever that she had him. She was frightened too over what Charles had said to her. And she wondered if he meant it. Would he take the boy, to force her to come with him? It was unimaginable. She knew they were empty threats. He would never do anything to hurt Teddy. "I'm sorry we met him today. I wanted to have a nice time with you at the boat pond."

"That's okay." He smiled up at her. "I always like to be with you." He always said the thing that melted her heart, and made her love him.

"How about if we go to see *Snow White* tomorrow?" It was Sunday, and usually Malcolm liked to do paperwork at home, which left her at loose ends. And the best part was that Miss Griffin was off, and there would be no interference whatsoever. Teddy would be with Marielle all day, with Betty's help if she needed it, and Edith would baby-sit for him in the evening.

"Wow! Can we do that? Can we really see *Snow White*?"

"We sure can. I'll arrange it." He leapt out of the car when they got home and raced up the front steps as Haverford opened the door for them, and almost smiled as young Master Theodore exploded into the house as he entered.

And as he did so, he almost collided with his father. For a moment, Marielle wondered if he would tell Malcolm about Charles, but he was in too much of a hurry to get to lunch and get ready for the party, and he was much too excited about *Snow White* to even think about

the odd man they had met in Central Park.
Teddy was halfway to the third floor before
Marielle even got her coat off.

"Where have you two been?" Malcolm
asked conversationally. He had been to the office and back. He liked going in on Saturdays,
and now he was going to his club for lunch
with an old friend visiting from California.
They were all rituals he enjoyed, and that
were important to him.

"We went to the boat pond, but it was frozen."

"It must have been awfully chilly," he said,
looking at her, and she nodded.

"You're going out?" she asked, wondering
where he was going.

"Yes," he gave her a businesslike kiss on the
cheek, "but don't forget dinner at the Whytes'
this evening." They were giving a Christmas
dance, and she was planning to wear a fabulous dress Malcolm had bought her from Madame Grès in Paris. It was all made of tiny,
tiny folds of shimmering white satin, and she
was going to wear it with diamonds at her
throat and ears, silver shoes, and a floor-length
ermine coat he'd given her for her birthday. It
was quite an outfit.

"Do we have anything tomorrow night too?"
Suddenly she couldn't remember. But it re-

minded him of the note he had just left on her desk that morning.

"I'm leaving for Washington a day early. I want to go down tomorrow afternoon, and have a quiet dinner with the Secretary of Commerce tomorrow night, and be ready for a full day of business with the ambassador on Monday." In fact, he was so serious about the trip, he was taking both of his secretaries with him. "Is that all right with you?" They both knew it didn't matter if it wasn't, but he was always good about asking, and she was equally so about playing the game, pretending to "allow him."

"It's fine. I have a date with your son to see *Snow White* tomorrow afternoon, and we'll have a quiet evening." She smiled at her husband. His courteous ways were such a relief, after seeing Charles act like a madman.

"You're sure you won't come?"

"We'll be fine here." She smiled again, and he kissed her forehead.

He signaled to Patrick that he was ready, and the driver went back out to the car to wait for him, as Haverford handed him his homburg. "See you later, my dear. Have a nice afternoon. Rest up for this evening. You don't want to get one of your headaches." Sometimes she thought they all treated her like a cripple. Of course, the meeting with Charles would have been the perfect spark to provoke one, but she was fine all afternoon. She saw Teddy before and after he went out, and she went upstairs to kiss him again before she went out for the evening. Miss Griffin growled when she did, she felt she had already seen enough of him for one day, but sometimes it was fun to let him see how she looked when she was dressed for the evening, and he loved it. He ooed and aahed over everything she was wearing.

The Madame Grès dress looked sensational on her. It clung to her figure like angels' wings, and Malcolm said she looked like a goddess when he saw her. She won the attention of the Whytes' dinner guests too, everyone was in awe of how she looked, and most of the men told Malcolm how lucky he was to have a wife half his age, and so incredibly lovely.

She was quiet that night on the way home from the party, and he told her again how beautiful she had looked. She smiled her thanks, but she was thinking about Charles and the threats he had made in the park about Teddy. She decided that Charles was just enraged, she was sure that he would never harm a child, hers, or anyone else's. He was just frustrated at her refusal to see him and he didn't know what else to do, except threaten. But she was glad she had decided not to see him. It would have just fanned old flames, and made them both unhappy. Had things been different between them, she would have told Malcolm, but under the circumstances, she knew she couldn't. He had no idea how important Charles had been to her, or that he'd even existed, let alone that they'd been married and had a child, who had died, or what reason Charles might have to resent Teddy.

"You seem preoccupied." He had noticed it too, but it gave her a dreamy look that made her seem even more beautiful, and for the first time in a long time, he found he wanted her, which surprised him.

"I was just thinking."

"What about?"

"Nothing special."

"Well, you look very special to me." She smiled again, still looking distracted, and for reasons of his own, Malcolm decided not to pursue it.

One of the maids had stayed up to help her undress, and Marielle put her jewelry away, and went to bed. And as she lay there, she thought about Charles and the things he had said in the park . . . but tonight, when she slept, she didn't dream about André . . . but of Teddy.

4

Marielle took Teddy to see Snow White *the* following afternoon. It was playing at the Radio City Music Hall, and they went to Schrafft's for hot chocolate afterward. It was a perfect afternoon for both of them. Teddy said he loved it when Miss Griffin had a day off, which made Marielle wish, more than ever, that she would leave them. It reminded her to broach the subject again with Malcolm. He still thought that Miss Griffin did the boy good, she instilled manners in him, and according to Malcolm, as far as governesses went, there was nobody like the British. But she was far from their minds as Marielle and Teddy drove home again, and tonight she gave

him a bath in her own enormous marble bathtub, and he loved it. They used tons of bubble
bath and got it all over the bathroom, and
Edith, the redheaded Irish girl, looked furious
when she saw it. She was supposed to be
baby-sitting for Teddy that night, but she had
long since made other plans with Patrick. They
were going to a Christmas dance at the Irish
Dance Hall in the Bronx, and she had already
gotten Betty, the young kitchenmaid, to agree
to come up and baby-sit for him while she
went out. And when she got back, she would
slip a five-dollar bill into Betty's hand, get into
the bed in the nursery spare room, and nobody would be the wiser. So she didn't appreciate the mess they had made, and the fact that
she'd have to clean it up before she went anywhere, unless she could get one of the others
to do it for her, which was unlikely.

Marielle had dinner with Teddy in the nursery sitting room that night, and she read him a
story before he went to bed. Later she sang
Christmas carols to him and stroked his hair,
and he fell asleep as he lay next to his mother
in his red pajamas. It was a far cry from his
swift, brisk good nights, and the freezing cold
open windows he experienced with Miss Griffin. And Marielle slid gently off his bed so as
not to wake him.

As she walked back downstairs to her own rooms, Marielle wondered if she was spoiling him, as Miss Griffin said, and if she was, if it really mattered. Lately, Marielle had been spending more and more time with him, and she seemed to be having trouble keeping her distance. Her old fears about getting too close seemed to have been cast to the winds, and she thrived on being with him. And if she loved him too much, what harm could it do? What difference could it make? She was so lucky to have him. And she refused to let herself believe that anything could happen. Malcolm was right, she worried about too many things, and it was time she stopped it.

She went to bed with a copy of *Rebecca*, and Malcolm called her from Washington when he returned from dinner. It was after ten o'clock, and he said he had had a delightful evening. He had dined with Harry Hopkins, who would be replacing Daniel Roper as Secretary of Commerce in the next two weeks, although it was still very much a secret. Louis Howe, FDR's right-hand man, had been there too. And they had talked extensively about FDR's feelings about Europe. He was beginning to feel that war was inevitable, but he still hoped that with any luck at all, it could be avoided.

The German ambassador had told Malcolm how well things were going in Berlin. There was no doubt that the German army was stepping up its activities, but he assured Malcolm that his investments were safe there. And when Malcolm questioned him, the ambassador admitted that the business of *Kristallnacht* had been an embarrassment, but on the other hand what Hitler was doing for Germany industrially could change the entire world for the better. Malcolm was deeply excited to be involved, and he told Marielle that it had been interesting sharing some of the latest developments with Howe and Roper, and the men they'd brought with them. Malcolm said he could see an extraordinary future ahead for Germany and all her allies, and Marielle was touched that he had called to share his excitement with her.

He was going back to Germany again soon, and as usual, she was planning to stay home with Teddy.

"How was the movie, by the way?" He loved hearing about the boy. Next to Germany, the child was his greatest passion.

"Teddy loved it."

"I knew he would. I hear it's terrific. Maybe we'll take him again." Even though he was away more and more, he still liked doing

things with them. She was so sweet to the
boy, and it was obvious that despite her other
anxieties, she was a good mother. Malcolm
yawned then, and Marielle smiled. It had been
a long day for him, and not as relaxing as hers,
going to the movies, and giving bubble baths
to Teddy. As they finished the conversation,
she heard an odd noise in the hall, like someone bumping into things, and then footsteps
on the stairs. She listened for a minute, but it
was quiet again and she decided it was nothing.

"You'd better get some sleep," she told Malcolm. "You must have a long day ahead tomorrow. Will you be back tomorrow night?" She
had forgotten to ask him when he'd left, they
had both been so busy.

"More like Tuesday. I may want to have dinner with the German ambassador tomorrow
night, if he's free. We have meetings tomorrow
afternoon, and we'll see then. But in any case,
I think it makes more sense to come back on
Tuesday. I'll call you tomorrow evening."

"I'll talk to you then. And Malcolm . . .
good luck with your meetings. . . ." She felt
grateful to him again suddenly. He had given
her so much, and he asked for so little.

"Take care of yourself, Marielle. We'll have
a nice evening together when I come home."

And soon there would be Christmas. With Teddy, it was a magical time which meant a great deal to both of them. For Malcolm, never having had children before, it was like a whole new life, and he couldn't wait to give the boy his train, and show him the room that had been specially built to house it.

She hung up after the call from Washington, and lay in the dark for a long time, thinking about him, and his many virtues. But two hours later, she was still awake, she couldn't sleep thinking of Charles and what he'd said at the boat pond. And she prayed this didn't mean she was getting one of her headaches. It had been a difficult few days after running into Charles twice, and sometimes insomnia meant that the next day she would be felled by a migraine. She decided to get up, and with a small smile, she began to mount the stairs to the third floor, silent and barefoot. She was going to give him one more kiss as he slept, touch his hair, and just watch him for a minute before she went back to her own bed. She noticed that someone had dropped a towel on the stairs, and realized that one of the maids had been careless. That was probably the noise she had heard a while before, someone bumping the laundry down the marble stairs, and perhaps they'd run into some of the furniture and dropped some of the laundry. She picked the towel up, and walked down the third-floor corridor to the nursery door. There were three bedrooms off the nursery living room and hall, one was Miss Griffin's, one was a spare, and would have been for the second child they never had, and the largest was Teddy's. And as she crossed the living room on silent feet, Marielle heard a stirring some- where, and assumed that it was probably Edith in the spare bedroom. She knew that Miss Griffin would be asleep in bed by then, back from her day off, but officially on Sunday nights, she was still off duty, so Edith was baby-sitting that night. But as Marielle took a step closer to Teddy's door, she fell over an unexpected obstacle and went sprawling across the nursery floor, and had to remind herself not to scream, so as not to wake Teddy. The object she had fallen over seemed large and soft, and as she sailed over it in her night- gown and bare feet, something touched her leg, and she let out a yelp of fear, and tried to jump clear of it before it touched her again. But the room was so dark, she could see noth- ing. And suddenly just near her, there was an ugly animal sound, and she was really fright- ened. Groping blindly along the wall, she found a table she knew was there, and switched on a light, wondering what she would do if she found herself face-to-face with an attacker. But she was not about to run from the room and leave her child unprotected. But what she saw as she turned on the light was not at all what she had expected. Betty, the second kitchen girl, was rolled up in a ball, her hands and feet tied with rope, and a towel had been shoved into her mouth and secured with more rope. Her face was red, and her cheeks were covered with tears, but she was able to make no sound other than a low moan as Marielle saw her.

"Oh my God . . . my God . . . what happened? . . ." In the shock of seeing the girl bound and gagged on the floor, she forgot to keep her voice down, or to worry about waking Teddy. Had there been a robbery? A fight? An intruder? What had happened? And what was this girl doing here? She worked in the kitchen. Marielle pulled the gag out of her mouth and fought to loosen her bonds, as she frantically asked her questions. But the knots were tight and the ropes strong, and for a moment she wondered if she would have to cut them as the hysterical girl screamed incoherently and at last Marielle was able to free her. "What happened?" she asked, shaking her, desperate for information. "Where's Edith?"

And where was Miss Griffin? But the girl was still too hysterical to explain, all she could do was sob and flail her arms wildly. And then, feeling terror creep into her heart, Marielle leapt past her to Teddy's room and flung open the door. Her worst nightmare had come true. He was gone, and the bed was empty. There was no sign of him, no note on his pillow, no threat, no demand for ransom. He was simply gone, and the bed was still warm when she touched it. Her whole body began to tremble as she realized what had happened.

She ran back out to Betty then, still sobbing as she rubbed her hands and feet and gasped for air as Marielle began to shake her.

"What happened? You have to tell me!"

"I don't know . . . it was dark . . . I was asleep on the couch when they grabbed me. All I know is that I heard men's voices." But where was Teddy, Marielle thought frantically . . . where in God's name was Teddy?

"What were you doing here?" Marielle was shouting at her and the girl was crying so hard she could hardly talk, but she knew she had to tell the truth now.

"Edith went out . . . to a Christmas dance . . . she asked me to stay with him . . . until she came back . . . I don't know what happened. I think there were a lot of them. They put a pillow over my face, and I smelled something terrible and then I think I fainted, and when I woke up I was tied, and they were gone, and that's all I know until you found me."

"Where's Miss Griffin?" Had she taken the child? Was she capable of that then? Marielle ran to the governess's room, feeling more than half crazy. Her baby was gone . . . someone had taken him . . . and she didn't know who, or where he was . . . but in the back of her mind a voice began to whisper . . . had he meant what he'd said in the park? Had he taken him? Would he do something like that? For revenge? She felt sick as she tore open Miss Griffin's door, and found her bound and gagged with a pillowcase over her head and the smell of chloroform everywhere, and as Marielle pulled the pillowcase off, she thought the older woman looked as though she were dead, but she stirred, and for a moment, Marielle left her. She ran to the nursery phone, and rang for the operator, praying that they'd find him quickly. In a voice that sounded like someone else's, she told the operator who she was and that she needed the police at once.

"And what is the problem?" the woman asked.

She hesitated for only a moment, fearing the

press, and then not caring, as her voice caught on the words. She had lost one child, and she knew she wouldn't survive the loss of another. "Please . . . please send the police at once . . ." She barely got the words out, and then regained her composure as she put words to every mother's nightmare. "This is Mrs. Malcolm Patterson. My son has been kidnapped." There was a brief silence at the other end, and then the operator sprang to life, got the address from her, and Marielle set the phone down with trembling hands, and stared at Betty sitting on the floor terrified of what would happen now, certain that the boy's disappearance was in some way her fault. And for a long moment, Marielle only stood there . . . thinking of him, the tiny face, the soft curls she had stroked as she sang him to sleep only hours before. And now he was gone, at midnight.

She heard a groan from Miss Griffin's room then and hurried to her aid. She removed the gag from the governess's mouth, and then she called to Betty to help untie her. The older woman was dazed and she began to vomit from the chloroform they'd given her, but when she was finally able to speak, she knew no more than Betty about her assailants. They had come into the room while she was asleep, and she thought she'd heard two men's voices, or perhaps more, but they said very little, and then the chloroform overtook her.

As she listened to her, Marielle felt numb. It was as though she were listening to a story that had happened to someone else. It was difficult to absorb what had happened. Then she heard the front doorbell ring, and hurried downstairs, still in her bare feet and her nightgown. She came down the marble stairs like a ghost in a dream, and Haverford was wearing a dressing gown and looking puzzled. He'd been asleep when the police came, and he was in the process of assuring them that all was well and there must be some mistake because they weren't needed.

"A practical joke perhaps, some mistake . . ." He looked grave, as though they had committed some frightful faux pas. But as she flew down the stairs toward them, her hair loose, her face pale, it was clear that there was no mistake, and the three policemen in her front hall and the butler stared up at her in amazement.

"There's no mistake." She looked at them as she stood in their midst, suddenly shivering, as Haverford went to find her a coat with which to cover herself. "My son has been kidnapped." They followed her rapidly upstairs to the nursery, with Haverford just behind them. He stopped in her room to find her slippers and dressing gown, and he was shocked when he reached the nursery and heard the two women's tale. There was no mistake. The child had vanished. One of the two policemen took notes, while the other two conferred, and one of them reached for the phone. Kidnapping was no longer just a state offense, ever since the kidnapping of the Lindbergh baby. It was federal now, and the FBI would want to be in charge of the investigation.

The man who appeared to be in charge spoke to Marielle first, and urged everyone else not to touch anything in the room, if possible, for fear of disturbing fingerprints the kidnappers may have left there. Everyone nodded, Betty continued to cry, and the governess still looked desperately unwell as Haverford went to call the doctor.

"Was there any ransom note? Any message left anywhere in the room?" The senior officer asked, he was an Irish policeman in his early fifties. He had five children of his own, and the prospect of losing any of them at any time filled him with terror. He could just imagine how she felt, and as he looked at Marielle he wondered. She seemed so calm, so cool, so totally in control she was almost frozen, and yet her hands shook terribly, and her whole frame trembled even in the warm dressing gown Haverford had brought. Her feet were still bare, her hair loose, and her eyes had the wild look of someone who does not quite understand what has happened. He had seen it before, many times, at fires, in an earthquake once, during the war . . . at murders . . . it was a kind of shock that set in to numb the mind and the soul, but sooner or later, no matter what she did, it would hit her. Her baby had been taken.

She explained that there had been no note, no message at all, no sign of anything except the empty bed and the two women bound and gagged by their attackers. He nodded, made notes, and the others called for more police. In half an hour, the house was ablaze with lights, and two-dozen policemen were searching the house inside and out, for clues of any kind. But so far, there was nothing.

The servants were all awake and lined up now, as Sergeant O'Connor questioned each of them, but no one had seen anything, or knew anything at all. And then suddenly Marielle realized that both Patrick and Edith were missing. She had never trusted them, and suspected they hated her, whatever their reasons. And now she wondered if their hatred would lead them to take Teddy. It was difficult to believe but anything was possible, and everything was worth looking into. She signaled their absence to the police, and a description of them, and of Teddy, was put out on the police radios.

"The quicker we find him, the better it is," Sergeant O'Connor explained. He didn't tell her that it gave them less time to do damage to him, to spirit him too far away, or worse, to kill him. Even then she remembered only too well that the Lindbergh child had most likely been killed the night they took him.

The sergeant warned her too that putting a bulletin on the police radio meant that the press would arrive soon, but if putting a police bulletin out for the child could mean finding him at once, she knew it was a risk well worth taking. She also knew she had to call Malcolm before he heard it on the radio or read it with his morning coffee, but the house was already swarming with police, and the FBI arrived before she had time to call him. It was all like a nightmare, or a very bad film, police running up and down stairs, throwing open windows, pulling back drapes, moving furniture, tearing up the garden, putting searchlights into bushes, stopping pedestrians, and questioning the servants. It was totally frantic and unreal, and through it all she had a continuing sense that it really hadn't happened. It was all a bad dream, and she would awake in the morning. It would turn out to be one of those terrible nightmares she had with her migraines.

"Mrs. Patterson." Sergeant O'Connor was standing next to her, surrounded by half a dozen men in dark suits. They all seemed to be wearing hats, save one, who was apparently their leader. He was about forty or forty-two, tall, lean, serious, with brown hair and piercing blue eyes that seemed to run right through her. He looked hard as steel as he stared down at her, and he looked as though he always got what he wanted. "Mrs. Patterson." Sergeant O'Connor spoke to her as gently as he could in the confusion. "This is Special Agent Taylor. He's with the Federal Bureau of Investigation, and he's been assigned to your case." Her case . . . what case? . . . what had happened? Where was she? Where was Malcolm? . . . and where was their baby? . . .

"How do you do." She shook his hand woodenly while he watched her, and like the rest of him, his eyes were cool. He gave away nothing as he listened to the few details she gave him. He'd been on the Lindbergh case too, but it was too late by then. It had all been so botched by the time they brought in the

FBI, and in the end it didn't make much difference. Kidnapping was his specialty, and at
least now they could get in on it from the first.
But so far there was very little to work with.
The chauffeur and maid had disappeared, and
there was an all points bulletin out on them,
but other than that, there was nothing. No ransom notes, no clues, no fingerprints, no description of the men, nothing at all except their
M.O., the chloroform and the fact that the
child was gone. He'd heard it all, but what
intrigued him was this woman. There was
something absolutely terrified in her eyes, as
though at any moment she would lose control,
and her hands shook visibly, but other than
that she seemed completely calm and collected, and she was painfully polite and delib-
erate when she spoke. But for a moment, he
was almost afraid she would snap and go crazy.
She was barely hanging on by her fingernails,
he knew. And she was genuinely terrified. Yet
through it all, standing there in her nightgown
and robe, she looked like an empress at a ball,
quiet, aloof, and unbelievably pretty.

"Is there somewhere quieter for us to talk?"
he inquired, looking around at the police tearing her house apart, while the servants stood
by and watched them.

"Yes." She motioned him to Malcolm's

study. It was a handsome room, filled with
rare books, leather couches and chairs, and the
huge desk Malcolm worked on, the desk
where he had sat only that morning. The sight
of the room reminded Taylor that he hadn't
seen her husband. He asked her about it, as
she invited him to sit down. She sat down,
shivering, on one of the couches as she answered.

"He's away. In Washington. I spoke to him
about two hours before I discovered . . . before I went upstairs. . . ." She could not
bring herself to say the words that Teddy had
been kidnapped.

"Have you called him yet?" She shook her
head, looking deeply troubled. How would she
tell him?

"I haven't had time to call him," she said
softly, suddenly feeling it was all her fault.

He nodded, watching her, deeply intrigued
by this woman. He came from a totally different world, and he had never met anyone quite
like her. So distinguished, so polite, and at the
same time so warm and gentle.

He had grown up in Queens, and came from
a desperately poor family. He'd been in the
Marines, in the big war, and came out and
joined the FBI right after. He'd been with
them now for twenty years, and he had just

had his forty-second birthday. He had a wife
and two kids, and he loved them deeply, but
as he sat facing her, trying to concentrate on
the case, he had to admit to himself, he had
never seen a woman like this one. Even in her
nightclothes, she looked aristocratic and dignified. Her face was so innocent, her eyes so full
of pain, that all he wanted to do was put his
arms around her.

"I'm sorry, Mrs. Patterson." He had to force
his mind back to the case, for her sake. "Tell
me about it again, exactly the way it happened." At first he just closed his eyes and
listened to her, and then from time to time
he'd open his eyes and watch her face, as
though to see if there was some discrepancy
there, something wrong, some untruth, the
kind he had an uncanny sense for. But there
was something different here, no lie, but some
intangible terror. He waited until she was
through, and then he asked her, "Is there anything else? Anything else you might have seen,
tonight, or in the last few days . . . anything
that frightened you, or that might make sense
to you now, in light of what has happened?"
But she shook her head again, unwilling to
share her private terrors with a stranger. "Is
there anything you'd like to share with me,
anything you want to say, before the rest of the

world gets in on this . . . even your husband?" At other times, he had asked women
about boyfriends, lovers, friends, but somehow
here it seemed wrong. She didn't feel like that
kind of woman . . . to him, she looked like
the kind of woman you wanted to die for. "Is
there anyone in your life, or even from your
past, who might want to do something like this
to you . . . anyone you can think of?"

There was a long, long silence this time, and
then she shook her head with a look of visible
pain. "I hope not."

"Mrs. Patterson . . . think carefully . . .
your child's life may depend on the information you give me." And as she thought of him,
her heart turned over. Was it possible that she
was still willing to protect him now? . . .
could it even be him? . . . but could she take
the chance and not tell Agent Taylor? Before she could say another word, Sergeant
O'Connor knocked briefly and walked into the
room to announce that the maid and driver
were home, and the child wasn't with them.
"Where are they?" The FBI man looked annoyed. He had sensed that she was wrestling
with herself, and had been about to tell him
something important.

"They're in the living room, and John . . ."
He looked conspiratorially at him, and then

apologetically at Marielle. "They're drunk as skunks, the pair of them, and she's wearing one hell of a ball gown." He glanced at Marielle again. "I'd bet my bottom dollar it's yours and you don't know she's got it." But all of that seemed unimportant now. The question was, where was her son, and who had him?

"Take them to the kitchen and give them as much black coffee as you can get into them till they puke, and then call me." The policeman nodded and disappeared, as John Taylor turned his attention back to the child's mother. And then the officer returned again, as though to tell her something.

"Mrs. Patterson, we called your husband." She wasn't sure whether to thank him or not. She felt guilty for not calling him herself, but relieved too. She had wanted to spare him the shock of hearing it from a stranger. There was no way to gentle this news, and all she could think was how much he loved Teddy.

"What did he say?" She looked terrified, as the inspector watched her reaction.

"He was very upset." He glanced at John, and didn't tell her that her husband had cried openly on the phone, but he hadn't asked to speak to his wife. O'Connor thought that was strange, but between people of their kind, sometimes things were different. He'd seen it all before, everything from kidnappings to murders. "He said he'll be here in the morning."

"Thank you." She nodded as he left the room, and she looked at the FBI agent again, and as he watched her, he knew that there was more than she had told him. He wondered how straightforward he could be with her, if she would lie, or swoon, or attempt to leave the room in a rage, but she did none of those, she only listened to him. And watched him. He was a powerful, compelling, very handsome man in a rugged way, but she wasn't paying any attention to his looks, only to what he was saying.

"Mrs. Patterson, sometimes there are things we don't want to say to people we don't know, things we don't want to admit about ourselves or people we love . . . but in a case like this, it could make all the difference. I don't need to tell you what's at stake here. You know . . . we all do. Will you please give it some thought, and see if there's anything else you want to tell me?" But before she could say anything, he left the room, and promised to come back as soon as he'd spoken to Patrick and Edith. And she sat there in Malcolm's den, wondering how much she should say to him, but knowing that she had to trust him.

Both Patrick and Edith were still very drunk when he walked in, but they were coherent enough to know where they'd been, what they'd done, and who they'd been with. O'Connor wrote it all down as Taylor talked to them, and Patrick acted outraged that an APB had been put out on him, he said it could ruin his reputation, which neither O'Connor nor Taylor cared about for a single moment. They both suspected he could be a nasty piece of work, given the chance, as could Edith.

"Why were you out with him tonight?" Taylor asked her as she crossed her legs and tried to look sexy in the dress she'd stolen. It was the one Marielle had worn the night before, to the Whytes', and she had asked Edith to send it to the cleaners. She was planning to send it to them, but she had worn it first, as she had with lots of other gowns before. She just hadn't had the courage to "borrow" the ermine. "Weren't you supposed to be on duty?"

"Yeah, so what?" Patrick said. "What difference did it make who sat with the kid? So if she'd been there she'd have wound up gassed and all trussed up like a chicken. What for? For the lousy salary they give us?" He was still too drunk to realize that what he said could damn them both, but Edith was sobering fast and looking very nervous.

"I didn't know . . . I should have . . . I guess . . . I just thought it being almost Christmas . . ."

"Where did you get the dress?"

"It's mine." She tried to brazen it out. "My sister made it." Taylor nodded understandingly, and then sat down across from her, as though he knew her better than he did, and had no intention of buying her story.

"If I ask Mrs. Patterson to come in, will she agree with that, or is the dress hers?" The girl bowed her head and started to cry in answer, as Patrick became increasingly belligerent.

"Oh for chrissake, you sniveling bitch, cut it out . . . so what . . . so you borrowed her dress. You always give 'em back. Shit, you'd think we was working for the Virgin Mary. And listen," he waved a finger menacingly at John Taylor, "don't you buy any of that holy Madonna crap from her. Twice this week I seen her with her boyfriend. Once she even took the kid, so don't you go insinuating it was us. You talk to her and ask her about the guy she was kissing in the church on Friday, and in the park yesterday, with Teddy." Nothing registered on O'Connor's face as he made a note of it, and John Taylor stared at him with silent interest. He knew that if he kept his mouth shut, there would be more, and he was right, there was, less than a minute later. "The guy looks like a lunatic if you ask me, ranting and raving at her, shouting, he looked like he was threatening her, then trying to kiss her. Poor Teddy looked scared out of his wits he did, if you ask me, the bastard is crazy."

"What makes you say that he's her boy-friend?" The voice was cool, but the eyes were icy. "Have you seen him with her before?"

Patrick thought about it and then shook his head. "No . . . just the other afternoon in church and yesterday in Central Park. But she could have seen him other times, and he really seemed to know her. She don't always let me drive her."

"Does she drive herself?"

"Now and then," he thought it out again, "she goes for walks sometimes. But she don't go out much. Feels sorry for herself a lot, I think. She gets a lot of headaches." It was certainly an interesting portrait he painted. Somehow, John Taylor had gotten the impression she was stronger.

"Have you ever seen her with other men?" He seemed sorry to admit that he hadn't, except this one. And then Taylor threw him a curve, with a question he didn't want to answer. "Have you ever seen Mr. Patterson with other women?"

There was a long, pregnant pause, when Patrick looked at the still sobbing Edith. She was sure she was going to lose her job over the dress she had taken. She was far more concerned with that than the disappearance of the little boy when she was supposed to have been there to watch him.

John Taylor repeated the question again, in case Patrick needed to be reminded. "Have you ever seen your employer with another woman?"

"Not that I can remember . . ." And then, ". . . except his secretaries of course." But that was all information Taylor knew he could delve into later. The matter of the boyfriend, however, did intrigue him. She seemed too cool for that, too smart, too clean, and too decent. But you never knew, and now he certainly had to ask her. He hated these things, forcing answers, causing pain. But the entire situation that had brought him here was painful, and if he could help find the boy for them, then it was worth it.

He stood up and looked at the driver he had come to loathe in a single moment. They were a slimy pair. But instinct also told him that it was unlikely they were involved in the kidnapping. It was possible they'd taken a bribe, had left a door open somewhere for a hundred bucks, but he wasn't even sure they'd done that. They were just out, taking advantage of their employers, in a purloined dress, a borrowed car, having shirked their duties to the child, but he doubted if there was more to it than that. Lucky for them, or he'd have been glad to nail them.

He went back to the library after telling O'Connor to let them go. He'd interrogate them again in the morning. They had both already insisted that they'd seen nothing unusual that night, or in the days before. The only thing unusual, Patrick repeated, was Marielle's meeting with her "boyfriend."

"What did you make of that?" O'Connor asked in an undertone before Taylor left the kitchen.

"It's probably all lies, but I'll ask her."

"She don't look the type." O'Connor shook his head. Maybe the boyfriend had taken the kid. It was certainly a possibility if she was involved with someone other than her husband. And you never knew. It was always the quiet ones who surprised you.

"No, she doesn't look the type," Taylor agreed almost sadly. But if it was true, he was even more anxious to talk to her before the return of her husband. As he walked into the library, he saw her sitting there, almost as though she hadn't moved, but she seemed to be shaking harder than ever. The house was warm, but she was clearly in shock, and in spite of himself, he felt sorry for her.

"Would you like a drink, or a cup of tea?"

"No thank you," she said sadly. "Did they know anything?" she asked him hopefully, but he shook his head. "Do you think it's possible they took him and left him somewhere, and came back?" It was a thought she'd had while he was talking to them, and she was anxious to share it.

"Possible, but not likely. I'll see them both again tomorrow morning. But I think they've probably just been out dancing and drinking." Like her, he was disappointed. It would have been so simple if they had him.

"Neither of them is very fond of me." Few people were, in Malcolm's house, but she was embarrassed to say it. Malcolm was their only boss, as far as they were concerned. No matter how kind she'd been to them, they were still cold and rude and surly, and more than they knew it, it hurt her.

Being married to Malcolm wasn't always the easy life it appeared. There had been many long nights when she'd been unhappy and lonely. There'd been years of them now, and yet she was faithful to him, and honorable, decent, and a good mother to Teddy. But no one gave her credit for that. Sometimes, she thought, not even Malcolm.

Taylor was watching her face then, and wondering something. "Why do you think they don't like you?" It wasn't that he disagreed with her, he had seen the hatred in Patrick's eyes, and the look on Edith's face when she talked about her dresses.

"I think they're jealous. Most of them have been here since before we were married. I was an intruder, as far as they were concerned. They had their arrangements with my husband, and suddenly there I was, and they didn't want to be bothered. Everyone has an angle in a house like this, something they're doing, something they want, something they shouldn't have done, but did, and they don't want to get found out. I'm a headache for them, and they don't like it." Something about what she'd just said reminded him about her headaches. It was an odd thing that had stuck in his mind, and he couldn't help wondering, in light of everything else the driver had said, if she and Malcolm were happily married.

"Maybe you're right." The investigator from the FBI was noncommittal. "What about what I asked you before I left the room?"

"I can't think of anything else." She was still

struggling with her conscience and her terrors, and her unwillingness to believe that Charles would take Teddy, no matter what he had said. He couldn't have meant it.

"You're sure?" Two uniformed policemen wandered by, and Taylor gave them a high sign and asked for a cup of tea for her, and coffee for himself, if they could find it. It was three o'clock in the morning by then, and just watching her shiver made him feel cold and tired.

"Do they have any news at all?" She had to fight back tears as she asked, and he shook his head. She still couldn't let herself believe that if she went upstairs, she wouldn't find Teddy. He had to be there . . . but in her heart, she knew he wasn't.

"Mrs. Patterson," he said slowly, after the tea had arrived and the policeman who'd brought it had left again, leaving the library door ajar. Taylor stood up and strode over and closed it. "I want to tell you something your driver said. I want to discuss this with you myself. Because if the press get hold of this, it's going to make a hell of a story." She knew before he said anything what the story was going to be, and maybe in some ways it would be a relief to tell him. "Mr. Reilly says you have a 'boyfriend.'" His face was without expression as he said the word, and Marielle smiled. It was so absurd that she had to smile, but she also knew how vicious Patrick was, and she could imagine the story.

"That's an interesting term."

"Is it accurate?" She could feel him pressuring her. He wanted to know everything about her, for the sake of her child's life. And if he had to, no matter how pretty he thought she was, he would be ruthless.

She sighed, and looked at him. "No, it's not accurate." It was almost funny to even think of Charles as her "boyfriend." "He's my ex-husband, and I hadn't seen him in almost seven years until two days ago. We ran into each other at Saint Patrick's Cathedral."

"Was the meeting prearranged?"

She shook her head solemnly, and the way she looked at him, he believed her. Her eyes were full of grief, and he sensed that behind the new sorrow was old grief.

"It was totally coincidental that we met. He's been living in Spain . . . fighting against Franco."

"Oh Christ, one of those." Taylor took a long sip of coffee. It had already been a long night, but he needed to be alert as the night grew longer. He wanted to talk to her himself, and to hear her story before her husband came home. "Is he a Commie?"

She smiled again. That was another funny word to apply to Charles, although nothing was funny now. Now that Teddy was gone, nothing would ever be funny again . . . or happy . . . or nice . . . or even worth staying alive for . . . but he would return. It would be different this time. It had to be. The story would have a happy ending. "I don't think he's actually political. He just spends his life tilting at windmills. He's an idealist and a dreamer and writer. He's gone to Pamplona to run with the bulls. He's close to Hemingway. I think he just saw a fight in Spain, and he went to fight it. I don't know. I haven't seen him in years. I haven't spent any real time with him since 1929 . . . I haven't seen him at all since 1932 when I came back to the States, and married Malcolm."

"And why now? Why is he suddenly here? To see you?"

"No." She shook her head. "Family obligations. His father is very old, and probably dying, or close to it."

"Did he call you when he arrived, or write to you?" She shook her head. "Do you think he followed you? Is he angry at your remarriage?"

She sighed and looked at the inspector long and hard. "I don't know if he has followed me, I don't think so. He hasn't called . . . and yes . . . I think he is angry at my remarriage . . . and about Teddy . . . he didn't know. I told him on Friday that I'd remarried, but I didn't . . . say anything . . . about Teddy. And then yesterday, he saw him."

"Yesterday?" John Taylor looked intrigued as she continued.

"In Central Park. We went to the boat pond, but it was frozen." Taylor nodded and wondered about the second meeting.

"Did you agree to meet him there?"

"It was coincidence again. His home is just outside the park, at the level of the boat pond."

"Did you want to meet him there?"

"I never thought about it." She looked straight at him, and she was still trembling.

"Did you think about him?"

She nodded, her eyes boring holes in his. She had thought about nothing but since she'd seen him at Saint Patrick's.

"Don't you think that two coincidental meetings is a bit much to believe after seven years? You don't see him in seven years, and suddenly there he is twice in two days. Don't you think he was looking for you on purpose?"

"Perhaps." It was possible. She had asked herself the same questions.

"Did he want anything from you?" Taylor's eyes searched everything about her.

She hesitated, and then nodded. "Yes . . . he wanted to see me."

"Why?"

"I'm not sure . . . to talk . . . to talk about things that no longer matter. It's all over now . . . it's gone . . . it was a long time ago. I've been married to Malcolm . . . my husband . . . for six years . . ." Her words drifted off as she looked sorrowfully at John Taylor. He had come into her life at a terrible time, and she barely saw him. She saw his face and heard his voice but she didn't know who he was, she didn't know anything. She felt numb, and desperately frightened every time she thought of Teddy.

"When were you married to him?" His voice droned on, gentle but ever probing.

"In 1926 . . . when I was eighteen . . ." She looked at him very hard then, and decided that she had to tell him. "My husband doesn't know about this, Inspector. He believes that I 'misbehaved' in Europe when I was eighteen. I think my father implied to all his friends that I had a 'serious flirtation with an inappropriate suitor.' Nothing more. My father was a dreamer. The truth was, as my father well knew, that I was married for five years, and we lived in Europe. I tried to tell Malcolm that when he asked me to marry him, but he didn't want to hear it. He said we each had a past, and it was better left untouched and undisclosed. What he had heard was the story my father had circulated to save himself embarrassment, I don't think he ever admitted to any of his friends that Charles and I were married. We lived in France . . ." There was a faraway look in her eyes . . . "And we were very happy." She looked even more beautiful as she said it.

"And what changed that?" His voice was deep and husky as he asked, trying not to be distracted by her.

"A number of things." She was evading him and he immediately sensed it. Only one thing had happened to shatter their dream. One thing. One hideous afternoon, from which neither of them had ever recovered.

"Mrs. Patterson . . . Marielle . . . I need to know what happened . . . for your sake . . . for Teddy's." What he said went straight to her heart, and tears filled her eyes as she looked at him.

"I can't talk about it now. I never

have . . ." except with her doctor at the clinic.

"You have to." He was determined and powerful, but she continued to resist him.

"I can't." She got up and walked around the room, and for a long time she stood and stared out the window. There was darkness outside, and somewhere out in that darkness, there was Teddy. She turned to look at the inspector then, and he had never seen so much pain in his life. More than ever, he wanted to reach out and touch her.

"I'm sorry. I hate doing this to you." He had never said that to anyone before, but he had never felt like this about any woman. There was a purity and a gentleness to her, and at the same time a fragility that genuinely scared him. "Marielle." He allowed himself the use of her first name without even asking her, but he had to do everything he could to bring her closer. "You have to tell me."

"I have never told my husband . . . perhaps if he knew . . . if he had known . . ." Perhaps there would never have been Teddy, or even a marriage.

"You can tell me." He wanted her to trust him.

"And then? You tell the press?" Her eyes bored into his, but he shook his head slowly.

"I can't promise you anything. But I give you my word. I'll do my damnedest to keep your secrets, unless they mean Teddy's safety. Is that a deal?"

She nodded in answer, and looked away again out into the garden. "We had a son, Charles and I . . . a little boy named André . . ." She could feel her throat tighten as she said his name. "He was born eleven months after we were married . . . he had shining black hair, and big blue eyes. He was like a little angel . . . a little fat cherub, and we adored him. We took him everywhere." She turned to look at John again, suddenly she had to tell him the story. "He was so beautiful, and he was always laughing. Wherever we went with him, people knew him." John was watching her as she spoke, and he didn't like the look in her eyes, or the way she told the story. "Charles adored him . . . and so did I . . . and one year we went to Switzerland for Christmas. André was two and a half years old, and we had a wonderful time, playing in the snow. We even built a snowman." There were tears beginning to slide down her cheeks, tears of pain, and he didn't interrupt her. "One afternoon, Charles wanted to go up the mountain to go skiing, but I wanted to stay in Geneva. So André and I took a walk around the lake, we talked and we played, and the lake was frozen, and there was a group of women and children, and we stopped and chatted. And I was talking to one of them, about little boys his age . . ." She could barely speak now, but she still went on, fighting for air as she struggled with each word. "You know how women are, they love to talk about their children, so she and I were talking about how mischievous two-year-old boys are, and as we spoke . . . as we spoke . . ." she touched her eyes with a trembling hand, and without thinking, he reached out to her, as though to help her on, and she clung to his fingers ". . . while we were talking, he ran out on the ice with some other children, and then suddenly, there was this terrible . . . terrible . . ." She could barely go on, the room seemed so airless, but John squeezed her hand as tightly as he could and she continued. She was unaware of him now, she was lost in a time that had almost killed her. ". . . There was a terrible crackling noise . . . almost like thunder . . . and the ice cracked . . . three of the children fell in . . . one of them was André . . . I rushed out on the ice, with the other women, and people were shouting. I was the first one to reach the hole . . . I got both of the little girls out . . . I got them," she

sobbed . . . "I got them . . . but I couldn't
get him . . . I tried . . . I tried so hard
. . . I tried everything I could . . . I even
climbed into the water, but he had slipped under the ice, and then I found him . . ." Her
voice was distorted by pain, and as he listened
John Taylor was crying. . . . "He was all
blue, and he lay in my arms so tiny and cold
and so still. . . . I tried everything . . . I
tried to breathe for him, I tried to warm him
. . . the ambulance came and we took him to
the hospital, but . . ." She looked up at John,
seeing him again then, and they were both
crying for the little boy who had died beneath
the ice in Geneva. "They couldn't save him.
He had died in my arms, they said, when I
first pulled him out . . . but he wasn't even
breathing then . . . how could they know
when he died?" And what did it matter? "It
was all my fault . . . I should have been
watching him, and I wasn't. I was talking to
those damn women . . . about him . . . and
then he was gone . . . one moment of talking
to them, and I killed him. . . ."

"And Charles?" He had asked the key
words, and he had barely recovered from what
he'd just heard, but he could see there was
more from her face, still ravaged by the story
she had just told him.

"He blamed me of course. They kept me in the hospital, and I wanted to be there anyway . . . with André . . . they let me hold him for a long, long time. I held him so close to me, I kept thinking that if only I could get him warm again, but of course . . ." She sounded a little mad, as she went on with the story.

"What did Charles do when he got to the hospital?" His voice was gentle. He had asked an important question, and she looked at John Taylor without seeing him as she answered.

"He hit me . . . hard . . . again and again . . . afterward . . . they said . . . I thought . . . it didn't matter . . . they said that when I jumped into the ice . . ."

"What did he do to you, Marielle?"

"He tried to beat me . . . he said I'd killed André, that it was all my fault . . . he hit me . . . but I deserved it . . . and . . ." She gulped on a terrible sob, and made a sound that he had never heard another human make, it was a keening of pain that was almost like baying. ". . . I lost the baby. . . ." She looked up at him again, and this time, he put an arm around her and pulled her close to him to let her sob against his shoulders. He held her against his chest, and stroked her hair without thinking.

"Oh my God." He suddenly understood. ". . . You were pregnant . . ."

"Five months . . . a little girl . . . she died that night, on the same day as André." She sat then for a long time, in silence, crying quietly, as John Taylor held her.

"I'm so sorry . . . I'm so sorry for what happened to you . . . and to put you through this now." But he had had to. He had to know what she was hiding. He had seen it in her eyes, but he hadn't known it would be like this.

"I'm all right," she said quietly, and in a way she was, but in another way, she wasn't. She had suddenly remembered that Teddy was gone . . . and that added to the others made it too much. That was why John Taylor had to find him. "I wasn't all right then. For a long time. I guess . . . I guess you'd call it a nervous breakdown, or something more. I suppose Charles went more than a little mad too. They had to tear him off me that night, and he collapsed at the funeral, I was told. I don't know . . . they wouldn't let me go. They put me in a private clinic in Villars, and I was there for twenty-six months. Charles paid for it, but I never saw him. They finally let him come to see me before they let me go, and he asked me to come back, but I couldn't. I knew we both thought that I had killed our child, if not both of them. Not only had I let André drown, but I had jumped into the icy water and killed the baby."

"And what were you supposed to do? Let him drown?"

"No, I did what I had to do, but it took me two years to figure that out, and it's taken me another six to live with it since then. I think that," she began to cry harder again, "I decided . . . when Teddy was born that God had decided to forgive me. I had a terrible time getting pregnant with him, and I always thought I was being punished."

"That's crazy. You were punished enough. What did you ever do to deserve that?"

She smiled sadly at the man she had just shared her life with. "I've spent most of my life trying to figure that out." He touched her hand again, and poured a small amount of brandy into the cup of tea she'd been sipping. He had helped himself to one of Malcolm's decanters, and he still had a hard time believing she'd never told her husband. What a lonely burden she'd had to live with, no wonder she suffered from migraines.

"And the meeting in the church?" But he had figured that out now.

"It was the anniversary of . . . the chil-

dren's death. I always go to church and light
candles for them, and my parents. And suddenly there was Charles, rather like a vision."
Taylor wondered if it was a welcome one. He
was fascinated by her now, and all she had
been through, and yet she had survived it. She
was much stronger than she looked, and much
deeper.

"Are you still in love with him?" He wanted
to know now.

"Yes, I suppose part of me always will be."
She was so honest with him, so open, there
was something about her which seemed so
fair. It made his skin crawl now when he
thought of the chauffeur's accusation that she
had a "boyfriend." "But that part of my life is
over." She sounded as though she meant it.

"Is that what he wanted? For you to come
back to him?"

"I don't know. I only saw him at Saint Patrick's for that little while, and we were both
upset. He kept telling me it wasn't my fault,
but I know he always thought it was. He accused me of murdering our son, of being neg-
ligent. . . ." She looked away from John
again, and this time he forced her to take a sip
of the brandy, "The truth is that I was. I was a
twenty-one-year-old girl, and I made a terrible
mistake. I talked to that woman for only a mo-

ment, and he was gone. . . . I'm surprised Charles is willing to forgive me at all, given how he felt about me then."

"Are you sure he has?"

She looked honestly at the inspector. That was the big question. "I don't know. I thought he had when I saw him at Saint Patrick's on Friday. I told him I was married again, and I think he was surprised, and perhaps not pleased, but he seemed to accept it. But the next day, when we saw him at the park . . . he was furious about Teddy, furious that I have another child . . . and he doesn't. He said I didn't deserve it, and I felt as though he were threatening me, but I think they were just words. He said he could take the child, in order to make me come with him." John Taylor had just heard the music he wanted to hear, and he was almost sure they had their man now. All they had to do was find him. Thank God she had confided in him. With any luck at all now they'd find the boy, and they could lock her ex-husband up and forget him. As sorry as he felt for her, with all she'd been through, Taylor felt far less sympathetic for Charles, who had beaten her up in the hospital when she was pregnant, and instead of consoling her, had accused her of murdering their children. He had left her in a hospital for two

years, and had somehow let her carry the burden for the rest of her life that it was her fault
their son had died. As far as John Taylor was
concerned, the guy deserved to be punished.

"Do you think he was serious when he said
those things?"

"I'm not sure. I just don't know. I can't
imagine him harming anyone, least of all a
child. But I'm not sure how angry he still is,
and I was afraid not to tell you what had happened." In the end, it had turned out to be a
blessing that the chauffeur had accused her of
having a boyfriend.

It was six o'clock in the morning by then,
and there were no further developments, no
new clues about Teddy. But the information
she'd just given him would go far. He carefully
wrote down Charles's name and address, and
promised to have a discreet talk with him in a
couple of hours. If he was satisfied with his
alibi, and believed what he said, the matter of
Charles Delauney would be closed, and nothing more needed to be said. But if not, he
would have to act on what he found. Secretly,
he hoped that he was going to find something.
If nothing else, the guy was a fool, and he had
clearly threatened her. It was entirely possible
he had taken the boy, even as revenge for the
children he had lost and because he still

blamed her for their deaths, or just because he misguidedly wanted to draw her to him. But he had promised her not to tell the press, or the FBI, or Malcolm, until he had spoken to Charles Delauney. It was the best he could do for her, and she appreciated his efforts.

It was almost seven o'clock when they left the library, and it was still dark, as they stood in the front hall and talked for a long time. He looked down at her, wishing that he could promise her he would find Teddy. If nothing else in this life, she deserved it. He had a feeling that her marriage to Malcolm Patterson was nothing more than an arrangement. All she had was Teddy, and he was gone. And Taylor could sense how much she adored him. It was clear that she was never going to return to Charles, wisely so as far as Taylor was concerned, but she really had no one in her life to help her. It was impossible to understand how the boy had disappeared at midnight that night, without a trace or a sound. He had simply been taken from his bed with his red pajamas on . . . and vanished.

5

After her lengthy conversation with John Tay-
lor, Marielle wandered through the house like
a ghost. At first, she went back to her room but
she found she couldn't bear to be there. The
walls seemed to be closing in on her, and she
almost couldn't breathe. And without even
planning to, she found her feet on the stairs,
and she was back in Teddy's room before she
knew it. It was the only place she wanted to
be, the only room where she could feel him
close to her. It was impossible to believe . . .
impossible to understand. Who would do this
and why? But it was obvious, it had to be for
money. Extra phone lines had already been
put into the house, and there were police ev-

erywhere. They were waiting for a call, or a ransom note. The morning newspapers were already being scoured for messages from the kidnappers. All the usual methods were being used. And more men from the FBI were waiting to talk to Malcolm. But she felt useless now. There was nothing she could do, except pray that her son was still alive. She knelt next to his bed, and laid her head down, as she remembered the feel and touch of him, only hours before when she had put him to bed in his little red pajamas with the embroidered blue collar. Miss Griffin had made them for him, and Marielle wondered if he was cold now, or afraid . . . if they were kind to him, or if he had eaten. It was unbearable not knowing where he was, and Marielle had to gasp for air as she knelt there. She heard a sound in the room, and turned suddenly, in time to see Miss Griffin standing behind her, still looking pale, but starched in her uniform, and for the first time in years she looked kindly at Marielle. There was something she felt she had to say to her, and like Marielle, she could hardly get the words out.

"I'm. . . ." Her lips trembled, and she looked away from her. She couldn't bear to see the agony in the young woman's face. It mirrored all too clearly exactly what she herself was feeling. "I'm sorry . . . I should have been . . . I should have heard . . ." She burst into tears as she said the words that were torturing her. "I should have been able to stop them."

"You couldn't know . . . and there must have been too many of them." Armed with ropes and chloroform, and perhaps guns, they were well equipped for what they had come for. "You mustn't blame yourself." She rose slowly to her feet, so dignified and so kind, and without a word she went and put her arms around the older woman. She was crying too, but she stood and held the old woman like a child and tried to reassure her. It made the governess feel even worse, knowing how hard she had always been to her. But she had always thought her so weak, so self-indulgent, so foolish. And now she saw something she had never known was there, a silent strength not only for herself, but for everyone around her to draw on.

The two women stood together for a long time, deriving strength from each other without speaking, and then Marielle went downstairs again. And as she did, there was a stir, she heard voices shouting and realized there were reporters outside, trying to force their way in past the police as the front door opened.

"He's here!" She heard a shout from the police, wondering who it was, praying that it was someone who would make a difference. And as she looked over the banister, she realized that it was Malcolm. He was home, looking aristocratic and pale, in his black coat, his dark suit, and his homburg. He looked so funereal as he came up the stairs and they met halfway up, she still in her dressing gown, and still barefoot. He opened his arms to her, and for a long time he just stood there and held her, and then finally they went upstairs and he spoke to her once they were in her bedroom.

"How could this have happened, Marielle? How could they force their way in and take over so completely? Where was Haverford? Where were the maids? Where was Miss Griffin?" It was as though he had expected her to keep their child and their home safe, and she had failed him. She saw now that his eyes were full of reproach and pain, and the look he gave her cut her to the core. There was no excuse she could give, no explanation. She couldn't even explain it to herself. She could barely even allow herself to understand what had happened.

"I don't know . . . I don't understand it either . . . I heard a sound while we were speaking, but I didn't think anything of it . . . it never occurred to me that someone was in the house, other than the servants, I mean . . . I didn't even know Edith was out. . . ." The dress had been returned to her by then, dirty, stained, with lipstick on it, and smelling of cigarette smoke and cheap whiskey. But she didn't care about the dress. She only cared about her baby.

"I should have hired guards," Malcolm said, as he looked at her in agony. "I never thought . . . I always thought you were so foolish to be hysterical about the Lindbergh case . . . who knew you would be right?" He stared at her, a broken man, his only child was gone, and with him went hope and happiness and well-being. Malcolm looked suddenly older and as though he might not survive this. It made Marielle feel as though she herself had destroyed the man by being so careless. And yet it wasn't her fault . . . it wasn't . . . or was it? It was all so confusing, just as it had been years before. So confusing as to whose fault it was, and why. Had he drowned because he'd run away onto the ice, and why had she been able to reach the two little girls and not her own child? Had she killed the baby by leaping in after André . . . or had the baby died because Charles had hit her? And now this . . . was it her fault . . . or his . . . or someone else's? She looked distraught and her hair was disheveled as she ran her hands through it distractedly and Malcolm watched her, realizing that she suddenly looked a little crazy.

"You should dress," he said quietly, letting himself down heavily into a chair, "there are policemen everywhere, and the press are in throngs outside. For the next few days, if we go out, we'll have to try and get out through the garden." He looked at her even more somberly then. "The police say there's been no request for ransom. I've already called the bank, and they're ready with marked bills when we get a call, or a note." It was all they could do as they waited, and suddenly Marielle was relieved that he was home. He would take charge, he would make the right things happen. He would force them to bring Teddy home. She looked up at him then, feeling more than ever that she had let him down, which was something he had never done to her. He had never let her down. Never. Not in all the years that they'd been married.

"I'm so sorry, Malcolm . . . I don't know what to say. . . ." He nodded, not telling her that she wasn't to blame. And Marielle knew

then, as she looked at him, that he did blame
her. He rose slowly, and walked away, and as
he stood looking into the garden where Teddy
used to play, she saw that he was crying. She
was almost afraid to comfort him, to say anything, to reach out to him in his pain. If he
blamed her for not guarding Teddy closely
enough, what could she possibly say to console
him? As she stood watching him helplessly,
she felt the familiar vise begin to crush her
head, and for a moment she almost fainted. He
turned and looked at her then, and he recognized the symptoms. She looked terrible, but
he wasn't surprised. He felt as awful as she
did.

"You look pale, Marielle. Are you having a
headache?"

"No," she lied. She wouldn't allow anyone
to see how weak she was now, how afraid, how
vulnerable, how broken. She had to be strong,
for him, for the child, for all of them. She tried
to keep her balance as she fought a familiar
wave of nausea. "I'm fine. I'll get dressed."
She should have gone to bed, but she knew
she wouldn't sleep. And she couldn't have
borne the nightmares.

"I'm going to speak to the men from the
FBI." Malcolm had called some of his connections in Washington and they had promised to

call J. Edgar Hoover. The director had provided a police escort that had allowed Malcolm to get home as fast as his Franklin Twelve
would allow. The German ambassador had
also called to express his shock and concern
over what had happened.

"They've been very kind," Marielle said in a
barely audible whisper, wondering now if
Agent Taylor would tell Malcolm about
Charles. But if it would help them find Teddy,
she was willing to endure it. Taylor had promised her that he would keep her secrets if he
could, but not if it would harm the boy, and
she had readily agreed to it. She was willing to
sacrifice herself, her marriage, her life, for
Teddy.

Malcolm looked at her long and hard then,
and for a moment he felt guilty. "I don't mean
to blame you, Marielle . . . I know it's not
your fault. I just don't understand how it could
have happened." He looked so mournful, like
a dying man. He had lost the love of his life,
but so had she. And yet she could not help
him.

"I don't understand it either," she said quietly. And then he left the room, and she
changed into a gray cashmere dress and gray
silk stockings. She brushed her hair and
washed her face, and put on black alligator

shoes, and prayed that she would be able to control the headache.

She went to the kitchen after she dressed, and was planning to organize the cook into providing meals for the police and the FBI working in the house, but she discovered as soon as she arrived that Haverford had already done that. Sandwiches were being sent up on trays, with platters of fruit, and cakes, and huge mugs of steaming coffee. When she went back upstairs, she discovered that there was a buffet set up in the dining room, but it was barely touched, the men scarcely had time to eat, they were still so busy.

"Is there anything I can do?" she asked the sergeant in charge. O'Connor had gone home hours before, and the shift had changed. She recognized none of the men from the night before, as they continued to dust the house for fingerprints, and wait for calls requesting the ransom. Only she had not gone to bed. And as she wandered past the library, she saw that Malcolm was in deep conversation with two of the FBI men. He glanced briefly up at her, and then away, and for an instant she wondered if they were talking about her. The men looked at her strangely as she stood there, and then she walked away. What could they have said? What was there to say? It wasn't her fault that Teddy had been taken . . . or was it? Did they blame her because of Charles? Were they right? Were they telling Malcolm?

As she walked back to the front hall, she was startled to hear a tremendous scuffle. There were voices raised outside, and as the front door opened only a few inches, suddenly there were half a dozen shouting strangers standing near her, flashbulbs exploded in her face, and a phalanx of police rose like a shield and pushed them back outside, but only one small redheaded woman escaped them. She was pretty and young and very tiny, and she was wearing a ridiculous black hat and a very ugly outfit. She stood looking at Marielle as though she knew her, and before Marielle could realize what was happening, the little redhead was asking her questions.

"How do you feel, Mrs. Patterson? Are you all right? Is there any news? Have you heard anything from little Teddy? What does it feel like? Are you afraid? Do you think he could be dead?" And all the while, there were lights exploding in the distance, blinding her with the light and pain, almost like part of her headache. And as she struggled to get away, a powerful voice roared next to her, and a strong pair of hands moved Marielle away by the shoulders. It was John Taylor.

"Get that woman out of here!" And suddenly the redhead was gone, the front door was closed again, and the noise was far, far in the distance. And she realized that John Taylor was supporting her arm, and leading her to a chair in the hallway. As he had come back into the house, the press had forced their way in with him. "Damn scum. Next time, I'll come in through the kitchen." He was looking down at her with obvious concern, and he looked very tired. But she looked worse, and as he handed her a glass of water he had signaled one of his men to get, she took a small sip and tried to smile, but she couldn't fight back the tears this time. The headache was too much, Malcolm's anger, her terror over Teddy and just sheer exhaustion. And the redheaded woman had asked such awful questions. What if he was dead? What if they had killed him? And yes, she was afraid. Desperately. And Malcolm had seemed so heartbroken, and so angry when he returned. She looked at John Taylor and sighed, embarrassed at having lost her composure.

"I'm sorry."

"What for? Being human? Those bastards make me sick." And then he lowered his voice as he looked at her. He had just been to see

Charles Delauney. "Is there somewhere we can speak alone? The library again?"

She shook her head. "My husband is there, speaking to two of your men." And then she thought for a moment. "I know." She led the way to a small music room they never used. It was filled with old books and instruments, and some of Malcolm's files. Once in a great while, Brigitte used it as an office. There was a desk, and two chairs, and a small settee, where he settled her, and then he pulled up one of the chairs, and looked at her for a long moment. He had only known her since the night before, but he was willing to believe every word she said and stake his reputation on it. He had never met another human being like her. She was like someone in a book, or a dream, with the kind of inner strength and ideals that real people didn't have, or not the ones he knew. And yet at the same time she was a powerfully attractive young woman. And she'd had nothing but raw deals, from two men, neither of whom he had much use for. Delauney had struck him as a spoiled rich boy, drunk, self-indulged, and deluded in his political ideals, and still whining about what had happened to him almost ten years before, and the fact that she hadn't been willing to come back to him again after he'd almost killed her. Taylor felt that, given the opportunity, he could be impetuous and crazy, possibly even dangerous, and he could have done it for revenge. And Taylor had no use for Malcolm either. So far, he only knew him from the press, and he had always appeared to be very cold and pompous.

"Is something wrong?" More wrong than it already was? Was that possible, she wondered. "Have you heard anything?" She looked at him with huge eyes, suddenly frightened, but he was quick to shake his head, and reassure her.

"Not about Teddy." He felt as though they had shared the secrets of a lifetime the night before. And he wanted to do anything he could to protect her now. She'd been through enough, she had trusted him, and he didn't want to betray that. But he also didn't want to endanger the child, and John Taylor was worried. "I've just spent three hours with Charles Delauney." Marielle watched him with anxious eyes, wondering what Charles had said.

"Did you tell him I told you everything?"

"Yes. He blames himself, or so he says, for being crazed after it happened and reacting very badly. But he also claims that when he saw you in the park with Teddy the other day, he was still drunk from the night before, and he says he's not sure what he said, but he's

willing to admit it was probably pretty out of
line. But he insists he meant no harm, and he
would never do anything to hurt Teddy."

"Do you believe him?" She searched his
eyes, needing to know the truth, and willing to
believe him. She trusted him. There was
something about him that seemed innately
fair, and she sensed correctly that he would
not betray her. She remembered how he had
held her hand the night before, and taken her
in his arms as she cried for André.

"That's the problem." He looked back at
her, and then shook his head as he leaned back
in the chair. "I don't. I don't think he'd hurt
him, not like the Lindbergh case or anything
like that. But I think he's a spoiled young man.
I think he'd do almost anything to get what
he wants—threats, coercion, maybe worse.
Maybe he would take Teddy to bring you
closer to him. Maybe in his mind that's an all-
right way to do it. I'm not sure. I don't even
know what I think. But I can tell you that I
don't think I believe him. Telling me he was
drunk, and trying to excuse the threats he
made didn't wash with me when I listened."
His eyes had been wild, and his black hair
uncombed, he'd been unshaven, and there was
the smell of booze in the air. He looked like a
wild dissolute type whose life had not gone

well, and maybe he was capable of some pretty frightening things, all in the name of justice. He was involved in a war, after all, that wasn't his, just for the sheer pleasure of killing, or at least that was how John Taylor saw it. He didn't understand political causes, or noble wars, or running with the bulls in Spain, or beating his pregnant wife up when they had just lost their little boy. He didn't understand any of these people. The only one he understood or cared about, God only knew why, was Marielle, and he wanted to help her.

"I'm worried about him, and I want you to know it. It means we're going to watch him, and I'd like to go back and search the house. But it also means that I may not be able to keep your secret, and I wanted to warn you. You may want to tell your husband some of this before it gets to him some other way."

She nodded, grateful for the warning, at least he was allowing her to tell him herself. He was every bit as decent as she had suspected, and she tried to smile at him, but her head hurt so badly she couldn't. She winced in sudden pain, and he saw it. "Are you all right?"

"I'm fine." They were words that no longer meant anything, but they were expected.

"You'd better get some sleep at some point.

Or you're going to fall apart when we really need you." She nodded, but she couldn't imagine ever sleeping again . . . not until Teddy was returned. How was she going to live without him? She couldn't touch him or hold him or know where he was, or if he was safe, or decently cared for . . . she suddenly longed for the powdery smell of his neck and his hair . . . his laughter . . . the chubby little arms around her neck, or the way he looked at her that told her just how much he loved her. How was she going to survive without him until they found him? As she thought of it, she almost swooned, and then she felt a firm hand on her arm, as though pulling her back from her own terrors. "Marielle, hang on . . . we're going to find him." She nodded and stood up, realizing that she had some very difficult things to say to Malcolm.

"Are you going to say anything to my husband about Charles?" She looked concerned, but not really worried. If she had to tell him, she would. It was as simple as that. This was no time to hide anything, if it could hurt Teddy.

"I'm going to tell him that, like many people at this point, Charles Delauney is a possible suspect. I'm not really sure he would do anything. But I can tell you right now, I don't like

him. I don't like the threats he made, or the
idea that he's so angry you have a child again,
and he doesn't. I think in his own crazy way,
he still loves you. He says he wants you back.
And in his mind that's enough reason for you
to come running back to him, because he says
so." He didn't tell her what Charles had said
about her marriage to Malcolm, that it was all
a fraud and a sham, and everyone in town
knew that he had other women, that people
said she lived like a nun, and Malcolm didn't
give a damn about her. Charles Delauney
seemed to feel that that was all reason enough
for her to leave him. He had also said that he
didn't think Marielle loved Malcolm, and that
she had married him for all the wrong reasons,
because she had no one in her life at the time
and she was afraid and shaky after her release
from the clinic in Switzerland. He said she'd
been looking for a father and not a husband.
But seeing Delauney with his wild looks, and
crazed airs, it was easy to see why she would
have. Taylor could see the appeal of a man like
Malcolm Patterson and yet he could also understand why a girl of eighteen would have
been drawn to Delauney. He was colorful and
handsome and wild and full of romance, but
men like that were dangerous too . . . men
like that did foolish things . . . like beat their

wives . . . or make terrible threats and accusations. But did they kidnap other people's
children? Was that part of it? That was the
question. Taylor didn't know the answer to
that one. But one thing was certain, if he had
done it, he hadn't done it for the money. And
perhaps that was why there was no request for
ransom. He would have just hired people to
take the boy away from her, and conceal him.
But what would he do with him once he had
him?

John Taylor stood up then and walked her
slowly out of the room, and she thanked him
again for the warning about what he was going
to have to tell Malcolm. She turned and
looked at John Taylor for a last moment, with a
worried frown. It was all so confusing. "Do
you really think he'd do a thing like that?
Charles, I mean." It was hard to believe. He
had always been wild and uncontrolled but not
like this . . . she couldn't believe he would
really take Teddy. Did he hate her that much
then? It was hard to imagine.

"I don't know." Taylor was honest with her.
"I wish I knew the answer."

She nodded, and went back to the chaos in
the main living room. Malcolm was standing
there, looking grim, with an FBI man on ei-

ther side, and she introduced him to John Taylor.

"I've been waiting to see you," Malcolm growled, seemingly unimpressed by Taylor.

"I've been out talking to some people about the case." His eyes never looked once at Marielle. He knew better than that. But he also wasn't sure, as he watched Malcolm, that he disagreed with Delauney. There seemed to be no warmth toward Marielle, no visible support, only Malcolm's own concern, and his grief at losing his only son. Instead of asking for John's help, he demanded that he find him. "We're all set for a possible ransom request, sir," John Taylor said with a respect he didn't feel. In fact, he had already decided, he didn't like him.

"So am I," Malcolm said. "The U.S. Treasury Department is sending us marked notes this morning."

"We'll have to be very careful how that's handled." It had been a disaster in the Lindbergh case, and John didn't want anything going wrong this time. "I'd like to speak to you this afternoon, if you have time." John wanted to know if there was anyone he suspected, or was afraid of. And as he had with Marielle, he wanted to see him alone, but he also wanted to give Marielle time to tell him about Charles Delauney.

"I'll see you now," Malcolm said with a frown. He had slept in the car coming up from Washington, and he was more rested than either Marielle or John Taylor.

"I'm afraid I have some other matters to attend to first." If nothing else, he wanted to get back to his office and shower and shave, have another stiff cup of coffee, and take some time to think about what they were doing. The truth was, they had no leads at all. All they had was Charles, and the fact that the driver had admitted that morning that someone had called him a few weeks before and offered him a hundred dollars if he'd choose that particular night to go out with Edith. He had figured the joke was on them anyway, because they'd been planning for ages to go to the Irish Christmas dance in the Bronx, so it was no effort for him. But the hundred had arrived in a plain envelope at the back door the week before, and he'd thrown the envelope away and spent the cash, and never given it another thought. He said he hadn't recognized the voice on the phone, except that they'd had an accent, what kind of accent he wasn't sure, maybe English, maybe German. He insisted he couldn't remember. But even if Delauney had taken the child, he wouldn't have done it himself. And supposedly the week before, he hadn't seen Marielle, and didn't know she had a child . . . or did he? Was it all a clever plan? Had he been watching her for weeks? Months? Had he been getting news of her while he was in Europe? Had he planned his revenge for years? It was hard to make sense of it, there was so little to go on, and it was still way too early. But why hadn't the driver been suspicious of the call? It could have meant a robbery was being planned or an attack on Malcolm or Marielle. But it was clear to John Taylor that the driver didn't care about his employers.

Malcolm looked annoyed that Taylor wasn't ready to speak to him just then, and just so he understood who he was dealing with, he mentioned his trip to Washington again. But Taylor understood perfectly. The message was, do it right, do it now, do it my way, or you're going to regret it. The trouble was, Taylor wasn't that kind of man. And he wasn't about to take any pressure from Malcolm.

"I'll see you this afternoon, sir. Say around four?"

"That'll be fine. I assume your men know how to find you, if a call comes in before that?" It was a very gentle slap in the face, an inference that he was "disappearing."

"Of course."

"Very well. Is there anything you can do with those vultures on our front doorstep, by the way?"

"I'm afraid not. They all think they're out there defending the First Amendment. We can back them up a little bit though, get them away from the house. I'll have my men see to it."

"See that you do," Malcolm said with a stern look, instead of "thank you." Taylor left them then, as Malcolm looked down at his wife and muttered, "I don't like him."

"He's a nice man. He was very kind to us last night." She didn't tell him how kind, but it had made a lasting impression on her, in the absence of her husband.

"I'd be more impressed if he found your son. You might keep that in mind, Marielle." As though she could forget it. She wondered why he was being so cruel to her, except that she knew he was upset, and somehow he seemed to feel that it was all her fault. Or was she just imagining it? Was she feeling responsible again, as she had for André and her baby girl? Was everything always going to be her fault? It was that that usually set off the headaches, that and the terrible helplessness she always felt when things went wrong and she couldn't change them. But she couldn't allow herself to think of that now, couldn't allow herself to think of what might be happening to Teddy. She had to be strong. And she knew that before John Taylor returned that afternoon, she had to tell Malcolm.

"Could we go upstairs for a little while?" She looked nervously at her husband, and he glanced at her with a strange expression, as though she had propositioned him and he couldn't believe it. "I have to talk to you."

"This isn't the time." He tried to brush her off, he wanted to return the German ambassador's call. He was touched that he had called him.

"Yes, it is. Malcolm, it's important."

"Can't it wait?" But he could see from the look in her eyes that she meant it. She was surprising him actually. For a woman who seemed to go weak at the knees whenever life became even slightly difficult, she seemed to be holding up remarkably well in this crisis. She looked tired, of course, and pale, but she seemed calm and reasonable, and other than the pathetically trembling hands he had noticed at once, she seemed to be controlling her emotions. What he hadn't seen was the terrible scene in the boy's room only that morning, the crying that seemed to have no end as she held his teddy bear to her and felt terror rise in her throat every time she thought of her son. But she was fighting it, because she knew she had to. If she didn't, she would panic and collapse completely.

"Malcolm, will you come upstairs with me?" She was insistent.

"All right, all right. I'll be there in a moment." She waited for him in her dressing room, because she didn't know where else to be, and she paced the small room while she waited. She didn't know where to start, or what to say, and she wished she had forced him to listen before she married him, but he hadn't wanted to hear it then, and now he had to.

He came up half an hour later, just as she was ready to go downstairs looking for him. But finally he appeared, and he seemed huge in the small room, as he took a chair, and looked at her with obvious irritation.

"All right, Marielle, I don't know what you can possibly want to talk about now. I hope it's important, and has something to do with Teddy."

"It might. I hope it doesn't," she said quietly, sitting on a small settee across from him.

It was odd how far away from him she felt,
how distant they were, even in this crisis. In
fact, suddenly, it seemed worse than ever. "It
has to do with me. And I think it's important.
Years ago, when we were getting married, I
told you that there were things about me you
might not like, and you said that everyone had
a past and it wasn't important. You felt it was
best left untouched, but I felt I owed it to you
to tell you." She sighed and had to fight for air
again. All of this was so difficult that she always seemed to have trouble breathing. But
she knew she had to tell him. And this time he
had to listen. "Do you remember?" she asked
him softly, and for a moment, his eyes gentled.
Maybe he was only in pain, she told herself.
Perhaps the shock of losing Teddy was so great
that he could offer Marielle no comfort, just as
she and Charles had been unable to comfort
each other nine years before. Sometimes when
the common agony is too great one can only
struggle alone. She wondered if that was what
was happening now, and it wasn't that he held
her responsible after all. But she had to go on
now.

"I do remember," he answered her. "But
what does that have to do with what is happening now? Or with Teddy?" There was a

look of accusation on his face and she forced herself to ignore it.

"I don't know. I'm not sure. But I must tell you what I do know." She took a breath and went on, unaware of how beautiful she was. "My father told his closest friends that I had had a youthful flirtation and gone a little mad when I was eighteen and we were on the Grand Tour. And then he told everyone that I'd decided to stay on and study in Paris. Well, some of that was true but very little. I had much more than a flirtation. I ran away, I eloped, with Charles Delauney. I'm sure you must know his father." Malcolm nodded. He had known him, better than he had known her own. He was a crusty old man, but a smart one, with a huge fortune. But he had never met the son. They said he was a renegade of the worst sort, a writer. And he'd run off to the war when he was fourteen or fifteen, and after that he'd stayed in Europe. Old man Delauney said he was no good, and that was all he'd heard, but now he looked stunned at Marielle's confession. "I married him when I was eighteen, and by the time we came back from our honeymoon and my parents wanted to have the marriage annulled, I was pregnant. So they went home, and I stayed. The marriage was never annulled. And we had a little boy . . ." She had to fight back tears as she said it. After all these years, to tell the story twice in one day was almost more than she could bear. But she knew she had to tell him. Teddy's disappearance made it all different. "His name was André," she gulped again, "and he looked a little like Teddy, except that he had very black hair, instead of blond hair like you." She tried to smile, but Malcolm said nothing. He was not finding the recital amusing. And she knew that, for Malcolm, she had to keep it to the facts. He didn't have to know how much she loved him, or how desperately she had loved Charles, or how terrible it had been when André died. He just had to know that he did, and that Charles had seen Teddy and gone crazy. He had to hear this from her so he didn't think she was protecting Charles. The only one she wanted to protect now was Teddy. And Malcolm had to hear everything if they were going to find him.

"He died when he was two . . . in Switzerland. I was pregnant with another child, and that baby died too."

Malcolm looked desperately uncomfortable for a moment.

"How did they die?"

"André drowned." She squeezed her eyes shut and fought for composure, but unlike

John Taylor, the night before, Malcolm Patterson did not approach her. "He ran onto the lake . . . it was frozen . . . and he fell through . . . with two little girls. I saved them." Her voice was almost a monotone as she went on, trying not to see his face again, trying not to feel his icy face next to her own as she tried to blow life into him, trying not to smell the same powdery flesh she had loved so much . . . just like Teddy . . . and if Teddy died too . . . how would she survive it? She fought to go on as Malcolm watched her. "I couldn't reach him. He was under the ice." It was a breathless whisper, and then her voice grew stronger again. It was like climbing a mountain just telling him and the air seemed to be getting thinner and thinner and thinner. "Charles always held me responsible for it. He felt it was my fault, because I wasn't watching him. I was, but I was talking to someone . . . the mother of the two little girls . . . she said it wasn't my fault, but I suppose it was. And Charles thought so too. He was skiing that day, and when he came back, he tried to kill me . . . or maybe not . . . maybe he was just so out of his mind with pain . . . anyway, I lost the baby. I probably would have anyway, because of the icy water. I had jumped in to get André." Malcolm nodded, mesmerized by

the horror of her words, and in spite of himself, his face had gone pale as he listened.
"Charles always felt that I had killed both of
them, that it was my fault that we lost them.
And I . . . I . . ." Her voice trembled and
she couldn't go on as she bowed her head, and
then looked at him, her face filled with anguish, her eyes filled with a horror he could
never know and no one would ever take from
her. "I suppose you could say I had a nervous
breakdown. I was in a hospital . . . a clinic
. . . a sanatorium . . . for more than two
years. I was twenty-one when it happened,
and I tried to kill myself several times." She
had decided to tell him all of it. He had a right
to know now, and there could be no more
secrets. "I didn't want to live, without Charles
and my babies. I did everything I could to die,
and they did everything they could to save me.
I never saw Charles during that time . . . or
actually I only saw him once during that first
year. He came to tell me my father had died, a
few months after André. They say the shock of
the Crash killed him, and I suppose it did
. . . they didn't tell me that my mother killed
herself six months later. I suppose without
Daddy, and without me . . ." Her voice
trailed off, and Malcolm understood her meaning. "They didn't tell me that for another year,

and by then, I suppose I was better. They said I had to go finally, that I had to go back out in the world and live with what had happened. That it wasn't my fault, that I wasn't responsible, and if Charles still felt it was, then it was something that he had to work out for himself." She took another breath and seemed a little calmer as she looked unseeingly out the window. "He came to see me once at the end before I left, and he told me how sorry he was, that he had been out of his mind with pain, that it wasn't my fault, and he hadn't meant it. But I could see in his eyes that he did mean it, that he still believed I had killed his children. I still loved him." She looked back at Malcolm honestly. "I always had, but I knew that if I stayed with him, I would always feel guilty. It would always be between us. I couldn't go back to him. I had to be alone. So I left the hospital, and came back to the States, and that was the last time I saw him. And then I met you," she sighed, "and you were so good to me. You gave me a job, and you did so many things for me. You took care of me, and you were always so kind to me. And we got married. I never really wanted to get married again. I didn't think it would have been fair to anyone . . . I had so much on my conscience. But you seemed not to mind . . .

and . . ." She felt suddenly guilty. "I had no one . . . and I was so frightened sometimes. And you made me feel safe . . . I thought I could be good to you too . . . and maybe make you happy." She lowered her eyes then, thinking of when Teddy had been born, and the tears began to slide down her face again. She had given him a lot to absorb in a single moment. "I was so happy when Teddy was born."

"So was I." His voice was a croak in the small room. "He's all I lived for. I always thought there was some small mystery in your past, Marielle. But I never suspected it was quite so ugly." She was filled with shame as he said it.

"I know," she nodded, "that was why I thought you should know. I thought you should hear it before you decided to marry me, but you wouldn't listen." He nodded his agreement, and she went on. "I never saw Charles again when I came back to the States. I never saw him again until last Friday. I met him at Saint Patrick's Cathedral, by chance. I went to light a candle for the children and my parents. It was the anniversary of our children's death," she forced herself to say the words she hated, "and he was there. He said he was in New York to see his father."

"And what did he say?" Malcolm was interested in this part.

"He wanted to see me again, and I said I couldn't."

"Why not?" He was probing with his words, and she was hurt that he would ask her.

"Because I love you, because we're married. Because of Teddy."

"And he was angry?" Malcolm almost looked hopeful.

"No, not then . . . we were both so upset. It's a terrible day every year."

"And did he call you?"

"No, I ran into him in the park the next day with Teddy, at the boat pond. I think he'd been drinking, or was still drunk from the night before. He was wild-eyed, and he was shocked to realize we had a child . . . a little boy . . . and he was very angry," she admitted. This was the point of the whole story.

"What did he say? Did he hurt the child?" Malcolm looked terrified by what she was saying.

"Of course not. I don't think he's capable of it, and I'd never let him." She took a quick breath. "But he was very angry. He threatened me, I suppose. He said I didn't deserve to have another chance. And," she took a deep breath before she told him, "he talked some nonsense about taking Teddy in order to make me come back to him. But Malcolm, I'm sure he didn't mean it. But nevertheless, I felt you had to know. The police asked if anyone had threatened me, or had reason to be angry with me, and for Teddy's sake, I told them." It surprised Malcolm that she hadn't been more anxious to protect Charles Delauney, and he could see from the look in her eyes when she talked about him that she still cared deeply about him.

"You told this to the police? All of it?"

"Yes." She nodded slowly. She wasn't ashamed anymore. It was painful, but it was not her fault. She had finally come to accept that.

"That's a lovely tale to tell. I imagine that will make interesting reading in the papers."

"Mr. Taylor promised me he would do everything he could to keep it confidential. But he's already been to see Charles."

"You seem to know a great deal about the investigation."

She didn't answer him at first. "I wanted to tell you this myself. I felt you had a right to know." He nodded and stood up, still looking deeply troubled, and then he looked at her, and for a moment she wondered if he was angry.

"It would seem that your contact with Delauney may well have endangered our child,
Marielle. Have you thought of that?" Guilt
again . . . and responsibility . . . why was
it always her fault? Why did her life, or her
failings, or her stupidity, always cause pain to
others?

"I have. But I didn't plan to meet him. It
just happened."

"Are you so sure of that? Are you sure Delauney hasn't been following you and wasn't
waiting for you at the church?"

"He was as surprised as I was. And the boat
pond is just into the park from his father's
house."

"Then you shouldn't have gone there." Malcolm's voice was stern, he was accusing her.
And it was clear now that he did reproach her.
"You shouldn't have done anything to risk my
son," not *their* child, but *his* son, "and given
your history, I'm surprised that you would
take him to the boat pond at all, particularly in
this weather." It was the cruelest thing he
could have said. It had taken her years to be
able to do something like that, and she hadn't
let him near the water.

"How can you say that?" She was shocked.
His words hit her like a blow, but he didn't
care now. He was too worried.

He began to pace the room as he spoke to her. "How can you tell me this story and expect me to forgive you? You were involved with this terrible man, who you admit yourself tried to kill you, and may well have killed your unborn child, and you expose my son to him, you admit to me that he threatened you, that he threatened to take him, for whatever reason . . . and what do you expect from me, Marielle? Sympathy for your children who died? Or for my child who's been kidnapped? You brought this man into my life, you brought him right to my doors, you took my son to the park where they could meet, you exposed Teddy to him, and provoked this lunatic until he took our child, and what do you expect from me now with all this . . . *forgiveness*?" There were tears in his eyes and rage in his voice as Marielle stood in front of him, helplessly weeping.

"We don't know that he took him," she said in an agonized voice, she had told him everything and now she knew he would never forgive her. "We don't know anything."

"I know that you've been involved with people over the years who may well have cost me my only child . . . and you, your last one."

"Malcolm," she closed her eyes and almost swooned at his words, "how can you say that?"

"Because it's true," he roared at her, "because Teddy may be dead by now, buried in a shallow grave we'll never find, or if he isn't yet, he may be at any moment. You may never see your child again." He bore down on her like a nightmare with his booming voice and terrifying accusations. "And what you have to understand, what you have to tell yourself, is that you brought Teddy to him, you provoked this man, you brought Charles Delauney into our life . . . it's you, Marielle, who did it." She gasped at the pain he caused, but she couldn't tell him he was wrong. Perhaps she had done all that he said. Perhaps it was all her fault again, and as she listened to him, she sank into a chair, and the migraine came crashing through her brain so hard she could barely keep her balance. She heard all the voices again, felt all the familiar pain, and just as she used to, she heard the sound of the rushing water beneath the ice, and as she heard Malcolm leave the room, she was barely conscious.

It seemed hours later when she heard a sound, and she was startled to look up and see the little maid who had been bound and gagged by the kidnappers the night before. It was Betty, bringing her her laundry. Mr. Patterson had sent everyone back to work in an

attempt to get the house back to normal, with
the exception of Edith and Patrick, who had
been warned not to leave town. The FBI was
still very interested in their stories.

"Mrs. Patterson, are you all right?" Betty
hurried to her side, she looked as though she
had fainted, and she was halfway out of the
chair toward the floor, when Betty found her.
The sound of her voice roused Marielle to
consciousness again, and she looked around,
through the blinding pain, remembering all
too quickly what had happened and what Malcolm had said . . . it was all her fault . . .
she had brought Charles into their midst . . .
and he had taken Teddy . . . but had he?
And why? Did he really hate her that much?
Did they all? . . . and were they right? . . .
she suddenly wished she had died years before, when she should have . . . perhaps
even under the ice, with her babies.

"Mrs. Patterson . . ."

"I'm fine . . ." Marielle murmured, struggling to her feet, trying to straighten her dress
and smooth her hair, as the frightened young
girl watched her. Marielle looked as though
she had died she was so pale, and she looked
sick as she struggled to keep her balance.
". . . I'm not very well . . . just a headache
. . . nothing to worry about. . . ." She

walked slowly into her bedroom as Betty followed. She had been through her own ordeal
the night before, but the police had reassured
Betty that it wasn't her fault, that she couldn't
have done anything to stop them, and if she
had tried they probably would have killed her.
So she no longer felt guilty, only lucky. Unlike
Marielle, who felt guilty for everything in her
life for the past nine years. It was an awesome
burden.

"Would you like a cold cloth?"

"No . . . no . . . thank you . . . I'll just
lie down for a moment," but as soon as she
did, the room spun around and she thought
she might vomit. It was almost like being
drunk, but worse, because it was so painful.
"Is there any news?" She raised her head for
an instant after she lay down, but Betty only
shook her head and went to pull the blinds
down, and when she left a moment later, Marielle's eyes were closed in pain, but she wasn't
sleeping.

Betty ran into John Taylor downstairs who
asked her where Mrs. Patterson was. She told
him that she had a headache and was resting.

"Let her rest," he added. All he had wanted
was to make sure that she had told Malcolm
about Charles before their meeting, but the
moment he stepped into the library, he knew.

Malcolm Patterson looked grim as he greeted
John Taylor.

"My wife has told me about Charles Delauney," he said immediately. And John assumed she had told him the rest too, but he
didn't appear to be softened. "It's a shocking
story. Do you think that's our man?" He was
clearly frantic about his son, and wanted no
stone left unturned, no matter how great the
scandal.

"It could be. We have no evidence, no
proof. He has an alibi for last night, it's not a
great one, but he's sticking to it, and we've
checked it out and it holds. He was drinking at
a bar on Third Avenue. And before that he was
with friends at '21'. But he wouldn't have done
it himself anyway, he would have hired people
to do it for him, I would imagine."

Malcolm had given it a great deal of thought
ever since she'd told him the story. "If it was
done for revenge, there will be no ransom request. And for the moment, there isn't," he
said grimly.

"That's true. But the boy's been gone for
less than a day. A lot could happen in the next
few hours."

"I want Delauney arrested," Malcolm
roared. "*Now!* Do you understand?"

"Yes, sir, I do," John Taylor said in a taut

voice. "But we need evidence, and there is none. There is absolutely nothing except for the fact that he was drunk and he made some threats which may not have meant a damn thing. And he was once married to your wife." Malcolm glared at him, not amused by the gist of the conversation.

"Then it would seem to me, *Mister* Taylor, that you'd best go out looking for some evidence, hadn't you?"

"Are you suggesting I manufacture it?" Taylor was fascinated by him. No matter how powerful, or important, or intelligent, or allegedly charming the man was, John Taylor suspected that beneath it all, Malcolm Patterson was a bastard.

"I'm not suggesting anything of the sort. I'm telling you to find it."

"If it's there, I will."

"Good." He rose to his feet then, indicating that the interview was over, and Taylor would have been amused if he hadn't disliked him. And for an instant, he wondered if his own hostility was because he was jealous. The man had everything. Money, power, and a wife that Taylor would have given his right arm for. And something told him that for Malcolm Patterson, she was the one thing he had that was not precious to him.

"I'm afraid I have to ask you a few more questions."

"Certainly." Malcolm sat down again, look-ing cooperative and official. He wanted to do everything he could to get his son back.

"Is there anyone who could be out to get you? Anyone who's made threats against you, say in the past year, even foolish ones, things that may not have seemed important at the time, but in light of what happened last night jump to mind now?"

"I can't think of anything. I thought about it all night as I drove from Washington, but I can think of no one who would want to harm me."

"Any sensitive political associations? Any dissatisfied ex-employees?" Malcolm shook his head again. "Any women you may have been involved with? What you tell me will be kept confidential, to the best of my ability." It was what he had promised Marielle. "But it may be important."

"I appreciate that," he said coolly, "but that won't be necessary. I have not been involved with any women." He looked outraged that it would even be mentioned.

"Ex-wives who may be resentful that you've had a child with someone else after all these years?"

"Hardly, my first wife is married to one of

the world's leading concert pianists and lives in Palm Beach, and the other is married to the president of a bank and lives in Chicago." And then he threw in a blow that John thought was a cheap shot but he showed no reaction. "Unlike my wife apparently, my previous spouses are not dangerous people."

"Maybe Charles Delauney isn't either." He felt he had to say something to defend her.

"I don't care who it is, Inspector. I just want my child back." It was eleven days before Christmas.

"I understand, Mr. Patterson. We all do. And we're going to do everything we can to make that happen."

"Go back and talk to Delauney." Taylor did not like taking orders from civilians, but he nodded as he stood up and thanked Malcolm for his patience. Taylor noticed that he looked tired and worn, but for a man his age, he looked fairly healthy and composed, considering what had happened. And inquiries about Marielle before he left told him she had been felled by a migraine.

From her room, just above it, she heard the front door close as he left, and the shouts of the press as he made his way through them. And a little while later, the police cordoned off

the front of the house to keep them at a distance. But to Marielle, it was just noise, as she
lay in the dark in blinding pain, silently praying for Teddy.

6

The next day Taylor returned, and there was still no news of Teddy. The kidnappers had said not a word, made no calls, sent no letters, and there was still no request for a ransom. And the press was having a field day. Old photographs of Malcolm and Marielle were splashed all over the papers. Patrick, the driver, had given an interview, and intimated that there was a man involved with Marielle, and there was a photograph of him with Edith, wearing Marielle's white Madame Grès dress from Paris. It had been taken the night of the kidnapping when they were at the Irish Christmas dance in the Bronx, and they looked very grand as they posed for it. And in the afternoon paper the day before, there was a photograph of Marielle looking frightened and disoriented when the press had forced their way into the house, and another of her in her nightgown, which they'd taken through the library windows. But although Patrick had hinted there might be a man in her life, there was no actual mention of Charles Delauney.

"It's a pleasant piece to read," Malcolm said acidly over breakfast the day after his return. "I don't enjoy reading about my wife consorting with other men." He hadn't seen her since he had left her with her headache the day before, and she still looked wan, but she said she was better.

"I told you what happened." She looked crushed by what he was saying.

"Maybe you should have explained it to Patrick."

She looked up at him with a snap then, and for a moment she almost lost control of herself. But even that effort almost resparked her headache. "Maybe you should have your spies report a little more accurately to you, Malcolm."

"What's that supposed to mean?" He looked at her coolly.

"Exactly what it sounds like. None of your

servants have been civil to me since the day I arrived in this house, and you know it."

"Perhaps you don't know how to take command, Marielle. Or perhaps they know something I don't."

"How dare you!" She had been so faithful to him, so loyal, so decent. And now, because of Charles, he blamed her for everything. He had changed overnight. It was so unfair, she left the dining room with tears in her eyes, and collided with John Taylor.

"Good morning, Mrs. Patterson." He looked at her face and knew that the strain was taking a toll on her. He had been to see Delauney again, and warned him not to leave town, but they still had no evidence, and his alibi was solid. So far there were no leads to people he may have employed to kidnap Teddy. But the FBI was frantically trying to build a case, assuming too that Teddy might well have been taken out of state to New Jersey. And so far, Charles Delauney was their best suspect. The people who had paid Patrick a hundred dollars to spend the night out had vanished without a trace, and so far that was all they had. And Betty and Miss Griffin had seen and heard nothing and couldn't help them. "Feeling better today?" Taylor asked calmly.

She nodded. How much better could she

feel with Teddy still gone? "Is there any news at all?"

"Not yet. But we're working on it, and we're waiting. Sooner or later, we're going to get a call for ransom, and then we can move ahead. I want to speak to some of your staff members again today to see if anyone remembers anything they might have forgotten initially in the excitement." She nodded, it sounded sensible. And he also wanted to speak to Malcolm.

She went back up to the nursery then, and she was surprised when she ran into her husband. He was standing in Teddy's room, looking stricken as he touched the child's toys, and let a hand drift across his pillow. It brought tears to Marielle's eyes again when she saw him. She felt guilty for their sharp exchange downstairs. They were both under a terrible strain. As she looked around the room, it tore at her heart again. She remembered stroking his little cheek as he lay there in the red pajamas Miss Griffin had made, with the embroidery on the collar. There were tiny little trains sewn all around in Miss Griffin's careful blue stitching.

"It's impossible to believe that a child can just vanish into thin air, isn't it?" Malcolm said mournfully, and she nodded. He looked at her so sorrowfully, and he sounded gentler than he had an hour before. Here, in this room, you could be sad, but not angry. He sank slowly into the rocking chair near the bed, and stared at where his son had lain for the last time before they took him. "I keep thinking of the train downstairs, waiting for him." There were tears in his eyes when he spoke, and Marielle turned away so he wouldn't see her own, and then he reached out and touched her hand. "I'm sorry about this morning. I'm afraid I was overwrought. And yesterday too . . . it's just such a nightmare all this, Marielle. What are we going to do?" It was the first time she had ever seen him at a loss, and suddenly she felt sorry for him. He seemed suddenly so broken.

"We're going to pray that he comes home soon." She tried to say it calmly as she squeezed his hand. And a few minutes later, Haverford came to find him to tell him that Brigitte was waiting for him in his office at the house. He was still struggling to maintain his work load, and Brigitte had been enormously helpful and deeply sympathetic. She had cried for hours when she heard the news, and she still couldn't believe it.

Marielle followed him downstairs when he left for his office and then went back to her bedroom. At least they had made peace, after a fashion. She exchanged a few words with Brigitte, when she saw her. Both women cried, and Brigitte hugged her warmly, unable to speak for a moment, before she went off to work with Malcolm. Marielle had always known how Brigitte adored Teddy.

It was late that afternoon when John Taylor finished interviewing the help for the second time, and asked to see Malcolm. He wasn't surprised by what he'd heard till then, because she'd warned him, but he still didn't like it. They painted a portrait of a woman who was different from the one he'd seen the night of the kidnapping. A woman who was weak and indulged and frightened and always hiding. Miss Griffin had said that Mrs. Patterson was too nervous, too anxious, and that it wasn't healthy for the boy. In fact, she was so nervous sometimes, she didn't even want to see him, and it had taken her quite a long time to adjust to him in the beginning. At first, she had hardly shown any interest in him at all, as though she wasn't even sure if she wanted him. And it was only lately that she'd been spending time with him, "in between her headaches."

And when he'd last spoken to Edith she had called her a spoiled brat, and intimated that she could have said worse, that she spent so much on clothes it was a wonder she didn't ruin her husband. She said she spent all her time napping or resting, and didn't spend any time running the house, which was just as well, because no one would have listened. They all worked for *Mister* Patterson, she made very clear, and had since before *"she'd"* been there. And she even blamed the loss of her job now on Marielle and not Malcolm.

The housekeeper said almost nothing, and said she knew very little of Mrs. Patterson's habits. She made it equally clear that Mrs. Patterson herself was of no interest. Only *Mister* Patterson mattered.

Only Betty had a few kind things to say. And Haverford seemed to feel sorry for her, although he wouldn't say why, and he refused to open up to John Taylor. And of course, when they last interviewed him, Patrick the driver continued his tale about her "boyfriend," which Taylor suggested he keep to himself, as there was more to it than he knew and he could very easily find himself a material witness, which, for a moment at least, seemed to frighten him into silence.

But the picture Taylor got was one of a woman who was universally disliked for reasons he couldn't fathom. She was the outcast she had described herself to be, in her own house, and very few of the people who suppos-

edly worked for her seemed to know or like
her. He got the feeling that she was withdrawn
from all of them, and he suspected correctly
that she was very lonely. It was still puzzling
him when he walked into the library to see
Malcolm, and he mentioned it while Haverford brought them each a cup of coffee.

"Why is it," he put a spoonful of sugar in
and left it black as he glanced up at Malcolm,
"that so many of your servants seem to dislike
her?" He saw Haverford watching him, but
the old butler said nothing.

Malcolm let out a long sigh and stared out
the window. "She's not a strong person, you
know . . . she's weak, and frightened, and
perhaps they sense it. She's had," he seemed
to hesitate, "ahh . . . mental problems, shall
we say . . . in the past . . . and she still suf-
fers from terrible headaches."

"That's no reason to hate her." They all
seemed to have so little regard for Marielle as
a person, as though she didn't count, as though
she didn't exist, as though they worked for him
and not for her and wanted everyone to know
it. And John Taylor couldn't help wondering if
Malcolm had set it up that way, to keep her
powerless in her own house. She seemed to
have absolutely no control over anyone, not
her child, or her staff, and certainly not her

husband. Even Miss Griffin had admitted that she'd never followed Mrs. Patterson's orders. She took her orders, as she put it, from the boy's father. But when he asked her why, she couldn't explain it, except to say that Marielle was weak and didn't know her own mind, but that didn't make sense to him. She didn't seem weak when he talked to her. She made sense, she was intelligent, and polite, and even if she had headaches, that didn't make her crazy. But that was the feeling he was getting now, that they all thought she was a little "off," as though her mind and her judgment couldn't be trusted. And he couldn't help wondering what had made them think that.

"I don't think anyone hates her here. What a terrible thing to say." Malcolm smiled benignly, but then he looked at him almost sadly. "She's not a strong girl, and she's had terrible problems. Who's to say that she will even be able to endure the shock of all this? This could be the last straw in an already very tenuous picture."

"Is that what you think?" Taylor knew he was onto something, but he wasn't sure what. And there was something else he wanted to know. But he was saving that for later. "Is that what you're telling me?" Taylor pressed. "That she's crazy?"

"Of course not." Malcolm looked outraged at the insult to his wife. "I'm telling you she's fragile."

"Isn't that the same thing? Aren't you telling me she could crack because Teddy's been kidnapped? Has that been the implication in this house for all these years, that she's 'fragile,' as you put it, and not someone to take seriously? Have you told them that, or have they just guessed it?"

"I've told them that they should deal with me, and not trouble her." He looked annoyed. "But I see absolutely no connection between that and my son's kidnapping," he snapped.

"Sometimes the whole picture is very important."

"The whole picture here is that she's a delicate girl with a terrible history, as you know yourself, and I just found out. Two years in a mental hospital, and *nine years* of imaginary headaches." He sounded hard as nails and Taylor didn't like what he was saying. It was as though he was trying to discard her as a person, and somehow he had conveyed it to everyone who worked near them. Taylor suspected that only Haverford felt differently about her.

"Are you saying her headaches are imaginary?"

"I'm saying that she's neurotic." He had gone further than he wanted to and was suddenly very irritated at John Taylor.

"Neurotic enough to be involved with Charles Delauney in the kidnapping of her own child?"

Malcolm looked shocked but for a long moment he didn't answer. "I never thought of it. But I suppose it's possible. Maybe anything is. I don't know. Have you asked her?"

"I'm asking you. Do you think she would do a thing like that? Do you think she's still in love with him?" Taylor was wondering how far Malcolm would go in condemning his own wife, and he didn't like the answer.

"I have no idea, Inspector. You'll have to discover that for yourself."

John Taylor nodded. "And you, Mr. Patterson, how involved are you with Miss Brigitte Sanders?" It was a question he'd been saving for him, and to which he wanted an answer. And he loved the expression on Malcolm's face when he asked him.

"I beg your pardon." Malcolm looked outraged. "Miss Sanders has been my secretary for the past six years, as I'm sure you know, and I'm not in the habit of becoming involved with my secretarial assistants."

John Taylor looked amused at that. "I believe you married your last one."

Malcolm flushed a deep purple and did not look amused. "Miss Sanders has a character of the highest order."

"That's impressive certainly." Taylor looked unflustered, and was secretly amused. In fact, he loved it. "But the two of you travel together a great deal, even to Europe. And I notice that even on the ships you take, your cabins are always adjacent to each other." He had researched it carefully, even with deck plans.

"That is perfectly normal, if I expect the woman to work with me. Since you've done your research so well, I'm sure that you're aware I frequently take my other secretary as well, Mrs. Higgins. She's in her late fifties, and I'm sure she'd be extremely flattered by your suggestions." But it wasn't the older woman who interested John, it was Brigitte. And he also knew that Mrs. Higgins hadn't traveled with him in well over two years, but he didn't say that to Malcolm.

"I apologize if the question seems impertinent, sir. But just as we had to delve into your wife's history, it's important that we are aware of yours as well. Angry lovers can do some very nasty things."

"Miss Sanders is neither angry, nor my

lover, I can assure you." His face was still red from Taylor's suggestions. They went on talking for a short time about Malcolm's involvements in Germany, his business dealings in the States, and any people he could have angered with deals he had made. But there seemed to be nothing worth mentioning. All Taylor could figure out by the end of it was that Teddy had been taken either for money or for revenge. If it was money, they'd hear something soon. If it was revenge, it had to be Charles, and John just prayed that Delauney wouldn't hurt the boy.

They talked about Delauney again, and Taylor reiterated that there was no evidence against the man, there was nothing to link him to the child or the crime, except the foolish things he had said to Marielle. And you couldn't put a man in jail for being stupid. He had an alibi, there was no evidence, and even if he had a motive, it was all still pretty shaky.

"I still think he's our man," Malcolm said solemnly as he walked John to the front door, and the inspector nodded.

"Unfortunately, so do I. And if he is, let's just hope we get him."

Malcolm left him at the front door, and Taylor pushed his way through the throng of press outside. Finally, two hours later, as Malcolm and Marielle sat down to dinner in the dining room, the call came.

Two policemen took the call, pretending to be servants, the recording machine was set in operation instantly, and by the time Malcolm came on the line seemingly innocently, everything was rolling.

They had asked for him in an accent that screamed of South Bronx or East Jersey. "Yes, this is Mr. Patterson." Four policemen, and Marielle, were holding on at various extensions. "Who is this?"

"I've got a friend here . . . a little guy in red pajamas." Marielle felt dizzy as she held her hand over the phone and listened. They had taken him exactly forty-six hours before, and as she held the phone in her trembling hand, she was crying.

"How is he?" Malcolm closed his eyes as he listened.

"He's fine. Kinda cold, I think. We need some money to buy the little guy a blanket."

"May I speak to him?" Malcolm said calmly, but the policeman watching him saw that his hand was trembling.

"Nah . . . he's sleeping. Let's talk about the money first."

"How much do you need?"

"Oh . . . I'd say about two hundred thousand dollars would buy a nice blanket." It was four times what the Lindberghs had paid and well worth it. "In unmarked bills, Mr. Smart Guy. In a locker at Grand Central Station. You leave it there. No cops. No marked bills. No funny stuff. You leave it there as long as it takes for us to pick it up. And when we're ready, you get your kid back."

"How do I know he's all right now?"

"You don't." The voice was hard and ugly. "But you screw me around, you tell the cops, you do anything . . . we kill him." Marielle felt the room reel as she listened, and perspiration was pouring down Malcolm's face when he hung up. He had written down all the instructions, and in any case, the call had been recorded.

John Taylor arrived at the house less than half an hour later, Malcolm was still looking gray, and Marielle was shaking. They hadn't let them speak to the child, and he reminded them that there was no way of knowing if the call was for real, or from some crank, or someone who wanted to make some easy money. People were cruel, and sometimes they wanted to get in on the excitement. But at least it was a hope, something to cling to, and when Taylor left the room, Malcolm dropped his face in his hands and sobbed. It was their only hope of seeing Teddy.

The money was organized by midnight that night. The Intelligence Unit of the Treasury Department had placed half a million dollars in marked bills in Malcolm's account the day before, and Taylor called the president of the bank and asked him to release two hundred thousand of it. A small black alligator bag was filled and by two a.m., everything was in place in a locker in Grand Central Station. They'd been told to place an ad in the *Daily Mirror* when the bag was in place, and by the next morning, the ad was where it should be, and hundreds of plainclothes cops were swarming all over Grand Central Station, walking back and forth, sleeping on benches, eating hot dogs, reading magazines, looking like anyone else, and waiting for someone to pick up the ransom. But after three days, it was clear that no one was going to take it. The call was a cruel prank, and as hope waned, Marielle couldn't even make herself get out of bed. By Saturday, she looked gray, and Malcolm looked even worse than she did. The strain was telling on both of them, and somehow it all seemed worse because it was only six days till Christmas. The prospect of spending Christmas without him made it an added agony, as Malcolm stared at Marielle across their uneaten dinner.

"Why? Why didn't they come for it?" She was haunted by the call, and the threat to kill him if anything went wrong. What if they had? What if they'd panicked and killed him?

"Taylor says it was a prank, you know that." He was being sharp with her again. But he couldn't stand the strain anymore either. "I still think it was Delauney."

"Then why don't they find something, dammit? Why in God's name can't they find who did it!" She went back upstairs again then, unable to sit there any longer. Even the now familiar sight of John Taylor was no longer reassuring, and the next day Malcolm begged him to search Delauney's house again, and Taylor promised to do it.

It was Sunday afternoon, almost exactly one week after the kidnapping when they found it. It was in the basement of the Delauney mansion, in the wine cellar, hidden behind some old cases. One of the police found what he thought was a rag at first, it didn't look like much more than that, but when he moved the case aside he saw it, and he held it up with a look of astonishment, and then he knew he'd found what they had come for. It was a pair of red child's pajamas, with little blue embroideries on the collar. He walked upstairs as fast as he could, and asked to speak to Inspector Taylor, and then he showed him what he'd found. Taylor stood and looked at it for a long moment, and then wondered where the child had gone, what Delauney had done with him. There was a lot they had to find out now. He went back to where Delauney sat and told him what they'd found as Charles dropped his face into his hands and swore he hadn't done it.

"My own son died years ago." He looked up at John imploringly. "I know what it's like . . . why would I do that to someone else?" It didn't make sense, and in John's heart he hoped Charles hadn't done it.

John Taylor snapped handcuffs on him, and moments later he was downtown, the red pajamas carefully sealed in an envelope in Taylor's hand, and Charles Delauney was booked for kidnapping.

John called Malcolm and Marielle, and she cried when she heard they had found Teddy's pajamas.

"But where is he?" That was all that mattered.

"We don't know yet. We're going to question Delauney now. But I wanted to bring him downtown to do it. We can be rougher here." They both knew John Taylor meant business.

"I'll call you as soon as we know anything."
But this explained why there had been no real
requests for ransom. Charles had done it for
revenge, or out of anger, or to get Marielle and
he certainly didn't need any money from
them. He had the only thing he wanted: the
boy. But the real question was, what had he
done with him after he took him? And where
was he now? And worst of all . . . was he still
living?

Marielle looked heartbroken when John
Taylor hung up, and she couldn't help wondering what Malcolm was thinking. He said not a
single word to her. He simply walked upstairs,
and silently closed the door to his bedroom.

7

When news of Charles Delauney's arrest leaked out, the press went wild, and there were ten times as many reporters outside the Patterson home the next morning. Malcolm only went out under heavy police escort. The reporters hounded John Taylor now too, and the chief of police. They wanted to know everything. This was big news and they wanted the story. The heir to one of the most important fortunes in the country had been arrested for kidnapping . . . more than that, it was a crime of passion, a saga of revenge . . . the accused had been married to another scion's wife, and held her responsible for the death of their child. Despite all of John's efforts, word had leaked out, and the scandal was full-blown and out of control by Christmas. By then, Charles had been in custody at Federal Detention Headquarters for five days, and still there was no news of Teddy. Delauney still swore he had no idea where he was and had had nothing to do with it, which led John Taylor to fear that he had killed him. Much to his own chagrin, he told Marielle and Malcolm that on Christmas night. But he felt certain now that Delauney's stubbornness about the crime meant that he had done it as revenge, and Taylor thought it more than likely that he had killed him.

"Oh my God." Malcolm's whole body swayed when Taylor told him, but this time Marielle held firm, and put an arm around him as though to soothe him. She hadn't had a headache in days, and her whole life centered around waiting for news of Teddy.

"I can't believe that," she said quietly in answer to Taylor's news. "I can't believe we'll never see him again. No matter what Charles did, I can't believe he would have killed him."

"Come to your senses!" Malcolm shouted at her in front of John Taylor. "When are you going to understand that the man took him as revenge for his own child? His child is dead and so is mine. . . ." And somehow the way

he said it told her in no uncertain terms that
he blamed her. John Taylor heard the implication too, but there was nothing he could say to
help her. He wanted to whisper to her, "Be
strong," or hold her for a moment before he
left the room. But he could say nothing. He
only squeezed her hand, imperceptibly, and
then he left her with Malcolm.

Christmas didn't even exist for them this
year, there was no exchange of gifts, of warm
thoughts or feelings. There were no decora-
tions put up anywhere, and Teddy's room was
like a little altar to all they'd lost. They both
seemed to go there constantly, to renew their
hope and spirit. Marielle couldn't believe
she'd never hold him in her arms again,
couldn't believe he was gone . . . it wasn't
possible . . . Charles just couldn't do it.

She lay awake all that night after John had
gone, and she knew what she had to do. The
next morning when Malcolm went out, to attend to some business, she ordered the car
brought around and she asked one of the policemen to drive her downtown. They seemed
a little startled at first, but after consulting
with the sergeant in charge, they agreed to do
it. They spirited her out the servants' door, in
a black dress and hat and an old fur coat of her
mother's, and the car plowed through the re-

porters outside the house, and headed downtown as Marielle sat shaking between two policemen in the backseat. She hadn't been out
of the house since the kidnapping, and it was
terrifying pressing through crowds, and being
driven to a police station by four policemen.
But she knew that this was something she had
to do. No matter what they said, she had to see
him.

He was being held at Federal Detention
Headquarters and he had been there for six
days. Formal charges had been made almost
immediately, for kidnapping. Taylor was still
hoping to get a confession out of him, or at
least learn the whereabouts of the child, if
they could force that out of him. But so far, he
had given up nothing.

There were a handful of reporters on the
front steps when she arrived, and as soon as
they got a glimpse of her, they went wild, but
her escort forced their way through, and a moment later she was inside, breathless and shaking. She explained whom she had come to see,
and there were whispered conferences and
murmurings. It wasn't a visiting day, and this
was highly irregular, but she told them who
she was and that she had to see him.

Finally one of the sergeants in charge took
her in, and left her in a small bare room, and

ten minutes later, they brought him to her. He was wearing rough pants, one of his own shirts, what looked like combat boots, and he had a week-old beard, and an expression in his eyes she hadn't seen in years, an expression of pain and sorrow that told her what she had come to learn even before she asked him any questions. He began to cry the moment he saw her, and the guard left them alone in the room as he took her in his arms and held her.

"I didn't do it, Marielle . . . I swear . . . I would never do that . . . I was crazy . . . I was drunk that day . . . I don't know . . . just seeing you there with him . . . it reminded me of André. . . ."

"I know . . . I know . . . shhh . . . I had to talk to you." She pulled away from him so she could see him, and she was glad she had come. She had needed to hear from him just what had happened. Slowly, he sat down, and she sat down across from him, and looked at him. How far they had come, and how much pain there still was between them. "What happened?"

"I don't know. They said they found his pajamas in my basement. My God, Marielle . . . tell me you don't believe it's true. . . ."

"How did they get there?"

"I don't know. I swear to God, I don't . . .

I'm a fool . . . I was terrible to you . . . I
was wrong . . . I was crazy . . . but I've
spent the rest of my life trying to atone for it,
I've never hurt anyone . . . I've fought for
my friends, I was willing to die for their causes
because I have nothing more to lose . . . why
would I hurt him? Why would I hurt you? I've
done enough to you, and by God . . ." He
sobbed as she held his hands. "I still love
you."

"I know," she whispered, she still loved him
too. But she loved Teddy more. He was her
baby. "But where is he?"

"I swear, I don't know." He looked up at
her then, his eyes clear and deep and true, and
she believed him. "I swear, Marielle, even if
they kill me. I promise you, I know nothing of
the boy's kidnapping. I hope you find him, for
your sake. In spite of everything I said so stu-
pidly, you deserve to."

She nodded. "Thank you." How had they
gotten into this? How had it happened?

The guard came back to them then, and he
said she had to leave. She nodded and stood
up, and Charles looked at her long and hard
before he left her.

"Believe me" was all he said, and she nodded. It sounded like the truth. But if he hadn't
taken the boy, who had? She was no closer to

knowing anything than she'd been before she'd come. But at least she knew Charles Delauney hadn't done it. And as she left the tiny room, she was startled to see John Taylor coming toward her. He was FBI and not police and he had no business here, although she assumed he had come to see Charles, but he looked very stern as he led her to a private office.

"What are you doing here?" He seemed angry at her, almost the way Malcolm would have been, but she was glad she'd come anyway. It had been worth it.

"I had to see him."

"You're a fool."

She shook her head and knew she wasn't. "He says he didn't do it. And I believe him." She had had to know, had to ask, had to see him.

"And what do you think he's going to say to you? That he killed him?" She flinched as he said the words, but he was angry at her for coming to see him. "He's not going to tell you the truth. His neck is in the noose and right now he's going to do anything he can to save it."

"Why would he lie to me?"

"Why would he tell you the truth? There's too much at stake for him. Marielle, listen to me, stay away from here. Stay away from him. If we can, we'll find your son for you, but this man can do nothing for you. He's brought you nothing but pain . . . leave him alone. . . ." It was not his place to say, but he knew she was being duped. He knew too much about Delauney now. The wildness in Spain, the crazed furies he indulged from time to time, the wild drunks, the rage . . . the fact that he had hit her when he had . . . the fact that he still loved her. He wasn't even sure he was sane. That was going to be looked into too. But he didn't want her any more hurt than she had been. And when the press got wind of this, they were going to have a field day. "Come on, I'll take you home." She nodded, willing to go now. "And next time you want to do something like this, call me."

"And what will you say?" She smiled as he led her away. He had the policeman start the car, and all they had to do was make a wild dash for it, with the photographers blazing. Later, there was one picture of her swinging into the car with John Taylor just behind her. "What would you have said if I'd asked you to bring me down here?" she asked as they settled back in the car, and he frowned.

"I'd have said no." In no uncertain terms.

"That's why I didn't call you." She smiled.

But she was feeling relieved. She believed Charles. Maybe it wasn't all her fault. And John Taylor sat watching her, thinking that she was a terrific woman and how much he liked her. Much more than he should have.

"I'll take you out for a drive and give you a nice stern lecture next time you get an idea like that," he said as though scolding a child.

"That's what I was afraid of," she said quietly, and then said nothing more on the drive home.

As he watched her as they drove uptown, he felt distinctly sorry for her. He knew how desperate she was to find the child, and he was beginning to think they weren't going to. He had begun to feel that way in the Lindbergh case too, and he had wanted so badly to be wrong, but in the end he wasn't.

They ran in through the kitchen once she was home, and she thanked him for bringing her back. But Malcolm was far less grateful to him the following morning. The papers were smeared with Marielle's visit to Charles in jail, with photographs of her everywhere, and one of John with his arm around her as she got into the car.

When Malcolm came home he was livid.

"What was that about, Marielle?"

"He was shielding me from the press," she

said quietly. And he'd been right. The photographers had had a field day.

"He seems to be enjoying it. Was it his idea to take you to see Delauney?"

"No, mine. I ran into him there. And Malcolm . . . I'm sorry. I just had to see him . . . I wanted to hear what he'd say."

"And did he tell you how he killed your son? Did he tell you that? Or did he cry about his own son?" Malcolm was raging.

"Malcolm, please . . ."

"Please what . . . your lover . . . your ex-husband, your whatever you want to call him takes my son and you want me to feel sorry for him? Is that what you did? Go to tell him how sorry you are for him? You know who I'm sorry for? I'm sorry for Teddy . . . our little boy who is probably dead somewhere, who may have been kicked or stabbed or broken or hurt . . ." She was screaming as she listened, her hands over her ears, unable to bear it a moment longer.

"Stop! Stop! *Stop!*" She ran shrieking from the dining room and went to her own bedroom. It was too much to bear. Too much was happening. And everyone seemed to blame her. It was her fault for knowing Charles, for having been married to him, for not having been able to save her own child, Charles blamed her for that too, and now Malcolm blamed her for Teddy's kidnapping.

John Taylor came back to see her that afternoon, and was kind enough not to mention the furor in the press, but he didn't have any other news either. They were going to search Charles's house again, just in case. And this time when they did, they found one of Teddy's toys, it was a little teddy bear, concealed right in Charles's own bedroom. There was no longer any doubt at all. And this time, even Marielle believed them.

8

In mid-January, preparations for the trial were under way, and there was still no news of Teddy. It had been three and a half weeks since he'd been gone, and Malcolm had gone back to Washington for a few days to attend a joint secret session of the House and Senate Committees on Military Affairs, and to see America's ambassador to Germany, Hugh Wilson, who was home for a brief visit.

Marielle was alone in New York, in the house surrounded by guards, and it had been almost a week since she'd seen John Taylor.

She was going through some papers one afternoon, trying to keep her mind off Teddy, and stay out of his room. She couldn't bear

listening to the radio anymore. Either it was
news of the trial, which rattled her, or she
heard Teddy's favorite broadcasts, like *The
Lone Ranger,* which made her cry and de-
pressed her. And Marielle had come to hate
the sight of Shirley Temple because she reminded her of Teddy. They had finally sent
Miss Griffin off for a brief vacation to see her
sister in New Jersey. She too was almost hysterical by then. And it was a relief not to have
to look at her when Marielle went upstairs.
Now she could be alone in his room, with his
clothes, his toys, the little things he'd used,
like his hairbrush. Sometimes, she just stood
there for hours, and touched them, or sat in
his favorite chair, or lay on his bed, trying not
to think of his last night there.

Haverford appeared in the library that day,
as she put away the last of her papers. His
eyes were gentle and kind. He felt desperately
sorry for her, although he would never have
said it.

"There's someone here to see you. A Miss
Ritter. She says she has an appointment."

"I don't know anyone by that name."

"Yes, you do." At the sound of the words,
Marielle turned, and saw a young woman
enter the room where she was working. She
was small and had red hair and was about

Marielle's age, and she looked familiar but Marielle couldn't place her. And for an instant, she found herself praying that this would be some kind of threat, or extortion request, someone who could lead her to him, but those hopes were almost dead now. The ransom had never been picked up, and was still sitting in the locker in Grand Central Station.

"Who are you?" Marielle looked puzzled, and Haverford stood ready to defend her. And then suddenly Marielle knew. She recognized her as the reporter who had forced her way into the house early on, and the girl looked suddenly frightened as she glanced at the butler.

"May I talk to you alone?"

"No . . . I'm sorry . . . you can't." Marielle sounded far braver than she felt. The girl seemed very bold and sure, and Marielle was being very careful.

"It's important, please . . ." the young woman begged. She was wearing another of her incongruous outfits.

"I don't think so. How did you get in here?"

"We made an appointment for this afternoon." She tried to brazen it out but Marielle knew better. She hadn't had an appointment of any kind in over a month, except with investigators and policemen.

"I'm sorry, Miss . . ."

"Ritter. Beatrice Ritter. Bea." She smiled, trying to find some hook into Marielle, something that would catch Marielle's interest enough to ask her to stay, but Marielle knew better.

". . . you'll have to leave. . . ." For an instant, the girl looked bitterly disappointed, and then she nodded.

"I understand. I just wanted to speak to you about Charles." The sound of his name was like an electric current in the room and Marielle stared at her.

"Why?"

"Because he needs you." It was all much too complicated to discuss with a stranger.

"Madam? . . ." Haverford looked at her inquiringly, and she didn't know why, but she decided to let the girl stay, if only for a moment. She nodded, and he left the room, but he alerted two policemen as he left and Marielle saw them near the doorway.

"I don't understand why you're here. Did Charles send you to see me?" She had heard nothing from him since her visit to the jail, not since they found the bear that had finally convinced her he was guilty.

But Bea Ritter wanted to be honest with her, and realized she had to make her point quickly, before she was asked to leave. Charles had told her himself that Marielle would never see her. "I'm with AP. And I don't think he did it. I want to see if I can help find out who did. I want to know if you'll help me." It was as clear and concise as she could make it.

"I'm afraid I don't agree with you, Miss . . . Ritter." She groped for her name. "I didn't think he did it either, but two things have been found now to link him to my son, the pajamas my son was wearing when he left, and his favorite teddy bear. And no one else has come forward." Marielle had no doubts now.

"Maybe the real kidnappers are afraid to, or have good reason not to. There has to be some reason." She was so convinced of Charles's innocence. She had spent hours with him, and she could not believe him capable of the crime. But Marielle no longer believed in his innocence. She stood up quietly, wanting the girl to leave her.

"I'm afraid I can't help you." Her eyes were too full of pain, her heart too heavy. She didn't want to listen to this girl plead for Charles. All she wanted was her son back.

"Do you believe he's capable of it?" She had to know. She wanted to know if Marielle believed him. But Marielle was afraid of what this girl would put in the papers.

"I do believe he's capable of it. There's simply no other answer. And he threatened to do it." She was finally convinced, even if this young woman wasn't. After all these years, her heart had finally hardened to Charles Delauney.

"He was drunk." It was obvious that she'd talked to him, and Marielle was annoyed that she was so persistent. She was bright and strong and incredibly determined. She wore her hair in a short bob, and she was wearing a cheap navy blue coat and dress, and a ridiculous hat with a red flower, but in an odd, perky way, she was pretty.

"Being drunk is no excuse. I'm sorry . . ." She walked to the door and Bea Ritter didn't move.

"Mrs. Patterson, he loves you. . . ." The words stopped her in her tracks, and Marielle turned to stare at her in anger.

"Did he say that to you?"

"It's obvious."

"It hasn't been obvious to me in years, and I don't want to hear it." She was finally very, very angry at him, and mortally wounded by what he'd done. But Bea Ritter refused to share Marielle's point of view.

"He's innocent." She was so determined, so sure, that it almost haunted Marielle as she listened, but she didn't want to be haunted by Charles again. He had taken her baby.

"How dare you say he's innocent! If he is, where's my child?"

"He doesn't know. He swears." Her eyes never left Marielle's face. "If Charles knew, he'd tell us."

"You don't even know him." But she knew him better than Marielle thought. She had spent hours with him, in the jail, after bribing two policemen. At first it was just a story, an interview, but for some odd reason, she believed him. She was sure he was telling the truth, and she had promised herself that she would do everything she could to help him. In fact, she had gone to Tom Armour, at his request, and begged him to represent Charles. The two were acquaintances from years past, but until that point, Armour had refused all of Charles's letters and phone calls. It was Bea who turned the tide, who begged on his behalf, who convinced the young criminal attorney that Charles was in fact innocent, in spite of how grim things looked against him. And she had reminded Tom that if he didn't take the case, and Charles lost, he would be put to death . . . an innocent man. She insisted that

Tom could make all the difference. Thanks to Bea Ritter, Tom Armour had finally agreed to represent him.

"Will you help me?" Her eyes begged and Marielle didn't want to hear her, just as Tom Armour hadn't wanted to, but he had. Bea Ritter was uncomfortably convincing.

"Find my son and I'll believe you," Marielle said coldly.

"I'll try." Bea Ritter finally stood up. "May I call you if anything comes up?" Marielle hesitated, and then in spite of herself, she nodded. "Thank you." Bea stood for a moment, looking at Marielle, as though wondering about all she'd heard, and then she thanked her again and left, as Marielle watched her.

Marielle was still sitting at her desk, thinking about her unhappily, when John Taylor arrived with the U.S. Attorney. He was a tall, thin, spare, somewhat frightening-looking man, who seemed absolutely certain that Charles Delauney had kidnapped her child, and what's more, he was certain he had killed him. Marielle flinched as she heard the words, and John Taylor ached as he watched her. It was a far cry from Bea Ritter's plea to help him.

The U.S. Attorney told her they had scheduled the case for March, and he explained to her that they expected a guilty verdict, and hoped for every possible cooperation from her and her husband.

"What does that mean, Mr. Palmer?"

"It means that I expect you to be at the trial, to sit there and make the jury care. We want them to know what losing your boy has meant to you, so they convict Mr. Delauney. And if we're lucky, and can prove or even imply that he crossed state lines with the boy, we'll get the death penalty, Mrs. Patterson, and nothing less!" The way he said it made her shiver. He also made her feel that he was going to try to convict Charles on the emotions of the case, more than the evidence. And it worried her to be put "on display" during the trial. Taylor didn't like it either, but he understood it. William Palmer was a highly respected prosecutor, but not much of a human being. "Of course, if we find your son by then, we'd like to see him in court too, but only briefly." Marielle sat there thinking that she would have loved that. If only they would find him and he could be there.

"Anything else?" She was being flip with him because what he was saying was so awful, but he didn't seem to get the point as he stood up and prepared to leave her.

"We'll let you know." He readjusted his

glasses, stared at her as though evaluating how good a witness she'd make, and picked up his briefcase. "I'd like to see your husband when he gets back from Washington, if you'd let him know."

"I'll tell him." He left and Taylor stayed on, and she sighed as they sat down on the couch. It had been an endless month, a hideous time, and they still had no idea what had happened to Teddy. There had been no calls, no tips, only a few bum leads, and a handful of crackpot sightings from New Hampshire to New Jersey.

"He's sweet." She was referring to the U.S. Attorney, and Taylor laughed as he lit a cigarette and watched her. She was a good sport, among other things, when life wasn't crushing her to extinction.

"He's better in court than in the drawing room."

"Lucky for him." And then she looked inquiringly at John. In an odd way, they had become friends. Sometimes she felt as though he was her only ally. "I imagine the trial will be really awful."

"It'll be rough. And they'll bring out things you won't like . . . at least the defense will, maybe your time in the hospital, or something like that. They have to do what they can to discredit you."

"Why? I'm not accusing Charles." Although most of the time she now believed he did it. It was only now and then that she had doubts about Charles's guilt. She told him then about Bea Ritter.

"Stay out of it. You'll only get hurt. Whatever the press gets hold of, they're going to twist and use to stab you in the back with." She agreed. But what if the girl in the funny hats was right? She was so smart and so intense and so earnest. "I don't know what to think sometimes," she admitted to John dejectedly. "And what difference does it make anymore? Teddy's gone. The rest is all so unimportant." Her eyes were so big and sad as she said it. She had lost three children in one short lifetime.

"It isn't unimportant to Charles. His life is at stake. He's going to be clutching at straws for his survival."

"Who's his lawyer?"

"He picked a good one. A man named Tom Armour. Smart, young, he can be brutal in court, but if anyone can save Delauney's neck, he will."

"I don't know if I'm glad or not. I don't know what I think anymore. Malcolm says he

did it. And when they found the bear . . ."
Her eyes filled with tears and she blinked
them away. "But I don't know . . . when I
went to see Charles, I believed him when he
said he didn't. But if he didn't, where is
Teddy?" It was the one question no one could
answer, and as he watched her, he felt so
drawn to her, he could hardly listen to her
questions. He had never felt like that about
anyone, not even his wife, and certainly not
the women he usually dealt with in investiga-
tions, but there was something about her that
just drove him to distraction. Something so
vulnerable and soft that all he wanted to do
when he was near her was reach out and touch
her.

"I wish I knew the answer to that," he finally said, but his eyes caressed her as they sat
on the couch and it grew dark. It was another
cold night, and she was alone, as usual. Malcolm was away, and in spite of the police everywhere, the house seemed so empty and
lonely. He wished that he could take her to
dinner somewhere, somewhere where there
was noise and laughter and smoke and music.
He wished he could take her away from it all,
from men who beat her and broke her heart,
and others who ignored her. He knew more
about Malcolm Patterson now than he cared to

know, and one thing he knew for sure was that
Marielle was getting less than she deserved
from everyone. And John Taylor wished that
he could make things different. "I wish I could
make all of this go away for you, Marielle." It
was an unprofessional thing for him to say, but
it really touched her.

"That's sweet of you. So do I, I guess. . . .
I used to believe that difficult things happened
for a reason. I'm not sure I believe that anymore. Too much has happened to me." It was
impossible to believe that through totally un-
foreseeable and hideous circumstances, the
woman had lost three children. "Do you have
children?" She knew so little about him, and
yet she had known for a month now that she
liked him.

"Two. A girl fourteen and a boy eleven."
And then, suddenly he was sorry he'd said it,
but she seemed peaceful as she nodded.

"André would have been eleven" . . . and
the little girl eight . . . the baby who died
without ever taking a breath, and with no
name . . . just baby girl Delauney.

"Jennifer and Matthew." He filled in to dis-
tract her.

"Do they look like you?" She was smiling,
enjoying just talking to him about normal
things, not kidnapping and murder.

"I don't know. People say he does. It's hard to tell. What about you? What do you like to do when life is normal?"

She smiled at the question. "I like to swim, and go for long walks, and ride . . . I like music . . . I used to paint years ago, but I haven't in years . . ." Not since the hospital, but she didn't say that. "I like all the silly things I used to do with Teddy." Everything always came back to that, in the end, it was all she could think of. "We saw *Snow White*, the day . . . the day he . . ."

"I know," he said softly. He remembered. She nodded then, feeling sad, and he put a hand on hers, and she looked at him wondering why he cared, why he was so nice, but she was grateful that he was there. He always seemed to be there when it mattered. "Marielle . . ." He spoke her name softly, and the air seemed not to move between them, and then without saying anything, he leaned toward her and kissed her. She felt her whole body melt close to him as he took her in his arms and held her close, and all she could think of was the power of him, the excitement and the strength, and the kindness. She didn't know what to say to him when he pulled away from her and they both looked surprised, but it was obvious from her face that she was happy.

"I'm not sure what to say now . . . except that you mean a lot to me . . . and I'm not sure I could have survived all this without you."

"I want to be there for you . . ." He wanted to give her more than that, but he didn't know how to say it. He pulled away slowly, and sat back against the couch, wondering at what he had done, and why, except he knew he'd had to do it. He could never have given her any of the things she had. All he could give her was the one thing he knew she didn't have, and hadn't in years: love. And one thing he was sure of, Malcolm Patterson didn't deserve her. She was looking at John quietly, and she looked more peaceful than she had in a long time, as she touched his hand and then kissed it.

"Do you love your wife?" She wanted to know, more out of curiosity than anything else. She wanted to know him better. And he could never be anything less than honest with her. He hesitated and then nodded.

"She's very lucky." But he didn't want to talk about his wife with her.

"I haven't been able to think about anyone but you since the night I met you. All I wanted

to do that night was put my arms around you."
They exchanged a long intense look, and then
each knew what the other was feeling. They
didn't even need the words. All they needed
was each other. And they both knew he could
lose his job over what he was doing . . . and
his wife . . . but the truth was, he didn't care
now. All he wanted was to be with her, to take
care of her, and protect her as no one else had.
Marielle was drawn to him too, but she
couldn't imagine what would happen. They
were both married, whether happily or not,
and however angry Malcolm was at her now,
she couldn't leave him after losing Teddy.

"What's going to happen to us?" she asked
softly.

"What do you want to happen, Marielle?"
His voice was deep and gentle.

"I'm not sure." She looked worried. She
didn't want to hurt anyone, not John, or his
wife, or even Malcolm.

John touched the silky cinnamon-colored
hair. And the truth was that he was ready to
leave Debbie for her, but he knew that if he
told Marielle that, it would frighten her and
make her feel guilty. He didn't want to make
promises he couldn't keep, yet he wanted
her so badly. He wanted to be with her,
to help her, to hold her, to give her every-

thing she'd never had before. He wanted all of her . . . her soul . . . her life . . . and her body. . . .

"You haven't had a hell of a lot of lucky breaks, my friend." He said it with a rueful smile, and more kindness in his eyes than she had seen in a lifetime.

"No, I guess you could say that . . . Teddy was one of them . . . and now you . . . maybe that's all you get . . . maybe all you get out of anything worth having is a few years, a few days . . . a few moments . . ." She had had André for a brief two years. . . . Charles for three . . . Teddy for four . . . maybe that was it . . . maybe that was all. . . . Maybe there was no forever.

"You don't ask for much."

"I haven't had much choice." She looked him in the eye and he leaned toward her and kissed her again. This time it took their breath away, and he wasn't sure he could restrain himself much longer.

"I want you to be happy . . ." he whispered heatedly, but she looked at him sadly. Even though he had given her so much joy in these few precious moments, she didn't expect more, and she wanted him to know that. And all she wanted right now was to find Teddy.

"This has been such an awful time . . ." she said softly.

"I know." He took her hand in his own, wishing he could solve all her problems. Maybe in time . . . but he shuddered to think what would happen to her if they never found the boy, or they only found his body. "You have to be very strong, Marielle." He knew she was already. "I'm here to help you." And then he had a thought, because in truth, she asked so little of him. "Why do you ask so little of everyone? Why are you so decent?" Therein he knew he had found the key. That was why they all hated her. Because she expected nothing of them, because she gave without wanting anything in return, and it all made them feel so terribly lacking. She was too good, too kind, too pure, and too willing to endure the pain they gave her. "Don't be so good . . . even to me, Marielle . . . don't . . ." He kissed her again, and she kissed him hard this time, and finally she stopped and pulled away with a small smile that made his heart turn over as he watched her. With all her dignity and gentleness, she still exuded an aura of passion, and she was driving him crazy.

"If we don't stop soon, we're going to have a

serious problem." She looked at him know-
ingly as she said it.

"I'm not so sure that isn't what I want," he
answered hoarsely. And she was sure it was
what she wanted. She hadn't made love to a
man in three years, and the sinews beneath his
shirt looked powerfully appealing, but they
also didn't need that kind of complication at
the moment, and they both knew it.

"When this is all over, you and I are going
to have a serious talk, Mrs. Patterson. I don't
know what's going to happen. But I do know
I'm not going to let you off the hook so easily
then." He had never felt like this about anyone, not even his wife, and he wasn't willing to
give that up now. The moment he had met
Marielle, he had known his life was about to
change forever. But he also knew that what he
owed her now was to find her son, and if he
couldn't do that, to at least help her through
the trial and see Charles Delauney convicted.

"Would you like something to eat before
you go?" she offered, but he shook his head.

"I have to get back to the office," he said
reluctantly, hating to leave her. He seldom
went home before ten o'clock. Because he really didn't want to. He had told Marielle he
loved his wife and he did . . . he had . . .
he used to . . . But the truth was, he loved

his kids more, and that and their religion kept them together. "I'll call you tomorrow," he whispered to Marielle, wondering if she'd regret what they'd done, what they'd said, and if she'd be embarrassed, but there was a look of contentment in her eyes when she stood up, and she looked at him strangely.

"I know I should feel guilty, but I don't. I just feel peaceful." As though something very special had happened. And he felt it too. Something right. Something good. Something they both needed and wanted. But would they ever be allowed to have it? It was still too soon to know the answer to that question.

"Good night, Mrs. Patterson," he said softly, brushing her lips with his own before they left the room and were under the scrutiny of the policemen still assigned to her home night and day. "Good night, Marielle . . ." he whispered. She smiled as she walked him to the front door, and a few minutes later, she walked quietly upstairs to her own room. It was the first time in a month she had smiled, it was so wonderful to feel loved and wanted again, even if only for a moment.

9

Bill Palmer, the U.S. Attorney, became a fre-
quent visitor to their home, while he was pre-
paring his case, and for long periods of time he
would stay closeted with Malcolm. He spoke
to various members of the staff, and he had
had several conversations with the no longer
employed Edith and Patrick. And finally, in
early March, he spoke to Marielle again, this
time alone, with neither John Taylor, nor her
husband.

"I want you to be sure, Mrs. Patterson, before you take the stand, that you're perfectly
clear on what you believe happened. Do you
understand me?" She was sure she did, and he
was one of those people who spoke in a delib-

erate voice, and there was absolutely nothing endearing about him. His hair was slicked down, and his face was pale. He was probably John Taylor's age, a man in his very early forties. He was given to pin-striped suits and dark ties, he wore horn-rimmed glasses, and it was obvious that he was extremely impressed with Malcolm.

"I understand," she said quietly. But there was still very little to tell. She had heard a noise late that night, and at midnight she had gone upstairs to check on Teddy, just to kiss him, she explained for the hundredth time, but the attorney looked untouched by her recital. He was only interested in convicting Delauney. He hated men like him, a socialist lurking in the robes of a rich man, as he viewed it. A spoiled playboy who thought he could do anything he wanted. "I found Betty, and Miss Griffin, bound and gagged. Miss Griffin had a pillowcase over her head as well, and she'd been chloroformed. And Teddy was gone . . . that's all there was really . . . he had vanished." And there had been nothing since then, except the false alarm over the ransom left in Grand Central Station. It had never been picked up and they'd never called again, which convinced the police and the FBI that the call had been made by cranks in the first place.

"And the pajama suit found at Delauney's home, was that your son's?" She felt as though she were already on the stand as he paced the room and watched her.

"I believe so," she said softly.

"You're not sure." He stopped pacing and stared, as though in fury.

"I'm sure, but . . ."

"But what, Mrs. Patterson?" Malcolm had warned him that she was never sure, never certain, never brave enough to stand up for herself or have her own convictions.

"I don't know how it got there." Malcolm had said, unfairly, that you couldn't really trust her emotions.

"Delauney left it there of course. How else would it get to his house, along with the boy's teddy bear? Do you not believe Charles Delauney kidnapped your son?" There was a long pause as she pondered it again. She had asked herself the same question a thousand times in the past two and a half months, and she thought he had, the evidence was there, yet sometimes she was unsure, when she let herself think of Charles as a person. And everyone said he still maintained that he hadn't. But the

evidence . . . the evidence . . . the pajamas . . . the bear . . .

"Yes, I think so." She looked pained as she
said it.

"But you're not sure?" He bit off each word
as though it hurt him. "Is there anyone else
you think might have kidnapped your son?"
She shook her head. She felt as though she
were shrinking while she listened. "I don't
know. I don't think anyone knows, or we
would have found him."

William Palmer looked shocked. "Don't you
want justice, Mrs. Patterson? Don't you want
to see the man who took your son punished?
That's what your husband wants, isn't that
what you want?" He made it sound un-Ameri-
can of her not to want to see Charles executed.
But in truth that was not what she wanted.

"All I want is for my son to come home."

"Do you accept the possibility that he may
have killed him?" She closed her eyes as she
nodded, and then opened them again, wondering how she was going to survive the trial. The
past two and a half months had been a nightmare. The newspapers were hounding them
night and day, and almost every day there
were photographs of them, or Teddy, or
Charles, on the front pages. She couldn't even
listen to the radio anymore without hearing

tales about herself, or Charles, or Malcolm, most of them untrue, and many of them filled with imaginary scandal. She was supposedly seen dancing everywhere, Malcolm was divorcing her, Charles had escaped, Teddy had been seen. It was endless and totally untrue, and perfectly awful. And William Palmer was part of the nightmare. "You understand that this man may have killed your son, yet you're not certain that you believe he is guilty. Is that correct?"

"Yes," she finally spat at him, "yes, that's correct. . . . No . . ." She changed her mind again, "I think he did it." Palmer looked deeply annoyed as she turned and stood up and walked across the room, struggling with her own feelings. "I am not entirely sure that Charles Delauney kidnapped, and possibly even killed, my son. But I believe it is possible because of the pajamas and the teddy bear."

He smiled a small wintry smile at her. "That's my job, isn't it? Why don't you have a little faith in me, Mrs. Patterson, and let yourself be convinced. Your husband believes Mr. Delauney is guilty, you know." He was trying to soothe her. But she already knew what Malcolm thought, and why. He also thought it was all her fault, and that wasn't true either.

"He doesn't know him as well as I do."

"I suppose not. But Mr. Delauney beat you when you were pregnant, didn't he?"

She didn't answer for a long moment, as she stared out at the garden, wishing that she would see her son there. "More or less. I'm not sure I'd call it that. He hit me . . . but he was beside himself with grief. . . ."

"And didn't he kill your unborn child as a result?"

"I don't know. But he's not going on trial for murdering my baby."

"No, but perhaps for murdering your son. And if he could do it once, perhaps he could do it again."

"That's ridiculous. The two cases are entirely different."

"Are you defending him, Mrs. Patterson? Will you defend him at the trial?" That was what he wanted to know. He wanted to know just where she stood before she hurt his case, and he was already more than a little worried.

"That's not my job, Mr. Palmer. I'm not here to defend anyone. All I care about is my son."

"And all I care about is justice."

"Then justice will be served." She looked at him long and hard, and he was serious and unhappy when he left her. Patterson was right, she was unpredictable and unreliable, emotional, and he was beginning to wonder if the chauffeur was right after all. Maybe she still was in love with Charles Delauney. Maybe they'd been having an affair. Maybe there was more to this than met the eye. But his investigators had turned up absolutely nothing unsavory about her. The worst thing anyone could say about her was that she spent too much money on clothes, but Patterson didn't seem to mind that.

When Palmer left that afternoon, John Taylor had arrived only moments later. Visiting her had become part of his daily routine now. He enjoyed talking to her, or sometimes they just sat quietly over a cup of coffee. He liked just being there, somewhere near her. Sometimes he'd spend hours at the house pretending to keep an eye on his men, just so he could be around when she came downstairs. It was like being a kid again, but they'd smile at each other, or steal a look, or she'd bring him a sandwich, and he'd put a hand out quickly and touch her. He loved the smell of her, and the softness of her skin, and if he was very lucky, and no one was around, he might even have the chance to kiss her. He was dying to go outside with her, to go for long walks in the spring, or just go to the movies with her and eat popcorn. But they couldn't go anywhere.

The moment she opened her front door, she was like fresh meat in a pool of sharks. They had to stay inside, and hide, and talk. And it always intrigued him how seldom he saw Malcolm when he was at the house. The man was never there, but that suited John Taylor to perfection.

"How's it going?" he whispered as he took off his coat. He had seen Bill Palmer leave in a cab when he got there. "Palmer treating you okay?"

"I think he's disappointed I don't want to see Charles electrocuted. Or at least I'm not enthusiastic enough about it."

"I worry about that too," John said to her, touching her arm as they walked to the library. "What can I say to convince you?"

"Show me evidence . . . show me my child . . ."

"I wish I could. But are you really convinced he's innocent?"

"No," she admitted to him. "The trouble is I'm not a thousand percent convinced he's guilty either. I think he did it, but I'm not totally sure." She agonized about it sometimes, glad she couldn't be on the jury.

"Once we found the pajamas, it was open and shut, and you know it." But he also knew she didn't want to believe the child was dead, and not finding him suggested that, as they all knew. Maybe denying Charles's guilt meant believing Teddy was still alive. Maybe she couldn't afford to believe the truth. And sometimes John wondered if they'd ever find him. He had hated finding the Lindbergh child, hated telling them, hated what it must have done to them. Having children of his own, it didn't even bear thinking. And now maybe Marielle would have to face that too. All he could hope for her was that it had been quick and painless.

"The trial's going to be awful, isn't it, John?" she asked him over the coffee that Haverford had brought them. Even the old butler had grown fond of him. He was nice to Marielle, and it was comforting having him around. It made everyone feel safe to have him at the house. And only a couple of cops suspected that his interest in Marielle was something other than business. But they were smart enough to keep their mouths shut. So far, their secret was safe, but their feelings for each other seemed to be growing. They were still trying to live from day to day, concentrating on Teddy and the trial, but they each knew that the time would come when they'd have to face each other and their future. But for the moment, neither of them had to make any decisions. Instead, they continued to focus their attention on the trial which lay before them.

"I think it'll be rough, to be honest with you. I think they're going to drag out a lot of history that could be very painful," John told her quietly, over his coffee.

"I can hardly wait." She knew what he meant, and she also knew that Malcolm had treated her like a criminal ever since they had arrested Charles Delauney. It was as though he believed she had been in league with him, or that somehow she had provoked him into kidnapping Teddy. There was no getting close to him again, no reaching out to him, he had cast her adrift in a sea of loneliness and terror.

"Have you heard from Bea Ritter again, by the way?" She was the spirited young red-headed girl who had championed Charles's cause, and she was driving them all insane. She had mounted a campaign in the press to defend him. She called John Taylor every few days, his defense attorney, the investigators, the U.S. Attorney, and she knew Bea had called her several times, but she no longer took the calls. She had nothing more to say to her, and talking to her always made Marielle nervous.

"I think she called yesterday." And then, suddenly, she looked at John in amusement.

"Is she in love with him?" She was actually a very pretty girl, and she was about Marielle's age, but she had enough energy and fight for ten men and John found her exhausting.

"I wondered that myself, to tell you the truth. But you know, there are a lot of crazy broads who go nuts over guys like him, guys accused of some really ugly crime, and they become obsessed with the accused's innocence. She might be one of those, or maybe just another nosy reporter."

"She certainly seems to care about him. Whenever I've talked to her, she seems so determined to convince me."

"I know." John shook his head, finishing his coffee. "He could do a lot worse. He needs all the help he can get, and a little positive press won't hurt him. I just hope it doesn't hurt us, Marielle." He looked at her soberly as he stood up. "Be careful you don't unwittingly cooperate with the defense. No matter what you believe or don't believe, you don't want to help them." She wanted to ask him why not, but she already knew the answer. What they wanted was the truth, about what had happened to Teddy. A little while later, he left, and she was alone again. She went back upstairs to Teddy's room, to touch his things, and fold some of his clothes again, and arrange his

teddy bears differently. She could never stay
out of his room. But poor Malcolm could no
longer even bear to go up there.

It was the following day when Thomas Armour, the attorney for the defense, arrived,
shortly after noon. He had called and asked to
see her earlier that morning. She had called
John and asked him if it was something she
wasn't supposed to do, and he told her honestly that he thought it unwise, but it was not
illegal. But she was curious about the man,
and she wanted a little warning of what she
would be facing.

Malcolm had gone to Boston for a few days,
and she was alone when she met him. She was
wearing a black dress, which was all she
seemed to wear these days, as though she
were already in some kind of mourning. He
was wearing a dark blue suit, and he had dark
blond hair which must have been even lighter
in his childhood. He had warm brown eyes
that, at first, seemed very gentle. But his tone
was not gentle when he spoke to her. He was
polite and firm, and he didn't pull any
punches. And his eyes seemed to bore into
her, looking for answers.

Haverford brought him into the library, and
after the initial niceties, he looked her straight
in the eye and asked her a very pointed ques-

tion. "I'd like to have some idea, before the trial, of what you're going to say about my client." He hadn't wanted the case, he had expected Charles to be a spoiled brat at first. But he'd grown to like him and now that he'd taken it all his loyalties were with Charles Delauney.

"What exactly do you mean, Mr. Armour?" She knew from the newspapers that he had gone to Harvard, was the youngest partner of a very important firm, and was somewhere in his late thirties. Charles had hired the best, and he had every right to. But more than just his reputation, there was something very quiet and compelling about Tom Armour. He was handsome but it wasn't something Marielle noticed about him. She was more impressed by the intelligence in his face and an aura of determination.

"Mr. Delauney gave me some idea of what happened . . . several years ago. I think we both know of what I'm speaking." He meant when André died, but she appreciated the fact that he didn't just say it. "He admits that he behaved abominably, and that his behavior could be badly misconstrued now. You're the only person now who can testify as to exactly what he did, and why. Just how exactly do you view it?"

"I think he went mad with grief. So did I. We both did foolish things. It was a long time ago." She looked sad as she thought of it, and he watched her. She was a beautiful woman, but he thought she had the saddest eyes he'd ever seen, and she intrigued him. It had been clear to him all along that Charles Delauney was still in love with her, and he wondered just how much his sentiments were reciprocated, but Delauney had insisted ardently that they hadn't been involved before the kidnapping. In fact, because of Malcolm, she had refused to see him. Tom Armour was mildly impressed by that, but it was going to take a lot more than that to seriously impress him.

"Do you think my client is a dangerous man?" That was a loaded question, and she thought about it for a long time.

"No. I think he's foolish. Impetuous. Even stupid sometimes." She smiled but Tom Armour did not smile back. "But I don't think he's dangerous."

"Do you think he took your child?"

She hesitated for a long, long time, trying to be truthful. "I don't know." She looked him squarely in the eye, and she liked what she saw there. He looked like an honest man, someone you could trust. And had she met him in other circumstances, she knew that she

would have liked him. And she thought that
Charles was very lucky to have him as an attorney. "I don't know. I think he did. The evidence was there. But when I think of him, as
he was . . . as I knew him . . . I don't see
how he could do it."

"Do you think that if he took your child, he
would harm him?"

"Somehow . . ." She thought about it and
then looked at him again. ". . . Somehow I
just can't let myself believe that." Because if
she did . . . it would destroy her.

"Why do you think he might have taken
him? Out of revenge for the child you lost?
Anger at you because you wouldn't see him?
. . . because he still loves you?"

"I'm not sure." She wished herself that she
had the answers.

"Do you think someone could have framed
him?" It was what Charles had insisted to him
from the beginning. And Tom Armour had finally come to believe it.

"Possibly. But who? And how would he
have gotten Teddy's pajamas and bear, if he'd
never had him?" The defense had thought of
that too, and they were difficult questions to
answer, unless the people who had actually
taken the child had framed Charles, but that
was a long shot. And how would they even

know him? It was the weakest spot in their case. But the strongest one was that the child's mother herself wasn't totally convinced that Charles Delauney would do it. Armour had a feeling she could be swayed either way, which was dangerous for Charles.

He asked her a few more questions then, made a few notes, and thanked her for her time, as he snapped shut his briefcase. And as she stood up, she looked at him, and decided to be honest.

"I was told that I shouldn't speak to you today. That it was 'unwise, but not illegal.'" She quoted John, and she knew that Malcolm and the U.S. Attorney would have been livid.

"Then why did you?" He was fascinated by her, not by her looks as much as her quiet ways, and her inner peace. This did not appear to be a woman who had ever been in a mental hospital or gone crazy. Maybe she had just given up and wanted to die, as Charles had explained. But now she was definitely back again, and beneath the cool surface, there was a lot of fire, and a sharp brain. He had enjoyed talking to her.

"Mr. Armour, all I want is the truth. That's all I want. Even more than justice. If Teddy is dead, I want to know it . . . and yes, I want to know who killed him, and why . . . but if he's alive, I want him found. . . . I just want to know where he is, so he can come home."

Tom Armour nodded. He understood. And for his own reasons, he wanted that too. "I hope we find out, Mrs. Patterson . . . for his sake as much as yours . . . and Mr. De-launey's."

"Thank you."

Haverford saw him out, and Marielle watched as he went down the stairs. He looked like a man who was in control of everything he touched. And she envied him his confidence. But beneath the confident air, she had sensed something more. Something warm and strong and very caring. And as she walked back to the library, she realized again how fortunate Charles was to have him as an attorney.

10

The trial opened on a bleak wintry afternoon in March, with a bitter wind and a chill rain that went right to the bone, as the jurors, the public, and the press filed into the courtroom. It was the same week that Hitler swept into Prague, and announced to the world that Czechoslovakia was his now. But even Malcolm was less concerned with world news than usual. All they could think of was *The U.S. v. Charles Delauney.*

The trial was being held at the U.S. District Courthouse and at exactly one o'clock, Malcolm and Marielle arrived in the Pierce-Arrow limousine, driven by two policemen and accompanied by four FBI men, among them

John Taylor. He was glad he could be there to give her strength. She felt his presence close to her, and it made her feel braver. Malcolm had said not a single word to her since they left the house. His silent accusations had begun to wear her down in the past months. She looked as gray as her dress when they got out of the car, and Malcolm assisted her silently up the steps of the courthouse. She was wearing a pale gray coat and matching hat, and the wind nearly swept it off, just as the press descended on them in a wave, and the FBI men had to fight to make a path for them. And as they entered the courtroom, Marielle realized again how painful this was all going to be, and how pointless. At the end of it, they would not give Teddy back. What purpose did it serve? He was gone, and after three months their hopes of having him returned alive had grown dim now. All this was was an exercise in accusation.

The Pattersons took their seats in the front row behind the U.S. Attorney. John Taylor sat next to Marielle, and one of his assistants was next to Malcolm. There were two more FBI men just behind them, and two uniformed policemen on either side of them, and just ahead, so they were surrounded by more than adequate protection. And Brigitte was already in

the courtroom waiting for them when they arrived. She glanced warmly at Marielle, and
nodded politely at Malcolm. A few moments
later the bailiff appeared and demanded that
all rise as the judge entered in his black robes,
and gazed around the courtroom. He was a tall
man with a rugged face, and a shock of white
hair, not unlike Malcolm's. In fact, the two
men were vague friends, but he was known to
be a harsh judge, and Malcolm had made no
objection when he'd been selected.

Judge Abraham Morrison took his seat, and
scowled at everyone as he looked around his
courtroom. There was a long silence and people began to squirm in their seats, particularly
the press, whom he seemed to scrutinize, and
then the jurors, the Pattersons, the defendant,
and the attorneys.

"My name is Abraham Morrison." His
words rang out sonorously. "And I'm not going
to tolerate any nonsense in this courtroom. If
anyone here misbehaves, I'm going to throw
you out of here so fast your head will spin. Any
contempt of court, I'll put you in jail. Any
press gets out of hand, you're banned from
here, for good. Anyone attempt to coerce a juror, unduly influence a juror, or even talk to a
juror, I'll prosecute. Is that clear to everyone
in this room?" There were nodding heads and

a murmur of voices. "We're here for a serious matter. A capital offense. A man's life is at stake, and a child's life may have been taken. These are not matters I take lightly." He looked straight at the press section then. "And if you hound anyone here, either the jurors, the defendant, or the witnesses," he looked pointedly at the Pattersons, "you'll be out the door faster than my bailiff can throw you. Does everyone understand the rules here?" There was a long silence as everyone sat in awe of him. "Do you?" His voice boomed again, and there was a chorus of "Yes, sirs." "Good. Then maybe we can get started. I won't tolerate a circus in my court. Let's get that clear right from the beginning." More nodded heads, and he put on his glasses and carefully perused some papers. Marielle looked over at the defendant's table then, and she noticed that Charles was looking thinner and pale, and the hair at his temples seemed to have become grayer than when she last saw him. He was wearing a dark blue suit, a white shirt and dark tie, and he looked more respectable than most people in the room, but that wasn't the issue. Tom Armour looked extremely serious too, in a pin-striped suit with a vest. And he seemed suddenly younger than he had when she had seen him in her own

home. She had never told Malcolm about the
meeting.

Judge Morrison looked back up at the courtroom again, and his gaze swept the room. "I
think we all know why we're here today. This
is a kidnapping case. The kidnapping of Theodore Whitman Patterson, a four-year-old boy.
His parents are here today." He waved
vaguely in the direction of Marielle and Malcolm, and she could feel her heart pound. It
was difficult to believe that, after three months
of constant press, there was a person alive who
didn't know who they were, but it was as
though Judge Morrison wanted to introduce
them. He liked a great deal of decorum and
respect, but he also liked a personal touch in
his courtroom.

"The defendant is a man named Charles
Delauney. And the theory, ladies and gentlemen, and I am addressing prospective jurors
here, is that Mr. Delauney is innocent until
proven guilty. The burden of proof is on the
prosecution. The prosecutor, Mr. William
Palmer," he waved at him then, "must convince you, beyond a reasonable doubt, that
Mr. Delauney is guilty. It is then up to Mr.
Armour," he waved at Tom, "to convince you
that he is not guilty. If Mr. Palmer does not
make a convincing case, if you are uncon-

vinced, if you do not believe beyond a reasonable doubt that Mr. Delauney kidnapped this child, then you must acquit him. You must listen very carefully, and you must take your responsibility seriously. And I will tell you now that I am going to sequester this jury. You will be put up in a hotel, at the government's expense, for the duration of this trial. And you will not be able to speak to anyone except your fellow jurors. You cannot call your children, chat with your husband, visit with a friend, go out to a movie. You must stay with the other jurors, in the hotel, until your duty is done, without prejudice or distraction. The press won't make that easy for you, newspapers, radio, it's all very tempting, and very confusing. But you must make every effort to keep yourself pure of all that until this is over. And if there is anyone here to whom being sequestered would present an undue hardship for the next several weeks, for reasons of health or family responsibility, please speak up when your name is called. We are going to need twelve jurors and two alternates. And ladies and gentlemen, we thank you for your assistance." He turned to the bailiff then and told him to call the names of the prospective jurors.

The first woman was so frightened she almost tripped on the way to her seat, and she was shaking so hard Marielle could see it as she watched her.

The second juror was a woman too, an elderly black woman who had a hard time getting to her seat, she was so old and crippled. Then there were two men, both middle-aged, and a man about forty with one leg, a Chinese girl with incredibly long hair in braids, a good-looking young black man, two pretty young girls, and a middle-aged woman who kept staring at Malcolm and Marielle, two more men, and then two nondescript-looking women as alternates.

And as soon as they were seated, Judge Morrison introduced the attorney for the United States government, William Palmer, to the room. He turned, looked around the court-room, and then turned again to smile at the jury. "Hello, my name is William Palmer. I am the attorney for the United States government in this case, and I am here to represent the People. I represent *you* in this case, and I will need your help to convict this man," he waved vaguely at Charles, "whom we believe kidnapped a four-year-old boy, Teddy Patterson, twelve days before Christmas." As though that somehow made it worse, but actually it had, for his parents. "If any of you know this man, or me, or the defendant's attorney, Mr. Armour, or the judge, or anyone associated with us, you must speak up now, or it will prejudice the case, and you will be excused. Just tell the judge, when he calls on you and asks your name and occupation." He then sat down abruptly and Tom Armour stood up and introduced himself, and Marielle saw immediately that he had a far more winning way with the jury. He didn't talk down to them the way Bill Palmer had, and his manner was smooth, instead of grating, like the U.S. Attorney's. He explained that the case against Mr. Delauney was purely circumstantial, and there were two objects which connected his client to the case, but there was no proof that he had actually kidnapped the child, or had anything to do with it at all. And as he spoke, Marielle saw that several of the jurors nodded. He sat down again then, after thanking them for their help, with a warm smile that made the two young girls giggle, and the judge frowned as he watched them.

"May I remind you, ladies," he barked down at them, "this is not a social event, or an amusing matter. Now," he looked over the rest of them, "does anyone here have a health problem that would hinder them from being sequestered?" The elderly black woman held

up a hand, and Morrison looked down at her
with a warm smile. "Yes? Your name please,
ma'am?"

"Ruby Freeman."

"Yes, Mrs. Freeman?"

"It's my legs. I got terrible arthritis. It hurts
me all the time." She looked up at him sadly.

"I can see that." He nodded sympathetically.

"Some nights, I can't hardly move. And my
daughter . . . she takes care of me. . . . I
help watch her baby while she works." The
woman started to cry as she said it . . . "If I
don't go home to her . . . she can't go to
work . . . we won't eat . . . her husband
was killed at the factory where he
worked . . ." The saga of despair seemed to
go on forever.

"We understand. Perhaps your daughter
could find someone else to help her for a short
time. But Mrs. Freeman, do you feel you
might be in too much pain to do the trial justice?"

"I think so, Your Honor. You don't know
what a terrible suffering arthritis is until you
have it. I'm eighty-two years old, and I've had
it for twenty years, and it's almost killed me."

"I'm very sorry to hear that. And you may
be excused. Thank you for coming here to-

day," he said courteously. No one else raised their hand, so he continued. But the first juror was so nervous, she asked to be excused too. She said she had gallstones and her English wasn't so good, and her husband was very sick, and he needed her. She and her husband were citizens, but they were both German. And before she could tell him any more, Judge Morrison excused her. The Chinese girl with the braids spoke no English at all, and she was excused too. And the two young girls giggled through most of it, and the judge admonished them again. But then Bill Palmer stood up and began questioning the jurors, and after him Tom, and very quickly, the jurors began falling by the wayside.

The two middle-aged men were both businessmen and they stayed. Both were married and had grandchildren of roughly the same age as Teddy. The man with only one leg said he was forty-two, had lost his leg in the Great War, and he sold insurance now for Travelers Insurance. The young black man worked for the post office in the day, and played trombone at Small's Paradise at night, and said he didn't have time to get married, and everyone laughed. And the two young girls were excused because the judge said they couldn't behave. Both were twenty-two, neither one was married and they seemed to think it was a game, and their removal served as a warning to the others. The middle-aged woman who kept staring at Malcolm and Marielle was a secretary and had never been married either. She lived in Queens, and it was impossible to read if she was sympathetic to Charles or not. All she could seem to do was stare at the Pattersons, and once the judge had to remind her to keep her attention on the proceedings. As a result, the defense excused her in the end, as well as the two men who'd come after her. But both sides kept the two alternate women. Which left them eight seats to fill, and it took the next four days to fill them. And in the end, it was a very interestingly mixed jury. The two middle-aged men with young grandchildren were still on, although Marielle had been sure that Tom would want to get rid of them, because they might be too sympathetic to the prosecution. It had become fascinating to second-guess the attorneys. And had it been a trial about anything else, it might actually have intrigued her. Both the veteran with one leg, and the young black musician were kept on. And the last man was of Chinese origin and a professor of economics at Columbia University. The rest of the jurors, as well as the two alternates, were all women.

The youngest of them was older than Marielle, and had three children of her own, but all of them were much older than Teddy. There was a woman who had been a nun for thirty years and had recently relinquished her vows to come home and take care of her dying mother. And when her mother had died, she had decided not to go back to the convent again, but she was not married. There were two women who were friends and were on the same jury by coincidence, both were schoolteachers in the same school, and neither was married, and then there were three women who seemed very plain, were married, had no children at all, and were all either secretaries or employees of large corporations. One had worked for an attorney for a brief time, but she said she had no special knowledge of the law, and neither attorney objected. It was, for all intents and purposes, a jury of Charles's peers, and a group of supposedly normal, decent, fair people.

It was Friday, just before noon by then, and the judges ordered the jury to go home, tie up their affairs, and enjoy their last weekend, because starting on Monday they would be sequestered. He ordered them not to read any newspaper stories about the case, or listen to the radio over the weekend.

He recessed the court then until Monday morning, and Marielle was surprised by how exhausted she was, just by the process of five days of jury selection. It had seemed endless, listening to people's tales and watching the lawyers decide to bounce or keep them. As she and Malcolm stood up, Charles was led away to spend another weekend in jail, and Tom Armour walked past her with no sign of recognition.

The FBI men took them home, and Bill Palmer came to see Malcolm that afternoon. They spent a long time in the library, but they never included Marielle, and she had coffee in the living room with John Taylor. There was no news at his end, but at least it was a relief to talk to someone sympathetic after the difficult week it had been. Every time Marielle had moved an inch out of the courtroom, Bea Ritter had pounced on her and begged her to see her. She called later that afternoon, and Marielle didn't take the call. She was too drained to deal with her or listen to her pleas on Charles's behalf. And Marielle did not want to help her.

"She's quite a girl," Taylor remarked. "She must be crazy about him."

"Some people feel that way about him." Marielle smiled. She had no secrets from this

man. "I did once. But then again, I was eighteen then."

"And now?" John Taylor looked worried,
but not about the case, as Marielle smiled.

"I'm a lot smarter now." But that didn't
mean she wished the death penalty on him
either, if he didn't deserve it. She was still
having a hard time with that, and the FBI had
been able to shed no new light on the case.
There had been a sighting in Connecticut earlier that week, a little boy who supposedly
looked just like Teddy. But like all the other
leads they had had, when it was checked out,
it turned out to be bogus.

"You look tired." Taylor spoke softly as she
poured him a second cup of coffee.

"It's been a rough week."

"Not nearly as rough as next week's going to
be, and the week after." He knew what was
coming, he knew the people involved. The
U.S. Attorney was a tough son of a bitch and
he wanted to win this case. He knew the
whole world was watching, even FDR, and he
wasn't going to let the defense win, no matter
what it cost him. And Armour was tough too,
but in a cleaner, crisper way, he went right for
the gut, and then he destroyed you. And the
kinds of things they were going to drag up and
remind her of, weren't going to be pretty. "Are

you ready for it?" He worried about her, as resilient as she was, she was frail too, and he hated to see her go through that kind of pain. He remembered what it had been like when she told him about André. But she was holding up fairly well, considering the fact that she had gone three months without Teddy. "Whatever happens," he tried to warn her now, "don't let them frighten you . . . don't let them make you feel it's your fault." He knew that was the ghost that haunted her most, and had for years. "You know it isn't." He tried to reassure her.

"I wish Malcolm felt that way too. He still blames me for everything. For bringing Charles back in our lives, and costing us Teddy."

"You didn't want that any more than he did." What a fool the man was, and he didn't like him any better when he swept through the hall a little while later with Bill Palmer. John was talking to one of his men and Malcolm snapped his fingers at him like a dog, which didn't sit well with John Taylor.

"The U.S. Attorney is going to need some help from you, Mr. Taylor," he said. He had very little respect for him. He certainly hadn't been very effective in finding Teddy. "We need some information."

"About Delauney?" Palmer nodded.

"Why don't we go talk somewhere?" the attorney suggested, but when they did, Taylor didn't like what he heard. It was smear campaign stuff, ugly business about the past that had nothing to do with Teddy, and Taylor objected. The attorney wanted him to help dig up facts about Marielle and Charles that he knew would be painful to her.

"What does that have to do with this?"

"It's character stuff for chrissake, man. Don't get prissy on me now. We're talking about winning."

"Winning what? The conviction of an innocent man, or actually nailing the guy who did it? If he's guilty, you don't need this kind of shit, Palmer."

"If you don't get it for me, someone else will."

"Is that what this case is about now? Get him at all costs? And what about her? What are you going to do to her with this?" It had to do with André's death in Geneva and her time in the sanatorium afterward and Taylor knew, as Palmer did, that if Charles was guilty, they didn't need it.

"Mrs. Patterson is not my problem, Taylor. And her own husband wants it. Look, if it's no good to us anyway, we won't use it."

"How nice," Taylor said sarcastically, thinking to himself that he liked Tom Armour's tactics better. He was a lot cleaner. And he couldn't believe that Patterson was willing to sacrifice her just to nail Delauney. But Malcolm was convinced Delauney had kidnapped and killed his son, and he was willing to do anything to get Charles convicted. Maybe in some ways, Taylor told himself as he started making the calls, you couldn't blame him. At least if he got the information himself, he could figure out Palmer's next move and he could warn her what was coming. But what he didn't know was that Malcolm was making calls too, and he was going after the big stuff.

The weekend passed too quickly for her. And on Monday morning, they were back in court, and the trial began in earnest.

11

The following week, the opening statements seemed very dry, compared to their friendlier remarks previously to the jury. But some of the ugly things the two attorneys said were also very effective.

In his opening statement, the U.S. Attorney assured the jury and the courtroom at large that what they were dealing with here was very certainly a kidnapper, maybe even a baby killer, a man who had assaulted women in the past, killed men without batting an eye, a liar, a Communist, and a threat to all Americans. He told them that little Teddy Patterson had been torn from his parents' home in the middle of the night, in the dark, and the people who cared for him had been chloroformed and bound and gagged and might easily have been killed as well, and the child had disappeared without a trace, never to be seen again, and was probably dead, buried somewhere in a ditch, in a field, but for those who loved him, gone forever.

Marielle clutched her chair as she listened to the words, and he seemed to drone on for hours about what an evil man Charles had always been, what a sweet man Teddy would have become, and how we had all been robbed because this one child had died, and for nothing. And if it was true, if he was never to return, then Marielle had to agree with him. But it was still so painful to believe him gone for a lifetime.

Tom Armour's statement to them was only slightly more reassuring. He told them that Charles Delauney was a decent, honest, in some ways deeply troubled man, who had lost his own son nine years before, in fact his unborn daughter too, his entire family, and knowing how great the pain of that had been, he would never have hurt any child, or taken any man's children from him. He had fought honestly in the Great War and in the fight in Spain since then. He was no Communist. He was a man who believed in freedom. Edu-

cated, intelligent, decent, yet heartbroken by
the shattering of his youthful dreams, he was
admittedly misguided in some of his behavior,
or even his words, but this was not a man who
could kidnap anyone's son. And the defense
was going to prove that he hadn't. Further-
more, he reminded everyone, Mr. Delauney
was on trial for kidnapping here, and not for
murder. And if the jurors listened to the evidence carefully, he was sure they would acquit
him. As he spoke to them, Tom Armour walked
slowly before the jury, looking each one in the
eye, speaking directly to them, not in a conde-
scending way, but as equals, as friends, making sure they understood and believed him.
He was masterful at what he did, and it was
fascinating to watch him. He also explained to
them that the U.S. Attorney would be present-
ing his case first, from beginning to end, and
Tom would be cross-examining his witnesses,
of course, but he would not present his case
until the prosecution had completed theirs.
And he reminded them again that it was up to
the prosecution to *prove*, beyond a reasonable
doubt, that Charles Delauney had kidnapped
the Patterson boy, and if the prosecution could
not convince them of that, whether they liked
Charles or not as a man, they had to acquit
him. But Tom assured them that by the time

he finished his case, they would understand that he had been wronged by these charges.

There was a long silence when they were both through, and Judge Morrison instructed the U.S. Attorney to call his first witness, and Marielle was stunned when she heard her name. She had no idea he was intending to call her as his first witness. She raised an eyebrow as she walked past John, and he tried to look reassuring, but he was worried about what Palmer was going to do. He knew what had turned up in the calls he made, and none of it was very damaging. But he had no idea what Palmer and Malcolm had dug up without him.

She took the stand, and carefully smoothed down the plain black dress she had worn. She nervously crossed her legs as she glanced around the courtroom, and then uncrossed them again. And all the while, Bill Palmer strutted around the courtroom and watched her. He watched her as though there were something strange about her, as though he were suspicious of her, and more than once he glanced from her to the defendant, as though there was something he didn't understand about them. It was as though he was trying to convey something unpleasant or unsavory to the jury. And what he was doing was making Marielle very nervous. She glanced at the judge, then at Malcolm, who looked away, and at John, who looked serious as he watched her, and she waited for Palmer's first question.

"Please state your name."

"Marielle Patterson."

"Your full name please."

"Marielle Johnson Patterson. Marielle Anne Johnson Patterson," she smiled, but he did not smile in answer.

"Is there more?"

"No, sir." Two women on the jury smiled, and Marielle felt a little better. But her hands were shaking terribly as she held them in her lap where no one could see them.

"Have you ever had another name, Mrs. Patterson?" And then she knew what he was asking.

"Yes." Why was he doing this? What would it help? She didn't understand.

"Would you please tell us that name?" He boomed out the words as though to frighten her, and she couldn't see Malcolm's eyes.

"Delauney," she said quietly.

"Could you say that a little louder please, so the jurors can hear you."

She flushed bright red and said it louder for all to hear while Charles watched her in sympathy. "Delauney." He felt sorry for her suddenly. Sorrier even than John Taylor, because he suspected what was coming. Palmer was smarter than they had thought. He was going to discredit her early on, so anything she said later would be worth nothing. He wasn't going to take the chance she would question Charles's guilt in public, and weaken his case in front of the jury.

"Are you related to the defendant in any way?"

"I was married to him."

"When was that?"

"In 1926, in Paris. I was eighteen years old."

"And what kind of marriage was it?" He pretended to be friendly to her, he even smiled. But she knew now that he was going to destroy her. "Was it a big wedding? A small one?"

"We eloped."

"I see. . . ." He looked disturbed, as though somehow she had done something wrong, and he was sorry. "And how long were you married?"

"For five years actually. Until 1931."

"And how did the marriage end? In divorce?"

"Yes, that's correct." There was a thin film of perspiration covering her forehead, and she prayed that she wouldn't faint or vomit.

"Would you mind telling us why, Mrs. Delauney . . . sorry, Patterson . . ." He pretended to slip but she knew he had done it on
purpose, just to emphasize her having been
married to Charles, and yes she did mind telling him why, but she knew she had no choice.
"Would you mind telling us the reason for the
divorce?"

"I . . . we . . . we lost our son. And neither of us ever recovered from the shock." She
said it very quietly, and very calmly, and John
Taylor was proud of her and so was Charles.
Both of them felt their hearts torn in half,
watching her, but she didn't know that. "I suppose you could say it destroyed the marriage."

"Is that the only reason why you divorced
Mr. Delauney?"

"Yes. We were very happy before that."

"I see." He nodded again sympathetically
and she began to hate him. "And where were
you when you got the divorce?"

She misunderstood his question, but Taylor
didn't. "In Switzerland."

"Were you there for any particular reason?"
And then she knew. He was trying to discredit
her completely. But he couldn't. If losing
three children hadn't killed her yet, she knew
nothing would. Not this man, not this court,

and not these proceedings. She held her head high and looked directly at him.

"Yes, I was in a hospital there."

"You were ill?" She wasn't going to give him more than she had to. And he knew just what he wanted, and why, but so did she now.

"I had a nervous breakdown when our son died."

"Was there any particular reason for that? Was his death unusually traumatic? A long illness . . . a terrible disease?" Her eyes filled with tears as she listened to him, but she wouldn't give in to them. She brushed them away and spoke through trembling lips as everyone in the courtroom waited.

"He drowned." That was it. That was all she had to say. That was what it said on the death certificate. André Charles Delauney, two years five months, death by drowning.

"And were you responsible for this . . . *accident* . . ." He accentuated the word almost as though she had planned it, and Charles was frantically whispering something to Tom, who shot to his feet immediately, with an objection.

"Objection, Your Honor. Counsel is leading the witness, and implying that the child's death was her fault. That is not for us to decide here. Mrs. Patterson is not on trial here, my client is."

Judge Morrison raised an eyebrow at both men, surprised at Tom Armour's kindness. "Objection sustained. A little less zeal please, Counsel."

"Sorry, Your Honor. I'll rephrase my question. Did you *feel* responsible for the child's death?" But that was worse, because now they would never know if it actually was her fault or not and there was no way to save it.

"Yes, I did."

"And that was why you had the nervous breakdown?"

"I believe so."

"You were in a mental hospital there?"

"Yes." Her voice was growing softer and Charles felt sick, but so did John Taylor. Malcolm Patterson looked straight ahead, with an inscrutable expression.

"You were in effect mentally ill, is that right?"

"I suppose so. I was very upset."

"For a long time?"

"Yes."

"How long were you there?"

"Two years."

"More than two years?"

"A little." But Tom Armour was on his feet again.

"May I remind the court again that Mrs.
Patterson is not on trial here."

"Sustained. Mr. Palmer, where are we going
with this? It's going to take us six months if we
try every witness."

"If you'll bear with me, Your Honor, for just
a moment, I'll show you."

"All right, Counsel, speed it up."

"Yes, sir. Now, Mrs. Patterson." He turned
to Marielle again. "You were in a mental hospital for something more than two years, correct?"

"Correct." Palmer nodded at her, and for
once he looked almost happy with her.

"Did you ever try to commit suicide during
that time?" For a moment, she looked sick
while he asked her.

"Yes, I did."

"More than once?"

"Yes."

"How many times."

She thought for a moment, and unwittingly
glanced at her left wrist, but you could no
longer see the scars thanks to a very artful
plastic surgeon. "Seven or eight times." She
kept her eyes down this time, it was not something she was proud of. And she could have
told him she didn't remember.

"Because you felt responsible for the death of your child?"

"Yes," she almost shouted.

"And Mr. Delauney, where was he during this time?"

"I don't know. I didn't see him for several years."

"Was he as distraught as you?"

Tom Armour objected again, but even he couldn't save her. "You're asking the witness to guess my client's state of mind. Why not save it for later?"

"Sustained. Counsel, be warned please." Morrison was starting to look annoyed and Palmer apologized again, but you could see he wasn't sorry.

"Was Mr. Delauney with you when the child drowned?"

"No. I was alone with him." Charles was skiing.

"And did he blame you for the child's death?"

"Objection!" Tom shouted. "You're guessing at my client's state of mind again."

"Overruled, Mr. Armour," the judge intoned, "this could be important. Objection overruled."

"I repeat, Mrs. Patterson," he got her name

right this time, "did the defendant blame you for the death of his child?"

"I believed so at the time . . . we were both terribly upset."

"Was he very angry?"

"Yes."

"How angry? Did he hit you?" She hesitated in answer to the question. "Did he beat you?"

"I . . ."

"Mrs. Patterson, you're under oath. Please answer the question. Did he beat you?"

"I believe he slapped me."

"Your Honor." William Palmer held out a telegram to the judge, and then handed it to Tom Armour for inspection. "This telegram is from the administrator of the Sainte Vierge Hospital in Geneva, which states that according to their records, Mrs. Marielle Delauney was 'beaten,' they use the word *battue*, which translates to 'beaten,' by her husband on the premises of the hospital at the time of her child's death. She suffered extensive injuries, and a miscarriage later that night." There was a gasp from the courtroom, and then Palmer turned to her again as she grew paler by the moment. "Would you say this account is correct, Mrs. Patterson?"

"Yes." She couldn't say more. She could hardly speak now.

"Did Mr. Delauney beat you on any other occasion?"

"No, he did not."

"And had you ever suffered mental illness before the incident of your son's death?"

"No, I hadn't."

"Would you say you have recovered fully now?"

"Yes, I would."

There was a brief pause as Palmer consulted some notes and then went on, "Mrs. Patterson, do you suffer from severe headaches?"

"Yes, I do."

"And when did they start?"

"At . . . after . . . during my stay in Switzerland."

"But you've had them since then?"

"Yes."

"Recently?"

"Yes."

"How recently?"

She almost smiled but she couldn't. "This weekend."

"How many would you say you've had in the past month?"

"Maybe four or five a week."

"As many as that?" He looked sympathetic.

"And before your son's kidnapping? Just as many?"

"Maybe two or three a week."

"Do you have other recurring problems from the past, Mrs. Patterson? Are you unusually shy or withdrawn, are you afraid of people sometimes? Are you afraid of responsibility . . . of being blamed for things?"

Tom Armour stood up again in an attempt to stop what was becoming a slaughter. "My colleague is not a psychiatrist. If he feels he needs one, he should call an expert witness."

"Your Honor." Bill Palmer approached the bench again, and then waved another piece of paper at Tom Armour. "This telegram is from Mrs. Patterson's doctor at the Clinique Verbeuf in Villars, confirming that she was indeed incarcerated there."

"Objection!" Tom looked furious now, and she wasn't even his client. "Mrs. Patterson wasn't in prison!"

"Sustained. Mr. Palmer, please watch your language."

"Sorry, Your Honor. She was hospitalized there for two years and two months for a nervous breakdown and severe depression. She apparently attempted suicide repeatedly and suffered from severe migraines. That was the official diagnosis. Dr. Verbeuf goes on to add

that he is aware that her migraines have per-
sisted and that at times of great stress like the
present one, her mental health could be considered extremely fragile." Without meaning
to, the good doctor had killed her. And no
matter what she said now, they would think
her disturbed, and an unreliable witness. But
Palmer wasn't through yet.

After the telegram from Dr. Verbeuf was admitted as Exhibit B, he went on with his questions. "Have you had an affair with the defendant since your divorce?"

"No, I have not."

"Have you seen him in the past several
months, or rather before your son was kidnapped?"

"Yes, I ran into him in church on the anniversary of our son's death. And the following
day in the park."

"Was your son with you on either occasion?"

"Yes, the second one."

"And what was Mr. Delauney's reaction?
Was he pleased to meet him?"

"No." She lowered her eyes so she didn't
have to look at him. "He was upset."

"Would you say he was angry?"

She hesitated and then nodded. "Yes."

"Did he threaten you in any way?"

"Yes, but I don't know if he really meant it."

"And when was your son kidnapped, Mrs. Patterson?" If nothing else, he was making her out to be extremely stupid.

"The next day."

"Do you believe that there's a connection between Mr. Delauney's threats, and your son's disappearance?"

"I don't know."

And then he switched tacks again. "Have you kissed Mr. Delauney since your divorce from him, Mrs. Patterson?" She hesitated for a moment, and then nodded. "Please answer my question."

"Yes."

"And when was that?"

"When I saw him in church. I hadn't seen him in almost seven years and he kissed me."

"Was it just a peck on the cheek, or a kiss on the lips, like in the movies?" The audience tittered but Marielle didn't even smile. And John Taylor knew that Palmer had been talking to their driver, with his asinine tales about her "boyfriend."

"It was a kiss on the lips."

"And have you visited him in jail?"

"Yes. Once."

"Mrs. Patterson, are you still in love with

Mr. Delauney?" From then on, anything she said about him would be useless.

She hesitated again, and then she shook her head. "I don't believe so."

"Do you believe he kidnapped your child?"

"I don't know. Perhaps. I'm not sure."

"And do you feel responsible for that kidnapping in any way?"

"I'm not sure . . ." Her voice cracked as she said the words, and everyone in the courtroom was reminded of what the Swiss doctor had said, that under stress her mental health could be extremely fragile. Palmer had done exactly what he wanted to do with her. He had discredited her completely. She sounded mixed up and confused, unsure about Delauney's guilt, or her own, a woman who had tried to commit suicide several times, suffered from migraines and was probably responsible for her first child drowning. And if the defense wanted to use her now, she wouldn't do them any good, and Palmer knew it. It was exactly what he had set out to do, but he had wiped the floor with her in the process and John Taylor knew exactly who had helped him. It was Malcolm. And Taylor himself felt guilty for every call he'd made. But his had all been harmless.

"Thank you, Mrs. Patterson," Bill Palmer

said coolly, and then turned to Tom Armour. "Your witness."

"The defense would like to call Mrs. Patterson at a later time, Your Honor." He wanted to give everyone time to cool down, especially Marielle, who looked as though she'd died as she walked off the stand, and the judge called a recess until after lunch at two o'clock that afternoon. But as she tried to leave the courtroom with Malcolm and the FBI surrounding her, she was mobbed by the press at the door to the courtroom. Charles had tried to catch her eye as she left but she was too sick to even look at him, and the press physically tried to pull at her clothes and shout questions at her as she fled the courthouse.

"Tell us about the hospital . . . the suicides . . . your little boy. . . . Tell us everything . . . come on Marielle, give us a break!" Their voices were still ringing in her ears as they drove uptown, and John Taylor looked stonily out the window. Only Malcolm dared speak to her in a whisper, and she was startled by what he said.

"That was disgusting." She looked at him, not sure what he meant, certain he meant the way Palmer had treated her, but she could see from the look on his face that he meant what he'd heard about her. He said not another word, and tears filled her eyes as they rode home. Once in the library, alone with him, she asked him what he meant, but he could only look at her with disdain now.

"Marielle, how could you?"

"How could I what? Tell him the truth? What choice did I have? He knew it all anyway. You heard the letters from the two doctors."

"My God . . . the suicides . . . the migraines . . . two years in a mental hospital . . ."

"I told you all that in December." And she had, right after Teddy was kidnapped. In fact, the next morning.

"It didn't sound quite like that then." He looked genuinely aghast, and suddenly she was deeply embarrassed. She stared at the man she thought she knew, and ran upstairs to her own room, and locked the door. But a few moments later, she saw a slip of paper slide under the door. All it said was "Call your doctor." She thought it was someone being wicked at first, and then she recognized John Taylor's handwriting, and she wondered why he wanted her to call her doctor. And then she knew. Somewhere deep inside of her, she knew. She ran to her address book, picked up the phone, and asked the operator to call the number. It was nine o'clock in Villars, but she knew that he was there round the clock because he lived there. And he was in, of course, and startled to hear from her.

"What is going on there?"

She told him about the kidnapping, but assumed he knew, and he told her he had already answered many questions. She didn't tell him he'd ruined her with his telegram, she knew how upset he'd be to have his words misused. At one time in her life, the man had saved her.

"Are you all right?" he asked, with deep concern for her.

"I think so."

"Les migraines?"

"Better sometimes. Not right now. It's difficult with Teddy gone . . . and Malcolm . . . my husband . . . I had to tell him about Charles, and André . . . and the *clinique*. He never wanted me to tell him anything before we were married."

"But he knew." Docteur Verbeuf sounded surprised that she didn't know that. "He called me before you were married in . . . oh . . . when was it? . . . 1932? Yes, that was it. It was the same year you left here. You left in February, and he must have called in Octo-

ber." They were married three months after
that, in January, on New Year's Day.

"He called you?" She was confused. "But
why?"

"He wanted to know if there was anything
he could do for you . . . for the migraines
. . . to make your life a little happier . . . I
told him you should have lots of children." But
he was sad for her now that tragedy had found
her again. She was such a nice girl, and she
hadn't been very lucky. "Is there any news of
the child?"

"Not yet."

"Let me know."

"I will." She wondered if he even knew
what purpose his telegram had served, and as
she hung up, she wondered at Malcolm's motive. He had known for all these years, and
yet, when she'd told him he'd been shocked,
and he had even let Bill Palmer use the information.

But there was no time to ask him anything
as they sped back to the courthouse before
two. And she said nothing to John all that afternoon. She was lost deep in her own
thoughts and she had too many questions.

The U.S. Attorney put Patrick Reilly on the
stand that afternoon, and he described what
he'd seen at Saint Patrick's, and the look on

Delauney's face in the park the following afternoon. He said he'd been furious and Patrick said he'd seen Charles grab her and try to shake her.

And it seemed hours to her until she could confront Malcolm. They rode home in silence again that afternoon, and at last they were alone, and she found him in his dressing room. He was dressing for a quiet dinner at his club. He said he needed to get out and clear his head for an evening.

"You lied to me."

"About what?" He turned to her with obvious disinterest.

"You let me tell you the whole story after Teddy disappeared. And you knew. You knew everything . . . about André . . . about Charles . . . about the clinic. Why didn't you tell me?"

"Did you really think I would marry you without knowing where you came from?" He looked at her with derision. She had made a fool of herself on the stand that day, as far as he was concerned, and a fool of him . . . kissing Charles Delauney in church. It was disgusting.

"You lied to me."

"And you endangered my son. You brought that bastard into our life, and because of you, he took him." It looked as if he didn't care what they said about her fragile state of mind, as far as he was concerned, she had cost him everything he cared for. "And it's none of your business what I knew about you. That's my affair."

"How could you tell Bill Palmer?"

"Because if he didn't discredit you, you might support that fool that you were married to . . . that son of a bitch . . . that killer . . . but you, with your bleeding heart, you're still not sure he's guilty."

"So you did that to me? So I couldn't help him?" She didn't understand him anymore, and wondered if she had ever really known him.

"If he goes to the chair for Teddy's death, it'll be too good for him."

"Is that what all this is? A game of revenge between the two of you? He takes Teddy and you kill him? What's wrong with all of you?" She suddenly felt sick looking at him.

"Get out of my room, Marielle. I have nothing to say to you tonight."

She stared at him in disbelief. He had calculatingly ruined her, in order to destroy Charles. "I don't know who you are anymore."

"It's no longer important."

"What are you saying to me?" She was

shrieking at him, but it had been a hideous day and she could no longer stand it.

"I think you understand me."

"It's over, isn't it?" If it ever had existed in the first place. What had they ever had in common, except Teddy?

"It ended the day Delauney took my son out of here. Now you can go back to him when it's over, and you can both cry over what you've done. I'll tell you one thing. I'll never forgive you." And she knew he meant it.

"Do you want me to leave now, Malcolm?" She was ready to. She would have gone to a hotel that night if he had wanted.

"Are you so anxious for more scandal? You could at least have the decency to wait until the spotlight is off us after the trial."

She nodded, and a moment later, she went back to her own room. There was nothing left that could surprise her now. She was married to a stranger, a man who hated her for losing their son. Another one. Life had been cruel to her. And whatever happened next, whether they found Teddy or not, she knew the marriage was over.

12

The next morning, Marielle took breakfast in her room, and all she had was a cup of tea and piece of toast, as she glanced at the paper. It was all there, the horror of yesterday. The humiliation and the destruction she had suffered at the hands of William Palmer. The first article she read said that she had been a mental patient for years and she had had to be carried off the stand, screaming. It was so unfair what they were doing to her, and she still couldn't bring herself to believe that Malcolm had helped them do it. And then she turned to the last page, and saw the article written by Bea Ritter. She wasn't going to read it at first, but as her eyes glanced down the page, she stopped and began again, and tears filled her eyes as she read it.

"Aristocratic, elegant, dignified, Marielle Patterson took the stand yesterday, and never lost her dignity or her composure as the prosecution ravaged her for several hours and attempted to discredit her completely. Attempted but did not succeed, to the admiration of all who saw her. She endured the pain of recounting the circumstances of the deaths of two previous children in a tragic accident nearly ten years ago, which left everyone in the courtroom breathless. And she went on to explain her subsequent divorce from Charles Delauney. Her experience in a sanatorium in Switzerland was heard not with compassion or sympathy but instead with ridicule, and used to discredit her as a witness. . . ." The article went on for half a page, and concluded with the words, "One thing is certain after seeing the victim's mother on the stand, Marielle Patterson is through and through a lady. She left the courtroom with her head held high, and as every mother knew, her heart must have been breaking." It was followed then by Bea Ritter's byline.

Marielle wiped her eyes with her napkin then, and stood up to put her hat on. Bea Ritter's words had been kind, but it didn't change the fact that her own husband and the U.S. Attorney had set out to damage her so she could not help Charles Delauney. She'd had no intention of helping him anyway. But her uncertainty about his guilt clearly had them worried.

John Taylor and the other men were already waiting for her in the car when she got downstairs. She was wearing yet another black hat and black dress and a dark beaver coat as she climbed into the Pierce-Arrow. Nothing was said in the car on the way downtown. She spoke not a word to Malcolm or John, and Malcolm spent the entire trip staring out the window. Even John wasn't able to say much to her. He touched her hand briefly once as they sat down, but he didn't dare let his feelings show here. All he wanted was to offer her support, but it was difficult to do it in the courtroom.

Judge Morrison reminded everyone again that they were expected to behave with decorum. And with a pointed glance at the press, he reminded them that it was irresponsible to report things which did not actually happen. It had annoyed him to read the account of Marielle allegedly being carried from his courtroom.

And after that, the slaughter of the day be-

fore continued. Bill Palmer had apparently decided that it was not enough to have Marielle's
testimony but he would have others also take
the stand to help discredit her. Then, with no
sympathy for the child's mother, only Malcolm's voice would be heard, and Malcolm
never doubted Delauney's guilt for an instant.

Patrick Reilly, the driver, took the stand
again, and Edith, and even Miss Griffin. And
together they painted a portrait, with Bill
Palmer's help, of a nervous, hysterical unstable
woman, who was unable to run her own home,
take care of her child, or be of any real use to
her husband.

"Would you say that Mrs. Patterson is a responsible person?" Bill Palmer asked the governess, as Tom Armour jumped to his feet for
what seemed to be the thousandth time and
objected.

"This woman is *not* an expert witness. And
Mrs. Patterson's competence is *not* on trial
here. Call a psychiatrist if you want that kind
of testimony, Counsel, not a maid for chrissake!"

"I'll cite you for contempt if you don't watch
your language, Mr. Armour!" the judge roared.

"Sorry."

"Overruled." And the massacre went on,
with no one to support her. John Taylor and

Charles Delauney knew it wasn't true, but there was nothing they could do to put in a kind word, they were helpless. And even her husband had turned against her.

"Would you say she was a good mother?" William Palmer finally asked Miss Griffin, and the little woman hesitated for only a moment. But it was long enough to hurt Marielle deeply.

"Not really." Everyone gasped, and for a moment Marielle almost fainted. She seemed to pitch forward in her chair, and John Taylor pushed her swiftly back with a firm hand before the press could see it.

"Would you care to tell us why not?"

"She's too sickly to be of any use to anyone, and much too nervous. Children need stability around them, people who are strong. Like Mr. Patterson." She seemed proud of herself, and Marielle wondered again what she had done to make these people hate her.

"Your Honor." Thomas Armour stood up again, with a weary look. "This is not a custody trial. Mrs. Patterson's abilities as a mother are not the issue here. This is a kidnapping case, and I've yet to hear anyone so much as mention my client. In fact, these people don't even know him." They barely even knew Marielle, but Palmer had wanted to be sure that Marielle was totally ruined before he moved on. He wanted her discredited without a single doubt, so that if she was called by the defense later on, she would be useless. Who would listen to a woman who had been in a mental institution for years and was not even considered a good mother by her own staff? Palmer had done his job to perfection. And that afternoon, he completed the picture.

Malcolm Patterson took the stand immediately after lunch, for the prosecution.

"Were you aware of your wife's history, Mr. Patterson?"

"No." Malcolm's cold blue eyes looked straight ahead at William Palmer, and not for an instant did he allow Marielle into his field of vision.

"You had no idea that she had been in a mental hospital, is that correct?"

"Yes, it is, or I would never have married her." Marielle knew now that it was a lie. The only thing she didn't know was why Malcolm would want to destroy her. She sat very straight and tall, looking at a spot above him, somewhere on the wall, and thinking of happier moments . . . with little Teddy. She felt totally helpless now to defend herself, or expose Malcolm's deceit. And that was his intention.

"Did you know she had been married to Charles Delauney?"

"No. I did not. She never told me. I knew there had been some brief youthful interlude. I'd heard that she had a romance in Paris as a girl, but nothing more than that. She concealed the marriage from me." William Palmer nodded, sad for him that he had been so badly duped by this woman.

"Do you know anything about Mr. Delauney, sir?"

"Only his reputation. His father has kept him out of the country for many years.

"Objection!" Tom was on his feet again. "We would have to put Mr. Delauney Senior on the stand to tell us that, there is no evidence whatsoever that my client's family ever wanted him out of the country. In fact, quite the contrary. They wanted him to come home."

"Sustained. Hearsay. You may continue, Mr. Palmer."

"Have you ever seen Mr. Delauney?"

"Not until this trial."

"Has he ever called you, threatened you, harassed you, or any member of your immediate family?"

"Objection!"

"Overruled!"

Malcolm went on. "He threatened my wife

and son. He told her he would kidnap him if she didn't go back to him."

"And when was that?"

Malcolm bowed his head for a moment before he answered and then he looked full into the courtroom. "The day before my son was taken."

"Have you ever seen your son since that day?"

Malcolm shook his head, unable to speak.

"Would you speak up for the record, please, sir." He spoke with all the gentleness he should have used on Marielle and hadn't.

"I'm sorry . . . no . . . I have not. . . ."

"And how long ago was that?"

"Almost three months ago, to the day. My little boy was taken from us on December eleventh . . . shortly after his fourth birthday."

"Have there been any calls, or requests for ransom?"

"Only one, and it was a prank. The money was never collected." The implication was obvious. Delauney hadn't asked for ransom because what he wanted was revenge, and in any case, he certainly didn't need the money.

"Do you believe that your son is still alive?"

He shook his head again, but forced himself to speak this time. "No, I do not. I think if he were, he would have been returned to us by now. The FBI has searched for him across every state. If he were still alive, they would have found him."

"Do you believe that Mr. Delauney is the kidnapper?"

"I believe he hired people to take him, and probably kill him."

"What convinced you of that?"

"They found Teddy's . . . my boy's pajamas in his home . . . and a teddy bear the boy loved . . . he was wearing those same pajamas when he was taken." In spite of himself, he began to cry, and you could feel all the sympathy in the courtroom rush to him. The prosecutor waited politely while he regained his composure. And in her seat, Brigitte dabbed at her eyes with a lace hankie.

"Do you believe that your wife is still in love with Charles Delauney?" He had wanted to say "involved," but his investigators had been able to turn up absolutely nothing to support the fact that she was sleeping with him, and he decided to play it safe and not use anything that could be disproven.

"Yes, I do. I understand from my driver that two days before the kidnapping, they met in a church and she kissed him repeatedly. I suppose she's always been in love with him, during the entire time she was married to me. Perhaps that's why she's been so ill." They made her sound like an invalid, instead of a young woman with a troubled life, who suffered from headaches, a woman who had suffered tragedy and still managed to survive it.

"Do you think it's your wife's fault that your son was kidnapped?" He asked the question as though he expected a verdict, and Malcolm waited just long enough to answer so that everyone thought he was giving one.

"I think it is her fault that Charles Delauney kidnapped him. It is her fault that he holds her responsible for his own son's death, and wanted revenge with mine. It is her fault for bringing him into our lives." He looked woefully into the courtroom, and at her, but she did not look at him.

"Mr. Patterson, although you feel that to some degree Mrs. Patterson is responsible for . . . this tragedy, could you ever imagine yourself taking revenge on her in any way? Punishing her, or hurting someone she loved? Hurting her?" He already had, Marielle knew too well. With everything he had done in the past few days, and the way he'd behaved since Teddy was taken, and what he had just said on the stand. It was bad enough to lose her child, but then to be attacked by her husband could have destroyed her as well, but for the moment she was still struggling not to let it. "Could you ever see yourself taking revenge on her, or anyone?" William Palmer repeated, and Malcolm said a single word, as he sat there sounding like God, as his voice rang out in the courtroom.

"Never."

"Thank you, Mr. Patterson." He turned to Tom. "Mr. Armour, your witness."

Tom stood up and said not a word for an interminable moment, and then slowly he began to walk around the courtroom. He walked in front of the jury, and smiled at some of them, almost as though to relax them. And then, finally, he went to stand in front of Malcolm, but he was no longer smiling.

"Good afternoon, Mr. Patterson."

"Good afternoon, Mr. Armour." Malcolm looked unusually solemn, but Tom Armour seemed extremely relaxed, as the world watched him. It was an intriguing tactic.

"Would you say . . ." He seemed to draw the words out. "That your marriage to Mrs. Patterson has been a happy one?"

"I'd say so, yes."

"In spite of her illness . . . her unreliability . . . her headaches?"

For a moment, Malcolm wasn't quite sure

what to say, but he regained his energy
quickly. "They certainly didn't make it easy,
but I think I've been happy."

"Very happy?"

"Very happy." Malcolm looked annoyed, he
couldn't see where the defense attorney was
going.

"Have you been married before?"

Malcolm growled and stuck out his chin almost visibly. "Yes. Twice. It's well known."

"Is Mrs. Patterson aware of that?"

"Of course."

"Would you say it's hindered your current
marriage in any way?"

"Of course not."

"Would it have bothered you, had you
known that Mrs. Patterson was previously
married?"

This time he hesitated. "Probably not. But I
would have preferred it if she had been honest
with me."

"Of course." Tom readily agreed with him.
"Mr. Patterson, have you ever had any other
children?"

"No. Theodore is . . . was . . . my only
child."

"You say . . . was . . . you no longer believe him to be alive?" Tom looked surprised,
as though that seemed unlikely.

"No . . . I no longer believe him to be alive. I think Mr. Delauney killed him." He said it to inflame Tom, but it didn't.

"I understand that. But if he is dead . . . and all of us here certainly hope that's not the case . . . but if he is . . . how would you describe that event in your life?"

"Excuse me . . . I don't understand."

Tom Armour moved closer to him and looked him straight in the eye. "If your son is dead, Mr. Patterson, how will you feel? What will it do to your life?" The tone of Tom's voice was relentless.

But without hesitation, Malcolm looked back at Tom and answered, "It will finish me . . . my life will never be the same again."

"Mr. Patterson, would you say it would destroy you?"

Malcolm hung his head, and nodded before he looked at Tom again. "Of course . . . he's my only son. . . ."

Tom nodded sympathetically and then moved in a little closer. "It would destroy you, wouldn't it . . . then why are you so shocked that Mrs. Patterson was almost destroyed by the death of her previous children? Would you expect that to be any different?"

"No, I . . ." He looked uncomfortable for a moment and John Taylor tightened his lips, but Marielle was forcing herself not to listen. "I imagine that must have been very difficult."

"She was twenty-one at the time . . . and five months pregnant . . . her little boy dies . . . her father dies a few months later . . . her own mother commits suicide six months after that . . . her husband has turned on her, distraught with his own pain over the child's death. What would you do, Mr. Patterson? How would you feel? How well would you hold up?"

"I . . . I . . ." He couldn't answer, and the jury looked interested in what Tom was saying.

"Is Mrs. Patterson in the courtroom today?"

"Yes . . . of course. . . ."

"Would you point her out to me?"

"Your Honor," William Palmer got to his feet, ready to object to the question, "is this charade necessary?"

"Be patient, Counsellor. Mr. Armour, proceed, but not too much nonsense please, we have a great deal of testimony to hear, and our friends on the jury don't want to stay at a hotel at the taxpayers' expense forever." There was a titter of laughter in the courtroom and Tom Armour smiled. Compared to what Marielle had seen of him before, he suddenly looked surprisingly easygoing. But that appearance was deceptive. Inside him was a coil of incredibly well controlled tension.

"Mr. Patterson, will you please point out your wife to us." Malcolm did so. "She is here today, and yesterday certainly could not have been easy for her, talking about the death of her children, and the kidnapping of your son, or her time in the clinic in Switzerland . . . or her marriage to Mr. Delauney. . . . But she's here. She looks sane to me and in good control of herself." Marielle looked calm as she sat beside John Taylor. Malcolm was furious but he was trying hard to conceal it. "Would you agree with me, sir? She looks quite normal to me, and probably to everyone else here. Would you say she's holding up, in spite of everything?"

"I suppose so," he conceded halfheartedly.

"Would you say her previous problems are a thing of the past?"

"I don't know," he snapped. "I'm not a doctor."

"How long have you been married?"

"More than six years."

"Has she ever been in a hospital, for mental problems, during that time?"

"No, she hasn't."

"Would you say that she has ever done anything to endanger your child?"

"Yes." He almost shouted at Tom, and this time the defense attorney looked startled, and he wanted to clear it up quickly now, before he damaged her further. But Malcolm's answer had surprised him.

"What did she do that endangered your child?"

"She consorted with Charles Delauney. She even took him to the park and exposed him to that man! And then he took Teddy!" He was shouting and waving a hand, and Tom was relieved.

"Mrs. Patterson says the meeting was unplanned, that she ran into Mr. Delauney by accident."

"I don't believe her."

"Has she ever lied to you before?"

"Yes, about her mental history and her marriage to Delauney." Tom knew that was a lie but chose not to challenge him at this moment.

"If that's true, Mr. Patterson, has she lied to you at any other time?"

"I don't know."

"All right, other than that meeting in the park the day before Teddy was kidnapped, has she ever done anything to endanger the child? Taken him somewhere dangerous . . . left him somewhere unattended . . . even alone in the bathtub?"

"I don't know."

"Wouldn't you remember it if she endangered your child?"

"Of course!" Malcolm was slowly burying himself and John Taylor loved it.

"Do you believe your wife was faithful to you, sir?"

"I don't know."

"Did you ever have reason to suspect her of infidelity?"

"Not really." He shrugged, almost as though he didn't care.

"You travel a great deal, don't you, sir?"

"I have to. For business."

"Of course. And what does Mrs. Patterson do when you travel?"

"She stays at home." He blazed. "With a headache." A few people in the courtroom laughed, but the jury looked serious. They were trying to follow everything he was saying.

"Does she ever travel with you, Mr. Patterson?"

"Rarely."

"And why is that? Did you prefer not to have her along?"

"No. She preferred to stay at home with our son."

"I see." The bad-mother portrait was slowly

crumbling at Tom's hands and in spite of the fact that as an FBI agent he was part of the prosecution, John Taylor was relieved, for her sake. "And you, sir, do you travel alone?"

"Of course."

"You take no one with you?"

"Of course not." He looked highly irritated at the impertinence.

"Not even a secretary?"

"Of course I take a secretary. I can't do my work alone."

"I see. Do you take the same one, or different ones?"

"Sometimes I take both of my secretaries."

"And if you only take one, is there a preference?"

"I frequently take Miss Sanders. She has been with me for many years." Something about the way he said it suggested that she was a hundred years old, but Tom Armour had done his homework and he knew better.

"How long has she been with you, sir?"

"For six and a half years."

"And are you involved with her, Mr. Patterson?"

"Of course not!" he roared. "I never get involved with my secretaries!"

"And who was your last secretary before

Miss Sanders?" He was done for and he knew it.

"My wife."

"Mrs. Patterson was your secretary?" Tom Armour's eyes grew wide in surprise, as though he hadn't known, and the judge looked amused by the question.

"Only for a few months until we were married."

"Is that how you met her?"

"I suppose so, although I vaguely knew her father."

"Do you know Miss Sanders's father too, Mr. Patterson?"

"Hardly." He looked superciliously at Tom Armour. "He's a baker in Frankfurt."

"I see. And where does Miss Sanders live?"

"I have no idea." But even Marielle was intrigued now.

"You've never been to her home?"

"Perhaps a few times . . . for meetings . . ."

"And you can't remember where she lives?"

"All right, all right. I remember. On Fifty-fourth and Park."

"That sounds like a very nice neighborhood. Is it a nice apartment?"

"Very pleasant."

"Is it large?"

"It's big enough."

"Is it eight rooms, with a dining room, an office for you, two bedrooms, two dressing rooms, two baths, a very large living room, and a terrace?"

"Probably. I don't know." But his face was bright red now, to Marielle's amazement.

"Do you pay the rent for Miss Sanders's apartment, Mr. Patterson?" Marielle was staring at him in disbelief. Fool that she was she had never suspected. Brigitte had always been so pleasant to her, and so kind, and so generous with Teddy. And now, finally, Marielle understood it, and deep inside she felt angry. Brigitte and Malcolm had both taken her for a fool, and indeed she had been.

"I do not pay for Miss Sanders's apartment," Malcolm said sternly.

"How much salary does Miss Sanders make?"

"Forty dollars a week."

"That's a reasonable wage. But not very adequate to pay for an apartment that costs six hundred dollars a month. How do you suppose she pays the rent, Mr. Patterson?"

"That's none of my affair."

"You mentioned that her father is a baker."

"Your Honor." William Palmer stood up, feigning boredom. "Where is all this going?"

"This is all going," Tom Armour said, no longer amused, "to show that despite Mr. Patterson's poor memory, his bank statements, his checks, and his records show that he pays for that apartment." Tom's investigators had done well for him.

"And even if he does, so what?"

"Seamus O'Flannerty, the doorman there, will take the stand to tell us that Mr. Patterson goes there after the office every evening, and frequently spends the night there. When they travel, they frequently share the same bedroom. Miss Sanders wears a mink coat to the office, and this Christmas, two weeks after the kidnapping of his son, he gave Brigitte Sanders a diamond necklace from Cartier. It is clear to me, Your Honor, that Mr. Patterson has been lying."

"Objection overruled, Mr. Palmer," the judge said gently, all too aware of who Malcolm was. "I'd like to remind you again, Mr. Patterson, that you are under oath. Perhaps Mr. Armour would like to rephrase the question."

"Certainly, Your Honor." Tom was happy to oblige him. "Mr. Patterson, allow me to ask you again, are you, or are you not, having an affair with Brigitte Sanders?" For a moment, there seemed to be no sound in the courtroom.

But before he could answer, the prosecutor was on his feet again. "That's immaterial to this case, Your Honor."

"I don't think so," Tom Armour stated coolly. "The prosecution has totally discredited Mrs. Patterson as a witness, and claimed that she was having an affair with my client, which is not the case. My client has been out of the country for the past eighteen years until just before the kidnapping. But the presumption is that as a rejected lover, or wounded ex-husband, Mr. Delauney would seek revenge. If, indeed, Mr. Patterson is having a long-standing affair with Miss Sanders, it is equally possible that she might seek revenge."

"Revenge for a diamond necklace?" Palmer asked, and this time the whole courtroom roared with laughter.

"Answer the question, Mr. Patterson," the judge said regretfully. "Are you having an affair with Miss Sanders?"

"Perhaps I am," he said softly.

"Could you please speak a little louder," Tom asked politely.

"Yes, yes . . . I am . . . but she did not kidnap my son." Brigitte was looking pale in her seat, and Marielle was staring at her.

"How do you know that?" Tom Armour asked Malcolm.

"She wouldn't do such a thing." He looked outraged.

"Neither would my client. Do you intend to marry Miss Sanders, sir?"

"Of course not."

Tom raised an eyebrow. "Do you give all your secretaries mink coats and diamond necklaces?"

"Certainly not."

"Does she wish to marry you?"

"I have no idea. That has never been in question."

"Thank you, Mr. Patterson. You may step down now." But Bill Palmer wanted to ask him another question.

"Mr. Patterson, has Miss Sanders ever threatened you, or threatened to harm your son, or take him away from you?"

"Certainly not." He looked horrified. "She's a very polite, kind young woman." With fabulous legs, and some skills Marielle had never dreamt of.

"Thank you. No further questions."

Malcolm went back to his seat looking florid. And a moment later, Brigitte left the courtroom. She was mobbed by the press the minute she left, and her dress was torn when she finally climbed into a taxi, crying.

After that, the prosecution called a series of

forensic experts to establish the fact that the bear and the pajamas were in fact Teddy's. And the last witness of the day was a man who said he had gone to school with Charles Delauney, and Charles had threatened him once when they were fourteen. The witness, a nervous young lawyer from Boston, who had volunteered to testify in order to be helpful, said that he'd always thought Charles was a little crazy. Tom Armour objected, and it was sustained, and the jury was beginning to look bored. It had been a long day, and then finally, it was over, and everyone was relieved to leave the courtroom. John and Marielle exchanged a long glance on the way out, and Malcolm said not a word on the drive home. He went straight to the library when they got home, closed the door, and made several phone calls. And without a word to Marielle, he slammed out the front door half an hour later, as John Taylor and a handful of FBI men pretended not to watch him. They all knew what had happened that day in the courtroom.

John went to see her after Malcolm had left, and they sat and talked quietly. "Were you surprised?" he asked her gently, referring to Brigitte.

Marielle felt like a balloon the air had been

let out of. It had been another exhausting afternoon, and in many ways a sad one.

"Yes, I was. I suppose I'm incredibly stupid, but I've always liked her. She's a nice girl, and she's always been so sweet to Teddy." She looked thoughtful as she spoke, thinking back to all the little gifts, the things she had made, the candy, the toys, the sweaters . . . somehow, Marielle felt as though she had been a complete fool. She wondered how long it had been going on. Probably since the beginning, she realized, and she looked back over the past six and a half years, and that made her feel even more foolish. How stupid she had been, and how deceitful they were.

"She probably tried to make friends with Teddy to impress your husband."

"Maybe," Marielle said sadly. "I suppose it doesn't really matter." He had to have been going somewhere to address his needs, they hadn't slept with each other in years, and she knew that he was a very physical person. But she had just never thought of Brigitte. It had crossed her mind once, on a day when the young German girl was looking particularly pretty, and at first she had been a little jealous when they had started traveling together, but she had really never given it a thought after that. And now she knew that he went to her

apartment every day after work, spent the
night there frequently, and even paid for the
apartment. He was more married to Brigitte
than he was to her, or so it seemed to Marielle.
She had no tie to him at all anymore. No allegiance, no fondness, no loyalty, no fidelity
. . . not even Teddy.

John watched her quietly as she thought it
out, and he thought of his own wife, and what
might happen when the trial was over. He
knew better than anyone that they couldn't go
on like this forever. But despite the feelings
they shared, he and Marielle had shied away
from talking about the future. There was too
much happening in their lives now to think of
anything except the trial, and finding Teddy.

"I almost feel sorry for Malcolm," she said
later as she walked John to the front door. He
hated leaving her at night, and he had come to
cherish their hours together. "It must have
been difficult for him to be exposed." He had
looked furious on the stand, and Brigitte had
looked panicked.

"Not as difficult as it was for you yesterday."
How could she feel sympathy for him? She
was an amazing girl. "He lied through most of
it." But they'd caught him in the end. What he
hadn't admitted was that he had always known
about Charles, and her time in the clinic. But

the jury didn't know that. All they knew was that he was a cheat, and perhaps a liar. "He deserves what he got. He deserves worse for what he did to you. They didn't have to do that."

"Well they did. They don't have to worry that I'll be sympathetic to Charles and weaken the prosecution's case. My testimony is meaningless now." She wished she didn't have to go to court at all. It was all so painful.

"Are you still sympathetic to him, Marielle?"

She wasn't sure. She hadn't been in months. "I don't know. I just don't know what I think . . . all the evidence is there, and yet I thought I knew him better than that, even after all these years. No matter what he said, I didn't believe him when he said those things in the park . . . and then Teddy was gone . . . I don't know what to think." She couldn't bear thinking of it anymore . . . the empty bed that had still been warm when she touched it. It had been three months now since she'd seen him, three months since she'd held her little boy . . . the little boy they said she was too weak and unstable to take care of.

"If he were innocent . . . if we found Teddy again," and he still hoped they would, but he doubted it now. It had been too long. It was beginning to seem too much like the Lindberghs. "Would you go back to Charles?" He had wanted to ask her that for days. He wanted to know, because in his heart of hearts, he knew she still loved him.

"I don't know," she said honestly. "I don't think so. I couldn't. There's too much pain between us. Think of what we would feel when we looked at each other every morning. If he's innocent, and Teddy comes home again . . . Charles will never forgive me for this . . ." She looked up at him, and John was annoyed.

"Everything that goes wrong in the world is not your fault. You didn't make those threats in the park, he did. He's the damn fool who either did it, or put himself in a hell of a spot for shooting his mouth off. Last time I looked, all you did was go to the park with your boy. This is *not* your fault, for God's sake, just like Teddy's kidnapping isn't . . . and the other boy's drowning wasn't . . . stop believing all the shit these jerks give you." She smiled at him. She loved him for believing in her, and protecting her, and caring about her, and trying to find Teddy. But she wondered what else they would have when this was over. Probably very little. They would be friends, but they had met at a time that, for her, would be forever painful. But he was worried about something else now, since listening to the last few days' testimony in court. He knew what Patterson had up his sleeve now. If they found the boy, he was beginning to suspect that Patterson was going to sue her for custody and divorce, and accuse her of being an unfit mother. That's what the mental instability was all about, and the testimony by governesses and maids. John Taylor already saw where Malcolm was leading, but he didn't want to scare her. And maybe it would never happen. Maybe they would never find Teddy.

"Take care of yourself," he whispered as he hurried down the front steps a little while later, wishing he could kiss her. And as Marielle went back to her room, she correctly assumed that Malcolm was with Brigitte.

He didn't bother to come home that night, or to call. The pretense was over. She wondered where they were staying now, to avoid the reporters who were hot on their trail for a story. She wondered too how often his calls to her had come from Brigitte's apartment. It was amazing how little she had known about her husband. She had thought him so respectable, so kind, so gentle with her, and instead he had been building a case against her for years, he had always known about the hospital and Charles, and he had cheated on her for years with Brigitte. It was not a pretty picture. She was still thinking about it when the phone rang as she lay in the dark at ten o'clock. She almost didn't answer it, thinking it would be him. But there was always the possibility it would be a call about Teddy. She knew the police still in the house would pick it up, but nevertheless she wanted to listen. She was startled to hear Bea Ritter asking the policeman to put the call through to Marielle and he wouldn't.

"It's all right, Jack. I have it. Hello?"

"Mrs. Patterson?"

"Yes."

"This is Bea Ritter." Even her voice sounded nervous and energetic. She was an excited little woman full of life and the pursuit of a great story. But Marielle had wanted to thank her anyway, for the surprisingly decent article about Marielle's performance in the courtroom. She thanked her, and the little redhead sounded embarrassed. "They really did a job on you. It made me sick to watch it."

"At least I didn't get carried out of the court the way the others said I did."

"They're a bunch of jerks. If it doesn't happen the way they want it, they make it up, I don't do that." And then there was a pause. She had half expected not to get through to her, and now they were suddenly talking like old friends, but she was scared and this was important. "I'm sorry to call so late . . . I wasn't sure how to get through to you . . . Mrs. Patterson, can I meet you for a little while?"

"Why?"

"I have to talk to you. I can't tell you over the phone. But I really have to."

"Does it have to do with my son?" Was there a tip? . . . a chance . . . a hope . . . she almost felt her heart stop.

"No. Not directly. It has to do with Charles Delauney."

"Please don't ask me that. Please . . . you saw what they did to me yesterday . . . I can't help him."

"Please . . . just listen . . . I want to help find your son's kidnapper, and Charles isn't it. I believe that."

"Does he know you're calling?"

She blushed beet red at her end of the phone and shook her head. "He hardly knows me. I've been to see him a few times, but he's terribly distracted. But I think he's innocent and I want to help him."

"I want to find my son. That's all I want," she said sadly.

"I know . . . so do I . . . you deserve it

. . . please see me . . . just for a few minutes."

"When?" Just a meeting between them
would cause a furor in the press, and probably
a scandal. And they had enough scandal on
their hands, with the revelation of Malcolm's
affair with Brigitte.

"Could I come over right now? I mean . . .
I know . . . it's a terrible imposition." She
was scared to death, but she had to see her.

"I . . . I just don't think . . ."

"Please . . ." The girl was almost in tears,
and finally Marielle relented.

"All right. Come."

"Now?"

"Yes. Can you be here in half an hour?" She
would have gladly been there in half a minute.

When she arrived, Marielle was dressed and
waiting downstairs, and as Bea Ritter walked
in, the young reporter actually looked almost
frightened. She was twenty-eight years old,
and suddenly her brash, bold style seemed to
have melted and she was almost childlike. She
was a tiny girl, much, much smaller than Marielle, and she was wearing slacks, a heavy
sweater, and a raincoat.

"Thank you for seeing me," she said in a
voice filled with awe, as Marielle walked her
into the library and closed the door. She her-

self was wearing black slacks and a black cashmere sweater. Her hair was pulled back and
she had no makeup on, and there was something very clean and pure about her, which
was exactly what John Taylor had fallen in love
with.

"I don't know what you expect from me,"
Marielle said quietly as they sat down. "I told
you on the phone, there's nothing I can do to
help you."

"I don't even want your help," Bea Ritter
admitted to her as she looked at her thought-
fully. She had wanted to see this woman again
for weeks, and now she was here, and it felt
strange sitting there like two friends, two
women who wanted the same thing for different reasons. Bea wanted the boy found so
Charles would be cleared, and Marielle just
wanted her son back. "I just want to talk to
you, to know what you think . . . like this
. . . not for the newspapers . . . or in a
courtroom. . . . You don't think he did it, do
you?"

"I was honest in court yesterday," Marielle
said with a sigh, wondering why she had let
her come here. She was so energetic, so high-
strung, it almost made Marielle nervous, yet
she had felt she owed her one. But what good
would it do to rehash it all with her again? "Is

this for the press?" Bea shook her head, and Marielle could see that she meant it.

"No, it's for me. I have to know. Because I don't think he did it either." She acted as though Marielle believed the same thing, but she sensed that was the case, no matter how she denied it.

"Why?"

"Maybe I'm crazy, but I believe him. I trust him. I admire everything he stands for. I think he's a damn fool, he's done some awfully stupid things, and he never should have said the things he said to you that day in the park, but if he'd meant to take the boy, he'd never have said them."

"I thought so too . . . until they found the baby's pajamas . . ." It was funny, she still thought of him that way . . . "the baby" . . . at four . . . the baby she might never see again. She had to fight back tears suddenly as they sat there. "How did the pajamas get there if he didn't take him?"

"Mrs. Patterson . . . Marielle . . . may I call you that?" They were from two different lives, two different worlds, but for a brief moment they were friends, with one common goal, to find her baby. And Marielle nodded in answer. "He swears they were planted. He thinks someone was paid to put them there

. . . maybe even someone from here, from your own house."

"But those were the pajamas he wore. I saw them. The embroidery on them is little trains, and those are the same ones he was wearing the night they took him."

"Does he have other pajamas like them?" Marielle shook her head.

"Not exactly."

The young reporter shook her head with a look of despair. She wanted so desperately to help him, and Marielle wanted to ask her a question.

"Why do you care so much? Is it the story or the man?" She looked at her squarely, and Bea's eyes didn't waver.

"It's him," and then in a softer voice, "you still love him, don't you?" Marielle hesitated for a long time, wondering just how far she could trust her, but for some reason she did. And she knew she wouldn't be disappointed.

"I always have. I suppose I always will. But he's a part of my past now." Little by little, Marielle was coming to understand that.

"Charles said that too, when I spoke to him. But he loves you too. I think he's less crazy now. I think all of this has brought him to his senses."

"A little late." Marielle smiled sadly.

"He thinks the boy is alive somewhere." She wanted to give her hope, if not the answers.

"I wish that were true. The FBI think it's getting late. They're afraid . . ." She couldn't say the words, and her eyes filled with tears as she turned away. It was all so pointless. What purpose would the trial serve? Whatever they did to Charles, it would not bring back her baby.

"I don't believe that." Bea Ritter didn't move as she looked at her, and she reached out a tiny firm hand and took a grip on Marielle's fingers. "And I'm going to do everything I can to help them find him. Whatever the press can do, whatever ins I have, I'm going to use them." She had some very odd underworld connections, she explained, due to a series of articles she'd done, and the local mob boss had loved them. She'd made him a hero in his own way, and he'd promised her that he'd always be there for her, and lately, after talking to Charles, she had wanted to call him.

"What did you want from me?" Marielle asked tiredly. She liked the girl, but it was late, and it all seemed so hopeless. "Why did you come here?"

"I wanted to look you in the eye and see for myself what you believe. I think you don't know . . . but you're not sure that he did it either."

"That's true."

"That's fair enough. Maybe in your shoes I'd feel that way too. He must have given you a pretty rough time when . . ." They both knew that she meant when their son died.

"He was crazy then," she smiled sadly, "maybe he still is."

"A little bit." Bea smiled. "He'd have to be to fight in Spain." But she admired him for that, and she loved what he had written. He had showed some of it to her. They had talked for hours at the jail one day, and he had cried when he told her he didn't do it. And she believed him. She had vowed to help him then, and she knew that Marielle was an important key. No matter what they did to her, she was someone who could help him. "I'm sorry about your husband," she said carefully.

"So am I. It's not going to be pretty in the press tomorrow morning."

"No, it won't be." Bea had already seen some of the early tear sheets. "But it raises a little more sympathy for you. They really beat you to death the other day. It made me sick, that's why I wrote the piece I did." She was kind of a Robin Hood, always defending the underdog, the beaten, the poor, the defeated.

She and Charles seemed to have so much in common.

"Why Charles?" Marielle asked softly. "Why him? Why do you care so much?"

"I don't want to see him killed for nothing. I never believed entirely that Bruno Hauptmann was guilty either. I know some of the evidence was there, but so much of it was circumstantial. So much of it was hysteria created by the press. It was my first story, I was twenty-one, and I always felt that I could have made a difference, but I didn't. Maybe this time, I can. Or at least die trying."

Marielle didn't dare ask her more than that, but there was something more in the girl's eyes, and after a long moment she decided to ask her. "Are you in love with him?" There was no jealousy there, nothing proprietary. It was only a question. And Bea Ritter looked at her for a long time before she answered.

"I'm not sure. I don't want to be. That isn't the issue." But it was why she cared so much and Marielle knew it.

She smiled at her. "Does he know, or is he as stupid as he used to be?" Sometimes he could be dense when he wanted to be. And of course now he was involved with something much more important. But Bea laughed with her.

"I think maybe he is as stupid as he used to be, but maybe he's a little too busy." The man was fighting for life. Then suddenly Bea looked worried. "Would you ever go back to him?" But Marielle shook her head without hesitation. Too much pain gone by, too much time, too much sorrow. She loved him, she knew she always would. But he was gone for her now. Marielle thought the little redhead would be perfect for him, if ever the time came, and he was acquitted. He owed a lot to her, but according to Bea, he didn't even know it.

"What are you going to do now, Bea?"

"I don't know . . . I'm going to call up some debts . . . talk to some old friends . . . hang out with some private investigators I know. . . ." And maybe talk to Tom Armour, if she needed money. Maybe he would be willing to pay for some tips, or special favors. She was willing to do anything, call anyone, go anywhere, pay anyone she had to. "Maybe nothing will turn up, but at least we'll have tried . . . and maybe it'll lead us to Teddy."

"You'll let me know if you hear anything, won't you?"

"The minute I do." The two women stood up and Marielle walked her to the door. She knew they would never be friends. But she liked her. She was an unusual girl, and a smart one. Charles was luckier than he knew to have found her.

Bea Ritter slipped away into the night, and when Marielle went back upstairs, it was long after midnight. And as she turned the light off, she lay in her bed thinking of Malcolm, probably in an apartment on Park Avenue . . . and her little boy, she prayed, asleep in a bed somewhere, with strangers.

13

The trial went on for weeks after that, as Hitler seized Memel on the Baltic. The trial seemed to have pushed the world news off the front pages, in New York anyway. But Britain and France had announced that they stood ready to support Poland. And at the end of March, much to Charles's chagrin, the Spanish Civil War ended at last, when Madrid fell to General Franco. There were over a million dead by then, in three years an entire population had fallen. It was a tragedy to Charles, as he knew it would be to his friends in Europe. The fight was over. The war was lost. But Charles Delauney had his own war to fight now, the battle for his survival.

Marielle never heard from Bea Ritter again after her late-night visit. But she continued to read her articles in the paper, and was touched by her sympathetic viewpoint.

Predictably, there had been a huge hue and cry in the press about Malcolm and Brigitte for several weeks, but despite constant inquiries, Marielle stayed aloof about it, and made no comments. She and Malcolm had scarcely spoken to each other in weeks, and she had only seen Brigitte once since then. The girl had covered her guilt by looking haughtily at Marielle, and clinging to Malcolm, as though trying to prove that she was the winner. It seemed a poor defense to Marielle, and she didn't envy her awkward position. She felt betrayed by their lies, and Brigitte's false kindness, but she was hardly even angry anymore, or even jealous. He hadn't been hers in a long time, but she was deeply hurt by Malcolm's long-distance deception. Her only attempt to discuss the matter with him had been rebuffed, and Malcolm had pretended to be "outraged." He told her that after her behavior with Charles he owed her no explanations, which told her absolutely nothing, except to confirm his guilt. But that fact had already been established.

She reminded him coolly that if he contin-

ued to stay at the apartment with the girl, the
press would continue to hound them. After
that, she noticed that he stayed at their house
again, and not at Brigitte's apartment. But in
spite of that, she still scarcely saw him.

The tension between them was unbearable,
but so was the trial, as a trail of expert witnesses, detectives, and irrelevant people took
the stand, endorsing Charles's guilt, and one
by one being attacked by Tom Armour.

It was three full weeks before the defense
had their chance. And Tom Armour called
Marielle as his first witness. At first he led her
across the same terrain carefully, rebuilding
her where Bill Palmer had destroyed her. And
the portrait that began to emerge at his hands
was far different from the one colored by Malcolm and Bill Palmer. Instead of a mentally ill
invalid, a woman not to be trusted with her
own child, he showed more clearly what had
really happened, how destroyed she had been
at the death of her son, and the loss of her
baby, and then her husband. Tom Armour admitted openly that Charles had been more
than a little crazy, and had treated her badly.
They were both racked with pain, he explained, and there was not a dry eye in the
courtroom when he asked her to describe
groping for André beneath the frozen ice of

Lake Geneva. She explained how she had been able to save the two little girls, but not her own son, because he had slipped farther under the ice, and how he had lain lifeless and gray in her arms when she found him. She had had to stop several times as she described the scene to him, and then the hospital that night and losing the baby. In one fell swoop, they had lost their family, and Charles hadn't been equal to it, Charles even more than she. Then she had snapped, and all she wanted for months afterward was to die and be with her babies.

"Do you feel that way now?" Tom asked her quietly, as several jurors blew their noses.

"No," she said sadly.

"Do you believe Teddy is still alive?"

Her eyes filled with tears again, but she went on, "I don't know . . . I hope he is . . . I hope it so much . . ." She looked at the press then and into the courtroom. ". . . If anyone knows where he is . . . please, please bring him home . . . we will do anything . . . just don't hurt him . . ." A photographer ran up, and a camera exploded in her face as she said it, and the judge ordered the bailiff to throw the photographer out of the courtroom.

"And if anyone does that again, you'll go to

jail, is that clear?" Judge Morrison boomed as Marielle regained her composure. He apologized to her, and she waited for Tom's next question.

"Do you believe that Charles Delauney took your son?" It was a dangerous question, but he wanted the world to know what she thought because he didn't think she was convinced that he took him.

"I'm not sure."

"Do you think he would do a thing like that? You know him better than anyone here. He has loved you, and hurt you, and cried with you . . . he's even hit you . . . he has probably done worse things to you than to anyone he knows." Charles had admitted that to Tom himself, and yet what Marielle had told Tom of him told him that Marielle did not believe him guilty. "Knowing what you do of him, Mrs. Patterson, do you believe that he took Teddy?"

She hesitated for an eternity, and then finally shook her head and dropped her face into her hands, and Tom Armour waited.

"Are you still in love with this man, Mrs. Patterson?"

She looked at Charles sadly. What terrible things had come to them. What misery they had shared, and yet long ago, they had been so happy. "No," she said softly. "I love him. I probably always will. He was the father of my children. I loved him very much when I was young . . . but now . . . I am only sad for him, and if he has done this terrible thing, then I hope he returns my son safely. But I am not in love with him anymore. We've caused each other too much pain for too long." Tom Armour nodded, and he respected her more than she knew. She was one hell of a terrific woman. She had held up under questioning, shared her guts, her life, her soul, she had lost two children to the hands of fate, and now one more, and she was still standing. He admired her more than anyone he had ever met, but nothing showed in his face as he went on with his questions.

"Have you had an affair with Mr. Delauney since your marriage to Mr. Patterson?"

"No," she said calmly.

"Have you had an affair with anyone? Have you *ever* been unfaithful to your husband?" He looked her straight in the eye, and as her eyes met his, they did not waver.

"No, I have not." It was true. She had kissed John Taylor but that was all, and by now her marriage was over.

"Thank you, Mrs. Patterson, you may step down. I have no further questions." He helped her from the stand, and, feeling drained, she went back to sit down, but she didn't have the beaten feeling she'd had when she'd been interrogated by Bill Palmer.

Tom called Haverford to the stand next, their butler. He described her as decent, fair, and intelligent, a woman of integrity, and a true lady, he said proudly, which touched her. He said she'd been wonderful to her son, and he, Haverford, had always been shocked by how badly she was treated by Mr. Patterson's servants. It was as though everyone felt they owed nothing to her, and only to Mr. Patterson. Haverford himself felt that Mr. Patterson never stood behind her. He acted as though she was not in charge, and simply a guest, and that was how she was regarded. He said Miss Griffin had been abominable to her, the housekeeper was worse, and Edith stole her clothes, and everyone, including Mr. Patterson, knew it. He said that all of the servants ridiculed her in the kitchen.

"Are you saying there was no respect for Mrs. Patterson in her own home?" Tom Armour pressed him, to make sure the jury understood it.

"I am, sir," Haverford said, looking dignified in a dark suit that had been tailored for him in London.

"Would you say that her own behavior led to that attitude, Mr. Haverford? Is she, as has been suggested in this courtroom earlier, an irresponsible, weak woman, essentially without merit?" The old butler bristled visibly at the suggestion, thinking Tom had misunderstood him.

"What I said, sir, is that she is one of the finest people I've ever known. She is wise, kind, fair, decent, good, and after what she's been through, I don't see how anyone can call her a weak woman." It was Miss Griffin who had had the vapors and fainting spells, and had to have tablets prescribed by her doctor, ever since the kidnapping.

"Would you venture an opinion as to why no one in the Patterson household respected her then? Was there any logical reason?" Bill Palmer started to object, and then decided it wasn't worth the trouble. The old man was harmless.

Haverford nodded, anxious to tell the jury. "Mr. Patterson let us know early on that . . ." he tried to remember the exact words, but couldn't ". . . she wasn't all there, well, not precisely that. But he told us she was very frail and very nervous. And he implied that her orders were to be listened to politely, but basically disregarded. Said she didn't know any-

thing about running a house, and later, about
children. That let all of us know where she
stood with Mr. Malcolm." It led Marielle to
know it too, as she listened. But she still didn't
understand why he had done it. He had made
her an object of disdain and ridicule right from
the beginning. Maybe he just wanted to keep
control of everything, and there had never
been a real place for her in his house, except
as Teddy's mother, and even at that, they
hardly let her be useful.

"Were you aware of Mr. Patterson's affair
with Miss Sanders?" Tom asked him then.

"I was, or at least I suspected it," Haverford
said with an air of frigid disapproval.

"Did you ever mention your suspicions to
Mrs. Patterson?"

"Certainly not, sir."

"Thank you, Mr. Haverford." Tom offered
his witness to the prosecution, but Bill Palmer
chose not to ask him any questions. He didn't
consider him of any importance. But Marielle
had been touched by his testimony, and so had
the jury.

She felt avenged somehow after what he'd
said. But it was embarrassing to hear it all
spelled out, and also comforting to realize that
what she'd felt was real and not delusions.
What she still didn't understand was why Mal-

colm had undermined her with everyone. There had to be a reason. Or was it that he'd been in love with Brigitte almost since the beginning? Was he trying to get rid of Marielle? Did he hope she'd run away, or just give up and leave Teddy with him? She would have died first. But why humiliate her, lie to her, cheat on her? Why bother to marry her in the first place? Had it all been a lie from the beginning? But remembering their sweet, early days, she couldn't believe that.

The next witness Tom called to the stand was Brigitte Sanders. And there was a considerable stir in the courtroom as she came forward. She was a beautiful girl, there was no denying that, and there was an air of definite sexuality about her, more than Marielle had ever noticed before. Perhaps it was because she had nothing to hide now. Their secret was exposed, and in some ways, Brigitte seemed proud of it. She wore a sleek black dress, and Marielle noticed that it looked expensive. Her hair was perfectly coifed in the familiar bob, and she wore the usual bright red nails and lipstick. And everyone agreed that she was very striking. She made Marielle feel like a small brown wren in comparison, but what she didn't understand was how cold Brigitte seemed, how calculating, and how hard she

seemed to everyone in the courtroom in comparison to Marielle. Tom Armour thought she
was unbearably German in her manner. And
there was an insolent tone to her voice as she
answered his questions. It was a style Marielle
had never seen her use before, and she wondered if she was feeling defensive, now that
the secret was out, and she'd been exposed to
the whole world as Malcolm's mistress.

She admitted that Malcolm spent most of
his evenings with her, and some nights, and
said that he had never been happy with his
wife, and he had married her only to have children. What she said gave Marielle a jolt, and
she wondered if it was true. Was that it then?

"She couldn't even do that easily," Brigitte
said with derision. Gone the warmth, the concern, the kindness she had always shown Marielle, and Teddy. She was ready to tell all, and
Malcolm looked strained as he watched her.

"Would you care to explain that last remark,
Miss Sanders?" Tom asked politely.

"It took her a long time to get pregnant."
Tom Armour refrained from suggesting that
perhaps Mr. Patterson was spending too many
nights at her apartment. "In fact, he was so
tired of waiting, that he was thinking of divorcing her right around the time she got pregnant." There was a murmur in the crowd, and

Marielle cast her eyes to the floor, as the judge rapped his gavel. She could feel herself blush, as she sat next to John Taylor. He didn't move, or say anything, but he felt sorry for her, knowing how private she was, and how discreet. This couldn't have been easy for her.

"Were you already involved with Mr. Patterson then?" Tom Armour asked Brigitte, but for a long moment she didn't answer. "Should I repeat the question? May I remind you that you're under oath?"

"Yes, I was," she said a little less brashly.

"When exactly did that begin?" Marielle held her breath, she was curious now, as they waited for the answer.

"Two months after they were married. In February." And Marielle thought she knew when. It was the first business trip he had taken without her. He hadn't waited long. And it was then that he had become particularly chilly. She had thought for a while that it was his disappointment because she wasn't pregnant, but he was already under Brigitte's spell, and apparently he had stayed there.

"Weren't you very angry that he was married to her, and not to you?"

"No, I . . ." She looked vaguely discomfited by his questions. "I knew he wanted a child, and he . . . Malcolm . . . Mr. Patter-

son . . . has always been very generous with
me." So they'd heard. Tom didn't press her
about why he wanted Marielle's baby and not
Brigitte's. He asked her instead if Malcolm
had promised to marry her if he divorced Marielle, and she hedged by saying that they had
never discussed it, which Tom thought was unlikely. It was obvious that something had been
said, as she glanced at Malcolm.

She explained that they traveled everywhere together, particularly to Germany,
where Mr. Patterson did a lot of business. She
said it did not embarrass her to be his mistress. But she said it with a defiant air, and
Tom Armour was not completely sure that he
believed her.

She said that she was very fond of the child,
and Malcolm adored him, that it had almost
killed him when the boy was kidnapped. She
also said that she hardly ever saw Marielle
with the child. "She was always in bed with a
headache." She had the same unpleasant, dis-
respectful tone that the servants had used
when talking about Marielle. Not one of them,
except Haverford, had spoken of her kindly.

Brigitte left the stand with a great show of
legs and a good swing of her behind as she
walked past Malcolm, and he looked away and
pretended not to notice. And after that, for al-

most a week, the proceedings got back to normal. More forensic experts were called, more detectives. No fingerprints had been found at the scene, no evidence that could be tied to Charles, only the pajamas and the toy found at his house, and Tom Armour maintained that they could easily have been planted. No one at the Delauney home had seen the boy, and Charles's alibi for the night of the kidnapping was airtight. It was difficult to pin on him, and finally, at the end of the fourth week of the trial, he took the stand, and as he walked to the witness box, there was not a sound in the courtroom.

Charles Delauney looked gaunt and serious as he solemnly took the oath and promised to tell the truth, glanced nervously at the jury. Tom Armour had already walked him through everything, and he had tried to warn him of every possible pitfall.

Tom asked him where he had been for the past eighteen years, while he lived in Europe. He explained that he had lived in France for years, and for the past several years Spain, while he fought against Franco.

"Did you serve in the Great War too, Mr. Delauney?" Tom asked and Charles said he had. He looked very handsome and very pale and suddenly much older than he had when

Marielle had seen him in Saint Patrick's. It
had been a hellish four months for him, ever
since he'd been arrested. And his attorney had
just told him his father was fading fast, to add
to his problems. "How old were you when you
volunteered?"

"I was fifteen."

Tom nodded approvingly. "And were you
wounded in the service of your country?"

"Yes, at Saint-Mihiel. And after that, I came
back here to go to school for three years. But I
went back to Europe in 1921. I went to Oxford, and Italy for a while, and then I moved to
Paris."

"Is that where you met your wife, the current Mrs. Patterson?"

"That's right." He glanced at her and in
spite of himself he smiled, and she looked so
worried. She wasn't sure what she wanted to
happen anymore. She wanted justice for him,
and her little boy, and she wasn't sure which,
if either of them, would get it. "I met her in
1926. She was eighteen, and we were married
at the end of that summer."

"Did you love her, Mr. Delauney?" Tom
looked at him as though it were an important
question. "Did you love your wife?"

"Yes . . . I loved her very much . . . she
was so young . . . she was wonderful . . .

like a bright, beautiful spirit. Everything was new and exciting to her . . ." His mind drifted for a moment and then he looked at Tom apologetically and spoke very softly. "We were very happy."

"And you had a baby?"

Charles nodded. "A little boy . . . André . . . we'd been married for almost a year when he was born. He was very special." All children were, Marielle thought to herself . . . Teddy was too . . . they all were.

"Would you say you were extremely close to the child?"

"Yes."

"Unusually so?"

"Perhaps. The three of us were together all the time. We traveled quite a bit, and I was writing, and at home. Marielle was wonderful with him. She took care of him entirely herself."

"With no governess?" Tom interrupted him.

"She didn't want anyone to help her." Marielle smiled at the memory. Life was so much simpler then, without people like Miss Griffin.

"So the three of you were very close. Extremely so?"

"I suppose you could say so."

"Would that have made the shock of losing him even more traumatic, do you think?"

"I suppose it must have been. And we were both so young . . . we just fell apart. I blamed her and she blamed me . . . and none of it made any difference."

"She blamed you?"

"Not really . . . I meant about the baby . . . but the truth was, Marielle blamed herself and I was so hard on her," his voice caught, filled with guilt, even now, and he looked her in the eye across the courtroom. "I was wrong. I knew that afterward. But by then, I couldn't reach her . . . she wouldn't see me. And the doctors thought . . . they thought it would upset her if I came to visit her at the clinic."

Tom wanted to take the bull by the horns so there were no secrets from the jury. "Did you hit her the night of your son's death, Mr. Delauney?" He spoke in terrible tones and Charles looked miserable as he nodded.

"I did. I was crazy that night . . . I had just seen him . . . and I couldn't believe she had let that happen to him . . . I wanted to break something . . . to die . . . I slapped her hard . . ." The memory and the sound of it would haunt him forever.

"Did she lose the child as a result of that?"

"No," he shook his head with an anguished look at her. "The doctor said the baby was already dead when she arrived at the hospital. The exposure to the icy water had killed the fetus. But they hadn't told her." Marielle gulped on a sob as she heard the words, she hadn't even known the baby was dead, all she had known was that she had lost it that night, in the midst of all the horror.

"Did you hold her responsible for losing both children then?" Tom Armour went on relentlessly with his client, and Bea Ritter winced as she listened to him, but she knew it all had to be exposed if they were going to save him. Like a terrible wound that had to be excised and cleaned if they were going to save the patient.

"Yes," Charles Delauney whispered. "Yes . . . and I was wrong. It wasn't her fault. But it was too late by the time I knew that."

"Would you have killed her that night, if you could have?"

"No!" Charles looked horrified. "I never wanted to hurt her. I was just so hurt myself."

"Did you have to be pulled away from her, when you were slapping her, or did you stop of your own doing?"

"I stopped myself, and then I left her there, and went out and got drunk all night. And when I came back in the morning to tell her how sorry I was, she was in surgery. She had lost the baby. And she never recovered after that. I never really saw her, or talked to her, or spoke to her sensibly." Tears were sliding down his cheeks and Marielle's as he testified.

"Did you attend your son's funeral?"

"Yes."

"Did your wife?"

He shook his head, unable to speak for a moment. "No. She was too ill. She was still in the hospital in Geneva." Which was different from the Clinique Verbeuf in Villars everyone knew by now.

"Have you ever wanted other children, sir?" Tom asked him, and Charles shook his head very quickly.

"No. I have no desire for any more children. That's one of the reasons why I've never re-married. I feel that I had my son, and he was taken away from us. I have spent my life in other pursuits, writing about things that seemed important to me, fighting for causes that I believed in, because I have less to lose than some men, if I'm killed no one will mourn me. I have led my life freely. With a wife and children, I couldn't do that."

"Do you resent people for their families?"

"No," Charles said calmly. "I never have. I have made my choices and lived by them."

"Have you ever wanted to return to your wife?"

"Yes," he admitted quietly. "Before she left the hospital, I asked her to come back to me, but she wouldn't. She said she would always feel responsible for what had happened, and she didn't believe that I no longer blamed her."

"Were you in love with her at the time, Mr. Delauney?"

"Yes, I was." He wasn't ashamed to say it.

"Was she still in love with you, in your opinion?"

"I believe so."

"Are you still in love with her today?"

"Yes, I am," he said quietly. "Perhaps I always will be. But I understand that our lives have gone in different directions. I don't even think we would suit each other anymore." He smiled gently at her from across the courtroom. "She doesn't strike me as the kind of woman who would be happy camping on a mountainside, while her husband fights in the trenches." There was a common smile around the courtroom. Few women were aching to do that, save one, who would have followed him in a moment to any mountainside of his choosing.

"How long had it been since you'd seen her

when you ran into her in Saint Patrick's Cathedral last December?"

"Almost seven years."

"And were you deeply moved to see her?"

"Very much so. It was the anniversary of our son's death, and it meant a great deal to me to see her."

"Was she happy to see you, sir?"

"I believe so."

"Did she lead you to believe that she would be willing to see you again?"

"No," he shook his head firmly. "She said that she couldn't because of her husband." It was in sharp contrast to Malcolm's testimony about his love nest with Brigitte. "She was very firm about it in fact."

"And were you angry?"

"No, I was sorry. All I could think of then was the past. And what we had had, and I wanted to see her."

"Did she tell you about her son?"

"No, she didn't, and I was shocked when I saw him the next day. I was terribly hung over from the night before, and still pretty drunk, and I was angry at her for not telling me about him the day before. He was a very nice-looking little boy. And I said a lot of very stupid things about her not deserving him. I think I was talking more about myself in my drunken haze, but in any case, I behaved very badly."

"Did you threaten her?"

"Probably," he said honestly.

"Did you mean it?"

"No."

"Did you call her and repeat the threats, or had you called her before?"

"No."

"Have you ever threatened anyone with physical harm and acted on it, ever, at any time in your life?"

"Never."

"And was this time any different? Did you act on those threats, Mr. Delauney?" Tom's voice was getting louder and stronger in the courtroom.

"No, I did not act on those threats. I would never have hurt her or the boy."

"Did you take Theodore Whitman Patterson, the Patterson's son, from his home on the night of December eleventh of last year, or did you hire or conspire with anyone to do so?"

"I did not, sir."

"Do you know where the boy is?"

"No . . . I'm sorry, I do not . . . I wish I did . . ."

"Were his pajamas and a toy of his found in your home a week later?"

"Yes."

"Do you have any idea how they got there?"

"None whatsoever."

"How do you think they got there, Mr. Delauney?"

"I don't know. I thought they must have been planted."

"Why do you think someone would do that?"

"So that I pay for the crime that they did, that's the only reason I can think of."

"Do you have any idea who that might be?"

"No."

"Do you have any enemies at all, anyone who has sworn to do you harm?"

"No . . . maybe only General Franco . . ." There was a communal smile.

"Are you a Communist, Mr. Delauney?"

"No," he smiled, "I'm a Republican, or I used to be. Actually, I suppose I'm more of a free spirit."

"Do you belong to the Communist party?"

"I do not."

"Do you hold a grudge against Mrs. Delauney . . . Mrs. Patterson now, for leaving you? Or against Mr. Patterson for being her husband?"

Charles looked at him man-to-man across the courtroom and he wanted to spit on him, but he controlled himself as he addressed the court. "From what I've heard in this courtroom, he doesn't deserve her. But I have no grudge against him, or against Marielle. She has suffered enough in this life. She deserves better than either of us, and she deserves to have her child back." There were tears in her eyes as she listened to him. He was a decent man, he always had been. She didn't believe now, as she heard his words, that he could have taken Teddy. And Tom Armour was praying that the jury felt the same way she did.

"Are you guilty of the crime of which you're accused, Mr. Delauney? Think carefully, and remember that you are under oath. Are you in any way involved in the kidnapping of the child in question?"

Charles looked at him solemnly, and shook his head slowly. "I swear that I had nothing to do with it."

Tom Armour turned to the prosecution then. "Your witness, Mr. Palmer."

The prosecution attempted to make mincemeat of him, to make him say he had lied, to make him look even worse for hitting Marielle after their child's death. But it was all out in the open now, there were no dark secrets anymore, and he stuck rigidly to his story. He continued to say that he had nothing to do with the kidnapping, and no idea how the pajamas had turned up in his basement. There had been no forensic evidence of the child there at all, no skin, no nails, no hair, no other clothing, no sign that he had been anywhere near Charles Delauney.

His testimony took an exhausting two days, and at the end of it, the mystery still wasn't solved, but Charles had remained adamant till the end. He wasn't guilty. The only real question was had he convinced the jury?

Malcolm left the courtroom separately that day, and Marielle stopped at church on the way home. She wanted to pray for a merciful outcome to the trial, whatever that would be, and for her little boy. Easter had come and gone, and other children had hunted Easter eggs and played with little chicks, and at home Teddy's nursery was still empty. It tore at her heart to go there, and yet she found some reason to every day, to look for something, to put something away, to fold some small item of clothing. Miss Griffin had long gone, still staying with her sister in New Jersey, and the housekeeper had told Marielle recently that Miss Griffin was taking a job in Palm Beach soon, with a new baby. How lucky for her, Marielle thought . . . how lucky to have a baby to go on to. But there were no new ba-

bies for her, and all she wanted was little
Teddy. Her heart ached when she thought of
the silky hair, the firm little cheek, the sweet
lips kissing her, and he was gone now . . .
vanished . . . probably forever. She was trying to accept that, day by day, but thinking of
him even made Malcolm's betrayal less important.

She knelt at the altar of Saint Vincent Ferrer
church for a long time, and finally John Taylor
came and knelt beside her. He had been in
court with her every day, and yet there was so
little he could do, so little they had found.
There had been nothing new in the case since
they'd found the pajamas and teddy bear at
Charles Delauney's.

The closing arguments in the case were the
next day, and he felt totally helpless. He
thought Delauney had done well on the stand
for the last two days, it even made him think
twice, but Taylor still believed him guilty.

He put a gentle hand on Marielle's arm. She
had gotten thinner lately and she looked so
pale, but she seldom had her appalling headaches. "Ready to go home?" She sighed and
then nodded. Sometimes she wanted to stay
here, on her knees forever, begging Him to
bring Teddy home. She had been asking for
months now.

She was quiet on the way home. The press were still thronging her door, but Taylor was adept at dodging them and getting her in through the kitchen. It was odd to think that the trial would soon be over. The police were going to stay on with them for a while, and the FBI was certainly going to check in from time to time, but there had been no leads, no calls, not even the crazies calling at midnight. There was no reason to stay there anymore. It was over. All that remained now was to see what the jury did with Charles Delauney. He wondered if that was troubling her now too. He knew she still cared about him, probably more than she admitted.

"Do you want to be alone?" he asked quietly when they got home, and she looked up at him gratefully and nodded. In the end, she would be left with no one. She and Malcolm were through, Teddy was gone . . . and if they executed Charles there would be no one left in her world who had ever loved her. It took her breath away when she thought about it sometimes, and Taylor knew she was having a hard time. He gently touched her arm and then her cheek. "Hang in there . . . it's not as bad as it feels sometimes." But they both knew this was about as bad as it got. He watched her walk slowly up the stairs, her head down, and suddenly he began to worry. What if she did the kind of crazy stuff she had done years before? He wondered if he should stay, or follow her upstairs, but one of the cops told him that Malcolm was upstairs, so Taylor just told him to keep an eye on her, and he went back to his office.

When she left John, Marielle went upstairs to Teddy's room. She sat down in a rocking chair, and closed her eyes. It was dusk outside, and there were a few stars in the sky, she could just see them through his bedroom curtains. She thought of the nursery rhymes they had said, the songs she had sung him the last night she put him to bed, and as the tears rolled slowly down her cheeks, she heard a noise and turned to see her husband.

"What are you doing here?" he asked coldly.

"I came here to be closer to Teddy."

"It won't do you any good," he said evilly, "he's dead. Thanks to your ex-husband."

"Why are you so cruel?" she dared to ask him this time. "And how can you be so sure he's dead. How do you know he won't come home to us sometime soon?"

Malcolm Patterson stood looking at her coldly. The mask had fallen since the trial had begun. He had lost his cover, and he no longer cared. He was going to divorce her. "If he comes back, Marielle, he won't come back to 'us,' or to you, you're not fit to be his mother." It was exactly what Tom Armour had seen coming. He had consulted on the Vanderbilt case, and he knew just how those cases were built. And that's just what he saw Malcolm doing. The testimony from the nurse, the maid, the telegram from the mental hospital, all of it showing that she was unfit . . . just in case they found him.

"Who are you to decide that?" Marielle said sadly. "And why do you hate me so much?"

"I don't hate you. I have nothing but contempt for you. You're weak . . . and you let that Communist into our life to steal our son and kill him. . . ."

"You know that's not true." She had never moved from the rocking chair as he approached her.

"You're a fool, Marielle. A fool, and a liar." His eyes blazed, but so did hers. "How do you expect anyone to respect you?"

"And Brigitte?" she said quietly. "Is she so much better?" The affront of it still hurt her. She realized now too that he had undermined her for all these years. But why? Why did he hate her? Had he done it for himself or Brigitte?

"Brigitte has nothing to do with this. We should never have gotten married."

"Then why did we?" She no longer knew. She no longer understood anything about him.

"Perhaps if I'd met Brigitte before you, we wouldn't have. But I met you first. And I so desperately wanted to have children." After two barren marriages, Marielle had seemed to be the answer to his prayers. And she had been so young, so helpless. He had liked the fact that she was alone in the world. She was his to control, and he liked that. In truth, he hadn't even minded about her history at the sanatorium. It would only serve to make her more dependent on him.

"Was it all about children then? About having a son?"

"Perhaps." She'd been used. That's all she'd been. A tool to give him a baby. But there had been more, she knew it, and he did too, whether he admitted it or not. In the very beginning, for a short time, she had been sure that he loved her. And then . . . there had been Brigitte. Now she understood it.

"And what will you do now? Marry Brigitte and have more children?" He didn't tell her that Brigitte was unable to have children, and theirs was a genuine passion.

"What I do now is none of your business, Marielle."

"I'll move out as soon as the trial is over," she said calmly. But she was going to take Teddy's things . . . she had to take them with her . . . in case he came home again . . . for the first time in years, she began to feel the same confusion she used to feel at the clinic in Villars . . . that same strange pain some- where in her head that made it impossible to think, or decide anything . . . all she could think of now was Teddy.

"Where will you move to?" His eyes seemed to take in her energy.

"It doesn't matter. I'll give the FBI my ad- dress, so they can find me . . . in case . . . when they find him."

He looked at her scornfully. She was going crazy again. He could see it. And it never dawned on him that he had driven her to it.

"They're not going to find him, Marielle. Ever. Don't you understand that?"

"I'll stay at a hotel." She ignored his ques- tion, and looked away, as Malcolm watched her. He had already told his lawyer how much money he was going to give her. He was going to buy her off, and she was probably going to wind up in an institution. Once he was gone, and Charles was executed, and she understood that she would never see the child again, it would probably kill her.

"I'm leaving on a trip anyway. You can get organized then."

"Where are you going?" Her voice was very faint, as though she had to concentrate, and her hands were shaking.

"That's none of your concern."

Suddenly, as she listened to him, she felt rising panic. Who would take care of her when he was gone? . . . who would help her take care of Teddy? But suddenly she knew she didn't need anyone. All she needed was time to recover from what had happened. She realized what was happening to her, and wrestled with all her strength to fight the demons. She made a superhuman effort to stand up quietly, and went downstairs to her own room. He could do anything he wanted. But he couldn't take away the memories of the child she had loved, or how much she had loved him. And knowing that, she suddenly knew she could survive it.

John Taylor called her that night. He was worried about her. He knew the toll the trial was taking. "Are you okay?"

"Yes. It was rough today." And Malcolm had been even rougher. She was exhausted as she spoke to him, but she was also happy to hear him.

"It's going to be worse for the next few days. The closing arguments and the verdict are going to be killers. You just have to stay calm, Marielle." And he would be there with her.

"I know . . . I'm all right . . . John, there's no news of him, is there? . . . I mean, of Teddy?"

"No," he said softly, "there isn't." He knew she was coming to terms with it now. After four months, there was really no hope, and he knew it. "I'll tell you if anything happens."

"I knew you would."

"Marielle . . ." He knew the phones were tapped but he wished he could tell her how much he loved her.

"I know . . . it's okay." Her voice was so small and sad and he ached for her as he longed to hold her. But she sat alone in her bedroom with two lonely tears rolling down her cheeks. They were tears of exhaustion, as much as sorrow.

"Just be strong for a few more days. Maybe we can spend some time together when this is over." He knew how badly she'd need to get away. He was afraid she'd break again, and she had come close to it that night, but she hadn't. "I'll see you tomorrow," he said softly.

"Good night," she whispered, and then she hung up the phone. And as she drifted off to sleep that night, Bea Ritter was thinking about calling Tom Armour.

14

Tom Armour had been polishing up his closing arguments since late that afternoon when he got home, and he was finally satisfied that they were exactly what he wanted. He stretched, yawned, read through it all again, one more time, and finally decided to make himself a sandwich. His apartment looked as though rats had been nesting everywhere, and when he opened the refrigerator, he remembered that it was empty. He was contemplating it hungrily when the telephone rang and he debated whether or not to answer. It was probably the damn reporters again, but then again it could have been something important.

"Yeah?" He picked it up absentmindedly.

He was trying to decide if it was worth going out to get something to eat, or if he was better off just going to bed and getting some sleep so he'd be rested in the morning. Rested, but definitely hungry. He had skipped lunch that day too, and he could hear his stomach growl as he held the phone to his ear, wondering who would call him at that hour. The only interesting woman in his life had announced that she was marrying someone else shortly before Christmas. She claimed that he was married to his work, and she was tired of hearing about his cases. But at thirty-six years of age, he had managed to establish himself as one of the city's most prominent criminal attorneys.

"Is Mr. Armour there?" It was a female voice he didn't recognize, but she sounded very pleasant.

"Who do you think this is at this hour? The butler?" And then suddenly he wondered if it was a crank call related to Charles Delauney. Representing him had been interesting, but early in the case it had also won him his share of crank calls and threatening letters . . . how can you represent a monster like that, etc. etc. etc. "Who is this?" he asked with a puzzled frown. Nobody had called him at home in weeks, months, let alone an attractive-sounding woman.

"This is Beatrice Ritter. Is this you, Tom?"

"None other." He knew who she was by then, and he liked her. He had liked her when she'd come to him and begged him to take Charles's case. And he liked the pieces she had written about Marielle, and Charles, and his trial, since then. It was easy to figure out that she was on his team.

"I need to talk to you." She sounded earnest and excited.

"Go ahead. You got me." With a growling gut and an empty refrigerator and nothing else to do until the morning.

"Can you meet me somewhere?"

He glanced at his watch and winced. He was an attractive man, and he was standing in the kitchen in his white shirt from court that afternoon and his trousers and suspenders, and all he'd had for the past fourteen hours was a hell of a lot of black coffee. "It's almost eleven o'clock. Can it wait till tomorrow morning?"

"No, it can't." She sounded desperate.

"Is something wrong?"

"I have to see you."

"Have you murdered anyone?"

"I'm serious . . . please . . . trust me . . . it can't wait till tomorrow morning."

"I assume that this is somehow related to

my client?" She had become the champion of
his cause for reasons Tom didn't quite understand, but he was willing to take advantage of,
if it served his client.

"Yes, very much so."

"And it can't wait?"

"I don't think so." She sounded very earnest.

"Are you willing to come to my apartment?"
Most girls weren't willing to visit a man at that
hour of the night, but she wasn't just any girl.
She was a reporter. She was used to doing
things no sane man or woman would do, and
he admired the gutsy way she did things. She
was a tiny woman with an enormous spirit.
And he liked her. One day they might even be
friends, but not right at the moment.

"I'll be there . . ." she said excitedly. "Just
don't tell me you live in New Jersey."

"How's Fifty-ninth street, between Lexing-
ton and Third?" He lived in a quiet brownstone.

"I'd say lucky. I live on Forty-seventh. I'll
catch a cab and be there in five minutes."

"Will you do me a favor first?"

"Sure."

"Could you grab me a roast beef sandwich?
I haven't eaten since breakfast."

"Mustard or mayo?"

"Both. Anything. I'll eat the bag. I'm starv-
ing."

"You got it."

His doorbell rang twenty minutes later, and
she stood there in navy slacks and a bright
blue sweater. She had a blue bow in her hair,
and she handed him a brown bag, with a beer,
two pickles, and his sandwich.

"You're a saint." He didn't even care what
she had to say to him, he was just grateful
she'd brought him dinner. "Do you want to
share the beer?"

"No, thanks." She shook her head, and slid
into a chair in his kitchen. It was as though
they were old friends, but he knew she had
watched the entire trial, and indirectly, they
had been through the war together.

"How do you think it's going?"

"I'm not sure. The jury's tough to read.
Sometimes I think the guys like him better
than the women, sometimes . . . I'm not
sure. At least you gave Marielle Patterson a
certain amount of credibility again. What a son
of a bitch Patterson turned out to be." He nodded, still cognizant of the fact that she was a
reporter and this could be a trick. "You've
done a great job for Charles Delauney."

"Thank you. He looked good on the stand
today, at least I thought so."

"So did I," she said softly. She had managed to catch his eye as he left the stand, and he smiled when she gave him the high sign. He had been touched by her interest and her faith in him, and a little puzzled by her zeal, but he liked her. Not nearly as much as she liked him, but in Bea's eyes, it was a beginning . . . unless . . . but that was up to Tom Armour . . . and the jury.

"So what's up? What brings you here at this hour with a roast beef sandwich? I assume you didn't just come here to tell me you admire my style in the courtroom."

"No," she grinned, "but you're very good. Better than most I've seen." But her eyes grew serious then. She had something important to tell him. And they both knew time was running out for Charles Delauney. Both attorneys would be making their closing arguments the next day and after that, it was up to the jury. "I did a very strange thing," she admitted to him, as she accepted a bite of one of his pickles. "I called someone I wrote a story on a long time ago . . . well, anyway . . . last year. You probably know who he is, Tony Caproni."

"The mob boss from Queens?" Tom Armour looked startled. "You hang out with a nice bunch of guys, Miss Ritter."

"I wrote a nice piece on him, and he liked

it. He said if I ever needed a favor, to call him. So I did."

"You called Caproni? Why?" He was impressed once again by her courage. Tony Caproni was one of the most dangerous men in New York, but also one of the most powerful in his own world.

"I wanted to know if he'd heard anything, if he knew anybody who knew anybody who . . . maybe someone in the underworld, so called, knew who really kidnapped the kid, or . . . I don't know, I just figured it was worth it."

"And? He came up dry, I assume. The FBI tried the same tactic. They tried all the informants, all their underworld contacts, and they got nothing."

"So did Tony, the first time he called." She put the pickle down and grabbed Tom's arm. "He called me tonight. All he gave me was the name of a guy and his phone number and told me to call him."

Tom stopped eating and watched her. "Did he know anything?"

"Someone . . . he doesn't know who . . . paid him fifty thousand dollars to plant the toy and the pajamas. He doesn't want to testify, but if we promise him amnesty, he will. He's scared, Tom. He's scared to death, but he feels sorry for Charles, and he says he'll do it. He also said he thinks the kid is alive, and he wants to speak up before something happens."

"Holy shit . . . oh my God . . . give me his number." She pulled it out of her handbag, and he picked up his phone, and then he looked at her. "This isn't a setup, is it? You use this in the papers, and I'll kill you."

"I swear. It's for real." And for reasons he never knew, he believed her.

15

Judge Abraham Morrison rapped his gavel and called the court to order at exactly ten-fifteen the following morning. Tom Armour was looking particularly bright-eyed in a starched white shirt and a dark blue suit and a new tie, and he had actually gotten up fifteen minutes early to shine his shoes. He liked to look his best at the end of a trial when it really mattered. And Charles was looking very sober in banker's gray and a tie of his father's.

"We'll be hearing closing arguments today, ladies and gentlemen," the judge explained to the jury. They had been staying at the Chelsea Hotel for the past month, and it had to be wearing thin. Some of them were beginning to look very peaked.

But as the judge spoke to them, Tom Armour stood up and asked to approach the bench, which he did, in the company of Bill Palmer.

"What is it, Counsellor?" the judge asked him with a frown, in an undertone.

"New evidence, Your Honor, and a bit of a problem. May I see you in chambers?" The judge looked anything but happy. They were almost ready to wrap it up, and now they were talking about new evidence. What the devil did that mean?

"All right, all right." He waved them in, and they were there until eleven-thirty, arguing with each other and the judge. He was perfectly willing to let the man testify, but he was not willing to give him amnesty. If what he said was true, planting the pajamas in Charles Delauney's home was a federal offense, and he probably had additional knowledge about the kidnappers that he was concealing.

"I say, arrest him," Palmer said, hands down.

"I can't violate my source," Armour told him.

"What if he's lying?"

"What if he isn't? If he planted the pajamas and the bear, then Delauney's not guilty."

"For chrissake. Who is this guy?" Palmer almost shouted.

"I can't tell you till we come to an agreement."

The judge looked miserable by the time he'd heard them both out, and he was anything but happy with the deal they finally came to.

"I'll give you forty-eight hours to check this out, to find out if it's bogus or not. Use the FBI, the Marines, the army. I don't give a damn what you do, but see if you can't get me more than this. And I won't promise the man anything. Check it out, find out what's going on. But in forty-eight hours, you'd better be back in this courtroom with evidence, or I'm citing you for contempt, and I'm throwing your hot tip in jail. You got that?"

"Yes, sir. Thank you." Tom Armour was beaming. He had two days to work a miracle, but maybe Bea's friend would help him.

"Are you amenable to a two-day recess, Mr. Palmer?" the judge asked.

"Do I have a choice?" Palmer looked annoyed but resigned. He'd been all prepared to give it his best shot with his closing.

"Not really." The judge smiled at him, and
Tom laughed.

"Then I agree, don't I? This better be good.
Personally, I think it's all a crock. Delauney's
guilty as hell, the lousy Commie bastard."

"Don't talk about my client like that," Tom
Armour said sternly.

"Then don't take people like him as clients."

The three men walked back into court, and
the judge explained to everyone that there was
possible new evidence and court was adjourn-
ing for a two-day investigation. Court would
reconvene again on Friday. He thanked everyone for being there, and court was duly recessed, as Tom whispered to Charles and
explained what had happened. And as soon as
he stood up again, he signaled to John Taylor.

"Can I see you for a minute? We need
help."

"Sure." Officially, the way things had
worked out, John was there to help the prosecution. But he was actually there to help all of
them, by finding Teddy.

"Can we go somewhere quiet for a few minutes?" He left Charles then, to be taken back
to jail, and followed Taylor to an empty office.

"What you got?"

"I'm not sure. But I think it's a good one."
He explained the source to him, and what the

man had said. "He's scared out of his mind. He took the dough from whoever left it for him, and he's an accessory now, or at the very least he'll get an obstruction of justice. He's got a record an arm long, the guy's on parole, and he's scared shitless to come forward."

"At least he's not dumb. Who is he? Maybe I know him."

"You probably do. But you've got to guarantee me amnesty for the guy if I tell you."

"I can't guarantee you shit, Armour. But I can guarantee you I'm gonna kick your ass if you don't share what you've got with me. We're not just protecting your client's ass here. We're looking for a four-year-old boy, who may or may not be dead by now, and if he isn't, he's in one hell of a lot of danger."

"I know that, dammit. But you can't blow my source. He also thinks the boy is still alive. You've got to promise me you're not just going to go and nail him."

"I'm not going to nail him. I want to talk to him. If you want, you can come with me. Who is he?" Armour was still worried he was going to get the guy in trouble.

"His name is Louie Polanski," Tom said hesitantly, praying Taylor wouldn't bust him.

"Louie? Louie the Lover? Hell, Louie and I go back years. I sent him to the joint fifteen years ago when I was a kid myself . . . I saved his life. His mob buddies were trying to kill him then, and we gave him a nice cozy cell and protection for about five years. He loves me." John Taylor was actually grinning.

"Are you serious?" Tom looked startled by the story.

"He'll talk to me. I swear it." And when Tom called Louie again, he was waiting by the phone, and he agreed to meet with Tom Armour and John Taylor.

They met at one o'clock in an Italian restaurant in Greenwich Village, it was run by the mob and had been a speakeasy for years, and Taylor knew it well, although it was new to Tom Armour. The man they met was short and obese, bald, and sweating profusely. He was a nervous wreck when he talked about what he'd done, but he actually seemed genuinely pleased to see John Taylor.

"I never shoulda done it. It was crazy. But it was so damn much money, and it sounded so easy." And it had been. Until now.

Taylor looked at Tom. "Who the hell would have paid him that much to frame Delauney? Somebody really has it in for your client."

"I wish to hell I knew who," Tom said sourly.

"The word is, the kid's still alive, but I don't

know where, or who's got him," Louie said in a whisper, glancing over his shoulder.

"What makes them think so? Can you find out?" Taylor was suddenly all business.

"I'll ask. But I think someone's keepin' it real quiet. There's a lot of money changed hands, and they must have hired good ones, because no one's talkin'." Except for Louie, thank God. Taylor found himself praying that Louie's pals were right, and that Teddy was still living.

"You have any idea where he is? Any hint? Any clue? Anything we can go on?"

"Maybe he's already out of the country." They had thought of that. But for months they had held a tight rein on the ports and the airport, and even the frontiers into Canada and Mexico. They had closed down everything tight, until very recently. By now they figured that Teddy was either dead, or no one was going to try moving him out of the country. But that suddenly made John wonder. The pressure on the ports had been lightened only the week before. It was worth another look. He looked at Louie with an interested expression.

"You just gave me an idea, Louie. I love ya."

"Yeah? Then what are you gonna do for me? Listen . . . I'll give the money back . . . I only spent ten grand. You can have back the

other forty. Give it to the FBI, Christ, give it
to the judge. But shit, I don't wanna do more
time for a lousy pair of kid's pajamas."

"Tell you what." Taylor looked at him seriously. "If we find anything, I'll make a deal for
you for helping us find the kid. If we don't find
him, you could be in deep shit. But I'll do
what I can. I'll call you."

"Yeah . . . let me know . . ." Louie the
Lover looked nervously at Tom, and John Taylor went to make a phone call.

"Thank you for talking to us," Tom said quietly. "This could mean my client's life."

"Yeah," Louie smiled nervously, "and my
ass. But . . . eh . . . I don't like to see people hurt a kid. Stinks. You know what I mean.
Like the Lindbergh thing. I was in the joint
then, doing time for a little bank robbery.
Made me sick, guys like that . . . killing a
baby."

"Do you think they could have killed him?"
Tom felt sick as he thought of it, not just for his
client. He had come to admire Marielle
through the trial, and he couldn't bear the
thought of her going through that. Especially
not after the other children she'd lost, and
what she was facing with Malcolm.

"Hard to tell," Louie answered seriously.
"Sometimes when there's a lot of money in-

volved, it could go either way. And word on the street is, this one's a big ticket."

"I wish I knew who did it." He knew for certain it wasn't Charles Delauney. He had believed him before, but now he had no doubts whatsoever. But if it had been this professionally done, he also wondered if they would ever find out who had done it. Or find poor Teddy.

And when Taylor came back, he looked grim.

"What's up?" Tom asked him.

"I don't know. Maybe it's a wild-goose chase, but we're going to tear the port apart for the next few days. You never know what you're going to find there. But I hear we've got ten freighters and six passenger liners to pull apart. That ought to keep us busy for a few minutes. And Louie, you do your stuff too, and see what you hear." And if nothing else they could get a statement from him about planting the bear and the pajamas. But Taylor knew it might prove not to be that easy, in the end, to protect him. "I'll call you."

"Thanks for lunch." Louie looked at both of them, and he wasn't sorry he had come. If they found the kid, maybe it would be worth it. A man had to do something he felt good about once in a while, even if it cost him.

And as they left the restaurant, Taylor slipped into a phone booth, and made another call. He called Marielle at the house, he hadn't wanted anyone to hear him. "Hi there. It's me." He knew she'd recognize his voice. "Will you meet me at the same church we went to yesterday, say . . . in twenty minutes?"

"Sure." She sounded surprised. And when he met her there, she'd come alone. She'd slipped out the back door, and walked down the street like anyone else before anyone noticed. She was wearing a scarf over her head, a wool jacket, and dark glasses.

"Is something wrong?" She looked worried, and he smiled to reassure her.

"No, but I'm going to be very busy for the next couple of days. If you don't see me, don't be worried."

"Does it have to do with the new evidence they mentioned in court this morning?" She seemed surprised. She had seen him literally every day since the night of the kidnapping. He was her only support now.

"Yes, it has to do with that."

"Is it . . . does it have to do with Teddy?" . . . had they found him . . . or worse, found his body? But she didn't dare ask him.

"I don't think it has to do with anything, but we're checking it out. Don't worry about it, I'll

let you know if anything turns up," he assured
her. He didn't want to raise her hopes, it
wasn't fair to do that. "But I want to ask you a
question first. Something my office turned up
accidentally this morning." It was what had
led him to think of the port, that and something Louie the Lover had said. The two together had started a bell ringing in his head.
Before that, he just figured it was a mistake, or
something she hadn't told him. "Are you and
your husband going anywhere in the next two
weeks?"

"Malcolm? He's hardly spoken to me in
weeks, and last night he told me he was going
to divorce me." But she didn't look upset. She
was taking it all pretty well considering what
she'd been through.

"Nice guy. So you're not planning a trip
with him?" He was sure she wasn't, but he'd
had to check it.

"No. Why?" She looked puzzled.

"You don't think he'd plan a little honeymoon, to try and patch things up?"

"Not with me anyway. He told me his lawyer would call me."

"When was all this?"

"Last night, after church," and then suddenly she remembered something he'd said in

Teddy's bedroom. "He said he was going away. Is that what you mean?"

"Maybe." But he didn't tell her that Mr. and Mrs. Malcolm Patterson were booked to sail on the *Europa*. He could only assume that Malcolm was taking Brigitte and planning to pass her off as his wife. It had been done before, and on shipboard, people tended to be pretty discreet. Nice little trip he'd planned for himself, while Marielle was waiting to hear from his lawyer. What a bastard. "Anyway, I just wondered. I figured it was a mistake."

"Did you think I was planning to slip out of town?" She smiled, but even when she smiled her eyes were sad now. She had been through too much in the past four months. He wanted to hold her in his arms, but it didn't seem the time or place to him and he was busy.

"Don't plan on leaving town without the FBI on your heels, Mrs. Patterson."

"Actually, that sounds very appealing." She smiled as they walked out of church. "When will I see you again?"

"As soon as I can get away. I'll come by the house, or I'll call you. Or I'll see you in court on Friday morning." He smiled gently and put an arm around her shoulders.

"Take care of yourself." He knew that when he wasn't busy, he would worry about her every moment. He followed her most of the way back to the house, and then watched as she ran up the street to the Patterson mansion. He took a cab then to his office.

And for the next two days, Marielle didn't hear from anyone. Malcolm went down to Washington to see the German ambassador and Brigitte went with him. Tom Armour had his hands full with polishing up his closing arguments and keeping Charles calm. He was a nervous wreck about what was going on, when Tom told him at least some of Louie's story. If he'd known all of it, Tom knew he'd have gone completely crazy. But he knew Louie had planted the bear and the pajamas. What he didn't know was that Louie might not be willing to testify, if the FBI wouldn't promise him amnesty and protection.

"But that proves I'm innocent," he almost shouted at Tom.

"I know. But the guy has to be willing to come forward."

"What's his name?" As though it mattered, but Tom Armour smiled.

"Louie the Lover."

"Great. Just the kind of guy I need in my corner."

"Listen, my friend, if he planted those pajamas and is willing to testify to that fact in court, he's exactly who you need in your corner."

"How the hell did you find him?" Hope was beginning to dawn but he knew he wasn't out of the woods yet. A lot of things were going to have to happen right before he could be acquitted, and if Louie the Lips, or whatever his name was, disappeared, Charles was as good as dead, and he knew it.

"Actually, I got a hot tip in the middle of the night, from a friend of yours, or an admirer anyway."

"Who's that?" Charles looked intrigued.

"Beatrice Ritter," Tom said noncommittally.

"She's quite a girl, isn't she? Lots of spirit," and then Charles looked pensive. "Sometimes she reminds me of Marielle when she was young. She was such a fireball then, so full of life and fun and mischief. I guess life kicked it out of her after that." He looked sad. "Or maybe I did." She was so serious now, so beautiful and kind, and so quiet. And yet there was a side of her that wanted to laugh and have a good time, and be happy again. Tom Armour could see it when he talked to her. "Do you think she'll ever recover from all this?" He asked Tom as though he knew her, but Charles had come to recognize that his attorney had a good instinct for people.

"I think she will. I don't think she'll ever be the carefree young girl of her youth that you describe, but few people are by the time they reach thirty. She'll get over it, but it'll still be there. She'll go on, because she's strong." But he sighed then, she deserved a lot better than she'd gotten.

"How come you're so happy most of the time?" Charles teased him. They had become friends in the last four months, Charles respected Tom, and Tom liked him.

"Just stupid, I guess." But he had had his share of tragedy too. He had told Charles early on, when Charles had told him about André. Tom had lost his wife and baby daughter ten years before in a car accident, right after he finished law school. Oddly enough, it was the same year Charles had lost André. And he had never remarried either. But he was crazy about his work, and he figured one day he would, when he had time . . . when he wasn't defending lunatics like Charles Delauney . . . when he felt brave enough to love someone again . . . but for Tom Armour, that time hadn't come yet.

Tom had a hell of a time keeping Charles distracted for two days and Charles kept asking Tom if there was any news from John Taylor. But there wasn't. Tom was anxious to hear from him himself, and he had only dared to call once, and was lucky enough to find him in the office. And Taylor sounded exhausted.

"Hell man, do you know what it's like to tear apart sixteen ships? We've torn up the whole fucking port, what do you mean 'hurry up'?" And they had asked for the same cooperation from the Port Authority in New Jersey, but it was easier for them. All they had in port at the moment were tankers. But Manhattan was a snakepit, and all the foreign ships were furious to be searched, until they heard what it was about, then they were a little more willing to cooperate, but not much. The news of Teddy's kidnapping was old, and in spite of the trial, people had already begun to forget, and stop caring. And the inconvenience of a major search, with all it involved, was monumental. They had even checked out the *Europa,* which Malcolm was sailing on later, but it was clean. And the Germans had been highly annoyed to have their ship searched.

"I told you. I'll call you if we get anything. I haven't been in my office since last night, and I only came in to take a shower because I couldn't stand myself anymore. You got any complaints, Mr. Armour?" Taylor was sharp, but Tom knew he didn't mean any harm, he was just tired.

"No complaints, just a nervous client."

"Tell him to keep his pants on. We're doing our best. And will you do me a favor?" He hesitated and then decided to ask him.

"Sure. Shoot. What is it? Call Louie the Lover?" He smiled and Taylor laughed.

"No. Marielle Patterson. She must be a wreck, wondering what's going on. I didn't tell her about Louie getting fifty grand to plant the pajamas. I just told her we had a new lead. I didn't want to get her excited."

"Sure. What'll I tell her?"

"I don't know . . ." Taylor hesitated, and Tom found himself wondering what his interest in her was, but he told himself he was too suspicious about everything, he was turning into a real bastard. "Just make sure she's all right. Patterson's giving her such a hard time. He's divorcing her, you know."

"Swell guy." Tom was disgusted, but not surprised to hear it.

"That's what I said. He doesn't know how lucky he is. But I think he's going to get what he deserves with little Miss Krautland. Underneath all that blond hair, she looks like one tough cookie."

"May I quote you, Special Agent Taylor?" Tom laughed, and Taylor chuckled tiredly in answer.

"Anytime, Counsellor."

"You've got to admit, the little kraut looked cute on the stand though." They both laughed and Taylor went back to work reorganizing his agents. They had already torn apart twelve ships and they had four to go before the next morning.

Tom managed to call Marielle, as he'd promised Taylor.

"Is there something particular going on, Mr. Armour?"

Marielle sounded really worried. "I keep thinking they've had some kind of information about . . . about . . ." She was afraid to say it. "I keep worrying that they're going to find Teddy's body. I guess we should know if . . . I don't know which is worse, not knowing, or finally knowing that it's over." Either one sounded pretty awful to Tom. He still remembered finding out about his wife and the baby. It had been beyond bearing. But this had dragged out for so long, maybe it would be a relief to finally know if he was gone, instead of just having him disappear into thin air, and never know. It had taken them two months to find the Lindbergh baby.

"I hope we'll have good news for you soon."

"Do you know what it is they're doing?"

He didn't want to tell her they were turning

the port upside down, looking for Teddy. "I think they're just looking into some final evidence before we close. It'll all be over tomorrow."

"How's Charles taking it?"

"Actually . . ." Tom leaned back in his desk chair and smiled. She had a nice voice, and he liked talking to her. He liked everything he'd seen of her during the trial, but he hadn't let himself think about her before, except in relation to his client. "Actually, he's driving me crazy, to tell you the truth."

"That sounds like Charles." And then she grew serious again. "Is he very worried?"

"As worried as he should be. This new evidence may be of some help to him though. We're hoping so anyway. The FBI is checking it out for us. We'll let you know if we hear anything at all."

"Thank you." She wasn't supposed to be on their side, but there didn't seem to be sides anymore. There was just everyone searching for the truth . . . and for Teddy.

The next two days seemed endless to her with Malcolm away, and John Taylor gone to help with the investigation. Suddenly, she had no one to talk to, and with Malcolm gone, the house seemed unusually quiet. It made her start to think about what she would do when

she moved out. She had nowhere to go, nothing to do, no family to turn to. In some ways it
worried her, but she wasn't as frightened as
she might have been years before. He didn't
frighten her anymore. Suddenly, she didn't
care about him at all. All he had done was hurt
her.

Bea Ritter called her once too on the second
day of the recess, but she didn't say what the
investigation was about either. She pretended
not to know, and she didn't admit that she had
brought the tip to Tom Armour. She just called
to say hello, and see if they had any more leads
about Teddy.

"No, nothing. Have you seen Charles
again?"

"A few days ago. He's incredibly tense since
they're so close to going to the jury." And she
was praying they wouldn't have to.

But by midnight that night, nothing had
changed. There were two more ships to go
through, and one of them was refusing. It was
German and they claimed they didn't have to
submit. It took another eight hours to get a
court order to force them. And at ten o'clock
the next morning, as Judge Morrison called
the court to order, John Taylor was boarding the last ship with the Coast Guard, the
Port Authority, and the FBI, and he was sure

they would find nothing. But if nothing else, he had to do it for Marielle. He called Tom Armour from the dock, just before he left for the courtroom.

"Well?"

"We got nothing. We came up empty. No Teddy, no more tips, no one will talk, no one knows anything. We touched base with every one of our informants. Nothing. And Louie the Lover's not answering his phone. I think he's scared. He may have run out on us." Taylor had nothing but bad news for him.

"Shit. What am I supposed to do now?"

"You close your case, just like you were going to do two days ago."

"But he didn't do it, dammit, man. You heard the man. Someone paid him fifty thousand big ones to plant the kid's pajamas."

"Yeah, I know. But who's going to testify to that? You, or me? Hell, it's hearsay."

"You can't do this to me!" Tom was practically in tears, but Taylor was too tired to care. He still had one last ship to tear apart, and he was almost too exhausted to do it.

"Fuckin' A, man, I haven't slept in two days and I've been all over every slimy rotten ship in this port," and a few fancy ones too, but they all looked the same to him by now, "and I haven't turned up shit. I think your guy probably didn't do it, but I can't give you the goods to get him off with, and we don't have the kid. What more can I tell you?"

"I'll ask for a mistrial." Tom's voice was shaking he was so upset. But so was Taylor. No matter how hard they pushed, no one was talking.

"A mistrial based on what?" Taylor asked tiredly as his men started boarding the German ship to look around, but their hearts weren't in it anymore. They knew they weren't going to find the boy. Either he was gone, so well hidden he would never be found, or he was dead and buried somewhere and wouldn't turn up for years. "How the hell are you going to get a mistrial?" Taylor repeated when Tom didn't answer.

"I don't know . . . give me time . . . can you give me any reason at all to ask for another recess?"

"None at all. And if Louie doesn't surface soon, the judge is going to have your ass and mine to replace him."

"Yeah. I know that."

"I'll send a message to you in court with one of my guys, after we check this ship, but don't get your hopes up." Tom's hopes were already dashed and he dreaded telling Charles that Louie the Lover had vanished.

"He *what*?" Charles shouted when Tom told him.

"He's gone," Tom whispered tersely as they walked into the courtroom.

"Son of a bitch. How could those assholes have let that happen?"

"Keep your voice down." The judge was rapping his gavel. "He had a lot to lose. He could have gone to prison for what he did. And he's on parole with a rap sheet as long as your arm. It's a rotten thing to do, but you can't really blame him."

"The hell I can't. They're going to execute me for this." Tom's eyes were like rocks, and there was a pain in the pit of his stomach.

"I'm not going to let that happen to you." Tom tried to sound confident but it was not what he felt as the judge asked him and Bill Palmer to approach the bench with a look of suspicion.

"Well, Counsellor? Your new evidence? Do we have a witness?"

"No, sir, we don't," Tom Armour said grimly. "The FBI have been investigating this lead and several others for two days, and so far they've gotten nowhere." He was brutally honest and the prosecutor looked pleased.

"And your informant?" the judge asked, looking displeased with Tom.

"Has vanished, Your Honor. For the moment."

"I can't believe you've wasted two days of the court's and the taxpayers' time, Mr. Armour." The judge was rapidly sliding from displeasure to fury.

"We had to check it out, sir. I was even hoping to ask for a further recess. But . . ."

"Don't even consider it, Counsellor." He glared at both of them and waved them back to their seats. Bill Palmer was looking extremely happy, and he glanced at Malcolm sitting staunchly in the courtroom, with Marielle next to him, very still and quiet. They never spoke in court. The judge rapped his gavel again, and told Bill Palmer to make his closing statement.

Tom Armour couldn't believe this was happening. They had almost had the key to it in their hands, and they had lost it. Charles looked as though he was near tears, and Bea Ritter was frantically wondering what had happened, but there was no one to tell her.

In his closing arguments, all of Bill Palmer's statements were predictable, and ugly. He reminded the jurors of every ugly thing Charles had ever done, every stupidity, every weakness, every threat, every drunken binge, every minor, or major, act of violence. His attack on

Marielle, his wanton destruction years ago, at nineteen, of a neighborhood bar in Paris. All of these were the early signs, according to Bill Palmer, of a lack of control, a self-indulgence, a tendency to violence that would eventually lead him to kidnap and *kill* little Teddy. His violence at war, his thirst for killing which had led him to the Great War at fifteen . . . His leaning to Communism, which had taken him to Spain . . . and the threats he had made in Central Park, which had been carried out only thirty-six brief hours later. And the little red pajama suit found in his basement, a sign that he indeed had kidnapped Teddy. The man was a kidnapper, the prosecutor raged across the courtroom, and he had almost certainly killed this helpless baby. And as he said the words, and looked at the jury, and then around the courtroom, there was a small flutter, and brief thumping sound. Finally, after all that had come before, it had been too much for her. Marielle Patterson had fainted.

16

As she came to, there was a terrible hum of noise, and blurred lights overhead, a feeling of something cold and damp on her forehead. She opened her eyes, and after a few moments, Marielle realized she had been carried into the judge's chambers. His secretary was standing over her with a damp cloth, and a doctor had been called, but she insisted that she was all right. She tried to sit up, but she felt weak, and then she saw that both attorneys were there, and her husband. Someone was pressing something cool against the insides of her wrists, and someone else handed her a glass of water. It was Bea Ritter. She had pressed right through the crush of photogra-

phers and literally climbed over them to get to
Marielle, and it was Bea who had called for
help as she knelt next to her on the floor, not
Malcolm. He only looked annoyed and embarrassed, and not one whit sympathetic.

"Mrs. Patterson?" the judge asked quietly.
"Would you like someone to take you home?"
Her head throbbed angrily as he asked her.

The truth was she would have liked to have
gone home, but she thought it cowardly not to
stay till the end. She felt she owed it to
Charles, or to Malcolm, or to someone. She
wasn't sure whom, but she thought she was
supposed to be there. Maybe just to prove to
the world that she wasn't a weakling. But everyone was looking so sorry for her now that
she hated to be there.

"I'm all right. If you don't mind . . . perhaps I can stay here for a few minutes." At
least long enough to regain her composure.

"Had you finished your closing statement,
Mr. Palmer?" The judge looked across his office and inquired, and Bill Palmer nodded. He
hadn't expected the additional drama to punc-
tuate his statement, but it hadn't done any
harm either. Actually, he rather liked it.

"Yes, I had, Your Honor. Just."

"Then why don't we recess for lunch? Mr.
Armour can close after the noon recess. Is that

all right with you, Counsellor?" It was already eleven-thirty, and he wouldn't have wanted to break into his closing statement anyway, so it was fine with him, and he agreed with a concerned look at Marielle. She was white as a sheet, and she looked really awful. But the judge had seen it too. "I think Mrs. Patterson should go home and rest for a little while, during the recess," he suggested to the room at large.

"Thank you, Your Honor," she whispered as Tom's heart went out to her, and Bea patted her hand in sympathy.

Malcolm made a show of assisting her to the car, but when they got to the house, he left her to her own devices. She lay down in her room, in the dark, with a cold cloth on her head, and tried to drink a little tea. But it was too late. She already had a crushing migraine. But she knew that no matter how rotten she felt, or how blinded by pain, she had to be back at the courtroom by one-thirty. But suddenly she could hardly force herself to go. It was as though she had expected something that only that morning she had finally come to understand wasn't going to happen. In some odd way, she'd thought it was all like a terrible game . . . and if they won . . . in the end, she'd get her child back. Someone would admit what they had done with him, or say they were sorry. There was going to be a reasonable end to it all, a prize for all the pain, some reasonable closure, only now she realized that there wasn't. There was nothing. There were only words and people and actors . . . and liars . . . and in the end, someone would say either innocent or guilty, and they would either execute Charles or set him free, but no one was ever going to bring Teddy back. Never. That had never been part of the bargain. And she felt as though she were in a haze of confusion as she lay there.

"Are you coming?" Malcolm walked into her darkened bedroom at one-fifteen, and looked with scorn at her lying on the bed. She felt too ill to move. And she couldn't even imagine getting to the courtroom.

"I don't think I can," she said weakly. She couldn't even open her eyes, or sit up now.

"That's nonsense," he snapped at her. "You *have* to. Do you want them to think that you're afraid to be there?" He said it as if it were a cardinal sin. Was fear so terrible then? The second deadly sin. Fear. The first one was weakness. And what about love? Was that a sin too? Had she sinned because she'd loved Charles . . . and André . . . and their baby girl . . . or even Teddy? Where was "love" in

Malcolm's vocabulary, or did it even exist? Were there only responsibility and obligation and duty? Her head was spinning. Or was love something he'd saved only for Brigitte.

"If you don't go, Marielle, they'll think you were in league with Delauney and you can't bear to watch him convicted. Is that what you want? Is that what you want smeared all over the press? Well, I don't. Get up for God's sake, and face it." He was shouting at her in the darkness, and she could feel her whole body tremble. But from somewhere, she drew on a strength she didn't know she had, and she sat up quietly and took the cloth off her head as she winced and looked at her husband. "I've been facing things all my life, Malcolm, things you couldn't begin to face, even now. So don't tell me what to get up and face." She spat the words at him in a way she hadn't dared speak to him since she'd known him. But he'd been vicious to her ever since Teddy's kidnapping, and she'd finally had it. It wasn't her fault, or his, or probably even Charles's. It had probably been done by some totally insane crazed stranger. And whoever had done it, they had, and it was over. Why did he continue to blame her?

"You look dreadful," he said, as he watched her comb her hair and pull it back in a bun in her dressing room. She went to wash her face and put on some lipstick, but she looked very severe, as she put on dark glasses and followed him to the car, thinking how long it had been since she'd seen John Taylor.

She sat quietly in the car next to Malcolm, with their guards and their policemen, and as usual they made their way through the crowds to the courtroom, dodging hands and people who wanted to touch them and ask questions, trying to avoid the press, and shield their faces from photographers. And with her headache, it seemed particularly awful. But they finally made it to their seats, and she took off her dark glasses.

For the first time during the trial, the judge was ten minutes late, and Tom was poring over his notes, while Charles sat with his eyes closed, looking grim. He had almost no hope left, in spite of Tom's skill. He was certain that without the informant's testimony about the pajamas and the bear, he would be found guilty.

The judge had just invited Tom to begin his closing argument, and he had just stood up, when John Taylor walked into the courtroom. He stopped for a moment and looked at the judge, who knew him well, and both prosecution and defense looked at him with profound expectation. And everyone in the courtroom wondered why the usually pristine FBI agent was so disheveled and filthy. He was wearing work pants and a rough sweater, and he was absolutely covered with oil and dirt, and it seemed a very odd appearance in court, but he went straight to Marielle, as everyone watched, and with an apologetic glance at the judge, John whispered to her to come with him. She followed him out of court silently, without even saying a word to Malcolm. Everyone watched them go, with turned heads and whispers, and the judge finally rapped his gavel again to get everyone's attention.

"May I remind you, ladies and gentlemen," he boomed, "that Mr. Armour is making his closing statement." Tom turned himself to what he was doing then, and attempted to concentrate and not think about why John Taylor had taken Marielle out of the courtroom. He had the terrible feeling that they had found Teddy's body and he wanted to tell her first. But wouldn't he have taken Malcolm with him too, or was it kinder not to? Tom forced himself to focus on the man with one leg . . . and the ex-nun . . . and the young black musician . . . and tell them what a fine man Charles was, how he had been unfairly accused, and the prosecution had *not* proven beyond a reasonable doubt that he was guilty. That if they examined their conscience there was no way they could send this man to the electric chair for things he had said, and never meant, in the heat of a drunken moment. Even to his own ears, he droned on, as he continued to wonder why Marielle had left the courtroom. It was all he or anyone else could think of. Only Malcolm looked calm as he continued to watch the proceedings.

And as she got in a car with John, she looked at him in terror. "What's happening?" she asked anxiously. "What's going on?"

"I want you to trust me. I have to take you somewhere. Are you all right?" He looked at her worriedly. She had swayed for a moment, and no one had told him she'd fainted that morning.

"I'm fine. I just have a very bad headache." She winced again, but she followed him into the car without hesitation.

"I'm sorry to do this to you. It won't be as bad as you think, and I'll make it as easy as I can for you . . . but I need to take you with me." He started the car, and they drove off toward the West Side, and she looked frightened.

"Are you arresting me?" Was that possible? Was he crazy? Did he think she'd been in collusion with Charles after all? Had Malcolm told him that? His final revenge on her? As they drove west, she looked really frightened.

"Of course not." He patted her hand gently, and then raised an eyebrow, trying to make light of the moment. "Should I be?"

"I don't know," she said nervously. "I don't know where we're going. Should Malcolm be here too?" Like Tom, she was suddenly afraid they were going to ask her to identify Teddy's body, and she knew she couldn't stand it, and maybe John thought he was being kind to her by taking her there alone, but he shook his head in answer to her question.

"No, he shouldn't. You'll be fine with me, Marielle. Trust me. You'll be all right. This won't be as difficult as you think." He looked at her gently, wanting to kiss her. But right now, they had serious business to take care of.

"Can't you tell me what this is about?" She was almost in tears. All he had said to her in court was "Mrs. Patterson, I have to ask you to come with me." And Malcolm had looked as startled as she did.

"I can't tell you, Marielle, I'm sorry. Right now, this is official business." But he patted her hand, and left a smudge of soil on her fingers.

She nodded, trying to be brave as she rode

along, but the headache was so bad now she could hardly stand it. He chatted with her on the brief drive, but it was obvious that he was preoccupied, and she couldn't help noticing that he was absolutely filthy, and she wondered why. And he was so distracted he didn't even notice her silence.

A few minutes later they reached the port, and he drove right onto the docks, where half a dozen FBI cars were waiting. And everyone scrutinized her intently as she got out of the car and he helped her.

"I hate to touch you, I'm so dirty." He smiled and the gentleness of his eyes seemed to help her.

He took her on board the ship then, it was a small German ship, and it wasn't particularly attractive or particularly clean, and there was a terrible smell of cabbage which did nothing to help her headache. It was a freighter which took passengers on too, and the captain was waiting for her in the small dining room, with a serious expression. Taylor introduced her, and half a dozen FBI men were standing by, and she was not sure if they were guarding her, or the captain, or John Taylor. But the captain came forward to her quickly.

"Mrs. Patterson. I am so very sorry. This will be a terrible sadness for my country," he

said solemnly with an awkward bow and an
attempt to kiss her hand, but as he said the
words to her, the room began reeling. She
knew from what he said, that they must have
found Teddy's body. She turned suddenly to
John Taylor in desperation, almost clawing at
him, begging him with her eyes to help her.
He pulled a chair up next to her and helped
her into it, and signaled to one of his men to
bring her a glass of water. And when it came
he held it to her lips and let her lean against
him, while he almost crooned to her like a
mother with a sick child, begging her to be
strong and let him help her. But all she could
do was shake her head and close her eyes, and
want to die again. She knew she just couldn't
go through it.

"You're all right, Marielle . . . you're going
to be fine . . ." She could hear his voice as
she closed her eyes, and then opened them.
"Just a few more minutes. I want you to look
at some people for me . . . that's all. I just
want you to look at them and tell me if you
know them."

"Are they dead?" She was whimpering like
a child and he gently stroked her hair with one
hand as he touched her shoulder with the
other.

"No, they're alive. You're all right. You just

have to look at them and tell me, yes or no, if you know them."

"All right." She was having trouble breathing she was so afraid, and she was grateful for the chair because she knew she could never have stood up, as everyone watched her. And a moment later, a man was led into the room, escorted by two FBI men. He was tall and blond and very thin, and he had a hard, angry face, and he tried to avert his face from Marielle, but the FBI men gave him a hard shove until he faced her. He stood some five feet away from her and she shrank back toward John, but his agents held him fast, and he didn't try to escape them.

"Do you know this man, Marielle? Have you ever seen him anywhere? Look at him carefully." She shook her head and said that she hadn't, and she had no idea why she was there, and now she was afraid to ask him. She knew it had something terrible to do with her child, but if they had killed him, she didn't want to know it.

They took the first man away, and then brought the second man in five minutes later. This one was dark and swarthy and he had an ugly scar that ran straight across his face and back down toward his chin, and he looked at Marielle as though he would have liked to kill

her. He said something to her in German, in
an angry, guttural tone, and she shrank toward
John and he was quick to reassure her.

"No one's going to hurt you, Marielle. I
won't let them." She nodded, childlike again,
and still so desperately afraid to know what
they'd done. And then a woman was brought
in. She was blond and heavyset, about thirty.
She was speaking frantically in German to the
captain of the ship as they brought her in, and
he finally shouted at her to be silent, and she
looked imploringly at Marielle, as though she
expected her to help her.

"What is she saying?" Marielle asked.

"She is saying that she has hurt no one," the
captain explained. She said a lot more then,
and the captain finally told her again to be
quiet.

"Who are these people?" she finally asked
John.

"That's what I wanted to know from you
first. You don't know any of them, Marielle?
You're sure?"

"Not a one. I've never seen them before."

"They've never worked for you, even briefly
. . . or for Malcolm."

"I don't know. I've never seen them," she
said again. She was certain. John nodded ex-
pressionlessly at his men, and signaled for the

three Germans to be removed. And when they were gone, he nodded at his men again, and then bent to say something to Marielle in earnest.

"I want you to be very strong . . . I want you to be strong, Marielle . . . hold my hand . . . we're going to show you someone . . . and I want you to tell me if you know him." But she was afraid the moment he said the words. She didn't have the courage to look at her dead baby. She had seen André when he was drowned, held him in her arms, clutched him to her heart, and she couldn't do it again . . . she knew it . . . she couldn't. She began to cry and turned, struggling to be free, as John held her.

"I can't . . ." she cried, and buried her face against him. "I can't do it . . . please . . . don't make me . . ."

"It may not be him . . . you have to help us . . . please . . . please, Marielle . . ." He was almost in tears himself, and he hated to hurt her. But the child they had found appeared to be a deaf mute, and did not seem to understand them. They weren't sure if he was drugged, or too frightened to speak to them, or simply didn't speak the language, and the captain didn't recall seeing him before, although the group had been aboard for days. The child looked different than the Patterson boy, but there was something about the eyes that had caught John's attention. The hair color was wrong, and he was much thinner than the photographs he'd seen of him, and older, but still . . . he knew he had to ask her. He couldn't let the ship sail without asking her to look at him. And some sixth sense had told him that there was something very wrong about these people. But she was clinging to him, and she refused to look at him. And then John's eyes met hers as he held her.

"You have to do this, Marielle . . . for Teddy's sake . . ." He held her hand, and slowly her head turned, and she stared at the child they brought in, and everything stopped for an endless moment. She got up and she stood staring at him, as though unable to believe what she was seeing. His hair had been cut, and he had short dark brown hair, but it was faintly blond at the roots, and if you looked carefully, you could see that they had dyed it.

And as she stared at him, he looked up at her, unable to believe that she had finally come to save him. She let out a heartrending scream and in two long strides she was clinging to him and holding him tightly against her. And slowly, like a forgotten sound, the child began to cry. He began to whimper at first, and suddenly there were great wounding cries, as he clung to the mother he thought he had lost forever. The captain began to cry, and there were tears streaming down John Taylor's cheeks as he watched them.

She looked at no one for an endless time. All she saw, all she knew, all she felt, was the child in her arms, the child she thought she had lost forever.

"My darling . . . oh my love . . ." She held him as though she would never let him go, and finally the captain assisted them off the ship, and the three Germans were taken away in handcuffs and leg irons by the FBI men. He apologized profusely again, and John informed him that the ship would have to be held in port, pending further investigation. Two-dozen men were left to guard the ship, and John helped Marielle and Teddy into the car. He had to get her back to court and tell the judge what had happened. But he had also called for additional men. He knew he was going to need an army of guards for them at the court-house.

He looked long and hard at the child sitting on his mother's lap. The boy hadn't smiled, but he clung to her as though he was afraid to lose her. And John touched the small fingers holding hers ever so gently.

"Hello, little man . . . we've been looking for you for a long time." Teddy stared at him, not sure whether or not to trust him.

"They said you were dead," he whispered softly as he looked up at his mother . . . "and then they put me in a box . . . with holes in it . . . and they fed me crackers."

"Nice folks, these krauts," John said tautly, "I've always loved them." They were going to do a lot of talking. They had insisted from the moment they'd been detained that they had been hired by the boy's father to take him to Germany, to "safety," but they would not disclose the boy's father's name. They said only that the boy's parents were German. But one of them had been carrying a card with Malcolm's name on it and a phone number John recognized as Brigitte Sanders's apartment. But John had said none of this to Marielle. It was going to be interesting what else the Germans had to say once they all started talking.

"I don't know what to say," Marielle whispered softly to John as she clung to Teddy on her lap and they drove swiftly toward the courthouse. "I never thought we'd find him . . . and I was so afraid . . . I thought you had taken me there to . . ." She couldn't even begin to say the words, and suddenly she realized her headache was gone. All she could think of was Teddy, held tightly in her arms, in the speeding car, beside the man who had found him.

"I know what you thought," he said quietly. "I wouldn't have done that to you . . . if that was the case, I'd have taken Malcolm. But I wanted you to see them first. They said they'd been hired by the child's parents."

"Malcolm's going to be so glad," she smiled. She was glad for him. He didn't deserve to lose his son. But John Taylor said nothing.

Twenty FBI men were waiting for them outside the courthouse when they arrived, and John had them surround Marielle and the child almost like a living cage, and the boy looked very frightened. All Marielle did was cling tightly to him in her arms, and promise him that everything was going to be all right. They were going to see Daddy in a minute.

And as John Taylor walked into the courtroom, surrounded by his men, everyone paused, as though they sensed that something important was about to happen. The judge stared up at them. And Tom Armour stopped in midsentence. The odd group made its way down the room, and it was only when they reached the judge that the men slowly peeled

away at Taylor's direction and what they saw
suddenly in their midst, completely hidden
there, was Marielle holding a small dirty little
boy with dark hair, and the judge rose to his
feet with a look of amazement.

"Is this? . . ." He looked at Marielle, smiling through her tears as she looked up at him,
and then at Taylor, and then in confusion
across the courtroom as suddenly a woman
screamed as she understood, and the specta-
tors and the press tried to stampede, but the
police held them back. They had been warned
as Marielle and Teddy entered the courtroom.
"My God . . . *it's the boy!*" someone
shouted. *"He's alive. It's Teddy!"* The judge sat
down again and began frantically rapping his
gavel, and ordering the police to clear the
courtroom. But it was Malcolm's reaction
which fascinated John. When he first saw the
boy, he didn't do what Marielle had done. He
stood, and then he sat down, and then he
looked around him as though for someone
else, and only then did he suddenly leap forward. But it was almost an afterthought by
then. His first reaction had not been to run to
hold his baby. And there was none of the rush
of emotion Taylor had seen in Marielle, that
terrible terror that he was dead, and the gut-
searing scream when she realized it was her

baby. It was Charles who stood crying as he looked at him, and he smiled at Marielle over the boy's head as they both cried. He remembered another time, another day, and he was glad that this time had been different.

"Thank God he's alive," he whispered to Tom Armour, who nodded, fighting back his own emotions, as he smiled at his client through tears. He also knew what it was to lose a child, and he too was grateful that that hadn't happened. Charles wasn't even thinking of himself just then, he was just glad for Marielle that they had found Teddy.

Malcolm looked extremely sobered as he came forward to Marielle and John and Teddy. "Thank God you found the boy," he intoned, almost piously, but his eyes were dry, and Taylor could see that he was angry. He tried to take the boy from Marielle, but the boy wouldn't let go of his mother.

"They said Mommy was dead," he said, still looking terrified.

"They must have been terrible people," Malcolm said with an odd expression. And at that moment, John Taylor asked Malcolm to join him in the judge's chambers.

The court had been cleared by then, and only the two attorneys, the defendant, Marielle, the child, the jury, and the countless FBI men remained in the courtroom. The judge had gone with Malcolm and John Taylor to his chambers. Marielle had no idea what was going on between them, but she sat talking quietly to Charles and Tom, and there was a feeling of peace and well-being in the room that she had never sensed in her entire lifetime. Two of the FBI men had gone out to get Teddy an ice-cream cone, and he was eating it happily while holding tightly to his mother. And she sat there holding him, feeling as though he had never left her. The last months shrank into the mists of the nightmare from whence they had come, never to return again. Teddy was home, safe and sound. After four months, and by the grace of God, and John Taylor, and maybe even Louie the Lover, Teddy was back with his mother.

It was a long time before Malcolm and the judge and John emerged, and when they did, Malcolm's mouth was set in a thin line. John had had two interesting calls from his office. There was still a great deal they didn't know, but what they did know was that the kidnappers, or at least the three people holding him on the ship, had been hired by Malcolm. There was no doubt of it now. They were even carrying papers to prove it and they had a false passport for the child that had allegedly been provided by Malcolm. It said the boy's name was Theodore Sanders.

"That's absurd," he had said instantly, moments after the call came. "They're trying to implicate me in something I have nothing to do with." He looked outraged, and reminded Taylor instantly of his connections.

"They used your name, Mr. Patterson," John said quietly. "And no one else's. You'll have every opportunity to identify them, and to defend yourself. We'll have to talk about this. But we're going to do it in my office. A lot of money has changed hands, a lot of people have committed crimes here while on your payroll. And if nothing else, I think you're looking at charges of conspiracy and extortion. Not to mention whatever civil matter may arise on the part of Mr. Delauney." Taylor did not look amused, nor did Malcolm.

The judge looked shocked. It was impossible to believe the man had kidnapped his own son, or hired criminals to do it. Why would he ever do it? But that was up to the FBI to find out. He had a jury to send home, and an innocent man to release. At least it appeared that way. It didn't seem as though Delauney was the kidnapper after all, and the child was back unharmed. It was certainly a step in the right direction.

"Ladies and gentlemen," the judge spoke solemnly to the very confused members of the jury. "It would appear that we have a miscarriage of justice here. Or we would have had, if we had gone any further. It would appear, at this time, that Charles Delauney is innocent of the crime he has been accused of. Pending further investigation, I am going to release him at this time, and I am going to send you home to your families. We are going to ask Mr. Delauney not to leave the city, and we will notify you if this case is indeed dismissed, which I believe it will be. We thank you for everything you have done here, for your good faith and your time." He nodded and they stood up, looking as though they were going to run from the courtroom. But they all managed to smile at Marielle, and a few wished Charles good luck. One of the women stopped to kiss Teddy.

"I am releasing you, Mr. Delauney, without bail, with the understanding that you will not leave the city of New York until this matter is settled. Is that clear?"

"Yes, sir." Charles looked as though the weight of the world had been lifted from his shoulders.

"And I'll wait to hear from you, Mr. Taylor," the judge said to John as his agents led Malcolm away without handcuffs. Malcolm said not a single word to Marielle as he left, and he had barely spoken to Teddy. John stayed behind to take Marielle and Teddy home, and Tom was smiling at his client.

"You're a free man. Would you like a lift home?"

"I'd like that a lot," he said to his lawyer. "I'm glad he's back," he said softly to Marielle . . . "I couldn't stand your losing him too. You don't deserve that." He kissed her gently on the cheek then and they looked at each other for a long moment. "I'll always love you," he said, as Teddy stared at him, and Marielle nodded. She would always love him too, but she had nothing left to give to him. She had given it all a long time ago, and now all she had left was for Teddy.

"Come on, I'll take you home," John said quietly, as he put an arm around her shoulders, and slowly they walked out of the courtroom, as Charles watched them go. Tom took him home a few minutes after that, and Bea Ritter was waiting for them outside on the steps of the courthouse. When she had seen Marielle walk in, flanked by FBI men, she had known that something incredible had happened. She had sat on the steps, crying as she waited.

"I owe you a hell of a lot," Charles said to her, almost shyly. "You and Tom were the only ones who believed in me. And for a while there it was pretty rough going." She nodded gratefully, and he gave her a warm hug, and then he drove home with Tom, who dropped him off at the Delauney mansion. The old butler who had worked there for forty years almost fainted when he saw him. The papers were filled that night with the tales of Teddy being found on a German ship, by FBI agents allegedly carrying machine guns.

And by the next morning, Charles Delauney was a free man. At eight o'clock that morning, Judge Morrison had officially dismissed the case of the U.S. against Charles Delauney. With the evidence gathered the night before, Tom Armour had called the judge at home to ask him to sign the order. And by then, John Taylor had enough evidence to bury Malcolm. It was a complicated tale, and his supporters would find it difficult to believe, but he had hired the cream of the underworld to kidnap his own son and paid them a fortune to do it. Over a million dollars had changed hands to keep the boy hidden until the pressure had eased up, and he could be gotten out of the country. And finally, a German team had been brought in, handpicked and carefully trained, to spirit him back to the country where Malcolm was planning to make his home with Brigitte.

He had planned it for a long time, almost as soon as the child was born. By then he already knew he had made a mistake marrying Marielle and not Brigitte. Marielle was distinguished, dignified, decent, and kind, and in many ways, she was the perfect wife. But it was Brigitte he longed for, Brigitte who excited him, Brigitte he wanted to make his life with, except for the fact that she couldn't have children.

The idea had come slowly at first, then they had only talked of a divorce. Marielle was too gentle for him, too frightened, too marked by her past. He had liked the fact that she had no other ties, when he married her, but in time, he felt her dependency on him as a burden. And in contrast to her, Brigitte was everything she was not, she was sharper, harder, more demanding, and totally independent. She made demands on Malcolm which terrified him, particularly when she threatened to leave him. But he had dragged his feet about the divorce, because he didn't want to leave Teddy. He had thought of suing for custody, but that was so involved, and unsure. And finally, Brigitte had suggested they just move to

Germany, and take the boy with them. It was then that Malcolm had taken the plan several steps further. If the boy was presumed dead, eventually everyone would stop looking for him, including his mother.

And if, eventually, he married his secretary, and adopted her child in Germany, who would know? Who would question it? It would seem perfectly natural that he would try to ease the pain of his loss. And who would even suspect it was really Teddy? After a year or two of keeping him well hidden in Germany, he would seem like a German child. It was an ingenious plan, and it would certainly have gotten rid of Marielle forever. But it had used countless people in the process, Charles, Marielle, the child, the people who had kidnapped the boy, those who had hidden him. A lot of people had suffered, and would suffer now, because of Malcolm. It almost made the judge sick when he heard it. And John Taylor wanted to kill him.

The plan was beautifully thought out. And Malcolm had already begun moving large blocks of his assets to Europe. No one seemed to have noticed it, because he had so many investments there. But he was planning to move to Germany within the year, with Brigitte.

Brigitte had been well paid too, for her complicity, to the tune of half a million U.S. dollars, which had been deposited for her in Berlin. And his other minions had been paid well too. It was a plan that had cost him a fortune. But to Malcolm it was a fortune well spent. What he wanted was to get rid of Marielle, have the boy to himself, and bring him up German. He had had it with America, he said. It was Hitler who was going to rule the world, Hitler, the only man who knew how to run a country. All his efforts and interests and passion, and even money, were devoted to Adolf Hitler. And in his eyes, the greatest gift he could give his child was to bring him up German.

It was an incredibly evil tale, and John Taylor, like the others involved, could scarcely believe it. And oddly enough, no one had squeaked except "Louie the Lover," but as the house of cards began tumbling down, the people he had hired began talking, to save their hides. They had no intention of going down the tubes for Malcolm. And in a matter of days, John Taylor had more testimony than he knew what to do with. They still couldn't charge Malcolm with kidnapping, because Teddy was his son. But they had charged those who had actually taken him. And Malcolm was charged with conspiracy, collusion, obstruction of justice, and consorting with known criminals, which was the best they could do against him.

The odd thing was that Charles Delauney had been an afterthought, a bit of serendipity that had come along at the perfect time for Malcolm. He was the perfect scapegoat to take the blame, after what Patrick had reported to Malcolm when Marielle had first seen him at Saint Patrick's. The timing couldn't have been better for him. And it only took another fifty thousand dollars to plant the pajamas and teddy bear at the Delauney home, to seal Charles's fate and confirm that he was guilty. Malcolm had easy access to the pajamas anyway, since he had the boy well hidden in New Jersey. He had kept him there for four months, waiting for the ports to open up again. And in May, he and Brigitte would sail after him on the *Europa,* after blaming Marielle for putting the boy at risk and causing him to be kidnapped. Malcolm was going to tell the world he was the injured party, and continue to find consolation in the arms of the devoted Miss Sanders. It was all so perfectly planned, and it would have gone off without a hitch if John Taylor hadn't ruined everything by finding Teddy at the last moment on the little German freighter. Two days later it would have sailed. The thought made everyone shudder. And somehow in Malcolm's mind, it was all a respectable plan, since the boy was his own son, and all he had really wanted was to get Marielle out of the picture, and allow the boy to become a German. For Malcolm it meant spending the rest of his life in Germany, but Malcolm loved it there anyway. He loved it better than his own country.

But for the moment he wasn't going anywhere. He was out on bail, pending trial in late July, and he and Brigitte were hiding out in upstate New York.

She had been charged with conspiracy too, and there was some talk of deportation.

And all Marielle wanted was to get out of town and spend some quiet time with Teddy. She didn't want to see Malcolm or Brigitte, and she was dreading the next trial, but she knew she had to be there, as a witness for the prosecution. In the meantime, she was thinking of going to Vermont for three months, but there were a number of things she had to do first, like see an attorney about divorcing Malcolm.

She was explaining some of it to John, when he came to talk to her before she made any firm decision to take Teddy away on vacation.

He had been busy for days, but he still tried to drop by almost daily. His agents were gone from her home by then, and the police, and most of the servants were gone too. And she and Teddy were looking for an apartment.

"I thought we were going to talk before you made any serious moves." He'd been in the press constantly since the trial, as the hero who found the Patterson baby. And other than that, he'd had his hands full with the case against Malcolm and Brigitte, and all their minions. There was a total of twenty-two people involved, all charged with various offenses. "And what's this about Vermont?" He looked worried and hurt. He hated the thought of her leaving, even for a few months. He wanted to keep her near him.

"I thought we could use some country air." Particularly before she went through another month of trial. But this time she was prepared, and John would be with her. But she looked at him cautiously as she said it. She had a lot to say to him. But the right time hadn't come yet.

"Are you really moving?" He eyed her hopefully. In some ways, things had worked out better than he'd planned. She had the boy back, and she was free of Malcolm. The question was, what was he going to do? His eyes met hers now as he asked her if she was really moving out of the Patterson mansion. And she nodded slowly. She wouldn't be sorry to leave this house. The only happy memories she had there were of Teddy, and he was coming with her. "The house is Malcolm's." Their eyes met and there were a thousand questions he wanted to ask her. "All we need is a small apartment," she said softly.

"And what else? What do you want from me now?" He knew he had to ask her. He knew what he wanted, but he was afraid he couldn't have it. He wanted her. Forever.

"Your friendship" . . . your love . . . your life. But she knew that she had no right to say that.

"Is that all?" His eyes were sad as he asked her. For weeks now he'd been putting off this conversation because he was afraid of what she'd say if he told her just how much he loved her. They had promised each other they'd wait until after the trial, before they let themselves think of what they wanted from each other. And now the time was here, and she had made her decision. She didn't want to be responsible for destroying his marriage. "What do you want from me, Marielle?" he repeated to her. "What will you let me give you?"

"The gift of time. The time to heal, and enjoy my son. But I owe you more than that, John . . . I owe you everything . . ." She smiled at him. She owed him still more, and they both knew it, or at least she did. "I owe you not to take anything away from you, not to destroy what you have . . . to steal you from your home, your wife, your children. What would you really have if you left them?" Her eyes were big and deep and sad as she asked. And he knew she was wiser than he was.

"I'd have you and Teddy . . ." he said softly.

"And guilt, and regret . . . and maybe one day you'd hate me for it."

"I could never hate you."

Malcolm had hated her eventually, and Charles for a time. She knew what it was like. And she valued John Taylor too much to lose him. She'd loved him more than he knew, more than she was ever going to tell him.

"You're not going to let me run away with you, are you?" He looked at her sadly, touching her hand, and wanting to kiss her. It was part of why she wanted to go away, to get away from him and how much she loved him, but she didn't tell him. She knew she loved him too much to be near him and not to get involved with him, and she cared too much about him to interfere with his marriage, or his children.

She whispered to him gently as he took her in his arms. "You need them. And they need you." But so did she, and other than Teddy, she had no one.

"I need you too," he said urgently. He had never known anyone like her, and for a mad moment he had told himself that he could make her go away with him. He could force her to if he had to, but as he looked at her, he knew he wouldn't.

She had a right to what she wanted. A time of solitude and peace and healing. And maybe she was even right about Debbie. "I don't want to lose you, Marielle," or what they had had, the promise of so much more to come, and now that promise was over.

"You won't lose me. I'll always be here." Her eyes tortured him with their tenderness and their wisdom.

"And when you're not there anymore? When you belong to someone else?" he said sadly, because he knew that day would come, better than she did. Because she deserved it, more than anyone, and much more than he did.

"We'll still be friends. I told you . . . you won't ever lose me." And then she smiled again, "Unless you want to." She kissed him gently on the lips then and he held her close, and they talked for a long time, and finally, hating to go, he left her and went home, wondering if she was very wise or very foolish. It would be years before they'd know. And yet he had always known that their worlds were just too different. It was something she had never acknowledged, but he knew he had to.

He felt lonely without her for days, and it amused him at times to take it out on suspects in the Patterson interrogations. But she felt lonely without him too. It wasn't as though she couldn't call. She knew she could. But for his sake, she was trying not to. And she was busy getting ready for the move to Vermont with Teddy. They had finally rented a house, sight unseen, and there were supposedly cows and chickens and a sheepdog. And Teddy looked more like himself again at last. He had gained weight, and he looked healthy and happy and clean, and most of the brown dye had come out of his hair, except in a few spots, but he still got anxious at night, and he had terrible nightmares. He was sleeping in Marielle's bed, and she took care of him herself. Haverford was the only one left and he was leaving them for good in a few days, and he was enjoying helping her with Teddy.

In fact, he was helping Teddy to a bowl of ice cream when Charles came to say good-bye to her and Teddy. He was going back to Europe in the morning.

"Spain again?" she asked as he followed her into the kitchen.

"Not now." He was thinking of going to England to enlist, but after all that had happened, he knew he wasn't ready and he wanted to go back to Paris before he went to war again. "We're going to the South of France first, just for the summer." He blushed, as though embarrassed by the indulgence, but they both knew that he had earned it. But something he had said amused Marielle, and she couldn't resist teasing him, as Teddy offered him part of the huge bowl of chocolate ice cream as they stood in the Patterson kitchen. He and the boy were almost friends, although Teddy was still confused about how he knew his mother.

"We?" she asked. "Are you taking a friend?" But she already suspected. She had seen them out walking together more than once, and Marielle was pleased. Perhaps more than anyone, they deserved it.

"All right, all right," he laughed. He knew that she had already guessed. He knew how wise she was, and the odd thing was, he still loved her.

"Anyone I know?" After so many years apart, it was odd to be so friendly again, except she knew now that they would never really be apart again. Suddenly, it was all so different.

"I'm taking Bea to Paris with me."

"You should. You owe her at least that," Marielle teased, and he laughed.

"She was awfully good to me during the trial." And even better to him since then. He stayed for a little while, and Marielle kissed him when he left, but he caused her no pain and she wished him well. She was free of him now. But she still loved him.

The one she didn't love was Malcolm. She feared what would happen after his trial. Somehow, she knew that, because of his connections, if he was hurt at all, it wouldn't be for long, and she wanted to be as far away from him as she could be. She didn't want him anywhere near Teddy. But John Taylor had promised her unlimited protection. But she knew that she couldn't run away forever either. At some point, she would have to stand and face him. But the FBI had sworn that Malcolm would never again take Teddy. He had pushed her for so long, had been so cruel, and had been so coldhearted in the terrible things he had done that he would even be denied visitation.

Sometimes she wondered if she would ever love and trust anyone again, except Teddy. He was everything that mattered. He was the joy and the life and the spirit that she lived for.

The day before they left for Vermont, she packed the rest of her things. She could hardly wait to leave Malcolm's home. They were taking all of their things with them. She had told Malcolm the house would be vacant when he got back with Brigitte. And Marielle was more than willing to stay at a hotel with Teddy. For her, the house was now haunted and she didn't want to be there.

It had been difficult explaining it to Teddy. He still didn't know that it was his father who had had him kidnapped. And instinctively, he had sensed something was wrong, and he had heard whispers here and there, but he was still so young, he didn't really understand it. Marielle had told him that Malcolm was away for a long, long time, and it was unlikely they would see him. Teddy was surprised, but not sad, and he seemed happy just being with his mother.

The doorbell rang the night before they left, and Haverford came to tell her it was Tom Armour. She was surprised he had come to see her. Charles was gone by then, and she hadn't seen Tom since the trial, but he had heard from John Taylor that she was leaving.

She walked slowly down the stairs to meet him. And he looked very handsome and young, and a little ill at ease as he stood there. Marielle was friendly and warm, as she greeted him, acting as though his visit had been expected.

"I heard in court today that you're leaving," he said awkwardly, as she shook his hand, and Haverford disappeared to make coffee. He had been meaning to come and see her for a while, but he'd been putting it off, till he could get up his courage. He'd wanted to come and say good-bye to her himself. He had wanted to say something to her ever since the end of the trial, and with everything that had happened, he had never had the chance to. "You're going to Vermont?" That was all that Taylor had told him, but his eyes told their own tale, and for an instant, Tom had wondered what had happened.

She nodded with a smile, as they sat down in the library, where, in recent months, so much had happened. She wondered why he had come by. But she was happy to see him. He had done a good job for Charles, and she had always liked him. He had been decent to her when she was on the stand, and she had always sensed his strength and innate kindness.

"Teddy and I need to get away," she explained, as Haverford appeared with the coffee, and then disappeared just as quickly.

"How is he now?" He inquired about the boy, as he looked around. It was a magnificent home, and he couldn't help wondering if she was sorry to leave it. But she smiled as she watched his face. She knew what he was thinking, and she had no regrets. She couldn't wait to leave now.

"He's fine. He still has nightmares sometimes, and he doesn't like to talk about what happened."

"Understandably." They both knew it was going to mark him forever. And he still had no idea that the kidnapping had been masterminded by his father. Marielle was hoping she wouldn't have to tell him for years, which Tom thought was incredibly decent of her, but from what he'd seen of her during the trial, it didn't surprise him.

She seemed peaceful now, very calm and subdued, and her eyes were serious, but in a quiet way, she looked happy.

"And you?" he asked gently, as he looked at her. "You're all right? No more headaches?"

She smiled in answer. She hadn't had one since the trial. For the first time in years, she felt totally healthy. It was as though she had survived some terrible test, and having come through it the ghosts had finally been laid to rest, and she was much stronger. "I'm fine." She wanted to thank him for his kindness during the trial, but she wasn't quite sure how to do it, and she tried not to notice how handsome he looked in white slacks, a blazer, and red tie, but he was a good-looking man, and she blushed as she turned away to straighten a book on the table.

"Marielle . . ." He knew it would have to come from him. But he didn't want her to leave town before he had spoken to her. "I . . . I'd like to call you when you're in Vermont . . ." She looked at him with wide eyes, surprised by what he had said, and suddenly wondering if he was representing Malcolm. But he saw the look in her eyes and he gently touched her hand to reassure her. "I'm not sure I'm making myself clear . . . I'm making a terrible botch of this." He suddenly looked embarrassed and boyish, and they both felt like two children. "It's been a long time since I've done anything like this." It had been a long time since he'd met anyone even remotely like her. She reminded him so much of his late wife. And yet, she was also very different. Marielle had more integrity than any woman he'd ever known, more strength, more fortitude, possibly more kindness. And she hadn't been very lucky in the last ten years. When she came back from Vermont, he was hoping to change that. "Will you have a phone in Vermont?" He was still stumbling around, trying to talk to her about the future, and suddenly Marielle laughed. She thought she understood, but it was difficult to believe it. He had always been so businesslike, so cool, and yet beneath the serious air ran powerful emotions.

"I think we'll have a party line."

"Good. Then we'll give your neighbors a thrill," he laughed. "I'll try to think up some really juicy news to tell you when I call you." But there had already been enough of that, they both knew, for the past several months. She was hoping that life would be ordinary now, and she looked at him with interest as they chatted about her new life in the country. She was only going to be there for a few months, until Malcolm's trial. And then she would have to come back and find an apartment for herself and Teddy. Haverford was leaving them the next day, when they left for their adventure in Vermont. And when they came back, life was going to be very different, but she didn't regret it.

"Would it be too soon if . . ." He ventured

on, feeling more awkward than a schoolboy,
". . . if when you got back, I . . . we . . ."
He almost groaned as he looked at her, he
couldn't believe this was as difficult as it was.
He had been thinking of her for weeks, in
ways he hadn't thought of anyone in years, and
he had never thought anything would ever
come of it, and now he was finding it impossible to tell her. He finally took a deep breath,
took her hand in his own with an earnest expression. "Marielle . . . you're an extraordinary woman. I'd like very much to get to know
you." There. He had finally said it, and he felt
relief sweep over him. Even if she told him
she never wanted to see him again, at least she
knew to some small extent how much he liked
her. "I've admired you since the first moment
I saw you."

She blushed again, feeling oddly vulnerable
and very young, and when she looked at him,
he saw something in her eyes that almost
made him feel that he was melting.

"It's amazing to think that from so much
pain . . . from such a terrible thing . . . so
many good things have happened." She was
very gentle as she spoke, and very grateful for
the blessings she had received. And as she
looked at Tom, wanting to say so many things,
there was a sound at the door of the library,

and her greatest blessing appeared in blue pajamas.

"What are you doing here?" she said as she grinned, and Teddy bounded into the room with a look of mischief.

"I couldn't sleep without you." He climbed up on her lap, and looked at Tom with interest.

"Yes, you could. You were snoring when I left."

"No, I wasn't," he denied it, and Marielle introduced Tom to Teddy, without explaining how she knew him. "I was faking," he announced. But he yawned happily as he said it, and leaned possessively against his mother.

"I hear you're going to Vermont," Tom said easily. He loved children, and after all they'd been through over him, more particularly this one.

"Yeah," Teddy said proudly, "and we're going to have cows and horses and chickens. And Mommy says I'm going to ride a pony."

"I used to spend my summers in Vermont when I was your age." Tom smiled at him, and then over his head at his mother. He had said enough. No matter how awkwardly put, she had clearly understood his intentions, and she liked them. A private look passed between them over the boy's head that brought them suddenly closer.

"Did you have a pony?" Teddy inquired, suddenly intrigued by him. He hadn't seen his Daddy in a long time, and sometimes he still missed him. And Mommy said he'd gone on a long, long trip. He was probably in Africa somewhere, or on a ship, and they couldn't even call him.

"I did have a pony. And I had a cow I had to milk all by myself. If I come to Vermont, I'll show you how."

"Are you coming to Vermont?" Teddy looked seriously interested, and in point of fact, so did his mother.

"I hadn't thought of it," he had planned on waiting till she got back, "but actually that's not a bad idea." He glanced at Marielle inquiringly and they exchanged another smile. He was happy he had been brave enough to come over and see her before she left. Otherwise, he might have tortured himself for months, and perhaps now he wouldn't have to. "Maybe I could come up for a weekend." He knew a lovely hotel near where they were going, and the idea suddenly held enormous appeal, as he watched the boy with his mother.

"Can you still ride a horse?" Teddy asked him seriously.

"I think so," Tom laughed.

"If you can't," Teddy offered generously,

"I'll teach you." The three of them laughed, as they wandered to the kitchen to find Teddy a cookie. Haverford had gone to his room. He had to pack the last of his own things, and Marielle knew he was sorry to leave them. But he hadn't wanted to continue in Malcolm's employ, and Marielle could no longer afford him. She had accepted a small settlement from Malcolm and that was all she wanted. Teddy would inherit the rest from Malcolm when he was older.

Tom poured him a glass of milk, and Marielle found the last of the chocolate chip cookies, and in the end, the three of them sat talking and laughing and eating cookies until long, long after Teddy's bedtime. It was almost eleven when Tom finally left. He helped her put Teddy to bed, and then they both came downstairs so she could let Tom out, and he stood at the front door, looking at her for a long, hungry moment.

"Thank you for letting me spend some time with you tonight," he said, wanting to touch her hair, and her cheek, and her neck, but it was too soon and he knew it.

"I'm glad you came by." She hadn't expected ever to see him again, and she had regretted it. Now his visit had opened a whole new horizon. She still missed John Taylor, but she knew she had made the right decision, for his sake. And spending some time with Tom was like an unexpected gift and she was grateful. "I always wanted to tell you how much I admired you in court," she said softly, but he didn't want her thinking of that anymore. He only wanted her to think of Vermont, and happy things, and summers in the country with Teddy. And when she came back for Malcolm's trial, he already knew he was going to be there to help her. He didn't want her to go through it alone. He didn't want her to go through anything difficult again, only happiness and peaceful things, if he could do anything about it.

"Don't think of that," he said gently. He couldn't stop himself from reaching a hand out to her and bringing her closer. "Don't think of it anymore." The past was over. Hers, as well as his own. There was too much pain there, and he wanted to close those doors firmly behind them. "Just think of Teddy and his pony." They both smiled and then his eyes grew serious as they stood very close to each other. "I'll miss you when you're in Vermont." The crazy thing was he meant it. They scarcely knew each other, and yet they did. He knew her better than most of his closest friends, better in some ways than he'd known any of the women he'd gone out with. And he loved everything he knew about her.

"I'll miss you too," she smiled at him, feeling hope for the first time in years, and totally at ease with him. "We'll call you on our party line."

"I'll call you first," he whispered. He had already written down the number. "Drive carefully." He pulled her closer to him then and she closed her eyes when he kissed her. "Good night, Marielle . . . see you soon . . ." He looked at her for a last time as he stood in the doorway, and then he was gone, and she closed the door, thinking of how odd life was. You never knew what was going to happen. She had thought so many things that had been untrue in her lifetime . . . that she and Charles would be together forever, that their life would be happy and exciting and full of children . . . and that Malcolm would cherish and protect her forever . . . that nothing terrible would ever happen to them because he was so decent and so solid . . . and then she had feared that Teddy would never come back to her again. She had been wrong about everything, and especially, thank God, about Teddy. He was home again. He was all that truly mattered. He was the shining star of hope that she had survived for. But

now, there was something more than that. The
others had gone. The nightmares were past.
The dreams had vanished in the mists. And
she and Teddy were alone, with their bad
memories and their good ones, and their
whole lives before them. The sorrows would
strengthen them, she knew. And the time in
Vermont would do them good . . . and when
they came home, they would begin a whole
new life . . . and Tom Armour would be
waiting for them, with all the decency and
kindness he had to offer. And maybe their
dreams would come true, and maybe they
wouldn't. She hoped they would, and so did
he, as he walked home to his apartment. She
hoped the nightmares would never come
again, to either of them. She hoped many
things, and most of them about Teddy.

In the morning, when they left, Haverford
stood there waving at them, as she and Teddy
drove off in Malcolm's old Buick. Haverford
had known her for all the years she had been
married to Malcolm, and Teddy since he was
born. And now they were gone, to whatever
life held for them. He silently locked the door,
thinking of the boy, and slipped the key into
an envelope to send to the lawyers. The house
was empty, the family was gone. And as he
walked down the steps and hailed a cab, he

felt hopeful for them, and that cheered him. And at that exact moment, Marielle was driving across the bridge, and Tom Armour was on his way to court, to a fresh trial, thinking of her and Teddy.